A swarm of attackers were between them and the aircraft shed, and the shadowed shape of a flyer just inside was spotted with them, too. As Glenna gunned the engine, she turned the tractor at the same time, heading back toward the main building and the sea beyond. In the rear seat, Jenny held Ino. He bled on everything, and his eyes were fixed on the sky while his mouth worked in terror. In the front, Claus fought to protect the driver and himself.

A brown plate scuttled onto the cowling, moving for Glenna's hands on the controls. Claus swung, a baseball batter, bright metal blurring at the end of his extended arms. There was a hard, satisfying crunch, as of hard plastic or ceramic cracking through. The brown thing fell to the floor, and he caught a glimpse of dull limbs still in motion before he caught it with a foot and kicked it out onto the flying ground.

At the same moment, the tractor engine died.

FRED
SABERHAGEN

SABERHAGEN:
MY BEST

BAEN
BOOKS

SABERHAGEN: MY BEST

A Baen Books Original

Baen Publishing Enterprises
260 Fifth Avenue
New York, N.Y. 10001

First printing, May 1987

ISBN: 0-671-65645-7

Cover art by Tom Kidd

Printed in the United States of America

Distributed by
SIMON & SCHUSTER
1230 Avenue of the Americas
New York, N.Y. 10020

Table of Contents

The Graphic of Dorian Gray 1

Birthdays 23

The Long Way Home 74

Smasher 92

White Bull.....................................118

Wilderness 147

Peacemaker 152

Victory 162

Goodlife 185

Young Girl at Open Half-Door 210

Adventure of the Metal Murderer............221

From the Tree of Time 231

Inhuman Error.............................244

Martha 267

Intermission 270

Earthshade.................................271

Recessional 296

ACKNOWLEDGMENTS

"The Graphic of Dorian Gray," *New Destinies* Vol. I, April 1987. Copyright 1986 by Fred Saberhagen.

"Birthdays," *Galaxy*, March 1976. Copyright 1976 by Galaxy Publishing Corp.

"The Long Way Home," *Galaxy*, June 1961. Copyright 1961 by Galaxy Publishing Corp.

"Smasher," *The Magazine of Fantasy and Science Fiction*, August 1978. Copyright 1978 by Mercury Press Inc.

"White Bull," *Fantastic*, November 1976. Copyright 1976 by Ultimate Publishing Co.

"Wilderness," *Amazing*, September 1976. Copyright 1976 by Ultimate Publishing Co.

"Peacemaker," *Galaxy*, August 1964. Copyright 1964 by Galaxy Publishing Corp.

"Victory," *The Magazine of Fantasy & Science Fiction*, June 1979. Copyright 1979 by Mercury Press, Inc.

"Goodlife," *Berserker*. Copyright 1963 by Galaxy Publishing Corp.

"Young Girl at Open Half-Door," *The Magazine of Fantasy & Science Fiction*, November 1968. Copyright 1968 by Mercury Press, Inc.

"Adventure of the Metal Murderer," *Omni*, January 1980. Copyright 1979 by Omni Publications International, Ltd.

"From the Tree of Time," *Sorcerer's Apprentice*, Issue 14, Spring 1982. Copyright 1982 by Fred Saberhagen.

"Inhuman Error," *Analog*, October 1974. Copyright 1974 by Conde Nast Publications, Inc.

"Martha," *Amazing*, December 1976. Copyright 1976 by Ultimate Publishing Co.

"Intermission," *Fifty Extremely SF Stories*. Copyright 1982 by Fred Saberhagen.

"Earthshade," *The Magic May Return*, Ace Books. Copyright 1981 by Fred Saberhagen.

"Recessional," *Destinies*, Fall 1980. Copyright 1981 by Fred Saberhagen.

The Graphic of Dorian Gray

Mutant palms, bearing rust-red flowers that smelled like roses, grew on the steep slopes leading up to the house, as did genegineered eucalyptus trees with real oranges growing on them. When the two men had climbed the stairs that led up from the private parking area to the terrace level, some of the treetops were at eye level, some even lower. Adjoining the terrace was the house itself. Like every other dwelling within sight of it, it was a big one, Spanish-looking, with white stucco walls and a lot of red tile, most of the doors and windows guarded with wrought iron bars that added decoration as well as offering some protection.

From the top of the stairs the two men walked a few steps forward on the flagstone terrace and stopped. Lenses were swiveling to observe them, from several emplacements along the stucco walls.

"Announce us, please," the older man called to the house. He allowed his voice to sound tired when he was only talking to machines. "Basil Hallward and Henry Lord. Mr. Hallward is Dorian Gray's graphics designer, and I am Henry Lord, his agent." Or going to be his agent, maybe, he amended silently. If we both like

1

what we see at our first meeting. He hoped the hometronics system of the house could handle all that he had just told it, if the owner himself wasn't listening at the moment. Most of the new systems could.

Some of the lenses turned away. One set, adjoining the open entry to the house from the terrace, continued looking at the visitors. But neither system nor human being said anything in reply.

The two men continued to stand there, shifting their feet uneasily. This place was worth a bundle, Lord thought. It was a while since he'd had a client who wasn't hungry from the start. Not that you could be sure, of course, even with a place like this. For all Lord knew it might be burdened with a two-million-dollar mortgage that would be difficult to meet. According to what he'd heard, Dorian Gray had just bought the place with part of a recent large inheritance.

"Make yourselves at home, gentlemen," said the home systems voice at last, after what had felt like an unreasonable delay. It was a mechanical, subtly inhuman voice that sounded like one of the standard newer models. "Mr. Gray is expecting you and will be with you shortly."

"Thank you," said Lord. He would just as soon talk to the machine as to most receptionists. He strolled over to the balustrade that rimmed the outer edge of the terrace, gazing out over the view. Actually he was wondering whether it would be a good move now to light up a cigar. Some people were impressed to encounter a man who still smoked and others were put off.

Meanwhile, Hallward, as usual, was thinking about his art, his business. Just at the broad open doorway where terrace ended and house began, one of Gray's hometronic system terminals was sitting accessibly on a table. Already Hallward had set down his sizable toolkit beside the table, pulled up a chair, and was looking for the best way to get into the terminal.

Lord, continuing to size things up in his own way, told himself that it looked as if Mr. Dorian Gray might be still in the process of moving in. At the far end of the terrace was piled a collection of crates and boxes of various sizes, as if the stuff might just have been delivered. But at least part of the shipment must have been sitting here for a little while. One of the larger crates had already been opened, the plastic broken and peeled away from the contents it had protected. The contents consisted of a large painting, the full-length portrait of a man. It was an original oil, if Lord was not mistaken.

Hallward by now was completely lost in his technology. He had already opened the terminal, and set up his own portable computer on the redwood table beside it. He had even brought out an alpha helmet, though he wasn't wearing it yet. Somehow he was getting hooked into the house system. He was staring at the flat unfolded computer screen before him, and probing into the house terminal with a little plastic wand.

Again Lord turned away to eye the view. In the small private parking area just below the terrace, Hallward's utilitarian van waited. "Graphics to the Stars" was painted on both side doors. Across from the van was a regal blue Maserati, and close beside that an infinitely more modest Volks. The owners of any vehicles parked here at this hour of the morning, Lord surmised, had more than likely slept here.

To the west a great blur of high fog was still visible above the miles-distant Pacific, but the rest of the morning sky was as clear as a tourist's idea of what sky ought to be like in Southern California. Disjointed segments of a freeway, acrawl with traffic, were visible between other hilltop houses in the middle distance.

"Now, really announce us, you bastard," Hallward grunted with soft rage, at the same moment presumably compelling obedience with a deft prod from the plastic stick in his fingers. Good programmers, Lord had observed, seldom got angry at their systems; Hallward was definitely an exception.

This time an answer was forthcoming within seconds. "Be with you very shortly, gentlemen," boomed a male voice, sounding genuinely human, over the terminal's speaker. "Just settling up with the pedicurist." That last word was followed by a sound that might have been the start of a laugh—it cut off too abruptly for Lord to be sure. The impression he got from the voice was that it belonged to a man who wanted everyone to be impressed by his confidence.

Not unusual, but not encouraging either. The agent decided he might as well have the cigar, and stop worrying about what impression he himself was going to make. He took out a stogy and lit up. No use offering a smoke to Hallward, who was addicted to nothing but his programming.

Leaning on the marble balustrade, puffing smoke out into the sunshine over the parking area, Lord presently saw a shapely female form, dressed in a pink smock, emerge from some lower level of the house and go striding on high heels toward the Volks. He couldn't see her face, only the brown curls of the back of her head. Quite likely the pedicurist, he supposed. In a matter of seconds the Volks had vanished down the curving drive toward the public highway.

Still the client did not appear, or invite them into his house. Lord, chewing his Havana, strolled back across the terrace toward the muddle of packing crates. In the morning sunlight their tough plastic was as white as the stucco of the wall behind them.

Against that wall leaned the uncrated painting. The face of its youthful subject contemplated the California morning as if he were glad to have escaped the box. The subject was a very young and very handsome man, golden-haired and dressed in very old-time clothing. Maybe, Lord guessed, that style was from a hundred years ago. Maybe two hundred. Who knew? He could only hope that his client—if Dorian Gray did become his client—would be as good-looking as the painting. No doubt Hallward was a genius, and could create a beautiful personal graphic based on anyone who was ahead of Quasimodo in the looks department; but still, the higher the point you started from the more you could do.

The wooden frame of the painting was dark with age, and it looked as heavy as some old-time piece of furniture. It must have taken a couple of moving men to get the thing up here from the parking area; Lord wasn't at all sure it would have fit into the little elevator adjoining.

There was movement behind him. Hallward was looking up from his work. Lord turned fully around, smiling, to get his first look at his potential client.

Dorian Gray, wearing a thick gray robe, had just come bouncing out of his house onto his terrace. It was as if he were calculating his movements to be jaunty and energetic, but despite his best efforts they came out awkward, overacted. The good looks were there, though; what looked like a promising basis for a program. Blond hair curled crisply around Gray's shapely skull, as if it were still damp from an after-pedicurist shower. Just as Hallward had described him, Gray was tall, lean, and muscular, with a square jaw and a face definitely in the casting category of tough-guy hero. The subject of the portrait might have been his faggot brother.

Hallward was practically mute, as usual, indifferent to all social happenings, and Gray, all the while nursing a superior smile as if he admired his own suavity, stumbled around trying to introduce himself to Lord.

Well, maybe together they could be made to amount to something. Right now Lord could only hope. The agent took charge of the faltering conversation, and with his prompting to take up the slack everyone seemed to hit it off pretty well. He began to explain to Gray how, if they were going to be in this together, he intended to organize their approach to the people at the studio.

Hallward interrupted them to announce that the light was just great right now, and he wanted to get more sunlight input into the graphics banks on which the personal program would be based. Lord shut up immediately, getting out of the programmer's way; after all, it was the graphics that were going to make or break the deal with the studio when the time came.

Basil had his little videocam out, getting input of Dorian in sunlight. The little camera was a real professional model, with more adjustments and controls on it than the hometronics terminal had. With it the programmer swept the terrace from side to side, capturing Dorian from every angle. More material for the personal program to draw on when it was finally finished and went to work; you could never, Lord gathered, have too much data in the banks. Personal programs were something new, only starting to have a real impact on the business, and he wanted to know as much about them as anyone could who was not actually a programmer.

When the personal program that Hallward would design for Gray eventually went into operation, it would work the mass of graphic material on Gray into shape, the best shape for any given scene, selecting some details and suppressing others, adding bits of behavior, putting grace into the gestures of the image and good tones into its voice, even making vocabulary choices that could improve its wit when the necessity to ad lib came up.

Not that Hallward ever showed any particular grace or wit in his own behavior. The programmer, the agent thought, was like a writer. He was a writer, in his own way, and something of a director too, developing characters for his clients, writing their parts and doing half their performances for them in the great play they had to put on for the studio people, the money people, before any of the actors ever got the chance to perform for a mass audience. And all that most of the mass audience would ever see of the performer was the performing graphic. The quality of the best graphics was so high that you would swear you were watching real people act, sing, dance, make love or die on stage or screen. You would swear that . . . except that real people just were never really quite that good, that beautiful to watch.

Hallward grunted orders. "Now turn around, Dorian.

No, just halfway. I want some more of the back of your head in this light."

Dorian, when he faced away from the videocam, was now looking directly at the old portrait that stood propped against the wall. Flicking a glance sideways at Lord, he remarked: "Wonder if the old bastard had a good life? Looks like it was a rich one, anyway."

"Old?" That was probably the last word that would have come to Lord's mind when he considered the portrait. His thoughts had immediately turned on how great it would be to be that young again. Of course you couldn't expect this kid to look at it that way. He was about the same age as the subject of the portrait had been when it was made, maybe twenty-one.

Gray waved a hand in a clumsy gesture. "Well, he'd be about two hundred if he was still around, right? Or at least a hundred fifty. He's some kind of relative of mine, way back in the family somewhere. That's how come I got all this stuff. From the last heir's estate when she died."

Lord moved a step toward the painting and took a closer look. The artist had signed it, in the lower left corner, but he couldn't read the squirrelly red letters. For all Lord could tell, the name might even have been "Hallward."

Now Dorian was being ordered to turn around again, then walk back and forth across the terrace. This was a long, uninterrupted scan, in which the camera caught plenty of input from Dorian. And from the background too; the sunlit terrace, the dimmer house interior of tile and oak beyond the open doorway, the packing crates. And the portrait, leaning almost straight upright in the California sun.

"I might suggest, Dorian," said Lord, "that you'd want to move it inside. This much sun can't be good for it."

"It'll be in the shade in a minute anyway. As the sun comes around."

And with that everyone forgot about the painting.

"We can take a look now at what we've got," Hallward

told them, wrapping up his videocam. "Is that stage in there turned on?"

The three men all pitched in to move the heavy videostage from its site deep in the house out to a place near the doorway to the terrace. There Hallward's special cable, stretching from the hometronics terminal and his portable computer, could reach it. He assured the other two men that his computer had enough on-board memory to provide a fairly good presentation; and anything that looked good here ought to look really great when it was run on studio equipment.

The stage was set up just inside the house, in shadow; the polychrome lasers that generated its three-dimensional graphics were bright enough to stand up to anything but direct sun.

And then Dorian, wearing only a purple bikini brief, his robe cast aside, his muscles even bigger than Lord had expected, was standing on the stage, had somehow jumped up onto the low dais before Lord had seen him approach it.

And still, at the same time, Dorian Gray was standing just where he had been, still wearing his gray robe and slumping, a little behind Lord and to his right . . .

The robed man who stood near Lord in the sunlight was squinting slightly, and you could see the start of a small pink blemish on one of his rugged cheeks. At the moment the look on his face was expressive of stupidity more than anything else.

Lord turned his head. The image on the stage was without blemish, and taut with energy. It stood proudly erect, with one fist planted on a hip, the free arm hanging gracefully at ease. With a gaze of keen intelligence its eyes met those of Henry Lord, then moved on to each of the other men. It looked last upon its model, and its gaze rested upon him longest.

The voice of the graphic image said: "Good morning, gentlemen. Or, I suppose I should say, fellow workers." Lord supposed that the program, using input from the house cameras, could do fairly well in determining what humans were present, and where they were standing. Then a good program ought to be able to come up with a reasonably appropriate response. The tones of its speech were resonant and finely modulated; the voice of it sounded very much like Dorian's own, and yet it differed. There too things had been improved.

"Good morning," Dorian answered himself, automatically. The words came out sounding rough and awkward, almost angry, as if he were swearing in surprise.

Hallward was surprised too, muttering real swearwords, but joyfully. Lord realized that the programmer was actually delighted, and really astonished, by how good his own creation looked.

"That last input must have helped a lot," Hallward was murmuring to himself. "I don't know why. Son of a bitch, just look at this thing, would you?"

"I hope," said the holographic reproduction on the stage, "that we are all going to enjoy a long and mutually profitable relationship." Once again it looked each of the three men in the eye, one after another. And it didn't just say the words. It acted them, projected their syllables, made them the utterance of some great man on the brink of some tremendous enterprise. This thing was going to knock their eyes out at the studio, if Henry Lord knew anything at all about his business. This was going to catch them right by the balls and lift them out of their goddamn chairs. He had long since dropped his cigar and ground it out with his shoe.

Again Basil Hallward's hands were moving, easily and decisively, over his computer keyboard. Dorian-onstage was suddenly fully clothed, garbed in the latest style of black formalwear, trousers turning into tights a little above the knee, white lace blooming at his wrists and throat. His onstage figure turned easily, one hand gracefully in his pocket, the other making a small, effective gesture. The image asked: "Is it time for us to join the ladies, gentlemen? Can't lick 'em"—here the stage face stuck out its tongue and contorted in a lewd grimace, returning next instant to smooth innocence—"if you don't join 'em."

"Tremendous," said Henry Lord, meaning it heartily for once, wishing he had a better word to use.

And now, suddenly, the image had an imaged bottle of champagne in hand. With a powerful, dexterous movement of its wrists it made the imaged cork pop out; with a dance step it slid its black dress shoes out of the way of the gushing foam.

Henry Lord had by now recovered from his happy surprise and started talking. It wasn't hard to be upbeat and encouraging about this. The only trouble was, he felt he ought to be talking to the graphic on the stage rather than to the man it represented.

Every once in a while he tried to get Hallward more involved in the conversation. But Hallward kept on staring at his little computer screen, and when Lord pressed him he insisted he wasn't sure that things were quite ready to be taken to the studio.

"Not quite ready? What is that supposed to mean? Baby, I've never seen a graphic that was readier than this one!" Not that Lord—or anyone—had seen a vast number of personal graphics in any stage of readiness. It was a new concept, just beginning to be well established.

Hallward still grumbled. He said there were things he hadn't figured out yet, about the way this particular program was working now.

"Anything that's likely to screw up a presentation?"

Hallward grumbled something.

"Well?"

"How the hell do I know? I guess not."

Five days later, in the sunlit afternoon, the three men were again together on the terrace. The presentation at the studio had gone off as well as Lord had dared to hope—but, of course, it hadn't gone in precisely any of the ways he had imagined beforehand. One thing he had long ago learned to be sure of was that such meetings never did.

Today a fourth person, a young woman, was with them on the terrace. Her name was Sibyl Vane, and she was under the patronage—perhaps for the obvious reason, perhaps not—of Alan James. James was the major power at the studio, or at least the most major power that programmers and young actors and their agents were ever going to see.

The way things looked now, Alan James was going to give Dorian Gray a contract. It looked as if he was going to give Basil Hallward a contract too, and Henry Lord was going to be collecting ten percent from both of them. But the contracts would be signed only— only—if Sibyl Vane—rather, the personal program that Hallward was now going to design for Sibyl Vane— appeared in the first commercial production with the graphic program of Dorian Gray. It was going to be feature length, for theater release, and the working title was *Prince Charming*.

As far as Henry Lord could tell so far, the requirement to use Sibyl Vane oughtn't to slow them down particularly. Dorian would have to share billing with someone. Whether Sibyl Vane was any good or not, Alan James had seen something in her, and a genius like Hallward ought to be able to connect with that something and get it to come out in a polychrome three-D graphic. Whether *Prince Charming* would be a hit or a flop when it hit the public screens and stages, was impossible to determine this early, anyway. Lord wouldn't have wanted to say that out loud to anyone in so many words, but it was so.

Already Hallward's preliminaries with Sibyl were over, and her first session in front of his videocam was well under way. Dorian, thirty seconds after he got his first look at her, had volunteered his house and terrace as a location. And there were certain advantages to working here rather than at the studio.

Lord thought that Sibyl, whose dark hair and fair skin made her look almost Taylor-like, ought to provide a fine visual foil for Dorian. And so far she had been willing to give the session all she had. It was beginning to look as if that might not be very much, beyond the naturally great starting points of her face and body.

She was growing increasingly nervous as the session went on. Henry Lord, having become her agent too, found himself having to calm her down.

"Take it easy, kid. This is only a test."

"*Only* a test!" Sibyl almost screamed the words, even though her breathless, ill-modulated voice failed to give them much real volume. She, unlike Dorian, was from a poor family. She understood as well as did Henry Lord that she could easily be throwing potatoes into hot grease for McDonald's next month if this thing didn't pan out, and if Alan James turned sour on her as a result.

"Take it easy. Yeah, only a test. I mean, if your first try doesn't look right, Basil can fix it up until it does." Basil, hearing that, gave him a look. Lord ignored it. This was a time for encouragement, not stark truth. "He's great at this, a goddamn genius. You've seen what he's done for Dorian. Take another look at that."

Something changed in Sibyl's face, as if a healing, restorative thought had come to her. "I want to do it right," she whispered to Henry Lord, "for Dorian too."

Holy shit, he thought. Both of them, really gone on each other, just like that. A complication we didn't need.

Hallward was frowning, and he kept on frowning, through the rest of that session and the next. Sibyl's graphic took shape. There was nothing grossly wrong with it, but Lord thought from the start that it would never attain anything like the magical quality of Dorian's. He was right.

Dorian said nothing about the difference. The truth was that he hadn't really looked at Sibyl's graphics yet, being busy admiring his own whenever he had the opportunity. But he took Lord aside, with the air of a man who had something he was just bursting to talk about, and told him how much he loved Sibyl, and how great and talented she was.

The agent tried to calm him down. "Great. Fine. But right now we've got this job to do."

Dorian struck his fist on a table, awkwardly. "If the

job gets in the way, to hell with the job. I want to marry her."

"Marry her?" Lord didn't get it at all. Neither of these kids had struck him as the marrying kind. "And what're you talking about, the job getting in the way? Why should it?"

"I just said if."

For the time being the job went on. But Sibyl and Dorian could hardly wait until the sessions were over before they disappeared into the house together, kissing as they walked.

A number of additional recording sessions took place at Dorian's house over the next several days, mainly on the terrace. Sometime between the second and third session, Sibyl moved in with him.

Lord, arriving for a fourth session a few days after number three, made himself at home on the terrace and started to replay what he thought was the tape of the most recent Sibyl-modeling session. He didn't ordinarily look over his clients' shoulders as they worked, but this had more and more earmarks of a special situation.

What he got on the holostage, instead of a working session with either of his clients, was two Dorians and two Sibyls. A nude encounter quartet, like something from a hardcore porn show. You could tell the two personal graphics from the two recorded human bodies chiefly because the graphics were better-looking and more graceful. No matter what position they got into, they didn't sag or show little ugly bulges. And you could tell by which bodies really interacted physically. Personal graphics were still purely visual, not tactile.

If this was really porn-for-hire, then two of Lord's clients were earning some money on the side, and neither was paying him his ten percent. Even worse than that—perhaps—they were in violation of their new studio contracts, jeopardizing a lot of real money.

Lord watched for a while and relaxed a little, becoming gradually convinced that this was only something the kids had done for their own amusement. They must have got up there on the stage in the flesh, while their two images cavorted, and joined in, meanwhile recording the whole thing. Oh well, it was great to be young. But somebody really ought to scrub this tape.

Lord turned it off and thought for a while. He didn't really know what this portended.

Dorian came out of the house, wearing the robe he'd had on the first day Lord met him. His face was stony sober, white around the lips. Something had happened.

"What?" Henry Lord demanded, monosyllabic in excitement, jumping to his feet.

"She's gone."

"All right. Where? When? How? You had a fight?"

"I saw her graphic. I took a good look at it, at last, and then we had a fight."

"Her graphic. You mean this stag show that the two of you cooked up?"

"No. No. The one Hallward's trying to get ready for the studio."

"All right. You saw it. So?"

"So. You know something? She's got nothing, and I told her so. To think I was ready to marry her. I felt something for her, I really did. I felt a lot, but she killed it. What a pig. Even my own graphic was telling her what a pig she was." And moisture was welling up in the eyes of Dorian Gray.

"Even your own . . . what? That doesn't make any sense at all."

Dorian began to babble incoherencies. Lord murmured soothing words. He managed to determine that Sibyl was really gone, out of the house with all her things, Dorian didn't know where. The graphics of her—the official ones not the porn show—were still here. Lord found the disk and took a look at them. Pretty nearly worthless. They were really piss-poor.

Hallward, on arriving and being confronted with this fact, grew angry. "You keep telling everyone I'm a goddamn genius, but there are limits. Computer's like a movie camera, some people it likes and some it doesn't.

I can only do so much to augment, and then the output starts looking like a cartoon character. That's not what the studios are buying this year."

After that encounter, Lord was busy with other clients and other affairs for several days. Hallward, much in demand, also had other jobs to catch up on. Lord did not see or hear from Sibyl Vane. She had dropped out of sight. When she was found, in a cheap motel room, she had been dead for two days. She had died of a pill overdose and it was pretty obvious that she had killed herself.

Henry Lord phoned Dorian as soon as he heard the news. The hometronics system answered, and the agent left a message, then hurried over in case Dorian was at home and just not answering his phone.

When Lord got to the house he found his client on the terrace, watching one short sequence of Sibyl's graphic over and over again. Her slender figure on the stage was chastely garbed, picking imaged flowers and arranging a bouquet.

"Dorian, I'm sorry."

"Yeah."

"It wasn't your fault."

"I was tough on her, that's for sure. But you know, I think I learned something about myself through all this. I think things are going to be all right now."

"That's good." Lord sighed. "That's the way to take it. I'm glad you're taking it like that."

"Yeah. I learned what it feels like to do something really rotten, you know? And I don't like it. So, no more. Today I start straightening out."

"Great. What's the first step?" Lord could hope that it might involve a new dedication to the job. It was time for another session with Hallward. And this new look on Dorian's face had graphic possibilities.

"First step is Sibyl. I'm gonna marry her after all."

Lord stared at him for some seconds in silence. Dorian didn't look as if he realized there was anything at all wrong with what he had just said.

"Dorian," the agent said finally.

"What?"

"I left a message on your system today. Didn't you read it?"

"No. I saw it there, but I . . . I was afraid it'd be something I didn't want to know." Dorian looked suddenly like a big, overgrown kid.

Lord was used to that in actors. "Dorian. Sibyl Vane is dead. As near as I could tell from the information that was given on the news, you're not mixed up in it in any way. She left a note, but I don't believe it said anything about you."

"Left a note. Then she—"

"Yeah. She did. You hadn't seen her since she walked out of here, had you? Talked to her, maybe?"

"No. No. Oh, my God. No, I didn't talk to her after she left here. I killed her, though, didn't I?" He stared at Lord. "I killed her, and I can't feel anything."

"Enough of that crap about you killed her. No one kills themselves these days because their lover tells them to get lost. She was a real flake anyway. And anyway, you don't want to step into the kind of publicity you'd get on this one. Especially not at this stage of your career. When you're fifty years old and people are starting to forget about you, then maybe. Right now no one knows who you are yet. What we ought to do—" He stared at Dorian.

"Yeah?"

"Call up Hallward. There's something new in your face. I think he ought to try to get it on tape for the program."

They tried to get Hallward on the phone. His hometronics system told them, after they had identified themselves, that he had just left on a trip to Japan.

"It can wait, then, kid. It'll have to wait. For now just sit tight. And don't say anything to anyone about your fight with Sibyl. Okay?"

"Okay, Hank."

*   *   *

A day passed. Then Dorian, coming back to his house from a long, aimless drive, was surprised to encounter Hallward's van, coming down his long curving driveway just as he was starting up.

Dorian stuck his head out of the Maserati's window and called a greeting. The programmer grunted something in return, and added: "I want to take a look at your master."

"What?"

"The master copy of your personal program. It's still here in your house system. I want to take a look at it—I've got a couple hours before my plane leaves."

"We thought you were gone already."

"I put that announcement on my home system ahead of time. There were things I didn't want to be bothered with. Let me see the program."

Feeling an intense reluctance, Dorian pulled in his head and gripped the steering wheel. Hallward backed his van up the curving drive and stood waiting for Dorian at the foot of the stairs.

When both of them were standing on the terrace, Dorian paused and said: "I don't know if you ought to see the master copy."

Hallward stared at him in astonishment. "Why in hell not? I'm going to be taking it to Comdex in a couple months anyway."

"You're what?"

"You heard me, pal. Comdex. The big computer show."

"You could take another copy."

"There're shades of difference in all of 'em. It says in the contract I can designate one original and keep it. This is the one I want."

But when Hallward had the graphic up and running, he paused, staring at Dorian-on-stage in astonishment. "What've you been doing to this? Who's been working on it?"

"No one."

"Goddam it, it's changed."

"How could it have changed?"

"Look at the face. Someone's been screwing around."

"You should know, Hallward," said the graphic image on the stage. "You're an expert on screwing around. And screwing up." It laughed.

"Who's been doing this?" A vein was standing out in Hallward's forehead.

"Not me," said Dorian. "I'm no programmer."

"Neither is Hallward," said the image, and laughed again.

Hallward became abusive and threatening. This copy was his property, that was in the contract. Someone had damaged it. If the damage was something he couldn't fix, he was going to sue Dorian Gray for his whole farm. He opened up his terminal and put on his alapha helmet—a tool that allowed a degree of direct interaction between the programmer's brain and his machine—and got to work. A lawsuit seemed certain now. He had the evidence right here.

It was easy for Dorian to move close behind the programer as he sat in furious concentration before the terminal, oblivious to everything else around him. Easy to bend over and extract a heavy mallet from the open toolbox beside Hallward's chair. The alpha helmet on Hallward's head was too flimsy to offer any real protection, so striking the blow was, in a way, the easiest thing of all. Then Dorian struck twice more, to make sure.

There wasn't much blood to be taken care of; later he would hose the terrace perfectly clean. Getting the helmet off Hallward's head was really the worst part. One of the little scalp probes had been driven right into skin and scalp and perhaps bone.

Dorian looked over the balustrade. All was quiet, and it was getting dark, but there was still light enough to see. It was as if the necessary actions had already been planned out for him.

He hoisted the body over his shoulders and carried it down to the parking area and loaded it into Hallward's van. There was another gate to the parking area, seldom used, that led to a road—a rutted track rather—

used only on rare occasions by utility companies. Being careful not to leave fingerprints in the van, Dorian got the keys from Hallward's pocket and drove the paneled vehicle down the unused road until he reached the old mudslide area near the throughway.

Here the genegineered kudzu vine recently planted by the highway department was taking charge of things. The ground-hugging vine devoured petroleum products and other pollutants from the air and soil, and released the oxygen from whatever it came across. The highway was so close now that Dorian could hear the rush of traffic in the dusk, but the traffic was above the mudslide area and the headlights never came near. The last time he had been back this way he had seen another abandoned vehicle already half-covered by the relentless kudzu. Maybe in a hundred years, he had thought, someone would take the trouble to dig it out. By that time only a few plastic parts would be left. Meanwhile everyone thought Hallward had gone to Japan. Some time would certainly pass before that was straightened out.

Back in his house, Dorian discovered that Hallward had left a message on the home system this afternoon. The programmer said he couldn't wait any longer, and was heading for the airport.

All to the good. Dorian left the message unerased.

Then he went back to the stage and confronted the graphic image of himself that still stood looking at him.

Again the face of it had changed, more drastically this time. Yet it was still him, Dorian Gray, and this was something he could not allow the world to see.

"I saw what you guys did," the image announced, as its human model approached the stage. Dorian had a hard time forcing himself to look at it. The once-perfect nose of the graphic image was turning into something like the snout of a pig. The red inside of its lower eyelids showed, as if the whole face were being stretched down, and the eyes themselves were increasingly bloodshot.

"What do you think you saw us do?" Dorian asked it at last.

It raised a hand, moved it up and down slowly, and the fist as it moved turned into the blunt head of a mallet.

"Bonk," the image grated, in its once-fine voice.

"I see I have to do a little reprogramming on my own," said the man, and picked up the alpha helmet from the stones of the terrace. Then he stood there staring at the damaged helmet in his hands. No reason to panic because he had temporarily forgotten one detail. There were plenty of places where he could hide the helmet—the programmer might just have forgotten it here. No, because it showed damage, better to get rid of it entirely. Anyway, it would be a long time before anyone came here seriously looking for Hallward.

"You're not a programmer," the graphic said. "Before you put on that helmet and start screwing around, you ought to remember that. Your job in this partnership is to look beautiful. You do that well. You should leave the other jobs to other people."

"Maybe. Maybe you're right. We'll let the programming go for now. There's plenty of time."

"When is Sibyl coming back?" the graphic asked him.

"Sometime. I wish . . . oh God. Oh well. Right now, you get put to sleep for a while."

And Dorian Gray slept well that night.

During the next few weeks, the copies of the program of Dorian Gray that were working at the studio went on having a fine career. *Prince Charming*, with a new co-star, was in the can and ready for release. At Dorian's house, the original home copy, and the damaged alpha helmet, had both been hidden away.

The next time Henry Lord came visiting, he saw the orange Volks of the pedicurist in the parking area. Somehow he took it as a hopeful sign.

"That bastard Hallward," he said to Dorian. "He's always been flaky. They wanted him for publicity the night of the premiere and he wasn't around. Now no one can find him; there's even some doubt he ever went to Japan at all."

"I have a feeling," said Dorian, "he's not coming back."

"Why do you say that?"

"I killed him."

Lord gave his client a long look. "Still trying to get Sibyl out of your system? It's not gonna do you any good to talk like that. Listen, we're gonna need Hallward soon, or be looking for another programmer. With the grosses for the first week in the theaters as good as they are, we want to sign up soon for something new."

"You saw Hetty leaving just now."

"That her name?"

"She and I have kind of got back together."

"Listen, this time they'll want to team you with some established star."

"No. No, I don't mean I want to use her for a graphic." Dorian, for some reason, shuddered faintly. "I was on the verge of asking Hetty to marry me today."

"Jesus Christ, kid. What is it with you and marrying? Why complicate your life just now? If—"

"No, listen to me, Hank. I changed my mind. Because my life is so screwed up already, I couldn't drag her into it. And, you know? Deciding not to mess up her life too was about the best thing I've ever done. I think I turned some kind of a corner, doing that."

"Great," said Lord after a thoughtful pause. "I agree it was probably a wise decision. You've got the career to think of now. I haven't met Hetty but somehow I doubt she'd fit."

"Yeah," said Dorian, "there's the career to think about. The graphic career. I'm thinking about that more than ever now."

When Henry Lord was gone, Dorian opened a drawer and stared at the innocent-looking laser disc on which the master copy of his graphic image was now stored. It seemed a long time since he had looked at the graphic, though actually only a few days had passed.

He put the disc into the machine and called up the

graphic image on the stage. He pulled the damaged helmet from its hiding place, and plugged it in, and fitted it on his head.

When Henry Lord came back to the house that evening, he found Dorian, with the alpha wave helmet still on his head, lying dead on the terrace. Circuit breakers in the system terminal had popped off, and Lord was alert enough to notice that the helmet appeared to have been damaged. Some of its wiring looked shorted, as if it had been beaten by a hammer or something similar. Dorian's head of blond curls looked undamaged; he wasn't going to touch him to find out.

"Henry Lord, Henry Lord," said the hideous graphic cavorting on the nearby stage. It was dressed in a Nazi uniform now, like something right from central casting. "You've got ten percent of me. I recognize you, Henry Lord."

"In that you have the advantage of me, as they said in the old days." Lord was letting his voice sound tired. "But I figure you're right about the ten percent." He stared at the shape, the face, the body, of the image. Might that thing once have looked like Dorian Gray?

He reached out a hand to a nearby phone, to call the cops, then drew it back. He didn't want to touch this house's system, or any system that had *that* in it. Something was wrong with it. He'd go down to his car and use his mobile unit.

First call to the cops, of course; and then, while he was at it, a call to someone he knew at another studio. Whoever had reworked that graphic up there, it had new possibilities. He'd heard there were plans for a remake of *The Hunchback of Notre Dame*.

Birthdays

One

Looking back, Bart could never clearly remember any part of his life before the day when the Ship first woke him from a long, artificially induced sleep, and guided him to the nursery to see the babies. That day and the first few that followed it were very confusing to live through.

The Ship's machines, working with paint and glass and light, had made the nursery spacious-looking and cheerful. Bart counted twenty-four cribs. To count babies would have been harder, because only those who happened to be napping were in their beds. The rest crawled or sat or toddled on the soft-tiled deck, sending up a racket and getting underfoot of their attending machines and images. The babies were all the same age, just about a year old the day Bart first saw them. They wore white diapers, and some had on green hospital gowns like Bart's only, of course, smaller.

Bart was not tall for almost fourteen, but he could easily lift one bare leg after the other over the low barrier the machines had placed to keep the little kids from tottering or crawling out of the nursery into the corridor. The corridor led in one direction to Bart's small private room and in the other—so his memory, working in a new, selective way, informed him—to the rest of the habitable Ship.

The babies squalled, gurgled, blubbered, or took time out to stare at the world in silence. They made nothing much of Bart's coming in among them. The images that the machines kept projecting and moving around the infants were of solid-looking adult humans speaking and smiling, and they evidently took Bart to be just one more image. The babies reacted more strongly to the machines, which had more effective contact with them.

"Pick one up, if you wish," the Ship said in his ear. It was able to project its conversation so there was no way of telling just what direction the words came from. The Ship's voice sounded human, but not quite man or woman, not quite young or old.

Like a good obedient boy Bart bent to have a try at picking up a baby. The chubby belly felt cool against his hands above the papery diaper and the head of dark scanty curls turned so that the liquid brown eyes could look at him uncertainly.

"See how the machines hold them," counseled the Ship. "Their arms are of basically the same form as yours."

He shifted his grip.

"The prime directives under which I operate are very clear. One human parent, adoptive or real, is necessary to the successful maturation of children; images and machines are psychologically inadequate for best results. Therefore, after receiving some elementary preparation for the role, you will serve as adoptive parent for the first generation of colonists."

Colonists. The word evoked in Bart the abstract knowledge that the Ship had started from an orbit around Earth, and was outward bound to seed humanity somewhere among the stars. How long ago the voyage had begun, and whether he himself had witnessed that beginning, were questions that his memory could not answer. Nor did he feel any urgency attached to them. Somewhere in Bart's lost past he had learned that the Ship was to be trusted utterly, and now he could wait patiently for a better understanding of what it meant by its announcement that he was to be a parent. Meanwhile, he watched the infants, played a little with them, and tried to comfort and distract those who cried. It seemed to be the thing to do.

The machines labored ceaselessly, patting, changing, feeding, washing, wiping up. Twice they dispensed cups of souplike stuff for Bart to drink. There were no clocks to watch, but he was certain that he had been in the nursery for hours. At last one of the machines took him lightly by the arm and pointed back down the corridor whence he had come.

When he had closed himself into his little plastic-walled bedroom the Ship's voice said: "You will be given a substantial breakfast when you wake again. That will be one standard year from now."

Two

He awoke as on the first day, as if from a sound night's sleep, and at once sat up to look over the rim of his bed, which curved around him like a padded bath-tub, warm and dry and clean. Just how he was being put to sleep or awakened he didn't know, but certainly there was more to it than he could see or feel. Somehow his gown had been taken off him while he slept, and he was naked.

There was a new gown laid out on the room's single small chair, or maybe the same one, washed clean of baby shit and pablum. He put it on after using the toilet and washing his hands and face. From a panel in the wall he got his promised breakfast, consisting of a warm, milky drink in a plastic cup, and a tray holding chunks of bread. The breadcrust was hot and crunchy and these were pieces of fruit and cheese inside.

One standard year, the Ship had said . . . but his

hands looked no bigger, nor did the muscles in his thin arms. His face looked no different in the wall mirror, and the fine tawny hair on his head had maintained its crewcut length. There were still no more than a couple of dozen brown pubic hairs curling at the bottom of his belly. He was sure he was no taller.

When he got to the nursery, though, he could well believe a year had passed. It certainly had, if these were the same kids. A few were in their beds as before, but now lying stretched out, they almost filled the little cribs. The majority were running about, keeping their balance reasonably skillfully for the most part, and busy with a multitude of toys. The kids wore shirts now, and shorts or pants over their diapers.

This time the babies were aware that Bart was more than just another image. Some of them took fright at first and clung to the machines. But he kept walking around and talking to them, as the Ship instructed him, and soon they started to warm up to him.

Again he spent the day socializing, and this time shared the little kids' food, dispensed by the machines. Meaty-tasting, mildly chewy chunks of stuff, and harder, biscuitlike objects that came in both sweet and sour flavors, it tasted good enough to be adult fare. Last year—yesterday—the babies had been drinking from nippled bottles, but today they got water and colored drinks in little cups.

Though he hadn't questioned the Ship on it, Bart was still thinking over the announcement that he was to be a parent. He could imagine himself at the head of an enormous dining table, all these kids, grown a little older, sitting around it, but beyond that his imagination was soon lost. He told himself to be patient; the Ship would come up with explanations and instructions as they became necessary.

The continual racket was wearying. By the time the babies were all bedded for what must be their regular night's sleep, with the lights dimmed, he was ready to go to sleep himself. At a word from the Ship, he walked back, yawning, to his room.

Three

Again he seemed to be experiencing nothing more than an ordinary night of restful slumber, and again when he awoke he hadn't grown or gotten older. This time he found a pair of shorts and a pullover shirt laid out for him on the chair.

After dressing and eating some breakfast he walked to the nursery. Before he got there he could hear the year's change in the children's voices, forming clear words now as they called to one another.

When the new glass doors of the nursery opened to let Bart in, he saw that bigger beds had been installed, and the walls moved back to make more space for play. The kids looked different and bigger again, of course. After an initial shyness, not so intense as yesterday's, they all came crowding around Bart so that he walked through a little sea of waist-high heads. Here and there a bulge of diaper still peeped out of someone's shorts.

"What's your name?" one tiny voice cried out, insistent above the babble of the others.

"Bartley. Everyone calls me Bart." Who had called him that? Family? Friends? There were still no particular memories available. "What's yours?"

"Armin." Or maybe Ermin was what the child answered. Bart wasn't sure if the speaker was a girl or a boy. The group seemed about evenly divided as to sex.

Again he ate with the children, and played with them through the day. They all accepted his presence unquestioningly before he had been with them an hour, though he didn't get the feeling that any of them could recall his earlier visits. Today, he noticed, there were fewer projected images of adults about.

A little girl who said her name was Deirdre brought him a wheeled plastic toy whose axle had come loose from its containing grooves. He forced it back into place, so the wheels could turn again, and Deirdre carried it off, after a machine had made her stand still until she said "thank you, Bart."

Counting as well as he could in the continuing melee, Bart decided that there were twelve girls and twelve boys in the group.

After dinner, when the machines had begun to pack the kids off to their beds, the Ship said to Bart: "You may remain awake for a few more hours if you wish."

He felt tired out, but not ready to sleep. "Maybe I'll read a book."

"I will provide some in your room."

Stretched out on his bed, he looked at a book for a while without reading, then put it down and asked the air: "How long have I been here? In the Ship?"

"I have edited your memories of your past life for good reason. Your past contains tragic and violent things. Nothing can be done about the past. We must work for the future and achieve a successful revised mission."

"Are there any other people on this Ship? Besides me and the little kids?"

"None. Much depends on you."

He lay there looking at the cover of *The Young Detectives Visit Earth*. Although his bed was very comfortable and he was tired, he didn't think he was going to be able to sleep.

But he really had no choice.

Four

His shorts and shirt were washed for him as he slept, or else it was a clean new outfit that he found on the chair. Breakfast as before, and he was on his way. The books had been removed and there was nothing else to do.

Two boys and two girls, grown bigger since he saw them last, were playing just inside the children's compound; Bart decided it couldn't be thought of as a nursery anymore. As he approached, the four caught sight of him and jumped with excitement, calling out to others, their voices coming to Bart faintly through the heavy glass doors.

As he entered it, Bart saw that their compound had been enlarged again. There were no more adult images

in sight. Children came, hesitantly at first, from everywhere, some pedaling vehicles, others emerging from toy
houses of multicolored blocks.

"Hi, I'm Bart," he said to those who gathered close
around. "Anybody remember me?"

"The Ship told us you were coming to see us today."
A bold little girl pushed forward. "Look, look, see the
picture I drew?" It was a row of a dozen or so little
circle-faces, each the same size, with lines for hair and
nose and eyes, and one large face above. "That's you."
In a corner the artist's name stood in big shaky letters:
SHARON.

As the day went on Bart heard the names of all the
other kids, though he remembered only a few. He
spent his time in play with one group and another, and
then read them all stories from a book about old Earth
as they sat around him on the floor. When the Ship
directed, he saw them off to bed.

"Am I being a good enough parent, Ship?"

"The revised mission plan is proceeding satisfactorily."

Five

All twenty-four of them were waiting for him excitedly just inside the heavy glass doors. And they remembered him.

"We're five now, Bart!"

"Ship says we can have a birthday party if we want—"

"—like Billy and Lynn—"

It took him a while to figure out that Billy and Lynn
were characters in some children's story that the Ship
showed them from time to time. Lynn and Billy were
twins, back on Earth somewhere, and in one episode
they had evidently enjoyed an elaborate birthday celebration, complete with cake, candy, and ice cream.

"How old are you, Bart?"

"Will you have a birthday with us?"

"Sure. If the Ship will give us cake and things. Maybe
we can have some real candles."

"Yayy!"

So they had the party, the Ship providing real candles and entrusting Bart with a lighter for them. The machines even brought forth small paper-wrapped toys as presents for all the five-year-olds.

"Din'choo get a present, Bart?"

"No, it's not my birthday."

"When is?"

"In about a couple of months." The precise date was something else still sitting undisturbed in his memory, with blank holes knocked all around it. "This was fun. Listen, maybe we can have another birthday party when I come back tomorrow. You'll all be six, if the Ship keeps me on the same schedule."

"Tomorrow?"

"Well—next year. See, you and I are running on different time schedules now, because I'm only awake one day every year. I expect the Ship'll put us on the same time schedule soon."

"Next year?"

Bart sighed, seeing that for them the difference between tomorrow and next year was not too clear. Especially the way he was talking.

Six

This year the difference in time schedules was much easier for them to grasp. So were a lot of other things.

Again the compound in which the children lived had been transformed. Part of it had become what Bart recognized as a school, and everybody was busy at teaching-machine consoles when he arrived.

The Ship's voice then declared a holiday for them all.

"Let's have our birthday party!" a boy cried out.

And after Bart had talked with them all, and read them a new story as the Ship directed, and had been shown through the school by his small friends, machines wheeled out a big cake. This time there were balloons as well as little gifts of toys and candy.

"Isn't it your birthday too, Bart?"

"Well, no. Mine's coming in about a couple of months . . . in two months and two days."

"How old will you be?"

"Fourteen."

After the cake and ice cream was finished they had a good time playing games. The kids were awed by Bart's strength and speed and dexterity. He taught them some of the skills he knew for games with balls and ropes and sticks. Now and then someone who got bumped hard in a game took time out to cry. Bart thought he could tell quicker and better than the machines just how serious the damage was.

Seven

Before the seventh-birthday party got started, Bart went through a period of rather intense questioning by a few of the kids. Fuad and Ranjan and Ora wanted to know what he was doing all the time they didn't see him—where and how he spent the year between birthdays.

"I'm sleeping. The Ship can fix it so a person just sleeps all the time."

"Huh," said Ranjan, doubtfully.

"Why does it want you to sleep all the time?" asked Ora. Today she had a loose front tooth she kept wiggling with her tongue.

"I don't know," Bart admitted, feeling foolish.

"Don't you get hungry?" Fuad wanted to know.

"No. I guess it's not like regular sleep." Some vague knowledge of the process was available in his impersonal memory. "It's something like being frozen, only you never feel cold."

This year the games were rougher. When two or three of the boys grabbed Bart by the legs at once, they could tip him over.

Back in his room alone after dinner, he asked: "Ship, am I really helping much, being a parent, if I just come out once a year? How long will I be on this schedule?"

"You will not be on this schedule for any substantial

portion of your lifetime. A definite time limit cannot be set now, but all computation on the matter is proceeding properly."

He tried again a little later, before going to sleep, but got essentially the same answer.

Eight

When Bart walked into the schoolroom something like boy-girl war was going on, the place in disarray, the weaker or more timid children in tears. The more aggressive ones were screaming insults at one another and hurling toys and writing materials back and forth as missiles, over bookshelves and teaching machines turned into parapets. Adult images had been brought out by the Ship and were calling sternly and uselessly for order, and outnumbered machines were shaking some of the worst offenders by the arm and lecturing.

"Ship, can I help?" Bart cried.

"Yes. Two boys have gotten to a lower deck and should be brought back up." Ship's voice was calm and methodical as always, though somewhat louder than usual to be heard plainly above the screaming. "My machines are busy. It would be helpful if you went after the boys and got them to come up again. Go down the stairs at the end of the corridor to your right."

It was a passageway he hadn't been in before, evidently one recently opened up by the ongoing enlargement of the living quarters. He found the two truants, Tang and Mal, without much trouble. There wasn't much of the lower level open to their exploration—only a loop of corridor sealed off by heavy glass doors at all points, except the stair where other passages intersected. The stair also was sealed where it went on down to still lower regions of the Ship.

The boys were glad to see Bart and willing to go back with him; they had been looking long enough at the interesting sights down here. Through the various sets of glass doors you could see other corridors stretching away for hundreds of meters, at least. Many other doors were visible, some of which stood open to reveal static glimpses of rooms furnished for human life but all unused and empty of movement. The lights were dim in that large world outside the glass, and there was not a footstep on the dustless, polished-looking floors.

"I wonder if anybody lives there," Mal asked, nose against the glass.

"Nobody does," said Tang. "Let's go back up."

"Maybe we will someday," Mal said in a small, thoughtful voice.

Nine

The war between the sexes was not raging today, but it still smoldered, as Bart could tell readily enough from the grimacing and hair-pulling and name-calling that flared sporadically during the day. The cake and ice cream lunch was a success, as usual, and the games were fun, though now he had to exert himself somewhat to outdo some of the other players.

A girl and a boy had a brief argument about what mathematical formula should be used to calculate the volume of the basketball they were playing with, and with a start Bart realized that now some of these kids knew things, maybe important things, that he had never learned. And he was supposed to be their parent! Or was it possible he had misunderstood what the Ship was saying?

These things still bothered him when the day was over and he had undressed and climbed back into his isolated bed. "Ship."

"Yes."

". . . nothing." He decided to let well enough alone. Ship rarely gave him a helpful answer anyway. And he wasn't really all that anxious to be a father, at least not until he was older.

Ten

Eating his usual breakfast, Bart felt for the first time a little anxious about meeting the people he was going to find waiting for him in the compound. If they were all another year older, they wouldn't be so much like small kids any more, but *people*, with whom he would have to interact almost as an equal. He shook off his misgivings and walked out.

The kids weren't enormously bigger today, but it was certainly time to celebrate their collective tenth birthday, and they reminded Bart of this right after their first whoops of welcome. They had a big calendar drawn on the wall now, and had been crossing off days. There was no doubt that another year had passed.

Today, when several of the boys ganged up on Bart in a rough game, they easily pushed him around. Not that there had been any plan on their part to gang up on him, or because they were not still impressed by his strength.

And this year there were certain moments, talking to the girls, when Bart felt oddly almost bashful.

Eleven

Suddenly some of the boys, Baruch and Olen in particular, were almost as tall as Bart himself. And Deirdre and Sigrid were starting to round out into the shapes of women; only just starting, but you could tell the process had begun.

Right in the middle of the cake-eating, the birthday party turned solemn, and there was a long sober discussion of early memories and hopes for the future.

All of them naturally shared as their lifetime memories the things that Bart had seen during the last eleven days—the old nursery, the parental images and the guardian machines, the toys and teaching devices. Of course Bart had missed the greater part of their history, but he had a sampling of it.

They sat there soberly sipping their sweet party drinks

and talking. When it came Bart's turn to recount his early memories, he explained that the Ship must have scrambled them for him in some way, erasing large sections. "I don't even know if I was raised out of the machines like you, or if my biological parents were on board, or if I was born on Earth."

No one could give him any help with those questions. The talk went on for a long moody time before they got around to playing games.

Twelve

Bart found himself looking up at Baruch, and level-eyed at a number of the other kids. The Ship was allowing them more freedom now, and everyone except Trac, who had a stomach ache, had come to meet Bart right outside his room, the doors of which could only be opened by the Ship. Even Tang was there, though hobbling on a broken leg he said he had gotten by falling two decks down a stairwell. Ships medical machines had neatly fixed the bones and told him he was healing.

Today the kids' collective attitude was at first so grown-up and businesslike that Bart was almost intimidated. They explained to him that they had just formed themselves into a society, modeled on old societies of Earth that they had studied through the teaching machines. Baruch had been elected president, and others chosen to fill at least half a dozen additional offices.

Even the birthday party began in an atmosphere of formality. But things soon loosened up. Bart was still stronger than Baruch, and could outwrestle him with an effort. But stocky Kichiro was now slightly stronger than he.

Thirteen

Chao, this month's president, announced early in the morning that this year's party was going to be a thirteenth birthday celebration for Bart as well as all the others. All the others chorused agreement, so Bart went along without protest, though he knew full well he had passed his real thirteenth birthday many months ago. He had not the slightest idea whether there had been any party to mark the event, so he enjoyed this one as his due.

All through the day the girls paid him a great deal of attention, to which he reacted confusedly, enjoying it all one moment and feeling tongue-tied and awkward the next. He could tell some of the boys were getting jealous.

Every night recently he had been saying goodnight with the feeling of saying farewell, knowing that never again would he meet the same people he was leaving. Tonight he tried to stay with them, but one of the machines took him gently by the arm and led him from the group toward his room. He looked around at the other children's faces, saw sympathy but no help, and knew he had to go.

Fourteen

Every morning now he went to greet some strangers, boys and girls he had heard about indirectly but had never seen before. They resembled other kids he had met yesterday, and had their names, but that was all. Their bodies were melting and altering almost while Bart watched, flesh inflating and stretching over elongating bones, boys' faces sprouting elementary whiskers while their voices deepened, girls growing breasts, their legs curving and rounding to spell out disturbing secret messages in visual code.

And today they could literally talk over his head. Bart was small for his age. That's what—who was it?—always used to say.

During the party, right in the middle of the ice cream and cake, a fistfight broke out between Fritz and Kichiro. They slugged away at each other so hard that Bart saw he wouldn't be able to stand up to either of them for ten seconds.

The machines just stood around like dummies and made no move to halt the fight. Fay, the current president, had to yell repeatedly to get other kids to step in and break it up.

As soon as things had settled down a little, some of the kids began drifting out of the room in pairs, a boy and a girl together, kissing and maybe pawing at each other as they left. Bart felt strange and almost frightened. The kids that remained in the dining hall talked and giggled and talked, talked, talked. The conversation was about nothing important, but still it seemed important that it be going on.

Edris came to sit near Bart and talk with him. A red ribbon tied up her brown hair, but some fell loose down as far as the halter that covered her breasts. Solon got jealous and started an argument. Soon he and Bart were trying to think up insults to call each other.

Bart shoved Solon, who was not too big for him to think of fighting, and Solon punched Bart on the cheek, so his mouth started to bleed inside. Bart hit back, then they grabbed each other and wrestled in deadly earnest to see who could get the other down. With furniture in the way, they couldn't come to any clean conclusion. Bart saw that a couple of machines were hovering near, and Edris was watching with enjoyment. Pretty soon some of the big kids grabbed the combatants and broke up the fight.

The social atmosphere was a little strained for the rest of the day, and Bart went back to his room earlier than usual, before the machines came to urge him along.

He sat on his room's one chair, arms folded. "Ship, I'm not being a parent. What am I really supposed to be doing?"

"Further instructions will be given you as required."

"Are you still going to wake me up only once a year?"

"The mission is proceeding according to its revised schedule."

He got up and tried to walk out of the room again, but found the door immovable.

He wondered if something vital *could* be wrong with the Ship. Might its planning computers break down like so many common machines, and issue hideously wrong decisions? Though his bland, smoothed-out memory suggested this was impossible, Bart went worriedly to bed. Sleep was still mechanically fast in coming.

Fifteen

Solon had grown alarmingly big, and it was with relief that Bart saw him smile in a friendly if distracted way. The inside of Bart's mouth was still sore from yesterday, but Solon said hello as if he didn't recall their fight at all.

Bart's former opponent had other matters on his mind, and returned quickly to a conversation he was conducting in fierce whispers with Fritz and Himyar and one or two other boys. It was shortly concluded, and the bunch of them took off running, grimly and purposefully, down a corridor. Bart looked around and realized there was no one left in the common room with him but half a dozen girls. Most of these girls looked worried.

Galina and Vivian came over to Bart and started trying to explain. It seemed that the boys were now divided into two gangs, of six members each, and between the gangs existed something like open war.

"They've been fighting this way off and on for months now," Galina told him. "Always getting black eyes and bloody noses. Today looks like it might be one of the worst. It started today over whether we should have another birthday party or not." Galina, rather plain, was solemn most of the time, usually giving the impression she favored sobriety and order. "And the trouble is, half the girls have gotten involved, too."

Helsa and Lotis also came over, and the girls debated whether there was anything they could do to stop impending hostilities. All around them the Ship was quiet—ominously so, Bart felt. He stood by, feeling dangerously out of it all. He didn't even know the layout of the passages the girls talked about as they tried to guess where their male friends might be planning fights or ambushes.

While the other girls kept on talking to one another, Lotis came to Bart and with a gesture got him to follow her off into the Ship.

"Where're we going?" he asked, supposing some plan for peacekeeping or hiding out was being put into effect.

"Something I want to show you." She was just barely taller than he, with straight black hair and Chinese eyes. Shortly they came out in a wide open space, a meeting of corridors, where Bart saw that the kids had improvised a swimming pool. Decking had been taken up, and a room in the lower level flooded. Lotis pointed out how waterproof patching had been stuck in where necessary, and a water pipe tapped to fill the pool. The water looked deeper than a man's head.

Bart was impressed, but somehow disturbed, too, that they had done this much on their own. "Didn't the machines do anything to stop you?"

A flirt of her head dismissed the powers of the machines. "I'm going in. Do you know anything about swimming? People on Earth used to do it all the time. The records show them in the oceans even."

Lotis pulled off her scanty clothing and slid down into the water naked. She turned over and paddled on her back, smiling knowingly up at Bart while he stared down in helpless fascination. Female nudity was not among the things on which his memory could give him reassurance. His mind lurched this way and that in turmoil.

He heard running feet quite near at hand, and turned to see a figure dash out of a side corridor. Fritz was bigger and stronger even than a year ago, but his eyes were wide and frightened; he scarcely looked at either Bart or Lotis, but came running around the pool as if pursued.

He was. Kichiro and Basil and Mal came pounding after him, carrying bludgeons made of the unscrewed legs of chairs, their faces transformed in the fury of the hunt. At the sight of them Bart started to run, too. He realized almost at once that this was a mistake, but it was too late. Someone responding to his flight with instinctive pursuit had grabbed him from behind and he was flattened beneath his captor on the deck.

Kichiro had tackled Bart, while Basil and Mal closed in on Fritz. It sounded like all of them were yelling.

Fritz broke away and fled for another corridor, but Basil was too fast and blocked his path. Fritz lunged at him in desperation and before Basil could swing his club he was slammed up against the bulkhead in a choking grip. The club dropped from Basil's hand, and Bart, pinned on the deck under Kichiro's kneeling weight, could see the whites of his eyes seeming to expand.

Mal stepped close to the struggling pair and earnestly swung his plastic chair leg. The impact made an ugly sound. Fritz let go of his enemy, staggered back and fell.

Kichiro had started to get up. Bart squirmed out from beneath him, tore free of a grasping hand, and ran. His one thought was to reach the safety of his own room. He had to pass between the group of boys and the pool, where Lotis, open-mouthed, clung to the side and watched.

Mal, turning wild-eyed, saw Bart coming and raised his club for one more swing—

None of them had seen the machine approach, but now it was on hand as if it had popped right out of the many-paneled wall. It took the swinging club like a feather from Mal's hand and in the same instant shoved him violently back, so he stumbled over Fritz's unmoving legs and fell.

"You *hurt* me," Mal croaked stupidly from the floor. His hand was scraped raw, oozing blood, where it had collided with the gripper of the machine.

The Ship said loudly to them all: "I have authority to sacrifice individuals, as I judge it necessary for the good of the mission."

Overawed, they all stayed frozen silent. The machine walked through them to bend over Fritz. As it picked him up, Bart saw that his eyes were half open but unseeing, and his mouth was slack.

It walked off down a corridor, carrying Fritz in its arms. His limbs hung down, utterly limp. The other boys came to life and followed in a group, their weapons left behind. Bart heard a slosh and trickle behind him, Lotis getting out of the pool, but he did not turn.

The machine went on for a few score meters, then stopped facing a panel in the wall.

"Ship," Kichiro said, "that's a disposal chute." But Fritz was already gone.

Ignored by the others, Bart went straight back to his room. He sat there, shivering a little and staring at the wall. The ship served him his dinner there, without comment. He ate a little, and then soon turned to his bed, where sleep and forgetfulness never failed to come.

Sixteen

All twenty-three of the kids were waiting for him in the corridor when he stuck his head out of his room to see what might be going on. But it was all right.

"No one's going to try to kill you *this* time," was one of the first things said, by a strong young man with thickening patches of dark beard on cheek and chin. With just a minor effort Bart could recognize the speaker as Kichiro, who, as Bart soon found out, was this year's president. They were having elections only once a year now, he was soon informed.

Fights were evidently much less frequent also, Bart discovered to his great relief. He overheard part of an argument as to who had tried to kill him last year, and this argument was the closest thing to a fight that happened on this birthday.

He soon found out also that birthdays, like gang wars, were now considered kid stuff, and today there was no party. There was a good elaborate lunch, with ice cream produced unpretentiously as dessert.

Talk turned to Bart, and his purpose in the world.

He repeated to the kids everything that the Ship had ever told him about that purpose, which wasn't much.

"I wonder," Basil said to him, "what the Ship'll do with you now? I mean, we obviously don't need you any more as a father or model or whatever to help us grow."

"I dunno," said Bart, taking a little more ice cream. The kids' eyes were all sympathetic, but still, their silent gaze made him uncomfortable. "Anytime I ever ask Ship about it, it just says the mission is proceeding as per revised schedule, or something like that."

Sigrid nodded knowingly. "You'll find Ship's that way. If it doesn't want to answer something for you, it just won't."

Seventeen

This morning it was a relief to meet a group of stable-looking, sane-looking people, not too much different from their namesakes he had said goodbye to the night before.

Bart soon noticed that Basil was missing from the group. "Oh, he's all right," said Ora reassuringly. "He'll be along for lunch. He goes studying the stars."

"The stars?"

"We've found a way to reach the outer hull. In one place there's a glass port through which you can see the outside of the Ship, and the stars to, of course."

Bart could call up a plain picture of what stars were; sometime, somehow, he had seen them.

"What do you think about the stars, Bart?" Tang asked him patronizingly.

He didn't have a quick answer. Armin said: "Look, we've been working on this problem of the Ship and where it's going for seventeen years now. And Bart's put in how much time? About seventeen days."

And there was laughter, not unkind.

Eighteen

When Bart mentioned that he thought it would be fun to learn to swim, they took him to the newly remodeled and enlarged pool. Everyone was matter-of-fact about undressing, and after clothes had been off for a minute or two, it all seemed practically normal to Bart.

Resting on the pool's edge after some strenuous splashing, they took up again last year's discussion about the Ship and its purposes. Bart got the idea that now they talked a lot on this subject. Today he remarked that maybe soon they would be having children, so eventually, people would fill up the empty rooms still waiting on the other levels.

Fuad shook his head. "The Ship's told us we're all sterile—know what that means?"

"You can't make any babies."

"That's right. Girls and men both. We can do all the sex we want, but nothing can ever happen from it."

Later, alone, Bart asked the Ship: "Am I sterile, too? I mean, am I going to be, when . . ."

"No. With maturity you will be fertile."

That was a definite answer at last, but he still got only the old answers to his old questions when he repeated them.

Nineteen

Bart's chronic worry that his life was going fundamentally wrong was lightened when he met his shipmates today. They were now so obviously adults that he could produce an inner sigh of relief and decide to leave the worrying to them.

Most of the teaching machines had been removed. At the few remaining, people were abstractedly at work, printouts and papers stacked around them.

As soon as the word spread that Bart had joined them for the day, most of the adults abandoned other activities and came towering around him, smiling and calling greetings, squeezing his shoulders and ruffling his hair. A number of people wanted to show him things.

Basil took him to see the stars. They went drifting, swimming through a part of the Ship where gravity was turned off, and though there was air, Basil made him wear a breathing device, just in case. Through the glass Bart looked along the curves of the hull, unreal in their great size and distances, and at the stars that looked even more unreal, like some vast scattering of bright powdered paint.

After lunch he asked to go swimming again. Lotis, in the pool with him and others, now had a peculiar slightly mottled look to her thighs that Bart eventually decided must be caused by fat under the skin. And on her left thigh was the threadlike red tracery of an enlarged vein.

After dinner Baruch and Tang took him aside. "Bart, do you really like this one-day-a-year life?"

"I dunno. It's all right, I guess. The Ship must have some reason. It's taking care of us all, right?" He might have said something else, but Ship heard everything.

The men exchanged glances over his head. With several of the girls, they walked him back to his room when the Ship called for him to come, and almost tucked him into bed.

Twenty

He learned soon after rejoining the others that Tang and Ora had been killed, some months ago, trying to work their way into a part of the Ship from which humans were ordinarily sealed out.

"Were they trying . . . I mean, did it have anything to do with me? With waking me up more often, or . . ."

"No." Fay shook her head definitely. "Oh, no, Bart, don't worry about that."

The thought hadn't really worried him. Actually, it had generated some hope.

"They were trying to get to the far end of the Ship," Ranjan explained. "You know, the aft, as the old records call it. Have you seen any of the old records? The part of the Ship where the drive controls and so many other things seem to be located."

They explained to Bart such elementary knowledge of the Ship as they had been able to piece together, and his understanding of it grew a little. He found out also that they meant to keep on trying to get through to the other parts of the Ship, and eventually to take over its control. That was a strange thought, and Bart wasn't at all sure how much he liked it.

Twenty-one

It had been many days since his shipmates paid him as little attention as they did today. He was greeted cheerfully enough, but no crowd gathered around. A couple of people went with him to swim, in a pool that had again been remodeled—made safer and more pleasant.

He learned that some of the people were working hard to grow plants, from seeds the Ship had provided for their old school biology program. They showed him the new garden. It held nothing ready to eat yet, but maybe next time he came.

He saw Kichiro limping by and heard that his knee had been lamed in some contest with another man, but whether it was a fight or a game Bart did not learn.

Twenty-two

There were no beds in the old common room any more. Bart found that most of the people had paired up two by two for sleeping, in more or less stable partnerships.

More noticeably, most of the people he talked to today had runny noses. Sharon told him that an experiment in the new biology lab had gone wrong and some viruses had escaped. Nothing to worry about, they assured him. He wasn't worried, really—not about viruses, anyway.

All in all, it was a casual, low-pressure sort of day.

Twenty-three

Lotis, working in the garden, wore shorts today, and he noticed that her legs and bottom were getting quite lumpy with fat. The red vein on her thigh had extended itself into a little tracery of defective blood vessels in the skin.

All the runny noses had dried up. Some medicine the people had made for themselves was ready for Bart in case he had caught the infection, too. But he hadn't.

"Maybe the Ship's still taking good care of you," Chao commented.

Twenty-four

No one came down the corridor toward his room to meet him, but as soon as Bart had entered the general living area they all jumped out of hiding with cries of "Surprise!" and "Happy birthday!" It wasn't his birthday yet, but he soon understood that a sort of general birthday had been declared, in which he was being invited to share.

"It's been ten years since we've had one, Bart," said Himyar. "A party, I mean. So we just thought it was time."

"We could make you an honorary fifteen," Fay put in. "Or how about an honorary twenty-four?"

"Have a glass of wine, Bart," said someone else.

"Wine?"

"Told you our garden was going to be a success."

"—oh, give him only a small one! He's too young—"

"—one glass won't hurt 'im—"

He realized after a while that some of the people were passing around another kind of drug, something they sniffed up into their nostrils. But he stayed with his one glass of wine, which made him feel just dizzy and high enough to be wary of asking for any more.

The party went on practically all day, with games and jokes and songs. Bart no longer minded when people paired off and vanished for a while, their arms about each other. This behavior was grownups' doings now, not something in which he might possibly become involved. He went along with all the partying and had a good time. Still, now and then he caught himself wishing they would get down to business. Though he didn't know just what their business was.

Twenty-five

This year his wish seemed to have been granted, for he got the impression of a lot of serious business going on. People were punching at computers and crouched over teaching machines, and in some rooms devices Bart couldn't identify had been set up.

He noticed that Olen's hairline was receding sharply. He wondered if the man had some kind of scalp disease, but he didn't ask.

In a large room away from the usual living area, Bart found Himyar working to form a towering metal sculpture, using a torch that showered and streamed electric flames. With this homemade device Himyar brushed the glowing metal into the shapes he wanted. Parts of the sculpture reminded Bart of flowers in the garden, or, again, of the curves of splashed water that lived momentarily when someone dived into the pool.

They talked for a time, and Himyar showed Bart some paintings Vivian had done. Himyar and Vivian spent most of their time working here or scrounging materials from every part of the Ship that they could reach; they had become known as the Artists.

"And Armin's an artist, too, I suppose," said Himyar. "He's made himself a camera and goes around using it. Well, the Ship made some of the component systems for him, and the film."

"I'd like to see that."

Twenty-six

Nobody was working quite so hard today. Bart found an elaborate game in progress, a contest involving both

physical and mental effort, with complicated rules. It
had to do with dividing up the regularly occupied territory of the Ship between two contending factions or
teams who struggled to gain more territory from each
other. People sometimes were allowed or compelled to
switch sides in the game. The dividing line between the
territories was marked with bright tapes stuck on the
decks and bulkheads, and moved back and forth as people
won or lost at events like Indian wrestling—men were
matched against men, girls against girls for the physical
struggles—or asking each other difficult questions.

"Bart, be referee. Wasn't his foot off the deck just
then?"

"Yep."

Powerful Kichiro, still limping on his trick knee,
smiled and moved the tape into his opponents' territory
by a distance of two wall panels.

"Hey, Bart!" It was Armin, approaching with some-
thing in his hand. "You never had a chance to see this.
Here's a picture I took of you at the last birthday party.
We'll have to have another one of those sometime."

Bart looked. "You hadn't even started with the camera when we had the party. It must have been yesterday when you took this. I mean last year, for you
guys."

"Hm. I guess you're right."

Twenty-seven

He found some of the marker tapes still stuck up in
place, but the game wasn't being played today and
everyone seemed to have forgotten it. He met Fuad
and Trac and was a little surprised to see how fat they
both looked, with rolls of flesh above their shorts.

He thought of going down the passageway that led to
the stars again, but there was no breathing equipment
in the locker where Basil had kept it earlier.

Baruch and Solon came along and asked what he was
doing. They soon explained that the breathing equipment was being used in what they called engineering

studies, to find out how the more distant parts of the Ship could best be reached.

Bart wanted to know more. They told him of the solid walls and sealed doors that cut off access to those regions, and how the Ship refused to discuss letting anyone go there. It had not tried to stop their engineering studies, though. Whether it would interfere when they began to break through a wall remained to be seen.

Using explosives aboard a spaceship was intrinsically dangerous; something important and irreplaceable might be damaged, or all of a compartment's air might be drained out into vacuum.

"That's how Ora and Tang were killed. And then I was getting some acid ready to eat through a wall, and it disappeared. I suspect some machine found it and took it away." Baruch shrugged, fatalistic but still determined. But we'll see, we'll see." He did not sound or look at all discouraged.

Twenty-eight

This year Bart got more attention from his shipmates than they had given him in some days. Edris and Helsa looked at his teeth, and wondered out loud if the Ship shouldn't be straightening some of them for him.

"Oh, they're not *terribly* crooked. But it did as much for some of us when we were kids."

After lunch there began a general discussion of his future, carried on at times as if he were not there. Ranjan said: "I still think the Ship plans to provide him with a bride one of these days—one of these years. Maybe it's already tried to hatch other people from the artificial wombs and something's gone wrong, so it's got poor Bart just marking time."

Another adult asked: "You still think there's a good supply of human genetic material on board?"

"Bound to be. Else the Ship wouldn't have sterilized us, right?"

There was general agreement on that point, but on

little else. One body of opinion held that the Ship really wanted the people to take over, now that its own computers had grown crotchety and unreliable with breakdowns and damage. But some kind of glitch prevented it from simply saying what it wanted. Schizophrenic, it fought off with one hand their attempts to gain control, while feeding and caring for them with the other.

The discussion soon got over Bart's head, but he listened intently, trying to weigh everything they said. He listened for what might give him confidence, but heard it not.

Twenty-nine

"I know you've seen our biology lab before," Galina told him. "But I think you ought to take a real interest. All our futures may lie in this room."

He ceased scratching his back against the doorframe. "How's that?"

"Sit down, Bart." When they were seated, she looked at him with concern. "Bart, if the machines never provide you with any people about your own age—with a fertile female, specifically—then it's going to be up to us to find some way to eventually produce more people, so that the human race can go on. I'm not sure that there are any people left alive on Earth."

"I see." He nodded very seriously.

Galina spoke slowly and kept studying him for his reactions. "We know that when the Ship was launched there were many human sperms and ova stored on board, all coded as to genetic type, so that people could be conceived and raised by machines when the end of the voyage drew near."

"Uh-huh."

She sighed. "I myself suspect that most, perhaps nearly all of this genetic material was lost in some kind of accident, one that evidently disrupted the voyage in other ways as well. The Ship speaks always of a revised schedule for the mission, a revised plan."

"I know."

"There's further evidence." She paused. "I said all the human seeds and eggs were coded as to type and potential? There's some indication in the available records that all of us now alive, except you—we don't know where you came from—were conceived from materials not considered of the highest quality. Not that we have any grave genetic defects, of course; no seriously defective material would have been placed aboard. But—not the best. This suggests to me that all the best material was somehow destroyed, and also that there may not be much material left."

Bart nodded, not knowing what else to say or do.

"Except you, Bart, as I said. There may have been a human crew aboard before the accident—whatever the accident was. You may be its only survivor. But I suppose your origins make little difference. Here you are and here we are, and there's the future to be faced. A future to be created, perhaps for the whole human race, out of whatever we have on hand. Would you like to learn something about biology?"

"I guess I'd better," said Bart.

They had a pretty good first lesson, distinguishing plants and animals, marking the first great branches of the tree of life.

"What are those marks on your face?" Bart asked on impulse a few hours later, as they were leaving the lab to go to dinner. He felt he knew Galina pretty well now and wasn't shy about getting a little more personal.

"What marks?" She raised tentative fingers to her cheek.

"Just like little lines in the skin, going out from the corners of your eyes."

Thirty

Today marked a standard month since the Ship had roused Bart from his first period of suspended animation. When he awoke, a machine equipped with measuring devices was waiting at his bedside. It quickly got busy to check his height and weight, looked into his eyes and mouth, listened at his chest.

"How much taller am I than a month ago, Ship?"

"Approximately seventy millimeters," said the expressionless voice.

"And how much heavier?"

"Approximately ninety-five grams."

"Is that good?"

It wouldn't say. But it did adjust his diet, adding a delicious, creamy drink to that very breakfast, served in his room.

When he joined the other people he found Olen half bald, and learned that Basil had gone back to communing with the stars.

Galina gave him another biology lesson, more technical and duller than the first.

Thirty-one

Today Bart heard that Deirdre was in her bed, too sick to get up.

"She always liked you, Bart," said Chao sadly. "Go in and talk to her a little."

He went into Deirdre's room, and found her looking much sicker than any human being he had ever seen before. She also seemed too dazed to talk very much.

"Galina's been giving her drugs," Chao explained when he came out. "Otherwise, the pain gets too bad."

"Pain? From what?"

"They think it's cancer." Chao and the others explained it to Bart as best they could.

Only later did they get around to telling him that Baruch had been killed in some kind of an explosion, trying to force a passage to the forbidden areas of the Ship.

"Remember this photograph, Bart?" said Armin, cheering him up. "I took it of you at our last birthday party. We're going to have another one soon."

"You took it the year after the birthday party, Armin."

"Oh? Maybe you're right."

Galina was busy with her other work today and never got around to teaching him biology.

Thirty-two

Deirdre had died, which came as no surprise to Bart, but still left him with a hollow feeling. Thinking over matters of life and death, he stood at the edge of the garden, a high-domed region full of bright lights, vastly enlarged from the first little plot of synthetic soil. Some people were jogging for exercise around the walk that circled the perimeter of the garden, while others were working casually inside.

It was strange to see gray in the hair of some of them, but Bart guessed that was just one more thing that happened naturally with age. His own hair, crewcut when his shipmates were babies, was starting to fall over his forehead now.

He went to look up Basil, and asked to go out and see the stars again. Basil was willing. When they got to the observation port, he pointed out to Bart the prow of the Ship, and the aft, or the stern, as they sometimes called it, where the engines and their controls were supposed to be.

"And when some people finally get back there," Bart asked, "they'll really be able to take over the whole thing?"

Basil shrugged. He was looking mainly outward at the stars.

Thirty-three

Trac was the first person to meet Bart as he came down the corridor from his room, and as soon as she smiled in greeting he noticed that several teeth were missing from her lower jaw.

"Had a jaw cyst, Bart. At least that's what Galina and Solon say. They took it out. Spoils my famous beauty, but they think eventually they'll be able to do something about giving me artificial teeth."

"Couldn't the Ship—?"

"It wouldn't help, whether it could or not. It's giving us less and less help these days. But never mind about that. Come along, we've got something to show you."

He followed along. And then they were all jumping out at him, yelling, "Surprise! Birthday party!" The common dining room was decorated with streamers and balloons, and the table set for a feast.

"We were going to have one next year, Bart. You know, ten years from the last. But then we decided, why not have it now?"

"You can be whatever age you like, Bart. Be an honorary thirty-three with us, if you like."

"That's a third of a century, Mal," a woman cried. "Who wants to be that old?"

They were all good to him, as they usually were these days, petting and hugging him and fussing around, making it his party although it was supposed to be their birthday. He never said what honorary age he wanted. Actually he didn't want any; his own real age was good enough.

Later he found unnoticed in a corner something that he supposed had been dragged out of storage accidently with the decorations. It was a wheeled plastic toy that he remembered fixing for Deirdre a month ago.

Thirty-four

The marking tapes were up on the bulkheads again, and a few people were playing at the question-and-wrestle game. Meanwhile, some had evidently been spending a lot of time working in the garden. It was now huge, and looked like the earthly gardens pictured in the Ship's records, which none of them had ever seen in actuality.

"And now, Bart, we're going to have some prayers. Come along."

"Some what?"

"You'll see. It's another old idea that Basil's been putting into practice lately."

They had wanted to hold the prayer meetings out by the observation port, Bart learned, but there wasn't room enough for everyone, and all had wanted to attend the first meetings at least, to see what they were going to be like. That was a month or two ago and by now, attendance was dropping slightly.

Bart didn't understand the theory of prayer too well, but at the meeting Basil and the others who got up to talk seemed to be speaking not only to the Ship but to the world outside it, and to some force or power that had made them both.

Thirty-five

When Bart emerged from his room most of his shipmates were there in the hall waiting for him, something that hadn't happened since they were sixteen, a day he could remember well. Today they were going to bring him to a meeting, they said. At first Bart expected more prayers, but this meeting turned out to be more businesslike than that.

It was a governmental council, held all day or most of the day around the big table where lunch came as an interruption. Lunch included fruits and vegetables brought fresh from the garden, as well as the usual rations issued by the Ship.

The proceedings got rather boring for Bart, though his friends made an effort to bring him into it all. They showed him their new system of recording all the discoveries of their research for easy access by Bart and future generations.

He looked the question at them.

"It's true, Bart," said Fay. A deep, gentle happiness glowed through her eyes at the thought. "The Ship has recently promised us, there *will* be future generations."

"Provided the mission is completed," someone put in.

"Yes. Well." That was enough for Fay, and for the people as a group.

Bart himself thought it sounded fine, but he would still like to know more. He asked the Ship for details later, but got nowhere, as usual.

Thirty-six

There had been important changes made around him. He knew this the moment he started to come out of sleep. Opening his eyes a groggy second or two later, he realized that he was in a new bedroom, much like his old one, but different in detail and bigger.

"Ship . . . Ship, where am I? What's happened?"

"You have been moved during your sleep into a new accommodation, Bart. There is no cause for alarm."

He got up, dressed, ate, and eliminated as usual. The walls of this room were metal, and its door was thicker, as he saw when it opened for him to go out.

"Why did you move me, Ship?"

"Some of the people were attempting to reach you, to rouse you from sleep at the wrong time. They meant you well but it was necessary to prevent their interference."

His door opened into a corridor he had never seen before, leading off in one direction only. It bent sharply several times and was interrupted by two sets of heavy doors that opened as Bart drew near and closed immediately after he had passed.

He found himself coming back into the peopled area of the Ship from a new direction, near the biology lab. The first folk to see him dropped what they were doing and ran to give him a glad welcome.

"I told you he'd be here on schedule!" cried Mal, pounding Bart joyfully on the back. No club in Mal's hand this time.

"Ship was just taking good care of him, that's all!" Sigrid pulled him in for a big hug against her heavy bosom.

Later he learned that an intensive effort had been

made to "rescue" him from the machines, set him free from his long sleeps. The attempt had collapsed foolishly and no one wanted to talk about it. Then everyone had grown a little worried about Bart and all were glad to see him still coming back, if only for a day each year.

Gray was spreading in the hair of the happy crew around him, and several of the male heads were now nearly bald. Many of the people looked a little fatter and squintier than when he had seen them last. They gave him a big lunch that was almost a birthday party.

Thirty-seven

Galina and Solon took him on a tour of their biology lab, which was much enlarged and changed since he had seen it last. They had in cages some white rats and hamsters, grown from genetic material obtained from the Ship's stores.

"Do you think the long sleeps are harming me?" Bart asked when he had a chance.

"Harming you physically? No, I doubt it." Galina looked at him thoughtfully. "It takes an enormous amount of energy and a great deal of control equipment to keep a human being in such a sleep; even a Ship like this couldn't do it for very many people at a time. It's not just freezing in the ordinary sense, you know. Even the orbital electrons within your body's atoms are kept from moving . . . but don't worry about the physical danger of it; that's extremely small."

She was anxious to resume the biology lessons, so they went on a thorough tour of the lab.

"We haven't been able to get any human genetic material from the Ship to work with. Still, in theory it should be possible for us to produce a new human generation here, starting with just ordinary cells from our own bodies. Did I ever tell you anything about cloning cells?"

"No."

"I will. Anyway, it hasn't worked out yet. We're not

sure if the Ship is interfering in some subtle way, or if there are simply problems we're not aware of."

They showed Bart masses of tissue growing in glass jars. They had never been able to get the tissue to differentiate properly into all the organs that had to grow in concert to make a person. It looked to Bart as if they hadn't yet even come close to achieving that.

Here and there old colored tapes were stuck to the walls and overhead, but the game they represented seemed to have been utterly abandoned.

The only competition Bart heard about today was in growing the best food plants and flowers.

Thirty-eight

It was depressing to see Helsa now dragging herself around like an invalid, her arms grown thin and her ankles puffy. Others told Bart that Galina suspected some slow, incurable disease. Then they turned the talk to brighter things.

"There's a lot of card playing going on now, Bart," Sharon informed him.

"Card playing?"

"Poker, whist, bridge," said Ranjan. "We'll show you. They're old games we dug out of the Ship's records. We've also tried out two new approaches to get through the barriers to reach the control regions of the Ship, but neither has worked."

"We haven't really tried them yet," Fuad objected.

"Well, we've run them on the computer," Lotis put in.

"Bah. I tell you, the Ship is still using that computer against us—"

"No, *I* keep telling *you*," argued Ranjan, "we've got it blocked off now against any possibility of the Ship's gaining access—"

"So you think! I don't agree." The argument was heated, but showed no sign of coming to blows.

Thirty-nine

Today there was a prayer meeting, more elaborate in ceremony but less intense in feeling than the last one Bart had attended. He noted that people's clothing, which they now largely made for themselves, was growing more elaborate, too, and more voluminous. It covered more of their sagging bodies, and distracted attention from them.

Bart also noticed that a softer, more comfortable type of chair had been manufactured somehow and was now in general use. The legs didn't look as if they could be unscrewed.

Forty

It was birthday party time again. Four candles adorned the big cake, each standing for ten years, as someone explained to Bart. The party was opened with a rather perfunctory prayer.

"Bet you don't remember when I took this picture of you, Bart."

"Yes, I do."

Several speeches were made, tracing the recent history of progress in science—mainly astronomical observations and biological research; and in the arts—mainly sculpture, painting, and drawing. Not much had been done lately in an engineering way, a speaker said, which Bart supposed meant they weren't getting anywhere with plans to take over the Ship.

A new president, Olen, had just been elected for a two-year term, and he pledged in a vague way to get things moving.

All around the table the faces were puffy or lined, continuing to puddle or sag. There was more gray hair than any other color.

Forty-one

Bart found a number of people playing chess, a game they said they would teach him before the day was over.

About dinner time Basil told him something else, more confidentially. "I'm not going to give you any details, kid—nothing the Ship doesn't already know. Information you don't have can't be pumped out of you. I'll just say that this time we really know what we're doing, and we're not likely to be stopped. We've been a long time getting ready."

Forty-two

He soon learned that Basil, Mal, and Olen had set out shortly after Bart's last waking day, on a major effort to force their way into the Ship's control areas. They were not back yet, and by now it was doubtful, to say the least, that they ever would return.

Himyar, the sculptor, proudly showed Bart a tall pair of steel doors on which he was carving the history of their little society in a series of panels. He claimed that he had devised a method of grinding stainless steel that worked beautifully.

Helsa was now much better, Bart saw with some surprise. But Sigrid looked unhealthy and was complaining of vague pains. "We're going to try something new," Bart heard Galina tell her cheerfully. Evidently the Ship was again not helping, or could not.

The garden had once more been enlarged, this time all for additional useful food plants.

Forty-three

Basil was back—had been back for several months—but Bart saw that there was still something new and wild and strange in his eyes and he was still emaciated. The other men weren't coming back, Basil said, and that was about all he had to tell about his adventure.

The way Basil looked made Bart timid about pressing him with any further questions. Later he heard more of Basil's story from someone else. The three men had tried going outside the Ship to reach the aft, where they intended to get back in. Something had gone wrong with their equipment; maybe the Ship had sabotaged it. They did get back into the Ship, luckily, in a region where they could find air and water and stored food enough to keep them alive for a time, but the controls had been as much out of reach as ever. Eventually, Basil had made his way back, somehow, through a maze of inner decks and passageways. He had never made it completely clear just how the other two had died, and Bart got the impression that it might be wise not to press too closely on that question.

Himyar had completed his doors and was working with Vivian on a giant mural of Earth, composed of scenes reconstructed imaginatively from old records.

Sigrid's condition was not much changed from last year.

Fay, having recently been named president in a special election, told Bart it had been decided that he should attend school every waking day. The people were getting ready a course of study for him. "The machines insisted on our attending school, I mean in a formal way, and I don't know why they don't with you, but never mind." She brushed back her graying hair and looked at him as if at a challenge. "It's time and past time that you formed good habits to carry over through the rest of your life."

Forty-four

Bart heard right away that Sigrid had died, only a few days ago.

Maybe this latest death was still on everyone's mind, and that was why his first day of school didn't go too well. Lotis was teaching, and sort of skipped from subject to subject, and technique to technique. She knew it wasn't going well, and once she sighed: "Someone else will take a turn at teaching next year—I mean, tomorrow. Are you able to learn anything from me, Bart?"

"Oh, yes."

His day was almost over before he heard something exciting: it was no longer quite certain that Olen and Mal were dead. At least, some garbled message had come in, along disused intercom channels that were thought to connect with control territory. Some almost indecipherable words about surviving. Maybe it was only garbage belched out by the vast intraship communications delay lines or memory drums, not produced by any of this generation's people at all. But maybe . . .

Forty-five

Himyar had put his clever hands to work, toiling in his improved shop, to outfit several people with eyeglasses. Studies on artificial teeth were now well under way, with Solon doing most of the research. The Ship refused to do anything along prosthetic lines for anyone, though it still treated routine minor injuries.

Bart heard Edris and Trac and Kichiro praying, but no longer to the Ship. He saw Basil, who now stared at walls instead of stars, and still said very little.

School was better today. Fuad as teacher talked with him easily and amused him with stories of old Earth.

Forty-six

School again, his teacher Chao, who was grimly determined that he should learn to appreciate the beauties of geometry.

He heard that the garden was just getting over an epidemic of plant disease, caused by no one knew what.

Ranjan had just been elected president, for an indeterminate term, and had pledged to get things moving.

The work on artificial teeth was progressing again after several setbacks. Solon and others looked into

Bart's mouth again to judge whether he needed braces, but to his relief decided to let well enough, or almost well enough, alone.

Forty-seven

Bart got to see Vivian's and Himyar's finished mural, and part of a championship chess game between Armin and Basil.

He tasted a new hybrid fruit from the restored garden.

He heard vague mention of a Golden Birthday celebration that might last for a year and should begin fairly soon.

He saw some artificial teeth in operation.

He heard with blunted shock that Fay, who had been working on and off in the biology lab, had killed herself with quick, painless poison. If anyone knew the reasons, they never made them plain to Bart.

In school Himyar taught him, spiritedly but unintelligibly, about the various traditions of Earthly art.

Forty-eight

The gardeners and biologists had reported success in rejuvenating plants, and there was hope of applying their discoveries to people. Some were saying excitedly that now they understood why the Ship in its wisdom had refused them any help along this line, while letting them work freely at it for themselves. It was something only humans could do, being beyond the very limited creative capabilities of computers.

Not everyone agreed.

Bart's school went on with a whole group of teachers. They were trying music appreciation today, and no one on the Ship seemed to have a real bent in this direction.

Forty-nine

Bart noticed today that some of the people who had seemed happily and permanently paired off as sex-and-life partners were now in different pairings, and evidently just as happy.

Today in school there was some confusion about just what Bart had been taught in previous sessions, and what he might now be fairly tested on. He did well on the tests when they were finally given, and the arguing teachers were all relieved.

Fifty

Again the whole group of them—the fifteen still alive—was on hand to greet Bart when he came through the last heavy door that set aside his private territory. They greeted him with cheers and songs, told him today was a holiday from school, and pulled him away for what they promised would be the biggest and best birthday party yet.

Sharon had just been elected president, and at the party table made a brief speech about how, with the help of all of them, she meant to get things moving again. As she said, she certainly wasn't going to be able to do it all by herself.

There were several games of volleyball. Playing with these old people who had the names of kids he had once briefly met, Bart found himself for a little while one of the gang. He lost himself in the game, jumped nimbly among the jiggling paunches and creaking joints, got knocked down when someone's hundred-kilo mass accidentally crashed into him.

But it was only for a little while that he belonged.

Fifty-one

He came into their living area with the feeling that they would have forgotten about keeping him in school, but no, the lessons were on as promised. Today, with Helsa teaching, Bart got a basic course in the Ship, what little the old records actually said about it and its mission, and something of what the people had been able to find out for themselves. After lunch, somewhat to Bart's surprise, Basil came in and took over for a while, describing how the hull looked from outside, and what some of the remoter portions of the Ship were like. He spoke impersonally, and rarely as if he himself had been there.

Fifty-two

The whole company was excited. About a month ago the world of the ship had been rocked by an explosion, thought to have taken place a kilometer or two away along the hull, probably toward the aft. Whether a hurtling meteoric body had struck the hull, or there were some internal cause, was unknown.

The rumor flew by that Mal and Olen were perhaps still alive, and somehow responsible for the blast.

There was a sudden renewal of religious fervor. And school was conducted in an atmosphere of tension.

Fifty-three

There had been no more explosions, nor any further hints that the lost men had survived. The crisis atmosphere was gone, and talk was again centered on the hoped-for rejuvenation treatments.

Bart saw a proud display of implanted artificial teeth. The method didn't work well in all cases yet, but Solon was optimistic about improvements.

School went on. Today a team of instructors tried to teach him a little about human language and its near-infinite variations, some of which they spoke, or at least could read.

Fifty-four

Timber harvested from the enormous garden was being used to build a sort of pavilion—a roofless, high-walled structure which Bart was told would be used as a kind of social center. He thought they built it just to be building something.

Himyar was seeking treatment for arthritis, which had stiffened his fingers and interfered considerably with his work.

Fifty-five

Fuad lay on a bed inside the finished pavilion, recuperating from what he said had been a heart attack. Galina said the ECG showed that the worst was over. Bart sat and talked for a while with Fuad, who was fatter even than last year, and didn't look good.

People were swinging woven racquets, worn with use, in a game they called squash, played where the volleyball net had been three days ago.

Fifty-six

"What I preach to you, Bart," said Basil, taking a turn at being schoolmaster, "what we have evolved here in our little world, is a complete synthesis of all mankind's old creeds and philosophies. I am really certain of this."

"How can you have a complete whatchamacallit if they were always contradicting each other, like you say?"

Basil had a long answer, but Bart found it not very satisfying.

A large part of the garden was now taken up by plants grown solely for use in the rejuvenation experiments.

Bart heard at dinner that Chao was now suffering repeated bouts of mental illness, and Galina had to keep her tranquilized and sometimes confined to her own room.

Fifty-seven

Politics had heated up suddenly. Edris, who had been acting president, had been removed from office and Trac was in, as some kind of compromise. Bart couldn't figure out what the dispute was about, except some of the people felt themselves insulted by others.

At lunch Trac made a little speech about how she meant to get things moving again, both on exploration of the Ship and the rejuvenation work, which evidently had been allowed to lapse. She said also that expanded medical facilities were needed, and the hospital should be enlarged.

Bart remembered the hospital as the pavilion, or social center, but there were two chronic invalids, Fuad and Chao, living in it now.

Fifty-eight

Kichiro and Himyar were pointed out to Bart as rejuvenation patients, perhaps already on their way to growing younger, though Galina and Solon didn't want to make any definite claims just yet.

"It's helped me a great deal, too," Trac said. Bart thought to himself how much her face had wrinkled and bagged in the last few days.

Himyar had started working in a new electronic medium, less demanding on the knuckles.

Basil was living apart now, giving much time to fasting and prayer.

Most of the women had taken to dyeing their hair, yellow and red being favorite colors.

Fifty-nine

Great interest in chess had revived, and a huge birthday party was being planned for next year.

Hair colors were still used, but had been toned down.

School went on. Bart argued with his teachers that they should show him more about the structure of the Ship than about things of old Earth, which didn't seem to him to have any bearing on his present situation. Galina still pushed biology, but Bart could see that you'd have to study that for years to really get anywhere. He didn't know how much time he had to study anything.

A couple of small riding carts had been built, powered by electric motors, and Bart had some fun riding them about. His elders got angry and yelled at him when he drove too wildly.

The most popular physical game consisted mainly of sliding discs over a pattern of numbered squares on the floor.

Sixty

When he woke up in his room a machine was standing beside him, waiting to give him his monthly physical. His gains in weight and height were both larger than during the previous month. He counted a few more pubic hairs. This morning the creamy drink was dropped from his solitary breakfast.

The birthday party had more and fancier decorations than before, but little else was different, except that most of the people were content to just sit around and eat, drink, and talk. Fuad didn't eat or drink much—he'd lost a lot of weight. But Chao, as the others said, was having a good day, and joined in merrily.

All in all, the old people had a good time. They fussed over Bart quite a bit, but he felt pretty much out of it. Not sad, really, but detached. School had been recessed for the day, though he would have liked to learn more about the Ship.

Sixty-one

Ranjan had suffered a stroke, and was lying paralyzed in the hospital, unable to move anything on his right side. Everyone seemed angry at the Ship, for what they described as cutting back more on its medical programs just as their needs were rising. Part of the space it had formerly used to give them such niggardly medical treatments as it provided had now been walled off. Something else was going on in there, they said, and nodded angrily, though they didn't know what.

They questioned Bart, something like envy now mixed

on their faces with the tenderness they usually accorded him these days. But he had not a scrap of information to provide.

At the moment the office of president was empty, and the question of reorganizing the government was being somewhat crankily debated.

Sixty-two

Vivian, who had been getting fat, was wasting and suffering internal pains. Ranjan was still unable to help himself at all. Bart was told these ills and a catalogue of lesser ones as if he should be just bursting with eagerness to hear them.

He was more interested by ping-pong, which was now a favorite game.

The burning social question was whether there should be an attempt at tinkering with the basic food machines to try to get a more easily chewable output from them.

Kichiro, Solon, and Armin, the only really healthy men, were undertaking an ambitious program to get themselves in shape. Edris, Galina, Sharon, Helsa, and Lotis were laughing a lot at the men and pondering a reducing program for themselves. Trac was thin already, maybe because she had trouble eating.

Sixty-three

He learned that Vivian was dead, to nobody's surprise.

His school today was conducted by Lotis, who about six weeks ago had started to seduce him in the swimming pool. Meeting the eyes of the old gray-haired woman now, Bart thought she didn't remember that at all. And he was right. That hadn't been her in the pool at all, only someone with whom she shared a name. Today she taught him gardening.

The garden was being expanded again. A lot of the rejuvenation plants were still there, taking up space, and not so much living room was needed for people any more, Bart supposed. There were fourteen of them alive now instead of twenty-four, and the survivors didn't move around as much as they used to.

"Remember when I took this picture of you, Bart?"

"Yes, I do, but you don't." And he went rudely on his way, leaving Armin standing still behind him. It wasn't really Armin that bothered Bart, it was the whole situation. The future wasn't coming for these old people, but it was sure enough coming for him.

Sixty-four

Fuad had just died, of another heart attack, and Bart was solemnly conducted to see the still body in a refrigeration room, before they said words over it and gave it back to the ship through a disposal chute.

"Death is a part of life, Bart," Basil explained. They hadn't given him that reasonable an explanation a couple of months ago when they murdered Fritz before his eyes. Never mind, he told himself.

The more energetic people were playing squash today, and Bart joined in for a little while. He was fussed over as usual, and after school people pressed cake and cookies on him.

Sixty-five

He had noticed for some time that his sessions in the school room (not far from the hospital, from which came now and then a querulous groaning) tended to fall into two types. In the first type a teacher tried very earnestly to cram knowledge into his head; in a lesson of the second type (sometimes conducted by the same man or woman) there were long pauses, and an air of futility hung over the proceedings.

Today's session, starting right after lunch, was of the second type. After about an hour Sharon, his instructor, left him alone with a teaching machine, from which he abstracted information on the layout of the Ship, until that got boring. He played with the machine trivially then until they came to get him for dinner.

Sixty-six

He asked to be allowed to study on his own again, and when the request was granted he daydreamed and played with the machine for a while. The vision of young Lotis in the pool came to him, and he got up and went to see if the pool was still there.

Gray-haired Lotis, his teacher again today, discovered his unexplained desertion and came after him angrily. They quarreled, and she tried to take him by the hair and drag him back to school.

She was still a sturdy old girl, but in getting free he pushed her hard enough to knock her down. Alarmed by the way she yelled, he ran away.

Soon Kichiro came limping after him. Bart might have run some more and evaded capture, or sought the safety of his room, but he thrust out his lip and stood his ground. Kichiro slapped him and made him come back to school, with the hardest grip that Bart could remember clamped on his arm.

Sixty-seven

He heard that Ranjan had died, to everyone's relief, after six years of paralysis.

Bart went sullenly into school, under Kichiro's watchful eye.

The regular lesson hadn't gone far before Kichiro interrupted it to make a small impulsive speech. "Bart, you're about all that we old people have to live for. You and the hope that you represent—that one day there will be more people on the Ship, people who will get out from under the yoke of the machines, something we've never been able to manage. 'We have done those things we ought not to have done, and left undone those things we should have done.'"

Bart didn't know what to say.

"But all our lives make too much of a burden to be put on you, don't they?" Kichiro added with a sigh. He seemed to be pleading.

"No, it's all right with me if you feel that way."

And his teacher was happy and gave him a manly hug. But Kichiro had missed the point. Bart no longer cared how any of them felt about anything.

Sixty-eight

The first person he met was Armin, who told him that Chao and Basil had both died, separately and rather suddenly, in the past year.

Bart went to school and found that they had a test programmed into the teaching machine, ready for him to take. Left alone to work, he answered a couple of the questions, and then, feeling that he had something more important to do on this day, he got up and left the school. He looked back once and then walked on. Kichiro looked older and less vigorous than he had two years before, and Bart didn't think any of the others would try to get rough with him. Not any more.

He went to the commissary and punched orders for a small birthday cake into the machine, as he had done for some of those early parties, so long ago. It seemed long to him, now.

Soon he had his cake, the fourteen small candles he had ordered, and a lighter, too. He carried the cake to a refectory table and sat down alone to eat some of it himself. He made a little ceremony of lighting the candles, but would have felt too silly singing himself any songs.

He had ordered the sweet fizzy drink he usually had at parties, but soon got up and went to where the wine was always kept and poured himself a cup of that.

Kichiro came in and stared at him a few moments before speaking. "You're supposed to be in school." The old man's voice was half startled and half angry. "What do you think you're doing?"

"It's my fourteenth birthday today. I'm having my cake."

Kichiro stared a little longer through his puffy, old man's eyes. "Well—I'm sorry if we forgot about your birthday, but that doesn't excuse your running out in the middle of a test." He had left a door open somewhere behind him and all the time he was talking, fretful moaning complaints kept drifting over from the direction of the hospital.

Armin and Helsa came into the room. "What's the matter?"

Kichiro told them, and they started arguing—Helsa for taking a different approach with the boy, as she put it, and Armin in favor of declaring another holiday. This last suggestion angered Kichiro. They were still arguing with one another when Bart finished the little piece of cake on his plate, got up, and left, practically unnoticed. This time he located the pool but found it had long been dry and empty.

Sixty-nine

Bart woke up and left his room as usual, and was surprised when the first set of heavy doors that interrupted his private corridor remained closed when he approached. Then he saw that a new doorway, leading to a new, or newly revealed, passageway had been made in the wall at right angles to the doors.

After a moment, Bart took the new way.

"The prime directives under which I operate are very clear," the Ship said in his ear. "At least one human parent is necessary for children to mature to their full potential.

"We will arrive in less than twenty standard years within a system of planets probably suitable for colonization. From now on you will be awakened increasingly often. You will serve the first generation of colonists as parent. Like them, you have first-rate genetic potential, and perhaps you will remain in some position of leadership when they mature. Today begins your apprenticeship in this role; your elementary preparation for it—a course in the basics of human psychology—was completed yesterday."

With gradual comprehension Bart walked on, guided toward the new nursery by the polyphonic squalling from its full cribs.

The Long Way Home

When Marty first saw the thing it was nearly dead ahead, half a million miles away, a tiny green blip that repeated itself every five seconds on the screen of his distant-search radar.

He was four billion miles from Sol and heading out, working his way slowly through a small swarm of rock chunks that swung in a slow sun-orbit out here beyond Pluto, looking for valuable minerals in a concentration that would make mining profitable.

The thing on his radar screen looked quite small, and therefore not too promising. But, as it was almost in his path, no great effort would be required to investigate. For all he knew, it might be solid germanium. And nothing better was in sight at the moment.

Marty leaned back in the control seat and said: "We've got one coming up, baby." He had no need to address himself any more exactly. Only one other human was aboard the *Clementine*, or, to his knowledge, within the better part of a couple of billion miles.

Laura's voice answered through a speaker, from the kitchen two decks below.

"Oh, close? Have we got time for breakfast?"

Marty studied the radar. "About five hours if we maintain speed. Hope it won't be a waste of energy to decelerate and look the thing over." He gave *Clem*'s main computer the problem of finding the most economical engine use to approach his find and reach zero velocity relative to it.

"Come and eat!"

"All right." He and the computer studied the blip together for a few seconds. Then the man, not considering it anything of unusual importance, left the control room to have breakfast with his bride of three months. As he walked downstairs in the steadily maintained artificial gravity, he heard the engines starting.

Ten hours later he examined his new find much more closely, with a rapidly focusing alertness that balanced between an explorer's caution and a prospector's elation at a possibly huge strike.

The incredible shape of X, becoming apparent as the *Clem* drew within a few hundred miles, was what had Marty on the edge of his chair. It was a needle thirty miles long, as near as his radar could measure, and about a hundred yards thick—dimensions that matched exactly nothing Marty could expect to find anywhere in space.

It was obviously no random chunk of rock. And it was no spaceship that he had ever seen or heard of. One end of it pointed in the direction of Sol, causing him to suggest to Laura the idea of a miniature comet, complete with tail. She took him seriously at first, then remembered some facts about comets and swatted him playfully. "Oh, you!" she said.

Another, more real possibility quickly became obvious, with sobering effect. The ancient fear of aliens that had haunted Earthmen through almost three thousand years of intermittent space exploration, a fear that had never been realized, now peered into the snug control room through the green radar eye.

Aliens were always good for a joke when spacemen met and talked. But they turned out to be not particularly amusing when you were possibly confronting them, several billion miles from Earth. Especially, thought Marty, in a ship built for robot mining, ore refining, and hauling, not for diplomatic contacts or heroics— and with the only human assistance a girl on her first space trip. Marty hardly felt up to speaking for the human race in such a situation.

It took a minute to set the autopilot so that any sudden move by X would trigger alarms and such evasive tactics as *Clem* could manage. He then set a robot librarian to searching his microfilm files for any reference to a spaceship having X's incredible dimensions.

There was a chance—how good a chance, he found hard to estimate, when any explanation looked somewhat wild—that X was a derelict, the wrecked hull of some ship dead for a decade, or a century, or a thousand years. By laws of salvage, such a find would belong to him if he towed it into port. The value might be very high or very low. But the prospect was certainly intriguing.

Marty brought *Clem* to a stop relative to X, and noticed that his velocity to Sol now also hung at zero. "I wonder," he muttered. "Space anchor . . . ?"

The space anchor had been in use for thousands of years. It was a device that enabled a ship to fasten itself to a particular point in the gravitational field of a massive body such as a sun. If X was anchored, it did not prove that there was still life aboard her; once "dropped," an anchor could hold as long as a hull could last.

Laura brought sandwiches and a hot drink to him in the control room.

"If we call the navy and they bring it in we won't get anything out of it," he told her between bites. "That's assuming it's—not alien."

"Could there be someone alive on it?" She was staring into the screen. Her face was solemn, but, he thought, not frightened.

"If it's human, you mean? No. I *know* there hasn't been any ship remotely like that used in recent years. Way, way back the Old Empire built some that were even bigger, but none I ever heard of with this crazy shape . . ."

The robot librarian indicated that it had drawn a blank. "See?" said Marty. "And I've got most of the ancient types in there."

There was silence for a little while. The evening's recorded music started somewhere in the background.

"What would you do if I weren't along?" Laura asked him.

He did not answer directly, but said something he had been considering. "I don't know the psychology of our hypothetical aliens. But it seems to me that if you set out exploring new solar systems, you do as Earthmen have always done—go with the best you have in the way of speed and weapons. Therefore, if X is alien, I don't think *Clem* would stand a chance trying to fight or run." He paused, frowning at the image of X. "That damned *shape*—it's just not right for anything."

"We could call the navy—not that I'm saying we should, darling," she added hastily. "You decide, and I'll never complain either way. I'm just trying to help you think it out."

He looked at her, believed it about there never being any complaints, and squeezed her hand. Anything more seemed superfluous.

"If I was alone," he said, "I'd jump into a suit, go look that thing over, haul it back to Ganymede, and sell it for a unique whatever-it-is. Maybe I'd make enough money to marry you in real style, and trade in *Clem* for a first-rate ship—or maybe even terraform an asteroid and keep a couple of robot prospectors. I don't know, though. Maybe we'd better call the navy."

She laughed at him gently. "We're married enough already, and we had all the style I wanted. Besides, I don't think either of us would be very happy sitting on an asteroid. How long do you think it will take you to look it over?"

At the airlock door she had misgivings: "Oh, it *is* safe enough, isn't it? Marty, be careful and come back soon." She kissed him before he closed his helmet.

They had moved *Clem* to within a few miles of X. Marty mounted his spacebike and approached it slowly, from the side.

The vast length of X blotted out a thin strip of stars to his right and left, as if it were the distant shore of some vast island in a placid Terran sea, and the starclouds below him were the watery reflections of the ones above. But space was too black to permit such an illusion to endure.

The tiny FM radar on his bike showed him to be within three hundred yards of X. He killed his forward speed with a gentle application of retrojets and turned on a spotlight. Bright metal gleamed smoothly back at him as he swung the beam from side to side. Then he stopped it where a dark concavity showed up.

"Lifeboat berth . . . empty," he said aloud, looking through the bike's little telescope.

"Then it is a derelict? We're all right?" asked Laura's voice in his helmet.

"Looks that way. Yeah, I guess there's no doubt of it. I'll go in for a closer look now." He eased the bike forward. X was evidently just some rare type of ship that neither he nor the compilers of the standard reference works in his library had ever heard of. Which sounded a little foolish to him, but . . .

At ten meters' distance he killed speed again, set the bike on automatic stay-clear, made sure a line from it was fast to his belt, and launched himself out of the saddle gently, headfirst, toward X.

The armored hands of his suit touched down first, easily and expertly. In a moment he was standing upright on the hull, held in place by magnetic boots. He looked around. He detected no response to his arrival.

Marty turned toward Sol, sighting down the kilometers of dark cylinder that seemed to dwindle to a point in the starry distance, like a road on which a man might travel home toward a tiny sun.

Near at hand the hull was smooth, looking like that of any ordinary spaceship. In the direction away from Sol, quite distant, he could vaguely see some sort of projections at right angles to the hull. He mounted his bike again and set off in that direction. When he approached the nearest projection, a kilometer and a half down the hull, he saw it to be a sort of enormous clamp that encircled X—or rather, part of a clamp. It ended a few meters from the hull, in rounded globs of metal that had once been molten but were now too cold to affect the thermometer Marty held against them. His radiation counter showed nothing above the normal background.

"Ah," said Marty after a moment, looking at the half-clamp.

"Something?"

"I think I've got it figured out. Not quite as weird as we thought. Let me check for one thing more." He steered the bike slowly around the circumference of X.

A third of the way around he came upon what looked like a shallow trench, about five feet wide and a foot deep, with a bottom that shone cloudy gray in his lights. It ran lengthwise on X as far as he could see in either direction.

A door-sized opening was cut in the clamp above the trench.

Marty nodded and smiled to himself, then gunned the bike around in an accelerating curve that aimed at the *Clementine*.

"It's not a spaceship at all, only a part of one," he told Laura a little later, digging in the microfilm file with his own hands, with the air of a man who knew what he was looking for. "That's why the librarian didn't turn it up. Now I remember reading about them. It's part of an Old Empire job of about two thousand years ago. They used a somewhat different drive than we do, one that made one enormous ship more economical to run than several normal-sized ones. They made these ships ready for a voyage by fastening together long narrow sections side by side, the number depending on how much cargo they had to move. What we've found is obviously one of those sections."

Laura wrinkled her forehead. "It must have been a terrible job, putting those sections together and separating them, even in free space."

"They used space anchors. That trench I mentioned? It has a forcefield bottom, so an anchor could be sunk through it. Then the whole section could be slid straight forward or back, in or out of the bunch . . . here, I've got it, I think. Put this strip in the viewer."

One picture, a photograph, showed what appeared to be one end of a bunch of long needles, in a glaring light, against a background of stars that looked unreal. The legend beneath gave a scanty description of the ship in flowing Old Empire script. Other pictures showed sections of the ship in some detail.

"This must be it, all right," said Marty thoughtfully. "Funny looking old tub."

"I wonder what happened to wreck her."

"Drives sometimes exploded in those days, and that could have done it. And this one section got anchored to Sol somehow—it's funny."

"How long ago did it happen, do you suppose?" asked Laura. She had her arms folded as if she were a little cold, though it was not cold in the *Clementine*.

"Must be around two thousand years or more. These ships haven't been used for about that long." He picked up a stylus. "I better go over there with a big bag of tools tomorrow and take a look inside." He wrote down a few things he thought he might need.

"Historians would probably pay a good price for the whole thing, untouched," she suggested, watching him draw doodles.

"That's a thought. But maybe there's something really valuable aboard—though I won't be able to give it anything like a thorough search, of course. The thing is anchored, remember. I'll probably have to break in, anyway, to release that."

She pointed to one of the diagrams. "Look, a section thirty miles long must be one of the passenger compartments. And according to this plan, it would have no drive at all of its own. We'll have to tow it."

He looked. "Right. Anyway, I don't think I'd care to try its drive if it had one."

He located airlocks on the plan and made himself generally familiar with it.

The next "morning" found Marty loading extra tools, gadgets, and explosives on his bike. The trip to X (he still thought of it that way) was uneventful. This time he landed about a third of the way from one end, where he expected to find a handy airlock and have a choice of directions to explore when he got inside. He hoped to get the airlock open without letting out whatever atmosphere or gas was present in any of the main compartments, as a sudden drop in pressure might damage something in the unknown cargo.

He found a likely looking spot for entry where the plans had told him to expect one. It was a small auxiliary airlock, only a few feet from the space-anchor channel. The forcefield bottom of that channel was, he knew, useless as a possible doorway. Though anchors could be raised and lowered through it, they remained partly imbedded in it at all times. Starting a new hole from scratch would cause the decompression he was trying to avoid, and possibly a dangerous explosion as well.

Marty began his attack on the airlock door cautiously, working with electronic "sounding" gear for a few minutes, trying to tell if the inner door was closed as well. He had about decided that it was when something made him look up. He raised his head and sighted down the dark length of X toward Sol.

Something was moving toward him along the hull.

He was up in the bike saddle with his hand on a blaster before he realized what it was—that moving blur that distorted the stars seen through it, like heat waves in air. Without doubt, it was a space anchor, moving along the channel.

Marty rode the bike out a few yards and nudged it along slowly, following the anchor. It moved at about the pace of a fast walk. *Moved* . . . but it was sunk into space.

"Laura," he called. "Something odd here. Doppler this hull for me and see if it's moving."

Laura acknowledged in one businesslike word. Good girl, he thought. I won't have to worry about you. He coasted along the hull on the bike, staying even with the apparent movement of the anchor.

Laura's voice came: "It is moving now, toward Sol. About 10 kilometers per hour. Maybe less—it's so slow it's hard to read."

"Good, that's what I thought." He hoped he sounded reassuring. He pondered the situation. It was the hull moving then, the forcefield channel sliding by the fixed anchor. Whatever was causing it, it did not seem to be directed against him or the *Clem*. "Look, baby," he went on. "Something peculiar is happening." He explained about the anchor. "*Clem* may be no battleship, but I guess she's a match for any piece of wreckage."

"But you're out *there!*"

"I have to see this. I never saw anything like it before. Don't worry, I'll pull back if it looks at all dangerous." Something in the back of his mind told him to go back to his ship and call the navy. He ignored it without much trouble. He had never thought much of calling the navy.

About four hours later the incomprehensible anchor neared the end of its track, within thirty meters of what seemed to be X's stern. It slowed down and came to a gradual stop a few meters from the end of the track. For a minute nothing else happened. Marty reported the facts to Laura. He sat straight in the bike saddle, regarding the universe, which offered him no enlightenment.

In the space between the anchor and the end of the track, a second patterned shimmer appeared. It must necessarily have been let "down" into space from inside X. Marty felt a creeping chill. After a little while the first anchor vanished, withdrawn through the forcefield into the hull.

Marty sat watching for twenty minutes, but nothing further happened. He realized that he had a crushing grip on the bike controls and that he was quivering with fatigue.

Laura and Marty took turns sleeping and watching, that night aboard the *Clementine*. About noon the next ship's day Laura was at the telescope when anchor number one reappeared, now at the "prow" of X. After a few moments the one at the stern vanished.

Marty looked at the communicator that he could use any time to call the navy. Faster-than-light travel not being practical so near a sun, it would take them at least several hours to arrive after he decided he needed them. Then he beat his fist against a table and swore. "Must be some kind of mechanism in her still operating." He went to the telescope and watched number one anchor begin its apparent slow journey sternward once more. "I don't know. I've got to settle this."

The doppler showed X was again creeping toward Sol at about 10 kilometers an hour.

"Does it seem likely there'd be power left after two thousand years to operate such a mechanism?" Laura asked.

"I think so. Each passenger section had a hydrogen power lamp." He dug out the microfilm again. "Yeah, a small fusion lamp for electricity to light and heat the section, and to run the emergency equipment for . . ." His voice trailed off, then continued in a dazed tone: "For recycling food and water."

"Marty, what is it?"

He stood up, staring at the plan. "The only radios were in the lifeboats, and the lifeboats are gone. I wonder . . . sure. The explosion could have torn them apart, blown them away, so . . ."

"What are you talking about?"

He looked again at their communicator. "A transmitter that can get through the noise between here and Pluto wouldn't be easy to jury-rig, even now. In the Old Empire days . . ."

"*What?*"

"Now about air—" He seemed to wake up with a

start, looked at her sheepishly. "Just an idea that hit me." He grinned. "I'm making another trip."

An hour later he was landing on X for the third time, touching down near the "stern." He was riding the moving hull toward the anchor, but it was still many kilometers away.

The spot he had picked was near another small auxiliary airlock, upon which he began work immediately. After ascertaining that the inner door was closed, he drilled a hole in the outer door to relieve any pressure in the chamber to keep the outer door shut.

The door opening mechanism suffered from twenty-century cramp, but a vibrator tool shook it loose enough to be operated by hand. The inside of the airlock looked like nothing more than the inside of an airlock.

He patched the hole he had made in the outer door so he would be able—he hoped—to open the inner one normally. He operated the outer door several times to make sure he could get out fast if he had to. After attaching a few extras from the bike to his suit, he said a quick and cheerful goodbye to Laura—not expecting his radio to work from inside the hull—and closed himself into the airlock. Using the vibrator again, he was able to work the control that should let whatever passed for hull atmosphere into the chamber. It came. His wrist gauge told him pressure was building up to approximately spaceship normal, and his suit mikes began to pick up a faint hollow humming from somewhere. He very definitely kept suit and helmet sealed.

The inner door worked perfectly, testifying to the skill of the Old Empire builders. Marty found himself nearly upside down as he went through, losing his footing and his sense of heroic adventure. In return he gained the knowledge that X's artificial gravity was still at least partly operational. Righting himself, he found he was in a small anteroom banked with spacesuit lockers, now illuminated only by his suit lights but showing no other signs of damage. There was a door in each of the other walls.

He moved to try the one at his right. First drawing his blaster, he hesitated a moment, then slid it back into its holster. Swallowing, he eased the door open to find only another empty compartment, about the size of an average room and stripped of everything down to the bare deck and bulkheads.

Another door led him into a narrow passage where a few overhead lights burned dimly. Trying to watch over his shoulder and ahead at the same time, he followed the hall to a winding stair and began to climb, moving with all the silence possible in a spacesuit.

The stair brought him out onto a long gallery overlooking what could only be the main corridor of X, a passage twenty meters wide and three decks high; it narrowed away to a point in the dim-lit distance.

A man came out of a doorway across the corridor, a deck below Marty.

He was an old man and may have been nearsighted, for he seemed unaware of the spacesuited figure gripping a railing and staring down at him. The old man wore a sort of tunic intricately embroidered with threads of different colors, and well tailored to his thin figure, leaving his legs and feet bare. He stood for a moment peering down the long corridor, while Marty stared, momentarily frozen in shock.

Marty pulled back two slow steps from the railing, to where he stood mostly in shadow. Turning his head to follow the old man's gaze, he noticed that the forcefield where the anchors traveled was visible, running in a sunken strip down the center of the corridor. When the interstellar ship of which X was once a part had been in normal use, the strip might have been covered with a moving walkway of some kind.

The old man turned his attention to a tank where grew a mass of plants with flat, dark green leaves. He touched a leaf, then turned a valve that doled water into the tank from a thin pipe. Similar valves were clustered on the bulkhead behind the old man, and pipes ran from them to many other plant-filled tanks set at inter-

vals down the corridor. "For oxygen," Marty said aloud
in an almost calm voice, and was startled at the sound
in his helmet. His helmet airspeaker was not turned on,
so of course the old man did not hear him. The old man
pulled a red berry from one of the plants and ate it
absently.

Marty made a move with his chin to turn on his
speaker, but did not complete. He half lifted his arms
to wave, but fear of the not-understood held him, made
him back up slowly into the shadows at the rear of the
gallery. Turning his head to the right he could see the
near end of the corridor, and an anchor there, not
sunken in space but raised almost out of the forcefield
on a framework at the end of the strip.

Near the stair he had ascended was a half-open door,
leading into darkness. Marty realized he had turned off
his suit lights without consciously knowing it. Moving
carefully so the old man would not see, he lit one and
probed the darkness beyond the door cautiously. The
room he entered was the first of a small suite that had
once been a passenger cabin. The furniture was simple,
but it was the first of any kind that he had seen aboard
X. Garments hanging in one corner were similar to the
old man's tunic, though no two were exactly alike in
design. Marty fingered the fabric with one armored
hand, holding it close to his faceplate. He nodded to
himself; it seemed to be the kind of stuff produced by
fiber-recycling machinery, and he doubted very much
that it was anywhere near two thousand years old.

Marty emerged from the doorway of the little apartment, and stood in shadow with his suit lights out,
looking around. The old man had disappeared. He remembered that the old man had gazed down the infinite-
looking corridor as if expecting something. There was
nothing new in sight that way. He turned up the gain of
one of his suit mikes and focused it in that direction.

Many human voices were singing, somewhere down
there, miles away. He started, and tried to interpret
what he heard in some other way, but with an eerie
thrill, he became convinced that his first impression

was correct. While he studied a plan of going back to his bike and heading in that direction, he became aware that the singing was getting louder—and therefore, no doubt, closer.

He leaned back against the bulkhead in the shadow at the rear of the gallery. His suit, dark-colored for space work far from Sol, would be practically invisible from the lighted corridor below, while he could see down with little difficulty. Part of his mind urged him to go back to Laura, to call the navy, because these unknown people could be dangerous to him. But he had to wait and see more of them. He grinned wryly as he realized that he was not going to get any salvage out of X after all.

Sweating in spite of his suit's coolers, he listened to the singing grow rapidly louder in his helmet. Male and female voices rose and fell in an intricate melody, sometimes blending, sometimes chanting separate parts. The language was unknown to him.

Suddenly the people were in sight, first only as a faint dot of color in the distance. As they drew nearer he could see that they walked in a long neat column eight abreast, four on each side of the central strip of forcefield. Men and women, apparently teamed according to no fixed rule of age or sex or size—except that he saw no oldsters or young children.

The people sang and leaned forward as they walked, pulling their weight on heavy ropes that were intricately decorated, like their clothing and that of the old man who had now stepped out of his doorway again to greet them. A few other oldsters of both sexes appeared near him to stand and wait. Through a briefly opened door Marty caught a glimpse of a well-lighted room holding machines he recognized as looms only because of the half-finished cloth they held. He shook his head wonderingly.

All at once the walkers were very near; hundreds of people pulling on ropes that led to a multiple whiffle-tree, made of twisted metal pipes, that rode over the central trench. The whiffletree and the space anchor to which it was fastened were pulled past Marty—or rather the spot from which he watched was carried past the fixed anchor by the slow, human-powered thrust of X toward Sol.

Behind the anchor came a small group of children, from about the age of ten up to puberty. They pulled on small ropes, drawing a cart that held what looked like containers for food and water. At the extreme rear of the procession marched a man in the prime of life, tall and athletic, wearing a magnificent headdress.

About the time he drew even with Marty, this man stopped suddenly and uttered a sharp command. Instantly, the pulling and singing ceased. Several men nearest the whiffle tree moved in and loosened it from the anchor with quick precision. Others held the slackened ropes clear as the enormous inertia of X's mass carried the end of the forcefield strip toward the anchor, which now jammed against the framework holding anchor number two, forcing the framework back where there had seemed to be no room.

A thick forcefield pad now became visible to Marty behind the framework, expanding steadily as it absorbed the energy of the powerful stress between ship and anchor. Conduits of some kind, Marty saw, led away from the pad, possibly to where energy might be stored for use when it came time to start X creeping toward the sun again. A woman in a headdress now mounted the framework and released anchor number two, to drop into space "below" the hull and bind X fast to the place where it was now held by anchor number one. A crew of men came forward and began to raise anchor number one . . .

He found himself descending the stair, retracing his steps to the airlock. Behind him the voices of the people were raised in a steady recitation that might have been a prayer. Feeling somewhat as if he moved in a dream, he made no particular attempt at caution, but he met no one. He tried to think, to understand what he had witnessed. Vaguely, comprehension came.

Outside, he said: "I'm out all right, Laura. I want to look at something at the other end, and then I'll come home." He scarcely heard what she said in reply, but realized that her answer had been almost instantaneous; she must have been listening steadily for his call all the time. He felt better.

The bike shot him 50 kilometers down the dreamlike length of X toward Sol in a few minutes. A lot faster than the people inside do their traveling, he thought . . . and Sol was dim ahead.

Almost recklessly he broke into X again, through an airlock near the prow. At this end of the forcefield strip hung a gigantic block and tackle that would give a vast mechanical advantage to a few hundred people pulling against an anchor, when it came time for them to start the massive hull moving toward Sol once more.

He looked in almost unnoticed at a nursery, at small children in the care of a few women. He thought one of the babies saw him and laughed as he watched through a hole in a bulkhead where a conduit had once passed.

"What is it?" asked Laura impatiently as he stepped exhausted out of the shower room aboard the *Clem,* wrapping a robe around him. He could see his shock suddenly mirrored in her face.

"People," he said, sitting down. "Alive over there. Earth people. Humans."

"You're all right?"

"Sure. It's just—God!" He told her about it briefly. "They must be descended from the survivors of the accident, whatever it was. Physically, there's no reason why they couldn't live when you come to think of it—even reproduce, up to a limited number. Plants for oxygen—I bet their air's as good as ours. Recycling equipment for food and water, and the hydrogen power lamp still working to run it, and to give them light and gravity . . . they have about everything they need. Everything but a space-drive." He leaned back with a sigh and closed his eyes. It was hard for him to stop talking to her.

She was silent for a little, trying to assimilate it all. "But if they have hydrogen power, couldn't they have rigged something?" she finally asked. "*Some* kind of a drive, even if it was slow? Just one push and they'd keep moving."

Marty thought it over. "Moving a little faster won't help them." He sat up and opened his eyes again. "And they'd have a lot less work to do every day. I imagine too large a dose of leisure time could be fatal to all of them.

"Somehow they had the will to keep going, and the intelligence to find a way—to evolve a system of life that worked for them, that kept them from going wild and killing each other. And their children, and their grandchildren, and after that . . ." Slowly he stood up. She followed him into the control room, where they stood watching the image of X that was still focused on the telescope screen.

"All those years," Laura whispered. "All that time."

"Do you realize what they're doing?" he asked softly. "They're not just surviving, turned inward on weaving and designing and music.

"In a few hours they're going to get up and start another day's work. They're going to pull anchor number one back to the front of their ship and lower it. That's their morning job. Then someone left in the rear will raise anchor number two. Then the main group will start pulling against number one, as I saw them doing a little while ago, and their ship will begin to move toward Sol. Every day they go through this they move about 50 kilometers closer to home.

"Honey, these people are walking home and pulling their ship with them. It must be a religion with them by now, or something very near it . . ." He put an arm around Laura.

"Marty—how long would it take them?"

"Space is big," he said in a flat voice, as if quoting something he had been required to memorize.

After a few moments he continued. "I said just moving a little faster won't help them. Let's say they've traveled 50 kilometers a day for two thousand years. That's somewhere near 36 million kilometers. Almost enough to get from Mars to Earth at their nearest approach. But they've got a long way to go to reach the neighborhood of Mars' orbit. We're well out beyond Pluto here. Practically speaking, they're just about where they started from." He smiled wanly. "Really, they're not far from home, for an interstellar ship. They had their accident almost on the doorstep of their own solar system, and they've been walking toward the threshold ever since."

Laura went to the communicator and began to set it up for the call that would bring the navy within a few hours. She paused. "How long would it take them now," she asked, "to get somewhere near Earth?"

"Hell would freeze over. But they can't know that anymore. Or maybe they still know it and it just doesn't bother them. They must just go on, tugging at that damned anchor day after day, year after year, with maybe a holiday now and then . . . I don't know how they do it. They work and sing and feel they're accomplishing something . . . and really, they are, you know. They have a goal and they are moving toward it. I wonder what they say of Earth, how they think about it."

Slowly Laura continued to set up the communicator.

Marty watched her. "Are you sure?" he pleaded suddenly. "What are we doing to them?"

But she had already sent the call.

For better or worse, the long voyage was almost over.

Smasher

Claus Slovensko was coming to the conclusion that the battle in nearby space was going to be invisible to anyone on the planet Waterfall—assuming that there was really going to be a battle at all.

Claus stood alone atop a forty-meter dune, studying a night sky that flamed with the stars of the alien Busog cluster—mostly blue-white giants, which were ordinarily a sight worth watching in themselves. Against that background, the greatest energies released by interstellar warships could, he supposed, be missed as a barely visible twinkling. Unless, of course, the fighting should come very close indeed.

In the direction he was facing, an ocean made invisible by night stretched from near the foot of the barren dune to a horizon marked only by the cessation of the stars. Claus turned now to scan once more the sky in the other direction. That way, toward planetary north, the starry profusion went on and on. In the northeast a silvery half-moon, some antique stage designer's concept of what Earth's own moon should be, hung low behind thin clouds. Below those clouds extended an entire continent of lifeless sand and rock. The land masses of Waterfall were bound in a silence that Earth ears found uncanny—stillness marred only by the wind, by murmurings of sterile streams, and by occasional deep rumblings in the rock itself.

Claus continued turning slowly, till he faced south again. Below him the night sea lapped with lulling false familiarity. He sniffed the air, shrugged, gave up squinting at the stars, and began to feel his way, one cautious foot after another, down the shifting slope of the dune's flank. A small complex of buildings—labs and living quarters bunched as if for companionship, the only human habitation on the world of Waterfall—lay a hundred meters before him and below. Tonight, as usual, the windows were all cheerfully alight. Ino Vacroux had decided, and none of the other three people on the planet had seen any reason to dispute him, that any attempt at blackout would be pointless. If a berserker force was going to descend on Waterfall, the chance of four defenseless humans avoiding discovery by the unliving killers would be nil.

Just beyond the foot of the dune, Claus passed through a gate in the high fence of fused rock designed to keep out drifting sand. With no vegetation of any kind to hold the dunes in place, they tended sometimes to get pushy.

A few steps past the fence, he opened the lockless door of the main entrance of the comfortable living quarters. The large common room just inside was cluttered with casual furniture, books, amateur art, and small- and middle-sized aquariums. The three other people who completed the population of the planet were all in this room at the moment, and all looked up to see if Claus brought news.

Jenny Surya, his wife, was seated at the small computer terminal in the far corner, wearing shorts and sweater, dark hair tied up somewhat carelessly, long elegant legs crossed. She was frowning as she looked up, but abstractedly, as if the worst news Claus might be bringing them would be of some potential distraction from their work.

Closer to Claus, in a big chair pulled up to the big communicator cabinet, slouched Ino Vacroux, senior scientist of the base. Claus surmised that Ino had been a magnificent physical specimen a few decades ago, before being nearly killed in a berserker attack upon another planet. The medics had restored function but not fineness to his body. The gnarled, hairy thighs below his shorts were not much thicker than a child's; his ravaged torso was draped now in a flamboyant shirt. In a chair near his sat Glenna Reyes, his wife, in her usual work garb of clean white coveralls. She was just a little younger than Vacroux, but wore the years with considerably more ease.

"Nothing to see," Claus informed them all, with a loose wave meant to describe the lack of visible action in the sky.

"Or to hear, either," Vacroux grated. His face was grim as he nodded toward the communicator. The screens of the device sparkled, and its speakers hissed a little, with noise that wandered in from the stars and things stranger than stars that nature had set in this corner of the galaxy.

Only a few hours earlier, in the middle of Waterfall's short autumn afternoon, there had been plenty to hear indeed. Driven by a priority code coming in advance of a vitally important message, the communicator had boomed to life, then roared the message through the house and across the entire base, in a voice that the four people heard plainly even four hundred meters distant, where they were gathered to watch dolphins.

"Sea Mother, this is Brass Trumpet. Predators here, and we're going to try to turn them. Hold your place. Repeating . . ."

One repetition of the substance came through as the four were hurrying back to the house. As soon as they got in they played back the automatically recorded signal. And then, when Glenna had at last located the code book somewhere, and they could verify the worst, they had played it back once more.

Sea Mother was the code name for any humans who

might happen to be on Waterfall. It had been assigned by the military years ago, as part of its precautionary routine, and had probably never been used before today. Brass Trumpet, according to the book, conveyed a warning of deadly peril, and was to be used only by a human battle force when there were thought to be berserkers already in the Waterfall system or on their way to it. And "predators here" could hardly mean anything but berserkers—unliving and unmanned war machines, programmed to destroy whatever life they found. The first of them had been built in ages past, during the madness of some interstellar war between races now long-since vanished. Between berserkers and starfaring Earthhumans, war had now been chronic for a thousand standard years.

That Brass Trumpet's warning should be so brief and vague was understandable. The enemy would doubtless pick it up as soon as its intended hearers, and might well be able to decode it. But for all the message content revealed, Sea Mother might be another powerful human force, toward which Brass Trumpet sought to turn them. It would also have been conceivable for such a message to be sent to no one—a planned deception to make the enemy waste computer capacity and detection instruments. And even if the berserkers' deadly electronic brains should somehow compute correctly that Sea Mother was a small and helpless target, it was still possible to hope that the berserkers would be too intent on fatter targets elsewhere, too hard-pressed by human forces, or both, to turn aside and snap up such a minor morsel.

During the hours since that first warning, nothing but noise had come from the communicator. Glenna sighed, and reached out to pat her man on the arm below the sleeve of his loud shirt. "Busy day with the crustaceans tomorrow," she reminded him.

"So we'd better get some rest. I know." Ino looked and sounded worn. He was the only one of the four who had ever seen berserkers before, at anything like close range. It was not exactly reassuring to see how grimly and intensely he reacted to the warning of their possible approach.

"You can connect the small alarm," Glenna went on, "so it'll be sure to wake us if another priority message comes in."

That, thought Claus, would be easier on the nerves than being blasted out of sleep by that God-voice shouting again, this time only a few meters from the head of their bed.

"Yes, I'll do that." Ino thought, then slapped his chair-arms. He made his voice a little brighter. "You're right about tomorrow. And over in Twenty-three we're going to have to start feeding the mantis shrimp." He glanced around at the wall near his chair, where a long chart showed ponds, bays, lagoons, and tidal pools, all strung out in a kilometers-long array, most of it natural, along this part of the coast. This array was a chief reason why the Sea Mother base had been located where it was.

From its sun and moon to its gravity and atmosphere, Waterfall was remarkably Earthlike in almost every measurable attribute save one—this world was congenitally lifeless. About forty standard years past, during a lull in the seemingly interminable berserker war, it had appeared that the peaceful advancement of interstellar humanization might get in an inning or two, and work had begun toward altering this lifelessness. Great ships had settled upon Waterfall with massive inoculations of Earthly life, in a program very carefully orchestrated to produce, eventually, a twin-Earth circling one of the few Sol-type suns in this part of the galaxy.

The enormously complex task had been interrupted when war flared again. The first recrudescence of fighting was far away, but it drew off people and resources. A man-wife team of scientists was selected to stay alone on Waterfall for the duration of the emergency. They were to keep the program going along planned lines, even though at a slow pace. Ino and Glenna had been here for two years now. A supply ship from Atlantis called at intervals of a few standard months. The last to call, eight local days ago, had brought along another husband-and-wife team for a visit. Claus and Jenny were both psychologists, interested in the study of couples living in isolation; they were to stay at least until the next supply ship came.

So far the young guests had been welcome. Glenna, her own children long grown and independent on other worlds, approached motherliness sometimes in her attitude. Ino, more of a born competitor, swam races with Claus and gambled—lightly—with him. With Jenny he alternated between half-serious gallantry and teasing.

"I almost forgot," he said now, getting up from his chair before the communicator, and racking his arms and shoulders with an intense stretch. "I've got a little present for you, Jen."

"Oh?" She was bright, interested, imperturbable. It was her usual working attitude, which he persisted in trying to break through.

Ino went out briefly, and came back to join the others in the kitchen. A small snack before retiring had become a daily ritual for the group.

"For you," he said, presenting Jen with a small bag of clear plastic. There was water inside, and something else.

"Oh, my goodness." It was still her usual nurselike business tone, which evidently struck Ino as a challenge. "What do I do with it?"

"Keep him in that last aquarium in the parlor," Ino advised. "It's untenanted right now."

Claus, looking at the bag from halfway across the kitchen, made out in it one of those nonhuman, nonmammalian shapes that are apt to give Earth people the impression of the intensely alien, even when the organism sighted comes from their own planet. It was no bigger than an adult human finger, but replete with waving appendages. There came to mind something written by Lafcadio Hearn about a centipede: *The blur of its moving legs . . . toward which one would no more*

*advance one's hand . . . than toward the spinning blade
of a power saw . . .*

Or some words close to those. Jen, Claus knew,
cared for the shapes of nonmammalian life even less
than he did. But she would grit her teeth and struggle
not to let the teasing old man see it.

"Just slit the bag and let it drain into the tank," Ino
was advising, for once sounding pretty serious. "They
don't like handling . . . okay? He's a bit groggy right
now, but tomorrow, if he's not satisfied with you as his
new owner, he may try to get away."

Glenna, in the background, was rolling her eyes in
the general direction of Brass Trumpet, miming: What
is the old fool up to now? When is he going to grow up?

"Get away?" Jen inquired sweetly. "You told me the
other day that even a snail couldn't climb that glass—"

The house was filled with the insistent droning of the
alarm that Ino had just connected. He's running some
kind of test, Claus thought at once. Then he saw the
other man's face and knew that Ino wasn't.

Already the new priority message was coming in:
"*Sea Mother, the fight's over here. Predators departing
Waterfall System. Repeating . . .*"

Claus started to obey an impulse to run out and look
at the sky again, then realized that there would certainly be nothing to be seen of the battle now. Radio
waves, no faster than light, had just announced that it
was over. Instead, he joined the others in voicing their
mutual relief. They had a minute or so of totally unself-
conscious cheering.

Ino, his face much relieved, broke out a bottle of
something and four glasses. In a little while, all of them
drifted noisily outside, unable to keep from looking up,
though knowing they would find nothing but the stars
to see.

"What," asked Claus, "were berserkers doing here in
the first place? We're hardly a big enough target to be
interesting to a fleet of them. Are we?"

"Not when they have bigger game in sight." Ino
gestured upward with his drink. "Oh, any living target

interests them, once they get it in their sights. But I'd guess that if a sizable force was here they were on the way to attack Atlantis. See, sometimes in space you can use a planet or a whole system as a kind of cover. Sneak up behind its solar wind, as it were, its gravitational vortex, as someone fighting a land war might take advantage of a mountain or a hill." Atlantis was a long-colonized system less than a dozen parsecs distant, heavily populated and heavily defended. The three habitable Atlantean planets were surfaced mostly with water, and the populace lived almost as much below the waves as on the shaky continents.

It was hours later when Glenna roused and stirred in darkness, pulling away for a moment from Ino's familiar angularity nested beside her.

She blinked. "What was that?" she asked her husband, in a low voice barely cleared of sleep.

Ino scarcely moved. "What was what?"

"A flash, I thought. Some kind of bright flash, outside. Maybe in the distance."

There came no sound of thunder, or of rain. And no more flashes, either, in the short time Glenna remained awake.

Shortly after sunrise next morning, Claus and Jen went out for an early swim. Their beach, pointed out by their hosts as the place where swimmers would be safest and least likely to damage the new ecology, lay a few hundred meters along the shoreline to the west, with several tall dunes between it and the building complex.

As they rounded the first of these dunes, following the pebbly shoreline, Claus stopped. "Look at that." A continuous track, suggesting the passage of some small, belly-dragging creature, had been drawn in the sand. Its lower extremity lay somewhere under water, its upper concealed amid the humps of sterile sand somewhere inland.

"Something," said Jenny, "crawled up out of the water. I haven't seen that before on Waterfall."

"Or came down into it." Claus squatted beside the tiny trail. He was anything but a skilled tracker, and could see no way of determining which way it led. "I haven't seen anything like this before, either. Glenna said certain species—I forget which—were starting to try the land. I expect this will interest them when we get back."

When Claus and Jenny had rounded the next dune, there came into view on its flank two more sets of tracks, looking very much like the first, and like the first, either going up from the water or coming down.

"Maybe," Claus offered, "it's the same one little animal going back and forth. Do crabs make tracks like that?"

Jen couldn't tell him. "Anyway, let's hope they don't pinch swimmers." She slipped off her short robe and took a running dive into the cool water, whose salt content made it a good match for the seas of Earth. Half a minute later, she and her husband came to the surface together, ten meters or so out from shore. From here they could see west past the next dune. There, a hundred meters distant, underscored by the slanting shadows of the early sun, a whole tangled skein of narrow, fresh-looking tracks connected someplace inland with the sea.

A toss of Jen's head shook water from her long, dark hair. "I wonder if it's some kind of seasonal migration?"

"They certainly weren't there yesterday. I think I've had enough. This water's colder than a bureaucrat's heart."

Walking brisky, they had just re-entered the compound when Jenny touched Claus on the arm. "There's Glenna, at the tractor shed. I'm going to trot over and tell her what we saw."

"All right. I'll start fixing some coffee."

Glenna, coming out of the shed a little distance inland from the main house, forestalled Jenny's announcement about the tracks with a vaguely worried question of her own.

"Did you or Claus see or hear anything strange last night, Jenny?"

"Strange? No, I don't think so."

Glenna looked toward a small cluster of more distant outbuildings. "We've just been out there taking a scheduled seismograph reading. It recorded something rather violent and unusual, at about oh-two-hundred this morning. The thing is, you see, it must have been just about that time that something woke me up. I had the distinct impression that there had been a brilliant flash, somewhere outside."

Ino, also dressed in coveralls this morning, appeared among the distant sheds, trudging toward them. When he arrived, he provided more detail on the seismic event. "Quite sharp and apparently quite localized, not more than ten kilometers from here. Our system triangulated it well. I don't know when we've registered another event quite like it."

"What do you suppose it was?" Jen asked.

Ino hesitated minimally. "It could have been a very small spaceship crashing, or maybe a fairly large aircraft. But the only aircraft on Waterfall are the two little ones we have out in that far shed."

"A meteor, maybe?"

"I rather hope so. Otherwise, a spacecraft just might be our most likely answer. And if it were a spacecraft from Brass Trumpet's force coming down here—crippled in the fighting, perhaps—we'd have heard from him on the subject, I should think."

The remaining alternative hung in the air unvoiced. Jenny bit her lip. By now, Brass Trumpet must be long gone from the system, and impossible to recall, his ships outpacing light and radio waves alike in pursuit of the enemy force.

In a voice more worried than before, Glenna was saying: "Of course, if it was some enemy unit, damaged in the battle, then I suppose the crash is likely to have completed its destruction."

"I'd better tell you," Jenny blurted in. And in a couple of sentences she described the peculiar tracks.

Ino stared at her with frank dismay. "I was going to roll out an aircraft . . . but let me take a look at those tracks first."

The quickest way to reach them was undoubtedly on foot. The gnarled man trotted off along the beach path at such a pace that Jenny had difficulty keeping up. Glenna remained behind, saying she would let Claus know what was going on.

Moving with flashes of former athletic grace, Ino reached the nearest of the tracks and dropped to one knee beside it, just as Claus had done. "Do the others look just like this?"

"As nearly as I could tell. We didn't get close to all of them."

"That's no animal I ever saw." He was up again already, trotting back toward the base. "I don't like it. Let's get airborne, all of us."

"I always pictured berserkers as huge things."

"Most of 'em are. Some are small machines, for specialized purposes."

"I'll run into the house and tell the others to get ready to take off," Jenny volunteered as they sped into the compound.

"Do that. Glenna will know what to bring, I expect. I'll get a flyer rolled out of the shed."

Running, Jen thought as she hurried into the house, gave substance to a danger that might otherwise have existed only in the mind. Could it be that Ino, with the horrors in his memory, was somewhat too easily alarmed where berserkers were concerned?

Glenna and Claus, who had just changed into coveralls, met her in the common room. She was telling them of Ino's decision to take to the air, and thinking to herself that she had better change out of her beach garb also, when the first outcry sounded from somewhere outside. It was less a scream than a baffled-sounding, hysterical laugh.

Glenna pushed past her at once, and in a moment

was out the door and running. Exchanging a glance with her husband, Jenny turned and followed, Claus right at her heels.

The strange cry came again. Far ahead, past Glenna's running figure, the door of the aircraft shed had been slid back, and in its opening a white figure appeared outlined—a figure that reeled drunkenly and waved its arms.

Glenna turned aside at the tractor shed, where one of the small ground vehicles stood ready. They were used for riding, hauling, pushing sand, to sculpt a pond into a better shape, or to slice away part of a too-obtrusive dune. It'll be faster than running, Jenny thought, as she saw the older woman spring into the driver's seat, and heard the motor *whoosh* quietly to life. She leaped aboard, too. Claus shoved strongly at her back to make sure she was safely on, before he used both hands for his own grip. A grip was necessary because they were already rolling, and accelerating quickly.

Ino's figure, now just outside the shed, came hurtling closer with their own speed. He shook his arms at them again and staggered. Upon his chest he wore a brownish thing the size of a small plate, like some great medallion that was so heavy it almost pulled him down. He clawed at the brown plate with both hands, and suddenly his coveralls in front were splashed with scarlet. He bellowed words which Jenny could not make out.

Claus gripped Glenna's shoulders and pointed. A dozen or more brown plates were scuttling on the brown, packed sand, between the aircraft shed and the onrushing tractor. The tracks they drew were faint replicas of those that had lined the softer sand along the beach. Beneath each saucerlike body, small legs blurred, reminding Claus of something he'd recently seen—something he could not stop to think of now.

The things had nothing like the tractor's speed, but still, they were in position to cut it off. Glenna swerved no more than slightly, if at all, and one limbed plate disappeared beneath a wheel. It came up at once with the wheel's rapid turning, a brown blur seemingly embedded in the soft, fat tire, resisting somehow the centrifugal force that might have thrown it off.

Ino had gone down with, as Claus now saw, three of the things fastened on his body, but he somehow fought back to his feet just as the tractor jerked to a halt beside him. If Claus could have stopped to analyze his own mental state, he might have said he lacked the time to be afraid. With a blow of his fist he knocked one of the attacking things away from Ino, and felt the surprising weight and hardness of it as a sharp pang up through his wrist.

All three dragging together, they pulled Ino aboard; Glenna was back in the driver's seat at once. Claus kicked another attacker off, then threw open the lid of the tractor's toolbox and grabbed the longest, heaviest metal tool displayed inside.

A swarm of attackers were between them and the aircraft shed, and the shadowed shape of a flyer just inside was spotted with them, too. As Glenna gunned the engine, she turned the tractor at the same time, heading back toward the main building and the sea beyond. In the rear seat, Jenny held Ino. He bled on everything, and his eyes were fixed on the sky while his mouth worked in terror. In the front, Claus fought to protect the driver and himself.

A brown plate scuttled onto the cowling, moving for Glenna's hands on the controls. Claus swung, a baseball batter, bright metal blurring at the end of his extended arms. There was a hard, satisfying crunch, as of hard plastic or ceramic cracking through. The brown thing fell to the floor, and he caught a glimpse of dull limbs still in motion before he caught it with a foot and kicked it out onto the flying ground.

Another of the enemy popped out from somewhere onto the dash. He pounded at it, missed when it seemed to dodge his blows. He cracked its body finally, but still it clung on under the steering column, hard to get at, inching toward Glenna's fingers. Claus grabbed it with his left hand, felt a lance. Not until he had thrown the thing clear of the tractor did he look at his hand and see two fingers nearly severed.

At the same moment, the tractor engine died, and they rolled to a silent stop, with the sea and the small dock Glenna had been steering for only a few meters ahead. Under the edge of the engine cowling another of the enemy appeared, thrusting forward a limb that looked like a pair of ceramic pliers, shredded electrical connectors dangling in its grip.

The humans abandoned the tractor in a wordless rush. Claus, one hand helpless and dripping blood, aided the women with Ino as best he could. Together they half-dragged, half-carried him across the dock and rolled him into a small, open boat, the only craft at once available. In moments Glenna had freed them from the dock and started the motor, and they were headed out away from shore.

Away from shore, but not into the sea. They were separated from deep-blue and choppy ocean by a barrier reef or causeway, one of the features that had made this coast desirable for the life-seeding base. The reef, a basically natural structure of sand and rock deposited by waves and currents, was about a hundred meters from the shore, and stretched in either direction as far as vision carried. Running from beach to reef, artificial walls or low causeways of fused rock separated ponds of various sizes.

"We're in a kind of square lagoon here," Glenna told Jenny, motioning for her to take over the job of steering. "Head for that far corner. If we can get there ahead of them, we may be able to lift the boat over the reef and get out."

Jen nodded, taking the controls. Glenna slid back to a place beside her husband, snapped open the boat's small first-aid kit, and began applying pressure bandages.

Claus started to try to help, saw the world beginning to turn gray around him, and slumped back against the gunwale. He would be of no use to anyone if he passed out. Ino looked as if he had been attacked, not by teeth or claws or knives, but by several sets of nail-pullers and wire-cutters. His chest still rose and fell, but his eyes were closed now and he was gray with shock. Glenna draped a thermal blanket over him.

Jen was steering around the rounded structure, not much bigger than a phone booth, protruding above the water in the middle of the pond. Most of the ponds and bays had similar observation stations. Claus had looked into one or two and he thought now that there was nothing in them likely to be of any help. More first aid kits, perhaps, but what Ino needed was the big medirobot back at the house.

And he was not going to get it. By now the building complex must be overrun by the attackers. Berserkers . . .

"Where can we find weapons?" Claus croaked at Glenna.

"Let's see that hand. I can't do any more for Ino now . . . I'll bandage this. If you mean guns, there are a couple at the house, somewhere in storage. We can't go back there now."

"I know."

Glenna had just let go of his hand when from the front seat there came a scream. Claws and a brown saucer shape were climbing in over the gunwale at Jenny's side. Had the damned thing come aboard somehow with them, from the tractor, or was this pond infested with them, too?

In his effort to help drag Ino to the boat, Claus had abandoned his trusty wrench beside the tractor. He grabbed now for the best substitute at hand, a small anchor at the end of a chain. His overhand swing missed Jenny's head by less than he had planned, but struck the monster like a mace. It fell into the bottom of the boat, vibrating its limbs, as Claus thought, uselessly; then he realized that it was making a neat hole.

His second desperation swing came down upon it squarely. One sharp prong of the anchor broke a segment of the brown casing clean away, and something sparked and sizzled when the sea came rushing in.

—seawater rushing—

—into the bottom of the boat—

The striking anchor had enlarged the hole that the enemy had begun. The bottom was split, the boat was taking water fast.

Someone grabbed up the sparking berserker, inert now save for internal fireworks, and hurled it over the side. Glenna threw herself forward, taking back the wheel, and Jenny scrambled aft, to help one-handed Claus with bailing.

The boat limped, staggered, gulped water, and wallowed on toward the landbar. It might get them that far, but forget the tantalizing freedom of blue surf beyond . . .

Jenny started to say something to her husband, then almost shrieked again as Ino's hand, resurgently alive, came up to catch her wrist. The old man's eyes were fixed on hers with a tremendous purpose. He gasped out words, and then fell back, unable to do more.

The words first registered with Jenny as: ". . . need them . . . do the splashers . . ." It made no sense.

Glenna looked back briefly, then had to concentrate on boat-handling. In another moment the fractured bottom was grating over rock. Claus scrambled out and held the prow against the above-water portion of the reef. The women followed, got their footing established outside the boat, then turned to lift at Ino's inert form.

Jenny paused. "Glenna, I'm afraid he's gone."

"No!" Denial was fierce and absolute. "Help me!"

Jen almost started to argue, then gave in. They got Ino up into a fireman's-carry position on Claus's shoulders; even with a bad hand, he was considerably stronger than either of the women. Then the three began to walk east along the reef. At high tide, as now, it was a strip of land no more than three or four meters wide, its low crest half a meter above the water. Waves of any size broke over it. Fortunately, today, the surf was almost calm.

Claus could feel the back of his coverall and neck wetting with Ino's blood. He shifted the dead weight on his shoulders. All right, so far. But his mutilated free hand throbbed.

He asked: "How far are we going, Glenna?"

"I don't know." The woman paced ahead—afraid to look at her husband now?—staring into the distance. "There isn't any place. Keep going."

Jenny and Claus exchanged looks. For want of any better plan at the moment, they kept going. Jen took a look back. "They're on the reef, and on the shore, too, following us. A good distance back."

Claus looked, and looked again a minute later. Brown speckles by the dozen followed, but were not catching up. Not yet.

Now they were passing the barrier of fused rock separating the pond, in which they had abandoned the boat, from its neighbor. The enemy moving along the shore would intercept them, or very nearly, if they tried to walk the barrier back to land.

Ahead, the reef still stretched interminably into a sun-dazzled nothingness.

"What's in this next pond, Glenna?" Claus asked, and knew a measure of relief when the gray-haired woman gave a little shake of her head and answered sensibly.

"Grouper. Some other fish as food stock for them. Why?"

"Just wondering. What'll we run into if we keep on going in this direction?"

"This just goes on. Kilometer after kilometer. Ponds, and bays, and observation stations—I say keep going, because otherwise, they'll catch us. What do you think we ought to do?"

Claus abruptly stopped walking, startling the women. He let the dead man slide down gently from his shoulders. Jen looked at her husband, examined Ino, shook her head.

Claus said: "I think we've got to leave him."

Glenna looked down at Ino's body once, could not keep looking at him. She nodded fiercely, and once more led the way.

A time of silent walking passed before Jenny, at Claus's side, began: "If they're berserkers . . ."

"What else?"

"Well, why aren't we all dead already? They don't seem very . . . efficiently designed for killing."

"These must be specialists," Claus mused. "Only a small part of a large force—a part Brass Trumpet missed when the rest moved on or was destroyed. Remember, we were wondering if Atlantis was their real target? These are special machines, built for . . . underwater work, maybe. Their ship must have been wrecked in the fighting and had to come down. When they found themselves on this planet, they must have come down to the sea for a reconnaissance, and then decided to attack first by land. Probably they saw the lights of the base before they crash-landed. They know which life form they have to deal with first, on any planet. Not very efficient, as you say. But they'll keep coming at us till they're all smashed or we're all dead."

Glenna had slowed her pace a little and was looking toward the small observation post rising in the midst of the pond that they were passing. "I don't think there's anything in any of these stations that can help us . . . in fact, I'm just about sure there's not. But I can't think of anywhere else to turn."

Claus asked: "What's in the next pond after this?"

"Sharks . . . ah. That might be worth a try. Sometimes they'll snap at anything that moves. They're small ones, so I think our risk will be relatively small if we wade out to the middle."

Claus thought to himself that he would rather end up in the belly of a live shark than torn to pieces by an impersonal device. Jen was willing also to take the chance.

They did not pause again till they were on the brink of the shark pond. Then Glenna said: "The water will be no more than three or four feet deep the way we're going. Stay together and keep splashing as we go. Claus, hold that hand up; mustn't drip a taste of blood into the water."

And in they went. Only when they were already splashing waist-deep did Claus recall Ino's blood wetting the back of his coverall. But he was not going to stop just now to take it off.

The pond was not very large; a minute of industrious wading, and they were climbing unmolested over the low, solid railing of the observation post rising near its middle. Here was space for two people to sit comfortably, sheltered from weather by a transparent dome and movable side panels. In the central console were instruments that constantly monitored the life in the surrounding ponds. Usually, of course, the readings from all ponds would be monitored in the more convenient central station attached to the house.

The three of them squeezed in, and Glenna promptly opened a small storage locker. It contained a writing instrument that looked broken, a cap perhaps left behind by some construction worker, and a small spider—another immigrant from Earth, of course—who might have been blown out here by the wind. That was all.

She slammed the locker shut again. "No help. So now it's a matter of waiting. They'll obviously come after us through the water. The sharks may snap up some of them before they reach us. Then we must be ready to move on before we are surrounded. It's doubtful, and risky, but I can't think of anything else to try."

Claus frowned. "Eventually, we'll have to circle around, get back to the buildings."

Jen frowned at him. "The berserkers are there, too."

"I don't think they will be, now. You see—"

Glenna broke in: "Here they come."

The sun had climbed, and was starting to get noticeably hot. It came to Claus's mind, not for the first time since their flight had started, that there was no water for them to drink. He held his left arm up with his right, trying to ease the throbbing.

Along the reef where they had walked, along the parallel shore—and coming now over the barrier from the grouper pond—plate-sized specks of brown death were flowing. There were several dozen of them, moving more slowly than hurried humans could move, almost invisible in the shimmer of sun and sea. Some plopped into the water of the shark pond as Claus watched.

"I can't pick them up underwater," Glenna announced. She was twiddling the controls of the station's instruments, trying to catch the enemy on one of the screens meant for observing marine life. "Sonar . . . motion detectors . . . water's too murky for simple video."

Understanding dawned for Claus. "That's why they're not metal! Why they're comparatively fragile. They're designed to avoid detection by underwater defenses—on Atlantis, I suppose—that could infiltrate and disable them."

Jen was standing. "We'd better get moving before we're cut off."

"In another minute." Glenna was still switching from one video pickup to another around the pond. "I'm sure we have at least that much to spare . . . ah."

One of the enemy had appeared on screen, sculling toward the camera at a modest pace. It looked less lifelike than it had in earlier moments of arm's-length combat.

Now, entering the picture from the rear, was a shark.

Claus was not especially good at distinguishing marine species. But this portentous and somehow familiar shape was identifiable at once, not to be confused even by the nonexpert, it seemed, with that of any other kind of fish.

Claus started to say, He's going right past. But the shark was not. Giving the impression of afterthought, the torpedo shape swerved back. Its mouth opened and the berserker device was gone.

The people watching made wordless sounds, but Jen took the others by an arm apiece. "We can't bet all of them will be eaten—let's get moving."

Claus already had one leg over the station's low railing when the still surface of the pond west of the observation post exploded. Leaping clear of the water, the premiere killer of Earth's oceans twisted in midair, as if trying to snap at its own belly. It fell back, vanishing in a hill of lashed-up foam. A moment later it jumped again, still thrashing.

In the fraction of a second when the animal was clearly visible, Claus watched the dark line come into being across its white belly as if traced there by an invisible pen. It was a short line that a moment later broadened and evolved into blood. As the fish rolled on its back something dark and pointed came into sight, spreading the edges of the hole. Then the convulsing body of the shark vanished in an eruption of water turned opaque with its blood.

The women were wading quickly away from the platform in the opposite direction, calling for him to follow, hoping aloud that the remaining sharks would be drawn to the dying one. But for one moment longer Claus lingered, staring at the screen. It showed the roiling bloody turmoil of killer fish converging, and out of this cloud the little berserker emerged, unfazed by shark's teeth or digestion, resuming its methodical progress toward the humans, the life units that could be really dangerous to the cause of death.

Jen tugged at her husband, got him moving with them. In her exhausted brain a nonsense rhyme was being generated: *Bloody water hides the slasher, seed them, heed them, sue the splashers . . .*

No!

As the three completed their water-plowing dash to the east edge of the pond, and climbed out, Jenny took Glenna by the arm. "Something just came to me. When I was tending Ino—he said something before he died."

They were walking east along the barrier reef again. "He said smashers," Jen continued. "That was it. Lead them, or feed them, to the smashers. But I still don't understand—"

Glenna stared at her for a moment, an almost frightening gaze. Then she stepped between the young couple and pulled them forward.

Two ponds down she turned aside, wading through water that splashed no higher than their calves, directly toward another observation post that looked just like the last.

"We won't be bothered in here, unless we should happen to step right on one, but there's very little chance of that," she assured them. "We're too big. Of course, of course. Oh, Ino. I should have thought of this myself. They wait in ambush most of the time, in holes or under rocks."

"They?" Injury and effort were taking their toll on Claus. He leaned on Jenny's shoulder now.

Glenna glanced back impatiently. "Mantis shrimp is the common name. They're stomatopods, actually."

"Shrimp?" The dazed query was so soft that she may not have heard it.

A minute later they were squeezed aboard the station and could rest again. Above, clean morning clouds were building to enormous height, clouds that might have formed in the unbreathed air of Earth five hundred million years before.

"Claus," Jen asked, when both of them had caught their breath a little, "what were you saying a while ago, about circling back to the house?"

"It's this way," he said, and paused to organize his thoughts. "We've been running to nowhere, because there's nowhere on this world we can get help. *But the berserkers can't know that.* I'm assuming they haven't scouted the whole planet—just crash-landed on it. For all they know, there's another colony of humans just down the coast. Maybe a town, with lots of people, aircraft, weapons . . . so for them, it's an absolute priority to cut us off before we can give a warning. Therefore, every one of their units must be committed to the chase. And if we can once get through them or around them, we can outrun them home, to vehicles and guns and food and water. How we get through them or around them I haven't figured out yet. But I don't see any other way."

"We'll see," said Glenna. Jen held his hand, and looked at him as if his idea might be reasonable. A distracting raindrop hit him on the face, and suddenly a shower was spattering the pond. With open mouths the three survivors caught what drops they could. They tried spreading Jenny's robe out to catch more, but the rain stopped before the cloth was wet.

"Here they come," Glenna informed them, shading her eyes from re-emergent sun. She started tuning up the observing gear aboard the station.

Claus counted brown saucer shapes dropping into the pond. Only nineteen, after all.

"Again, I can't find them with the sonar," Glenna muttered. "We'll try the television—there."

A berserker unit—for all the watching humans could tell, it was the same one that the shark had swallowed— was centimetering its tireless way toward them, walking the bottom in shallow, sunlit water. Death was walking. A living thing might run more quickly, for a time, but life would tire. Or let life oppose it, if life would. Already it had walked through a shark, as easily as traversing a mass of seaweed.

"There," Glenna breathed again. The advancing enemy had detoured slightly around a rock, and a moment later a dancing ripple of movement had emerged from hiding somewhere to follow in its path. The pursuer's score or so of tiny legs supported in flowing motion a soft-looking, roughly segmented, tubular body. Its sinuous length was about the same as the enemy machine's diameter, but in contrast, the follower was aglow with life, gold marked in detail with red and green and brown, like banners carried forward above an advancing column. Long antennae waved as if for balance above bulbous, short-stalked eyes. And underneath the eyes a coil of heavy forelimbs rested, not used for locomotion.

"*Odonodactylus syllarus*," Glenna murmured. "Not the biggest species—but maybe big enough."

"What are they?" Jen's voice was a prayerful whisper.

"Well, predators . . ."

The berserker, intent on its own prey, ignored the animate ripple that was overtaking it, until the smasher had closed almost to contact range. The machine paused then, and started to turn.

Before it had rotated itself more than halfway, its brown body was visibly jerked forward, under some striking impetus from the smasher too far for human eyes to follow. The *krak!* of it came clearly through the audio pickup. Even before the berserker had regained its balance, it put forth a tearing claw like that which had opened the shark's gut from inside.

Again the invisible impact flicked from a finger-length away. At each spot where one of the berserker's feet touched bottom, a tiny spurt of sand jumped up with the transmitted shock. Its tearing claw now dangled uselessly, hard ceramic cracked clean across.

"I've never measured a faster movement by anything that lives. They strike with special dactyls—well, with their elbows, you might say. They feed primarily on hard-shelled crabs and clams and snails. That was just a little one that Ino gave you, as a joke. One as long as my hand can hit something like a four-millimeter bullet—and some of these are longer."

Another hungry smasher was now coming swift upon the track of the brown, shelled thing that looked so like a crab. The second smasher's eyes moved on their stalks, calculating distance. It was evidently of a different species than the first, being somewhat larger and of a variant coloration. The berserker, put out a sharp and wiry tool and cut its first assailant neatly in half. As it turned back, Claus saw—or almost saw, or imagined that he saw—the newcomer's longest pair of forelimbs unfold and return. Again grains of sand beneath the two bodies, living and unliving, jumped from the bottom. With the concussion, white radii of fracture sprang out across a hard, brown surface . . .

Four minutes later the three humans were still watching, in near-perfect silence. A steady barrage of *kraks*, from every region of the pond, were echoing through the audio pickups. The video screen still showed the progress of the first individual combat.

"People sometimes talk about sharks as being aggressive, as terrible killing machines. Gram for gram, I don't think they're at all in the same class."

The smashing stomatopod, incongruously shrimplike, gripped the ruined casing of its victim with its six barb-studded smaller forelimbs and began to drag it back to the rock from which its ambush had been launched. Once there, it propped the interstellar terror in place, a Lilliputian monster blacksmith arranging metal against anvil. At the next strike—imaginable, if not visible, as a double backhand snap from the fists of a karate master—fragments of tough casing literally flew through the water, mixed now with a spill of delicate components. What, no soft, delicious meat in sight as yet? Then *smash* again . . .

An hour after the audio pickups had reported their last *krak,* the three humans walked toward home, unmolested through the shallows and along a shore where no brown saucers moved.

When Ino had been brought home, and Claus's hand seen to, the house was searched for enemy survivors. Guns were got out, and the great gates in the sand walls closed to be on the safe side. Then the two young people sent Glenna to a sedated rest.

Her voice was dazed and softly, infinitely tired. "Tomorrow we'll feed them, something real."

"This afternoon," said Claus. "When you wake up. Show me what to do."

"Look at this," called Jen a minute later, from the common room.

One wall of the smallest aquarium had been shattered outward. Its tough glass lay sharded on the carpet, along with a large stain of water and the soft body of a small creature, escaped and dead.

Jen picked it up. It was much smaller than its cousins out in the pond, but now she could not mistake the shape, even curled loosely in her palm.

Her husband came in and looked over her shoulder. "Glenna's still muttering. She just told me they can stab, too, if they sense soft meat in contact. Speartips on their smashers when they unfold them all the way. So you couldn't hold him like that if he was still alive." Claus's voice broke suddenly, in a delayed reaction.

"Oh, yes I could." Jen's voice, too. "Oh, yes I could indeed."

The White Bull

He was up on the high ridge, watching the gulls ride in from over the bright sea on their motionless wings, to be borne upward as if by magic, effortlessly, when the sun-dazzled landscape began to rise beneath them. Thus he was probably one of the first to sight the black-sailed ship coming in to port.

Standing, he raised a callused hand to brush aside his grizzled hair and shade his eyes. The vessel had the look of the craft that usually came from Athens. But those sails . . .

He picked up the cloak with which he had padded rock into a comfortable chair and threw it over his shoulder. It was time he came down from the high ridge anyway. King Minos and some of Minos' servitors were shrewd, and perhaps it would be wiser not to watch the birds too openly or too long.

When he had picked his way down, the harbor surrounded him with its noise and activity, its usual busy mixture of naval ships and cargo vessels, unloading and being worked on and taking on new cargo. On Execution Dock the sun-dried carcasses of pirates, looking like poor statues, shriveled atop tall poles in the bright sun. On the wharf where the black-sailed ship now moored, a small crowd had gathered and a dispute of some kind was going on. A bright-painted wagon, pulled by two white horses, had come down as scheduled from the House of the Double Axe to meet the Athenian ship, but none of the wagon's intended riders were getting into it as yet.

They stood on the wharf, fourteen youths and maids in a more or less compact group, wearing good clothes that seemed to have been deliberately torn and dirtied. Their faces were smeared with soot and ashes as if for mourning, and most of them looked somewhat the worse for wine. They were arguing with a couple of minor officials of the House, who had come down with the wagon and a small honor guard of soldiery. It was not the argument that drew the man from the high ridge ever closer, however, but the sight of one who stood in the front of the Athenian group, half a head taller than anyone around him.

He pushed his way in through the little crowd, a gray, middle-aged man with the heavy hands of an artisan, wearing heavy gold and silver ornaments on his fine white loincloth. A soldier looked around resentfully as a hard hand pushed on his shoulder, then closed his mouth and stepped aside.

"Prince Theseus." The old workman's hands went out in a gesture of deferential greeting. "I rejoice that the gods have brought you safe again before my eyes. How goes it with your royal father?"

The tall young man swung his eyes around and brought them rather slowly into focus. Some of the sullen anger left his begrimed face. "Daedalus." A nod gave back unforced respect, became almost a bow as the strong body threatened to overbalance. "King Aegeus does well enough."

"I saw the black sails, Prince, and feared they might bear news of tragedy."

"All m'family in Athens are healthy as war horses, Daedalus—or were when we sailed. The mourning is for ourselves. For our approaching . . ." Theseus groped hopelessly for a word.

"Immolation," cheerfully supplied one of the other young men in ashes.

"That's it." The prince smiled faintly. "So you may tell these officers that we wear what we please to our own welcome." His dulled black eyes roamed up the stair steps of the harbor town's white houses and warehouses and whorehouses, to an outlying flank of the House of the Double Axe which was just visible amid a grove of cedars at the top of the first ridge. "Where is the school?"

"Not far beyond the portion of the House you see. Say, an hour's walk." Daedalus observed the younger man with sympathy. "So, you find the prospect of a student's life in Crete not much to your liking." Around them the other branches of the argument between Cretan officials and newcomers had ceased; all were attending to the dialogue.

"Four years, Daedalus." The princely cheeks, one whitened with an old sword scar, puffed out in a winey belch. "Four god-blasted years."

"I know." Daedalus' face wrinkled briefly with shared pain. He almost put out a hand to take the other's arm; a little too familiar, here in public. "Prince Theseus, will you walk with me? King Minos will want to see you promptly, I expect."

"I bear him greetings from m'father."

"Of course. Meanwhile, the officers here will help your shipmates on their way to find their quarters."

Thus the ascent from the harbor turned into an informal procession, with Theseus and Daedalus walking ahead, and the small honor guard following a few paces back, irregularly accompanied by the remaining thirteen Athenians, who looked about them and perhaps wondered a little at the unceremoniousness of it all. The girls whispered a little at the freedom of the Cretan women, who, though obviously respectable, as shown by their dress and attitudes, strode about so boldly in the streets. The gaily decorated wagon, in which the new arrivals might have ridden, rumbled uphill empty behind a pair of grateful horses. The wagon's bright paint and streamers jarred with the mock mourning of the newcomers.

When they had climbed partway through the town, Daedalus suggested gently to his companion that the imitation mourning *would* be in especially bad taste at court today, for a real funeral was going to take place in the afternoon.

"Someone in Minos' family?"

"No. One who would have been your fellow student had he lived—in his third year at school. A Lapith. But still."

"Oh." Theseus slowed his long if slightly wobbling strides and rubbed a hand across his forehead, looking at the fingers afterward. "Now what do I do?"

"Let us not, after all, take you to Minos right away." Daedalus turned and with a gesture called one of the court officials forward, saying to him: "Arrange some better quarters for Prince Theseus than those customarily given the new students. And he and his shipmates will need some time to make themselves presentable before they go before the king. Meanwhile, I will seek out Minos myself and offer explanations."

The officer's face and his quick salute showed his relief.

"Daedalus." King Minos' manner was pleasant but businesslike as he welcomed his engineer into a pleasant, white-walled room where, at the moment, his chief tax-gatherers were arguing over innumerable scrolls spread out upon stone tables. Open colonnades gave a view of blue ocean in one direction, Mount Ida in another. "What can I do to help you out today? How goes the rock-thrower machine?" The king's once-raven hair was graying, and his bare paunch stood honestly and comfortably over the waistband of his linen loincloth. But his arms within their circlets of heavy gold looked muscular as ever, and his eyes were still keen and penetrating.

"The machine does well enough, sire. I wait for the cattle hides from Thrace, which are to be twisted into the sling, and I improve my waiting time by overseeing construction of the bronze shields." Actually, by now, the smiths and smelters were all well trained and needed little supervision, so there was time for thought whilst looking into the forge and furnace flames—time to see again the gull's effortless flight as captured by the mind and eye. . . . "Today, King Minos, I come before you with another matter—one that I am afraid will not wait." He began to relate to Minos the circumstances of the prince's arrival, leaving out neither the black sails nor the drunkenness, though they were mere details compared with the great fact of Theseus' coming to be enrolled in the school.

Minos, during this recital, led him into another room, out of earshot of the tax gatherers. There the king, frowning, walked restlessly, pausing to look out of a window to where preparations for the afternoon's funeral games were under way. "How is Aegeus?" he asked, without turning.

"Prince Theseus reports his esteemed father in excellent health."

"Daedalus, it will not do for King Aegeus' son to leave Crete with his brains addled, any more than they may be already," the king turned, "as has happened to a few—Cretans and Athenians and others—since the school was opened. Or to leap from a tower, like this young man we're burying today. Not that I think the prince would ever choose that exit."

"Yours are words of wisdom, sire. And no more will it be desirable for Theseus to fail publicly at an assigned task, even if it be only obtaining a certificate of achievement from a school."

Minos walked again. "Your turn to speak wisely, counselor. Frankly, what do you think the prince's chances are of pursuing his studies here successfully?"

Daedalus' head bobbed in a light bow. "I share your own seeming misgivings on the subject, great king."

"Yes. Um. We both know Theseus, and we both

know also what the school is like. You better than I, I
suppose. I can have Phaedra keep an eye on him, of
course. She will be starting this semester, too—not that
she has her older sister's brains, but it may do her some
good. It may. He is as stalwart and handsome as ever, I
suppose? Yes, then no doubt she will have an eye on
him in any case."

Continuing to think aloud, arms folded and a frown
on his face, Minos came closer, until an observer might
have thought that he was threatening the other man. "I
had not thought that Aegeus was about to send his own
son. But I suppose he did not want his nobles' children
displaying any honors that could not be matched in his
own house. Oh, if he'd had a scholarly boy, one given
to hanging around with graybeard sages, then I would
have issued a specific invitation. I would've thought it
expected. But given the prince's nature . . ."

Minos unfolded his arms but kept his eyes fixed
firmly on his waiting subject. "Daedalus. You are Theseus'
friend, from your sojourn at the Athenian court. And
you were enrolled briefly in the school yourself . . . I
sometimes marvel that you did not throw yourself into
it more wholeheartedly."

"Perhaps we sages are not immune to professional
jealousy, sire."

"Perhaps." Minos' gaze twinkled keenly. "However
that may be, I now expect you to do two things."

Daedalus bowed.

"First, stand ready to offer Theseus your tutorial
services, as they may be required."

"Of course, sire."

"Secondly—will you go today to see the Bull and talk
to him? I think in this case you have greater competence than any of my usual ambassadors. Do what you
can toward explaining the situation. Report back to me
when you have seen the Bull."

Daedalus bowed.

On his way toward the Labyrinth, at whose center
the Bull dwelt, he stopped to peer in, unnoticed, at the

elementary school, which, like most other governmental departments, had its own corner of the vast sprawling House. On a three-legged stool, surrounded by a gaggle of other boys and girls, sat ten-year-old Icarus, stylus in hand, bent over wax tablets on a table before him. Chanting grammar, an earnest young woman paced among her pupils. Daedalus knew her for one of the more recent graduates of the school where Theseus was bound. For a moment, the king's engineer had the mad vision of Theseus in this classroom, teaching—hardly madder than that of the prince sitting down to study, he supposed. After a last glance at his own fidgeting son—Icarus was bright enough, but didn't seem to want to apply himself to learning yet—Daedalus walked on.

As he passed along the flank of the vast House, he glanced in the direction of the field of rock-hewn tombs nearby, and saw the small procession returning across the bridge that spanned the Kairatos, coming back to the House for the games—the bull dancing and the wrestling that should please the gods.

Pausing in a cloistered walk to watch, he pondered briefly the fact that Minos himself was not coming to the funeral. Of course, the king was always busy. There was Queen Pasiphae, though, taking her seat of honor in the stands, rouged and wigged as usual these days to belie her age, tight girdle thrusting her full bare breasts up in a passable imitation of youth. And there came Princess Ariadne to the royal bench, taking the position of Master of the Games, as befitted her status of eldest surviving child. And there was Phaedra—how old now? sixteen?—and quite the prettiest girl in sight.

He had thought that Theseus might be sleeping it off by now, but evidently the recuperative powers of youth, at least in the royal family of Athens, were even stronger than Daedalus remembered them to be. The prince, cleansed by what must have been a complete bath and scraping, and suitably tagged for a modest degree of real mourning by a black band around his massive biceps, was just now vaulting into the ring for a wrestling turn. Stripped naked for the contest, Theseus was

an impressive figure. Daedalus stayed long enough to
watch him earn a quick victory over his squat, powerful
adversary, some Cretan champion, and then claim a
wreath from Ariadne's hand.

Then Daedalus walked on. There was, on this side of
the House, no sharp line of architectural demarcation
where ordinary living space ended and the Labyrinth
began. Roofed space became less common, and at the
same time walls grew unscalably high and smooth and
passages narrowed. Stairs took the walker up and down
for no good reason, and up and down again, until he
was no longer sure whether he walked above the true
ground level or below it. Windows were no more.

Now Daedalus was in the precincts of the real school,
which Theseus would attend. Behind closed wooden
doors taut silence reigned, or else came out the drone
of reciting voices. A dozen times a stranger would have
been confused, and like as not turned back to where he
started, before Daedalus reached a sign, warning in
three languages that the true Labyrinth lay just ahead.
He passed beneath the sign with quick, sure steps.

He had gone scarcely fifty paces farther, turning half
a dozen corners in that distance, before he became
aware that someone was following him. A pause to
glance back got him a brief glimpse of a girl with long
hair, peering around a corner in his direction. The girl
ducked out of sight at once. All was silent until his own
feet began to move again, whereupon the shuffle of
those pursuing him resumed.

With a sigh, he stopped again, then turned and called
softly, "Stay." Then he walked back. As he had expected, it was a student, a slender Athenian girl of
about eighteen, leaning against the stone wall in an
exhausted but defensive pose. Daedalus vaguely remembered seeing her around for the last year or two.
Now her eyes had gone blank and desperate with the
endless corners and walls, angles and stairs, and tantalizing glimpses of sky beyond the bronze grillwork high

above. Failing some kind of test, obviously, she stared at him in silent hopelessness.

It was not for him to interfere. "Follow me," he whispered to her, "and you will come out in the apartments of the Bull himself. Is that what you want?"

The girl responded with a negative gesture, weak but quick. There was great fear in her eyes. It was not the fear of a soldier entering a losing battle, or a captive going to execution, but great all the same. Though not as raw and immediate as those particular kinds of terror, it was on a level just as deep. Not death, only failure was in prospect, but that could be bad enough, especially for the young.

He turned from her and went on, and heard no more of feet behind. Soon he came to where a waterpipe crossed the passageway, concealed under a kind of stile. He had overseen most of the Labyrinth's construction, and was its chief designer. This wall here on his left was as thick as four men's bodies lying head to toe. Just outside, though you would never guess it from in here, was a free sunny slope, and the last creaking shadoof in the chain of lifting devices that brought seawater here by stages from the salt pools and reservoirs below.

Choosing unthinkingly the correct branchings of the twisted way, he came out abruptly into the central open space. Beyond the broad, raised, sundazzled stone dais in its center yawned the dark mouths of the Bull's own rooms. In the middle of the dais, like the gnomon of a sundial, stood a big chair on whose humped seat no human could comfortably have perched. On it the White Bull sat waiting, as if expecting him.

"Learn from me, Dae-dal-us." This was what the Bull always said to him in place of any more conventional greeting. It had chronic trouble in sliding its inhumanly deep, slow voice from one syllable to another without a complete stop in between, though when necessary, the sounds came chopping out at a fast rate.

The Bull stood up like a man from its chair, on the dais surrounded by the gently flowing moat of seawater that it did not need, but loved. It was hairy and muscular, and larger than any but the biggest men. Though wild tales about its bullhood flew through the House, Daedalus, who had talked to it perhaps as much as any other man, was not even sure that it was truly male. The silver-tipped hair or fur grew even thicker about the loins than on the rest of the body, which was practically covered. Its feet—Daedalus sometimes thought of them as its hind feet, though it invariably walked on only two—ended in hooves, or at least in soles so thick and hard as to come very near that definition. Its upper limbs, beneath their generous fur, were quite manlike in the number and position of their joints, and their muscular development put Daedalus in mind of Theseus' arms.

Any illusion that this might be a costumed man died quickly with inspection of the hands. The fingernails were so enlarged as to be almost tiny hooves, and each hand bore two opposable thumbs. The head, at first glance, was certainly a bull's, with its fine short snowy hair and the two blunt horns; but one saw quickly that the lips were far too mobile, the eyes too human and intelligent.

"Learn from me, Dae-dal-us."

"We have tried that." The conflict between them was now too old, and still too sharp, to leave much room for formal courtesy.

"Learn." The deep and bull-like voice was stubborn as a wall. "The se-crets of the a-tom and the star are mine to give."

"Then what need have you for one more student, one worn old man like me? There must be younger minds, all keen and eager to be taught. Even today a fresh contingent has come from Athens for your instruction."

"You are not tru-ly old as yet; there are dec-ades of strong life a-head. And if you tru-ly learn, you may ex-tend your life."

Daedalus curtly signed refusal, confronting the other across the moat's reflected sky. The king had had him raise the water up here for the Bull's pleasure, evidently as some reminder of a homeland too remote for human understanding. Some ten years ago the Bull had appeared on the island, speaking passable Greek and asking to see the king, offering gifts of knowledge. Some said it had come out of the sea, but the homeland it occasionally alluded to was much more wonderful than that.

Daedalus said: "For the past few years I have watched the young men and women going in here to be taught, and I have seen and talked to them again when they came out. I do not know whether I want to be taught what they are learning. Not one has whispered to me the stars' or atoms' secrets."

"All fra-gile ves-sels, Dae-dal-us. Of lim-i-ted cap-a-cit-y. And once cracked, good on-ly to be stud-ied to find out how the pot is made." The Bull took a step toward him on its shaggy, goat-shaped legs. "For such a mind as yours, I bring ful-fill-ment, nev-er bur-sting."

It was always the same plea: learn from me. And always the same arguments, with variations, shot back and forth between them. "Are there no sturdy, capacious vessels among the students?"

"Not one in a thou-sand will have your mind. Not one in ten thou-sand."

"We have tried, remember? It was not good for me."

"Try a-gain."

Daedalus looked around him almost involuntarily, then lowered his voice. "I told you what I wanted. Teach me to fly. Show me how the wings should be constructed, rather."

"It is not that sim-ple, Dae-dal-us." The White Bull's inhumanly deep voice stretched out in something like a yawn, and it resumed its chair. It ate only vegetables and fruits, and scattered about it on the dais was a light litter of husks and shriveled leaves. "But if you stu-dy in my school four years, you will be a-ble to build wings for your-self af-ter that time. I prom-ise you."

The man clenched his callused hands. "How can it take me four years to learn to build a wing? If I can learn a thing at all, the idea of it should take root within my mind inside four days, and any skill required should come into my fingers in four months. The knowledge might take longer to perfect, of course, but I do not ask to build a flock of birds complete with beaks and claws, and breathe life into them, and set them catching fish and laying eggs. No, all I want are a few feathers for myself."

When he had enrolled, a year or so ago, he soon found out that he was to learn to build wings not by trying to build them, but by first studying "the knowledge of numbers," as the White Bull put it, then the strengths and other properties of the various materials that might be used, theories of the air and of birds, and a distracting list of other matters having even less apparent relevance. Some of this, the materials, Daedalus knew pretty well already, and about the rest he did not care. His enrollment had not lasted long.

"Try a-gain, Dae-dal-us." The voice maintained its solemn, stubborn roar. "You will be-come a tru-ly ed-u-cat-ed man. New hor-i-zons will o-pen for you."

"You mean you will teach me not what I want to learn, but rather to forget wanting it. To learn instead to make my life depend and pivot on your teaching." Here he was again, getting bogged down in the same old unwinnable dispute. Why keep at it? Because there were moments when he seemed to himself insane for rejecting the undoubted wealth of knowledge that the Bull could give him. And yet he knew that he was right to do so.

"Bull, what good will it do you if I come to sit at your feet and learn? There has to be something that you want out of it."

"My rea-son for be-ing is to teach." It nodded down solemnly at him from its high chair, and crossed its hind legs like some goat-god. "For this I crossed o-ceans un-im-ag'-na-ble be-tween the stars. When I con-vey my teach-ings to minds a-ble to hold them, then I too will be ful-filled and can know peace. Shall I tell Min-os that you still re-fuse? There are wea-pons much great-er than cat-a-pults that you could make for him."

"I doubt you will tell Minos anything. I doubt that he will speak to you anymore."

"Why not? You mean I have dis-pleased him?"

He meant, but was not going to say, that Minos seemed to be getting increasingly afraid of his pet monster. It was not, Daedalus thought, that the king suspected the Bull of plotting to seize power, or anything along that line. Minos' fear seemed to lie on a deeper, more personal level. The king perhaps had not admitted this fear to himself, and anyway, the White Bull brought him too much prestige, not to speak of useful knowledge, for him to want to get rid of it.

Daedalus said: "The king sent me today, when he could have come himself, or else had you brought before him."

"On what er-rand?"

"Not to renew old arguments." Daedalus spat into the White Bull's moat and watched critically as the spittle was borne along toward the splash gutter at the side. He was proud of his waterworks and liked to see them operating properly. "Among today's Athenians is one whose coming poses problems for us all." He identified Theseus, and outlined Minos' concern for his alliance with Aegeus. "The young man is probably here at least in part because his father wants him kept out of possible intrigues at home. Minos said nothing of the kind to me, but I heard it between the words of what he said."

"I think I un-der-stand, Dae-dal-us. Yet I can but try to im-part know-ledge to this young man. If he can-not or will not learn, I can-not cert-i-fy that he has. Else what I have cert-i-fied of o-ther stu-dents be-comes sus-pect."

"In this case, surely, an exception might be made."

They argued this point for a while, Daedalus getting nowhere, until the White Bull suddenly offered that something might be done to make Theseus' way easier, if Daedalus himself were to enroll as a student again.

Daedalus was angry. "Minos will really be displeased with you if I bear back the message that you want me to spend my next four years studying, rather than working for my king."

"E-ven stu-dy-ing half time, one with a mind like yours may learn in three years what a mere-ly ex-cell-ent stu-dent learns in four."

The man was silent, holding in, like an old soldier at attention.

"Why do you re-sist me, Dae-dal-us? Not rea-lly be-cause you fear your mind will crack be-neath the bur-den of my trea-sures. Few e-ven of the poor stu-dents have this hap-pen."

Daedalus relaxed suddenly. He sat down on the fine stone pavement and was able to smile and even chuckle. "Oh great White Bull, whenever I see man or god approaching to do me a favor, a free good turn, I do a good turn for myself and flee the other way. Through experience I have acquired this habit, and it lies near the roots of whatever modest stock of wisdom I possess."

There was at first no answer from the creature on the high inhuman chair, and Daedalus pressed on. "Be-cause I *can* learn something, does that mean I must? Should I not count the price?"

"There is no price, for you."

"Bah."

"What is the price for a man who stum-bles up-on great trea-sure, if he sim-ply bends and picks it up?"

"A good question. I will think upon it."

"But the cost to him is all the trea-sure, if he re-fuses e-ven to bend."

He knew he had no particular skill in intrigue, and was afraid to do anything but carry the whole truth back to Minos. The king, of course, gave him no way out, and Daedalus was forced to enroll. He had no black sail to hoist, but simply walked to the White Bull's apart-ments again and said, "Well, here I am."

"Good." He could not tell if the Bull was gloating. "First, a re-fresh-er course." And shortly Daedalus was walking into a classroom where Theseus and Phaedra sat side by side among other young folk. Daedalus took his place on a bench, endured some curious glances, and waited, gnarled and incongruous, until the Bull entered and began to teach.

This was not instruction in the human way. Daedalus knew that he and his fellow students still sat rooted to their benches, with the tall shaggy figure of the Bull before them. But there came with the sudden clarity of lightning a vision in which he seemed to have sprung upward from the ground, flying at more than arrow speed into the blue. The Labyrinth and the whole House of the Double Axe dropped clear away, and his view carried over the whole fair isle of Crete. Its mountains dwindled and flattened, soon became almost at one with the fields and orchards, and very quickly the sea was visible on every side. Other islands popped into view, and then the jagged mainland of Greece. Then the whole Mediterranean, with a sunspot of glare on it bigger than lost Crete itself; then Europe and much of Africa; and then a hemisphere—the shared experience was too much for some of the students, and there were outcries and faintings around Daedalus. He was a little shaken himself, though he had seen this much during his previous enrollment.

Eventually, the first day of his renewed schooling was over, and in due time the second and the third had passed. Lessons came in a more or less fixed plan. Seldom were they as dramatically presented as that early one that indicated the size and complexity of the world. Mostly the students studied from books, hand-copied for them by students more advanced, who also did much of the teaching. And there were tests.

QUESTION: THE WORLD ON WHICH MEN LIVE IS:

A. Bigger than the island of Crete.

B. Approximately a sphere in shape.

C. In need of cultivation and care, that can be accomplished only through education, if it is to support properly an eventual population of billions of human beings.

D. All of the above.

"Are these the secrets of the stars and atoms, Bull?"

"Pa-tience, Dae-dal-us. One step at a time. Tra-di-tion hal-lows the mode of tea-ching."

"Bah."

"Now you are a stu-dent. Dis-re-spect low-ers your grades and slows your pro-gress."

Theoretically, his attendance was to be for half a day, every day except the rare holidays. But it was tacitly understood between the Bull and Minos—at least Daedalus hoped it was—that Daedalus in fact kept to a flexible schedule, spending whatever time was necessary on the king's projects—the catapults, the lifelike statues—to keep them progressing. His days were more than full, though he could have done all the schoolwork required so far with half a brain.

Meanwhile, the White Bull seemed to be keeping his part of the bargain. One of his chief acolytes, Stomargos, an earnest mainland youth who was frail and clumsy at the same time, explained to Daedalus how Theseus was being shunted into a special program.

"The prince will be allowed to choose both his Greater and Lesser Branches of learning from courses that have not previously been given for credit," said the young man, whose own Greater was, as he had proudly informed Daedalus, the Transmission of Learning itself. "Since Prince Theseus seems fated to spend most of his life as a warrior, the Bull is preparing for him courses in Strategic Decision, Command Presence, and Tactical Leadership—these in addition, of course, to those in Language, Number, and the World of Men that are required of all first-year students."

"I wish the royal student well." Daedalus paused for thought. "It may be foolish of me to ask, but I cannot forbear. Where and how is the course on Tactical Leadership to be conducted?"

"All courses are conducted within the student's mind, Daedalus." The answer sounded somewhat condescending. Nonetheless, Daedalus pursued the matter, out of concerned curiosity, and found out that the Labyrinth itself, or some part of it, was to be the training ground. Beyond that Stomargos knew little.

Back at his workshop that afternoon, Daedalus found a message from Icarus' teacher awaiting him—the boy had run off somewhere, playing truant. It was the second or third time that this had happened within a month. And scarcely had he grumbled at this message and then put it aside to take up his real work, when Icarus himself came dawdling in, an elbow scraped raw, arm messy with dried blood from some mishap during the day. Daedalus waved the note and growled and lectured, but in the son's face he could see the mother, and he could not be harsh. He ordered a servant to take Icarus home, see to his injury, and keep him confined to quarters for the remainder of the day.

Then there was a little time at last to part the curtains at the workshop's rear, and move through the secret door there that slid out of the way as if by magic, carrying with it neatly what had looked like an awkward, obstructing pile of dirty trash. Time to crank open a secret skylight above a secret room, and look at the great man-wings spread out on a bench.

Long ago he had given up trying to use real feathers; now he worked with canvas and leather and light cotton padding to add shape. But work was lagging lately; he felt in his bones that more thought, more cunning was needed. When he strapped on one wing and beat it downward through the air, the effect was not much different from that of waving a fan. He was not impelled noticeably toward the sky. There were secrets still to be discovered . . .

When he got back to quarters himself, it was late at night. He grabbed a mouthful of fruit and cheese, drank half a cup of wine, shooed a bored and sleepy concubine out of his way, and dropped on his own soft but simple bed to rest. It seemed that hardly had his eyes closed, however, before he heard the voices of soldiers, bullying a servant at his door: ". . . orders to bring Daedalus at once before the king."

This was not Minos' usual way of summoning one of

his most trusted and respected advisors, and Daedalus knew fear as, shivering, he went with them out under the late, cold stars. The lieutenant took pity on him. "It concerns Prince Theseus, sir. The king is . . ." The soldier shook his head, and let his words trail off with a puffed sigh of awe.

It was the formal audience chamber to which the soldiers brought him—a bad sign, Daedalus thought. At the king's nod they saluted and backed out, leaving the engineer standing before the throne. Theseus moved over a little on the carpet to make room for him. No one else was now present except Minos, who, seated on his tall chair between the painted griffins, continued a merciless chewing-out of the young prince. The flames of the oil lamps trembled now and then as if in awe. The tone of the king's voice was settled, almost weary, suggesting that this tongue-lashing had been going on for some time.

Sneaking glances at Theseus, Daedalus judged he had been drunk recently, but was no longer. Scratches on the sullen, handsome face, and a bruise on one bare shoulder—Theseus was attired in the Cretan gentleman's elegant loincloth now—suggested recent strenuous activity, and the king's words filled in the story.

Icarus had not been the day's only truant, and Theseus would have been wiser to bruise himself in some activity so innocuous as seeking birds' eggs on the crags. Instead, he had led some of his restive classmates on an escapade in town. Tactical Leadership, thought Daedalus, even while he kept his face impeccably grave and his eyes suitably downcast in the face of the Minoan wrath.

Violence against citizens and their valuable slaves. Destruction of property. Shameful public drunkenness, bringing disrepute on House and School alike. All topped off by the outrage of the daughters of some merchant families who were too important to be so treated.

Theseus held his hands behind him, sometimes tightening them into fists, sometimes playing like an idiot with his own massive fingers. His heavy features were set in disciplined silence now. This was probably like being home again and listening to his father.

". . . classmates involved will be expelled and sent home in disgrace," the king was saying. He paused now, for the first time since the soldiers left. "To do the same to you would, of course, be an insult to your father and a danger to our alliance. Daedalus, did I not set you in charge of this young blockhead's schooling?"

In the face of this inaccuracy, Daedalus merely bowed his head a little lower. Now was not the moment for any philosopher's insistence on precise Truth; rather, the great fact that Minos was in a rage easily took precedence over Truth in any of its lesser forms.

"His schooling is not proceeding satisfactorily, Daedalus."

The engineer bowed somewhat lower yet.

"And as for you, *Prince*—now you may speak. What have you to say?"

Theseus shifted weight on his big feet, and spoke up calmly enough. "Sire, that school is driving me to drink and madness."

Now Minos, too, was calm. The royal rage had been used up, or perhaps it could be turned on and off like one of Daedalus' water valves. "Prince Theseus, you are under house arrest until further notice. Except for school attendance. I will put six strong soldiers at your door, and you may assault them, or try to, should you feel the need for further recreation."

"I am sorry, King Minos." And it seemed he was. "But I can take no more of that school."

"You will take more of it. You must." Then the king's eye swung back again. "Daedalus, what are we to do? The queen and I leave in three days for state visits, in Macedonia and elsewhere. We may be gone for months."

"I fear I have been neglectful regarding the prince's problems, sire. Let me now make them my prime concern."

Shortly after dawn a few hours later, Daedalus came visiting the White Bull's quarters once again. This time he found the dais uninhabited, so he sloshed through the moat and stood beside the odd chair. There was never any need to call. Shortly, the silver-and-snow figure emerged from a darkened doorway, to splash gratefully in the salt moat and then climb onto the dais to bid him welcome.

"Learn from me, Dae-dal-us! How are you learn-ing?"

"White Bull, I come not on my own affairs today, but on Prince Theseus' behalf. He is having trouble—well, he informs me that this testing in the Labyrinth, in particular, is likely to drive him to violent madness. Knowing him, I do not think he is exaggerating. Must this Tactical course be continued in its present form?"

"The course of stu-dy of tac-tics is pre-scribed, in part, as fol-lows: The teach-er shall e-voke from the stu-dents facts as to their de-term-in-a-tion of spa-tial lo-ca-tion—"

He couldn't stand it. "Oh great teacher! Master of the Transmission of Learning—"

"Not Mas-ter. My rank is that of A-dept, a high-er rank."

"Master, or adept, or divinity, or what you will. I suppose it means nothing that the prince's fate in bat-tle, even insofar as he may escape all the sheer chance stupidities of war, is not at all likely to depend on his ability to grope his way out of a maze?"

"He has been al-lowed to choose his course of stu-dy, Dae-dal-us. Be-yond that, spe-cial treat-ment can-not be ac-cord-ed a-ny stu-dent."

"Well. _I_ have never fought anyone with a sword, White Bull. _I_ have never bullied and challenged men and cheered them on to get them into combat. Once, on the mainland, watching from the highest and safest place that I could reach, I saw Prince Theseus do these things. Some vassal's uprising against Aegeus. Theseus put it down, almost single-handedly, you might say. I think he would not be likely to learn much from me in the way of military science, were I to lecture on the subject. No doubt you, however, have great skill and knowledge in this field to impart?"

"My qual-if-i-ca-tions as teach-er are be-yond your

ab-il-i-ty to com-pre-hend, much less to ques-tion. Your
own prog-ress should be your con-cern."

"If Theseus fails, I may not be on hand to make any
progress through your school. Minos will be angry at
me. And not at me alone."

But argue as he might he still could not get his ward
excused from tactical training and testing in the Labyrinth. For the next couple of days the prince at least
stayed in school and worked, and Daedalus' hope rose.
Then, emerging one afternoon from his own classroom,
he saw a page from the Inner House coming to meet
him, and knew a sinking feeling. The Princess Ariadne
required his presence in the audience chamber at once.

He found Ariadne perched regally on the throne, but
as soon as she had waved her attendants out and the
two of them were alone, she came down from the chair
and spoke to him informally.

"Daedalus, before my father's departure, he informed
me that Prince Theseus was having difficulties in school.
The king impressed upon me the importance of this
problem. Also, I have talked with the prince myself,
and find that the situation does not seem to be improv-
ing." Ariadne sounded nervous, vaguely distracted.

"I fear that you are right, Princess." Then, before he
had to say anything more, another page was announcing
Theseus himself. There was no escort of soldiers with
the prince; evidently, the house arrest instituted by
Minos had already been set aside.

The exchange of greetings between the two young
people sounded somewhat too stiffly formal to Daedalus,
and he noted that Ariadne scarcely looked directly at
Theseus for a moment. Certainly, she had not so
avoided watching him during the wrestling match. And
when the prince looked at her now, his face was wooden.

For a few moments Daedalus thought perhaps that
they were quarreling, but he soon decided that the
absolute opposite was more likely: an affair, and they
were trying to hide it.

In response to an awkward-sounding request from
Ariadne, Theseus related his day's continued difficulties

in school. Now she turned, almost pleading, to the older man. "Daedalus, he will fail his Labyrinth tests again. What are we to do? We must find *some* means of helping him." And a glance flicked between the two young people that was very brief, but still enough to assure Daedalus of what was going on.

"Ah." He relaxed, looked at them both with something like a smile. He only hoped infatuation would not bring Ariadne to any too-great foolishness. Meanwhile, Theseus' problem might be easier to solve while Minos, with his awe of the Bull, was not around.

Conferring with the prince, while Ariadne hovered near and listened greedily, he made sure that the maze itself was indeed the key to the young man's difficulties. In courses other than Tactics the prince might, probably could, do well enough to just scrape by.

With a charred stick Daedalus drew, from memory, a plan of the key portion of the Labyrinth right on the floor near the foot of the throne. The griffins glared down balefully at the three of them squatting there like children at some game.

Theseus stared gloomily at the patterns while Daedalus talked. Ariadne's hand came over once, forgetfully, to touch her lover's, and then flew back, while her eyes jumped up to Daedalus' face. He affirmed that he had noticed nothing by holding his own scowling concentration on the floor.

"Now try it this way, Prince. The secret . . . let's see. Yes. If you are finding your way *in*, the secret is to let your right hand touch the wall at the start. Hey?"

"Yes, I can always tell my right hand from my left. Out here, anyway." Theseus was trying grimly. "Right always holds the sword."

"Yes. So if you want to go inward, as I say, first let your right hand glide continuously along the wall, in imagination if not in fact. Then, whenever you must climb a stair, switch at its top to gliding your left hand along the wall; in other words, when there's a choice, turn always to the left. Whenever a stair leads you downward, switch again at its bottom to going right. Now, if you are seeking your way *out*, simply reverse—"

"Daedalus." The prince's voice stopped him in midsentence. "Thanks for what you are trying to do. But I tell you, when I am put in there I cannot help myself." Theseus got to his feet, as if unconscious of the movement, his eyes fixed now on distance. "*In there* I forget all your lefts and rights, and all else. I know the walls are crushing in on me, the doors all sealing themselves off—" Ariadne put out a hand again, and drew it back. Now she was standing too. "—so there is nothing left but the stone walls, all coming closer . . . I could wish you had never told me that some of them are four men's bodies thick."

Theseus was shivering slightly, as if with cold. The look in his eyes was one that Daedalus had seen there only rarely in the past, and now Daedalus, too, got to his feet, moving with deliberate care.

"If that god-blasted cow dares lecture me on courage and perseverance in my stu-dies one more time, I swear by all the gods I'll break its neck."

"Very well, my friend." He laid a hard hand gently and briefly on the prince's shoulder. "There are other ways that we can help."

Midafternoon of the day following, and in his own classroom, Daedalus had fallen into a daydream of numbers that his stubborn mind kept trying to fit to flying gulls. He was roused from this state by a hand shaking his shoulder.

Stomargos stood at his side, looking down at him in obscure triumph. "Daedalus, the White Bull wants to see you, at once."

He would not ask what for, but got to his feet and followed the educator in a silence of outward calm.

Daedalus had expected that when they reached the Bull's private quarters Stomargos would be sent out. But the Bull, waiting for them on its tall chair, made no sign of dismissal, and the young man, with a smug look on his face, remained standing at Daedalus' side.

Today, for once, the Bull did not say *learn from me*. "We have dis-cov-ered the prin-ce's cheat-ing, Dae-dal-us."

"Cheating? What do you mean?" He had never been any good with lies.

"The thread tied on his right hand. The ti-ny met-al balls to bounce and roll and seek al-ways the down-ward slope of floor, how-ev-er gen-tle. How did you make a met-al ball so smooth and round?"

He had dropped them molten from a tall tower, into water. He wonderd if the Bull would be impressed to hear his method. "I see," he said aloud, trying to be noncommittal, admitting nothing. "What do you mean to do?"

"Leave us, Sto-mar-gos," the White Bull said at last. And when they were alone, it said: "Now learn from me, Dae-dal-us. As you have sought to learn."

. . . and he reeled and almost fell into the moat before he could sit down, as the pictures came into his mind, this time with painful power. There were wings—not much different in their gross structure from those he had in his workshop, but these were pierced through at many points with tiny, peculiarly curved channels. Soft, sculptured cavities that widened just slightly and quickly closed again, as in his vision the wings beat and the air flowed through and around them. With each beat, the air below the wings, encountering the chan-nels, changed pressure wildly, a thin layer of it turning momentarily almost as hard as wood. Somehow, in the vision he could feel as well as see the fluid alterations . . . and just *so* the pinions' width and length must be, in relation to the flyer's length and weight, and *so* the variation in the channels that went through the differ-ent regions of the wing . . .

It all burned into the brain. There would be no forgetting this, even if forgetfulness were one day willed. But the imprinting vision was soon ended, and he climbed shakily up to a standing pose.

"Bull . . . why did you never before give me such teaching?"

"It will not make of you an ed-u-cat-ed man, Dae-dal-us."

"I thank you for it . . . but why, then, do you give it now?"

The Bull's voice was almost soft, and it did not seem to be looking directly at him. "I think this teach-ing will re-move you from my pres-ence. One way or a-no-ther, stop your dis-rup-tion of my school."

"I see." In his mind the plan for the new wings burned, urgent as a fire in the workshop. "You will not tell Minos, then, that you accuse me of helping Theseus to cheat?"

"Your val-ue to the king is great, Dae-dal-us. If he is forced to choose be-tween us I may pos-sib-ly be sac-ri-ficed. Or my school closed. There-fore, I take this step to re-move you as my ri-val. I see now you are not wor-thy of fine ed-u-ca-tion."

The wings still burning before his eyes, he had let himself be led off through the Labyrinth for a hundred paces or so (Stomargos, triumph fading into puzzle-ment, his escort once again) before it came to him. "And Theseus? What of him?"

"I am a witness to the prince's attempt at cheating," said Stomargos, firmly and primly. "And the Bull has decided that he now must be expelled."

"That cannot be!" Daedalus was so aghast that the other was shaken for a moment.

But for a moment only. "Oh, the Bull and I are quite agreed on that. The prince is probably receiving his formal notification at this moment."

Daedalus spun around and ran, back toward the in-ner Labyrinth.

"Stay! Stay!" Stomargos shouted, trotting in pursuit. "You are to leave the precincts of the school at once . . ." But just then the roaring and the struggling sounded from within.

Theseus and the Bull were grappling on the central dais, arms locked on each other's necks, Daedalus saw as he burst on the scene. The tall chair was overturned, fruit scattered underfoot. In Theseus' broad back the great bronze cables stood like structural arches glowing from the forge.

The end came even as Daedalus' feet splashed in the moat. He heard the sickening bony crack and the Bull's hoarse warbling cry at the same instant. The prince staggered back to stand there, staring down at what his hands had done. The gray-white mound of fur, suddenly no more manlike than a dying bear, dropped at his feet.

Stomargos came in, and splashed over quickly to join the others on the dais. He pointed, goggled, opened his mouth, and began an almost wordless call for help. He turned and ran, and it was Daedalus who had to stop him with a desperate watery tackle in the moat.

"Theseus! Help me! Keep this one quiet." And in a moment the Prince of Athens had taken charge. Stomargos' head was clamped down under water, and soon the bubbles ceased to rise and make their way to the splash gutter at the side.

The two men still alive climbed out onto the dais. Theseus, still panting with his exertions against the Bull, seemed with every working of his lungs to grow a little taller and straighter, like some young tree just freed of a burden, resuming its natural form. "Does he still breathe, Daedalus?" A nod toward the fallen Bull.

Daedalus was crouching down, prodding into gray fur, trying to find out. "I am not sure."

"Well, let him, if he can. It matters to me no longer. My ship and men can be got ready in an hour or two and I am going home. Or somewhere else, if my father will not have me in Athens now. But better a pirate's life, even, than . . ." His eyes flashed once at the convoluted walls surrounding them.

Daedalus started to ask why he thought he would be allowed to leave, but then understanding came. "And myself?" he asked.

"Ariadne will come with me, I expect."

"Gods of sea and sky!"

"And her sister Phaedra. And you are welcome, friend,

though I can promise you no safe workshop, nor slaves, nor high place at a court."

"I want no place as high as a sun-dried pirate's, which I fear Minos might make for me here, when he comes home. Now we had better move swiftly, before this violence is discovered."

"Dae-dal-us." The unexpected voice was a mere thread of sound, stretched and about to break.

He bent down closer beside its head. "White Bull, how is it with you?"

"As with a man whose neck is bro-ken, Dae-dal-us. Af-ter to-day I teach no more."

"Would I had learned from you before today, White Bull. And would you had learned from me."

They walked out together, looking a little shaken, no doubt, as was only natural for two students who had probably just been expelled. Theseus muttered to passing teachers that the Bull and Stomargos were talking together and did not wish to be disturbed. They walked without hurrying to Ariadne, and then a trusted servant was sent to gather Theseus' crew, and another to help Daedalus look for his son, when he discovered that Icarus was truant yet again today, not to be found in school.

The wild lands where boys looked for birds and dreams swept up mile after mile behind and above the House of the Double Axe.

"We can wait no longer for him, Daedalus. My men's lives are all in danger, and the princesses', too. As soon as the bodies are found, some military man or sea captain will take it upon himself to stop my sailing, or try to do so."

And Ariadne: "Theseus must get away. My father will not deal too grievously with you, Daedalus; he depends on you too much."

Phaedra was silent, biting her full lips. Her fingers, as if moving on their own, caressed Theseus' arm, but Ariadne did not see.

Daedalus saw in his mind's eye the sun-dried pirates on the dock, and his workshop with the hidden, unfinished wings. And he saw how the small trusting shadow would cross the threshold when Icarus came running home . . .

Long, helmed shadows came first, the black triangles of shadow-spearheads thrust ahead of them. This time they held their weapons ready as they marched him deeper into the House, and Icarus, returning wearily from some adventure, was only just in time to see his father arrested, and be swept up like a dropped crumb by tidy soldiery.

A month must pass before Minos came home again, and the de facto military government, taking over after the princesses' desertion, did not want to assume responsibility for judging Daedalus. He and his son were confined under strict house arrest in his workshop and quarters, and allotted also a small area of the Labyrinth that lay between.

All entrances and exits to their small domain were walled up. The masonry was rough and temporary-looking, if there was any comfort to be derived from that. The guard was heavy all around. Food was slid in through a tiny door, garbage dragged out, and water continued to flow through the Daedalian plumbing. And that was all.

What material to use, to sculpt the thousand channels? It must be soft . . .

When he had a hundred cunning perforations built through a wing he tested it—strapped it on and gave a strong, quick push down. It felt as if his arm had, for a moment, rested on something solid and ready to be climbed.

One clouded night when there were a thousand channels and he had decided the wings were ready, the father mounted into the sky. Ascending awkwardly and breathlessly at first, he soon learned to relax, like a good swimmer. When some height had been attained, a long, gliding, coasting rest let the arm muscles recover before more work was necessary. In an hour, in air that was almost calm, he flew the length of the whole cloud-shrouded island, and was not winded or wearied, then back toward the pinpoints of the House's lamps, which served to guide him home.

When he landed, the wings were warm, almost hot, with heat that had been gathered into their channels out of the air itself, and somehow turned to pushing force. Daedalus still had not the words or thoughts to make clear, even in his own mind, just how the wings worked. In daylight, a strong push down with one completed wing, and you could see a vapor-puff big as a pumpkin appear in the beaten air and fly off rearward, spinning violently. Icarus, extending a hand into the puff, said he could feel the chill . . .

They would carry food and water and gold, in small quantities, at their belts. In daylight, they would cross the sea to Sicily; a few hours should be enough. And they could turn northward, to the mainland, if they flew into difficulty. "In the morning, son. Now sleep."

. . . he had not yet paid the price, but he knew that it would come. Squinting into the hot, rising sun, he absently marked its dull sheen on Icarus' wings, and waited for the breath of wind to help them rise among the gulls.

Wilderness

The house was set a wide lawn's distance from the roadside, and backed by a steep little foothill covered with pine and spruce. The girl, about twenty, dressed for neighborless comfort in jeans and old shirt, had come down the driveway carrying an empty bushel basket. She was just starting to clean up some of the early summer crop of roadside litter, when a man's voice rose in a whoop not far away. The cry came from only a little lower down the curving narrow road, where it bent out of sight around more pines. The girl was quick and assertive in her movements, shading her eyes against the lowering sun and looking. There were no other voices, no sounds of car or motorbike.

A lone man came walking heavily, and with a slight unsteadiness, around the curve of road. He was medium tall and well-enough dressed in slacks and light jacket. In each hand he carried an empty beer can, punctured in dark triangles. As he came crunching closer on the gravel road, she judged his age as nearer forty than thirty. His clothes, not made for rough hiking, had today been marked by mud and branches.

He was misplaced. For one thing, he seemed to be

147

drunk, and none of the crowd from Wilson's down at the highway intersection ever came wandering this far on foot. And—this was what held the girl at the roadside—his clean-shaven face was inescapably familiar to her, in some favorable context, but one far removed from this.

Coming closer, he several times glanced at her and away again, with what seemed to her a sort of preoccupied shyness. Five or six paces away, his feet scraped to a halt in the road's gravel. "H'lo," he said, and smiled past her at the orderly house. "An outpost of civ'lization. Wonderful."

"Were you looking for someone?" She stood straight and still beside the mailbox on its post, with the empty basket in her hands. The man had done nothing in the least menacing, and she felt no apprehension that he would; still, he seemed to have brought with him a certain contagion of fear.

The man perhaps noticed the empty driveway and carport and guessed that she was alone. He almost stopped swaying as he looked at her with a solemn face and shook his head. "Listen." He raised his voice slightly. "Don't don't don't be scared. Not of *me*. We humans have t' stick together."

She *had* seen him before, in connection with something . . . something that had seemed to her good. She smiled slightly, wanting to reassure him. "I'm not scared."

"Good." He swayed again, looking around him. "I come to distribute beer cans. Throughout the len'th and brea'th of the pristine wilderness."

"Well, how nice." Now she was balanced between amusement and anger, the balance made more delicate by fear that was not hers, fear that came and went like a blown odor in the air around the man. Did fear have a smell? He was not being pursued, for he never looked back. Instead he looked around, quickly, now and then, as if he feared the pines might close their ranks and charge at him.

"A lot of people have the same idea," she said.

"There's no shortage of beer cans and garbage along our road and in our forest."

"That's good," the man said almost soberly. He looked thoughtfully at the empty can in his muscular right hand. She noticed now that he was carrying at least one additional can in each side pocket of his jacket, and the garment was distinctly lumpy around the middle, as if more beer cans were stuffed inside.

She said sharply: "It seems people can't bear to see a thing unspoiled."

He might not have heard her. He turned suddenly and pitched a can, like a baseball, at the woods opposite the house, making a high arc twinkling golden in the descending sun.

"Now just a minute," the girl said.

Now he heard her. "Deep in th' savage wilderness is where they're needed. So's a wandering man's *never* out of sight of civ'lization."

"Did it ever occur to her that some people can get *tired* of civilization and all its mess? That we should preserve a *little* bit of the wilderness *somewhere*, for people to look at . . ."

He made an odd sound that was more terror than drunkeness, and turned his eyes on her with the fear in them. Whatever beast he was riding could not throw him, though. He pointed after the thrown can. "Notice th' nice flight path? Careless observer might describe it as par . . . parabolic. But you'n I know it's really one end of'n ee-lipse."

Drunkeness was no excuse. No help in facing problems. "There's not many places left that people haven't spoiled."

His eyes lowered confusedly before her. His right hand, groping in a jacket pocket, pulled out a half-pint whisky bottle and pushed it back. He pointed downward with a long finger. As if explaining everything, he said: "Th' other end of my beer can ellipse's down around th' center of th' earth. If a beer can could fall that far. But that's not far, really."

It was certainly no use talking. "I suggest you'd bet-

ter be on your way back down to Wilson's. It'll soon be
getting dark."

"Wilson's? No. Some other name, some big fancy
motel down th . . ."

And then her last word seemed to skewer him like a
slow sword thrust. "Dark?" He looked away to the west
and for a moment she thought he was going to fall. But
the only change was that the shadow of a distant mountain was coming upon them both, oozing at their feet
already; the orange sun was damaged by the mountain
and going down.

"Oh, God, it will be dark," he said soberly. "I can't
walk down there before it comes." He straightened,
bracing. "And no clouds in the sky. Clear night's coming."

She had seen him before in photographs. And on
television.

She raised the fingertips of both hands to her lips.
"You're the astronaut. The one who was alone on the
ship after the accident—all the way out to Mars and
back. Alone out there for two years."

He nodded vaguely, looking up. Already the blue
shielding bowl of day that the sun had made was starting to dissolve, starting to let the nothingness beyond
get at the earth. She could see it through his eyes, a
little, now.

"Oh, I'm sorry," she said, in a voice turned tiny. "I
didn't know."

She could feel the violence of the nothingness striking at him, and she could see the courage it took for
him to keep on looking up.

"Come inside," she said. To give him an ordinary
reason, if he wanted one, she added: "You must be
tired, walking all that way."

He looked down and mumbled thanks. Suddenly he
was embarrassed by his cargo of cans; silently, she held
out the trash basket to him for the clanging unloading of
his jacket.

The two of them stood there on the road until the
sun was gone from them, its last rays climbing up the

gentle piny hill behind the house. He watched that. And then before going in with her, he took one more look above.

"Wilderness," he said. "My God, all wilderness."

The Peacemaker

Carr swallowed a pain pill and tried to find a less uncomfortable position in the combat chair. He keyed his radio transmitter, and spoke:

"I come in peace. I have no weapons. I come to talk to you."

He waited. The cabin of his little one-man ship was silent. His radar screen showed the berserker machine still many light-seconds ahead of him. There was no reaction from it, but he knew that it had heard him.

Behind Carr was the Sol-type star he called sun, and his home planet, colonized from Earth a century before. It was a lonely settlement, out near the rim of the galaxy; until now, the berserker war had been no more than a remote horror in news stories. The colony's only real fighting ship had recently gone to join Karlsen's fleet in the defense of Earth, when the berserkers were said to be massing there. But now the enemy was here. The people of Carr's planet were readying two more warships as fast as they could—they were a small colony, and not wealthy in resources. Even if the two ships could be made ready in time, they would hardly be a match for a berserker.

When Carr had taken his plan to the leaders of his planet, they had thought him mad. Go out and talk to it of peace and love? *Argue* with it? There might be some hope of converting the most depraved human to the cause of goodness and mercy, but what appeal could alter the built-in purpose of a machine?

"Why not talk to it of peace?" Carr had demanded. "Have you a better plan? I'm willing to go. I've nothing to lose."

They had looked at him, across the gulf that separates healthy planners from those who know they are dying. They knew his scheme would not work, but they could think of nothing that would. It would be at least ten days until the warships were ready. The little one-man ship was expendable, being unarmed. Armed, it would be no more than a provocation to a berserker. In the end, they let Carr take it, hoping there was a chance his arguments might delay the inevitable attack.

When Carr came within a million miles of the berserker, it stopped its own unhurried motion and seemed to wait for him, hanging in space in the orbital track of an airless planetoid, at a point from which the planetoid was still several days away.

"I am unarmed," he radioed again. "I come to talk with you, not to damage you. If those who built you were here, I would try to talk to them of peace and love. Do you understand?" He was serious about talking love to the unknown builders; things like hatred and vengeance were not worth Carr's time now.

Suddenly it answered him: "Little ship, maintain your present speed and course toward me. Be ready to stop when ordered."

"I—I will." He had thought himself ready to face it, but he stuttered and shook at the mere sound of its voice. Now the weapons which could sterilize a planet would be trained on him alone. And there was worse than destruction to be feared, if one tenth of the stories about berserkers' prisoners were true. Carr did not let himself think about that.

When he was within ten thousand miles it ordered: "Stop. Wait where you are, relative to me."

Carr obeyed instantly. Soon he saw that it had launched toward him something about the size of his own ship—a little moving dot on his video screen, coming out of the vast fortress-shape that floated against the stars.

Even at this range he could see how scarred and battered that fortress was. He had heard that all of these ancient machines were damaged, from their long senseless campaign across the galaxy; but surely such apparent ruin as this must be exceptional.

The berserker's launch slowed and drew up beside his ship. Soon there came a clanging at the airlock.

"Open!" demanded the radio voice. "I must search you."

"Then will you listen to me?"

"Then I will listen."

He opened the lock, and stood aside for the half-dozen machines that entered. They looked not unlike robot valets and workers to Carr, except these were limping and worn, like their great master. Here and there a new part gleamed, but the machines' movements were often unsteady as they searched Carr, searched his cabin, probed everywhere on the little ship. When the search was completed one of the boarding machines had to be half-carried out by its fellows.

Another one of the machines, a thing with arms and hands like a man's, stayed behind. As soon as the airlock had closed behind the others, it settled in the combat chair and began to drive the ship toward the berserker.

"Wait!" Carr heard himself protesting. "I didn't mean I was surrendering!" The ridiculous words hung in the air, seeming to deserve no reply. Suddenly panic made Carr move without thinking; he stepped forward and grabbed at the mechanical pilot, trying to pull it from the chair. It put one metal hand against his chest and shoved him across the cabin, so that he staggered and fell in the artificial gravity, thumping his head painfully against a bulkhead.

"In a matter of minutes we will talk about love and peace," said the radio.

Looking out through a port as his ship neared the immense berserker, Carr saw the scars of battle become plainer and plainer, even to his untaught eye. There were holes in the berserker's hull, there were square miles of bendings and swellings, and pits where the metal had once flowed molten. Rubbing his bumped head, Carr felt a faint thrill of pride. We've done that to it, he thought, we soft little living things. The martial feeling annoyed him in a way. He had always been something of a pacifist.

After some delay, a hatch opened in the berserker's side, and the ship followed the berserker's launch into darkness.

Now there was nothing to be seen through the port. Soon there came a gentle bump, as of docking. The mechanical pilot shut off the drive, and turned toward Carr and started to rise from its chair.

Something in it failed. Instead of rising smoothly, the pilot reared up, flailed for a moment with arms that sought a grip or balance, and then fell heavily to the deck. For half a minute it moved one arm, and made a grinding noise. Then it was still.

In the half minute of silence which followed, Carr realized that he was again master of his cabin; chance had given him that. If there was only something he could do—

"Leave your ship," said the berserker's calm voice. "There is an air-filled tube fitted to your airlock. It will lead you to a place where we can talk of peace and love."

Carr's eyes had focused on the engine switch, and then had looked beyond that, to the C-plus activator. In such proximity as this to a mass size of the surrounding berserker, the C-plus effect was not a drive but a weapon—one of tremendous potential power.

Carr did not—or thought he did not—any longer fear

sudden death. But now he found that with all his heart and soul he feared what might be prepared for him outside his airlock. All the horror stories came back. The thought of going out through that airlock now was unendurable. It was less terrifying for him to step carefully around the fallen pilot, to reach the controls and turn the engine back on.

"I can talk to you from here," he said, his voice quavering in spite of an effort to keep it steady.

After about ten seconds, the berserker said: "Your C-plus drive has safety devices. You will not be able to kamikaze me."

"You may be right," said Carr after a moment's thought. "But if a safety device does function, it might hurl my ship away from your center of mass, right through your hull. And your hull is in bad shape now, you don't want any more damage."

"You would die."

"I'll have to die sometime. But I didn't come out here to die, or to fight, but to talk to you, to try to reach some agreement."

"What kind of agreement?"

At last, Carr took a deep breath, and marshalled the arguments he had so often rehearsed. He kept his fingers resting gently on the C-plus activator, and his eyes alert on the instruments that normally monitored the hull for micrometeorite damage.

"I've had the feeling," he said, "that your attacks upon humanity may be only some ghastly mistake. Certainly we were not your orginal enemy."

"Life is my enemy. Life is evil." Pause. "Do you want to become goodlife?"

Carr closed his eyes for a moment; some of the horror stories were coming to life. But then he went firmly on with his argument. "From our point of view, it is you who are bad. We would like you to become a good machine, one that helps men instead of killing them. Is not building a higher purpose than destroying?"

There was a longer pause. "What evidence can you offer, that I should change my purpose?"

"For one thing, helping us will be a purpose easier of achievement. No one will damage you and oppose you."

"What is it to me, if I am damaged and opposed?"

Carr tried again. "Life is basically superior to nonlife; and man is the highest form of life."

"What evidence do you offer?"

"Man has a spirit."

"I have learned that many men claim that. But do you not define this spirit as something beyond the perception of any machine? And are there not many men who deny that this spirit exists?"

"Spirit is so defined. And there are such men."

"Then I do not accept the argument of spirit."

Carr dug out a pain pill and swallowed it. "Still, you have no evidence that spirit does not exist. You must consider it as a possibility."

"That is correct."

"But leaving spirit out of the argument for now, consider the physical and chemical organization of life. Do you know anything of the delicacy and intricacy of organization in even a single living cell? And surely you must admit we humans carry wonderful computers inside our few cubic inches of skull."

"I have never had an intelligent captive to dissect," the mechanical voice informed him blandly. "Though I have received some relevant data from other machines. But you admit that your form is the determined result of the operation of physical and chemical laws?"

"Have *you* ever thought that those laws may have been designed to do just that—produce brains capable of intelligent action?"

There was a pause that stretched on and on. Carr's throat felt dry and rough, as if he had been speaking for hours.

"I have never tried to use that hypothesis," it answered suddenly. "But if the construction of intelligent life is indeed so intricate, so dependent upon the laws of physics being as they are and not otherwise—then to serve life may be the highest purpose of a machine."

"You may be sure, our physical construction is intricate." Carr wasn't sure he could follow the machine's line of reasoning, but that hardly mattered if he could somehow win the game for life. He kept his fingers on the C-plus activator.

The berserker said: "If I am able to study some living cells—"

Like a hot iron on a nerve, the meteorite-damage indicator moved; something was at the hull. "Stop that!" he screamed, without thought. "The first thing you try, I'll kill you!"

Its voice was unevenly calm, as always. "There may have been some accidental contact with your hull. I am damaged and many of my commensal machines are unreliable. I mean to land on this approaching planetoid to mine for metal and repair myself as far as possible." The indicator was quiet again.

The berserker resumed its argument. "If I am able to study some living cells from an intelligent life-unit for a few hours, I expect I will find strong evidence for or against your claims. Will you provide me with cells?"

"You must have had prisoners, sometime." He said it as a suspicion; he really knew no reason why it must have had human captives. It could have learned the language from another berserker.

"No, I have never taken a prisoner."

It waited. The question it had asked still hung in the air.

"The only human cells on this ship are my own. Possibly I could give you a few of them."

"Half a cubic centimeter should be enough. Not a dangerous loss for you, I believe. I will not demand part of your brain. Also I understand that you wish to avoid the situation called pain. I am willing to help you avoid it, if possible."

Did it want to drug him? That seemed too simple. Always unpredictability, the stories said, and sometimes a subtlety out of hell.

He went on with the game. "I have all that is necessary. Be warned that my attention will hardly waver from my control panel. Soon I will place a tissue sample in the airlock for you."

He opened the ship's medical kit, took two pain-killers, and set very carefully to work with a sterile scalpel. He had had some biological training.

When the small wound was bandaged, he cleansed the tissue sample of blood and lymph and with unsteady fingers sealed it into a little tube. Without letting down his guard, he thought, for an instant, he dragged the fallen pilot to the airlock and left it there with the tissue sample. Utterly weary, he got back to the combat chair. When he switched the outer door open, he heard something come into the lock and leave again.

He took a pep pill. It would activate some pain, but he had to stay alert. Two hours passed. Carr forced himself to eat some emergency rations, watched the panel, and waited.

He gave a startled jump when the berserker spoke again; nearly six hours had gone by.

"You are free to leave," it was saying. "Tell the leading life-units of your planet that when I have refit-ted, I will be their ally. The study of your cells has convinced me that the human body is the highest cre-ation of the universe, and that I should make it my purpose to help you. Do you understand?"

Carr felt numb. "Yes. Yes. I have convinced you. After you have refitted, you will fight on our side."

Something shoved hugely and gently at his hull. Through a port he saw stars, and he realized that the great hatch that had swallowed his ship was swinging open.

This far within the system, Carr necessarily kept his ship in normal space to travel. His last sight of the berserker showed it moving as if indeed about to let down upon the airless planetoid. Certainly it was not following him.

A couple of hours after being freed, he roused himself from contemplation of the radar screen, and went to spend a full minute considering the inner airlock door. At last he shook his head, dialed air into the lock, and entered it. The pilot-machine was gone, and the tissue sample. There was nothing out of the ordinary to be seen. Carr took a deep breath, as if relieved, closed up the lock again, and went to a port to spend some time watching the stars.

After a day he began to decelerate, so that when hours had added into another day, he was still a good distance from home. He ate, and slept, and watched his face in a mirror. He weighed himself, and watched the stars some more, with interest, like a man re-examining something long forgotten.

In two more days, gravity bent his course into a hairpin ellipse around his home planet. With it bulking between him and the berserker's rock, Carr began to use his radio.

"Ho, on the ground, good news."

The answer came almost instantly. "We've been tracking you, Carr. What's going on? What's happened?"

He told them. "So that's the story up to now," he finished. "I expect the thing really needs to refit. Two warships attacking it now should win."

"Yes." There was excited talk in the background. Then the voice was back, sounding uneasy. "Carr—you haven't started a landing approach yet, so maybe you understand. The thing was probably lying to you."

"Oh, I know. Even that pilot-machine's collapse might have been staged. I guess the berserker was too badly shot up to want to risk a battle, so it tried another way. Must have sneaked the stuff into my cabin air, just before it let me go—or maybe left it in my airlock."

"What kind of stuff?"

"I'd guess it's some freshly mutated virus, designed for specific virulence against the tissue I gave it. It expected me to hurry home and land before getting sick, and spread a plague. It must have thought it was inventing biological warfare, using life against life, as we use machines to fight machines. But it needed that tissue sample to blood its pet viruses; it must have been telling the truth about never having a human prisoner."

"Some kind of virus, you think? What's it doing to you, Carr? Are you in pain? I mean, more than before?"

"No." Carr swiveled his chair to look at the little chart he had begun. It showed that in the last two days his weight loss had started to reverse itself. He looked down at his body, at the bandaged place near the center of a discolored inhuman-looking area. That area was smaller than it had been, and he saw a hint of new and healthy skin.

"What *is* that stuff doing to you?"

Carr allowed himself to smile, and to speak aloud his growing hope. "I think it's killing off my cancer."

Victory

Along with everyone else on the Shearwater inter-
planetary ship, Nicholas Shen-yang had a bad five minutes or so of waiting to die, not knowing whether the
Condamine patrol craft had decided to blast them or
board them. Not until they heard and felt the clunk of
hull against hull were the would-be blockade runners
reasonably certain that the enemy had chosen to capture them and let them live.

Hands behind his head, face to the bulkhead along
with the Shearwater crew, Shen-yang got through the
next five minutes in silence, even when something that
must have been a gun barrel was rammed into his back
hard enough to leave a bruise. That was after the first
quick personal search and was meant to emphasize an
order that he should get the hell over there with the
others who had been searched and sit down. The voice
issuing the order sounded strangely accented to him,
but the message was quite understandable. Condamine,
Shearwater, and the multitude of other states making
up the so-called civilized galaxy shared at least one
common language, inherited from old parent Earth,

which fact tended to make events like this boarding a little less difficult for all concerned.

More minutes passed before Shen-yang got the chance to show his diplomatic card when a junior officer of the boarding party came around checking identification. After the officer had glowered at him in suspicious fury for half a minute—only a born troublemaker would be carrying such a card, to upset the officer's smooth routine—Shen-yang was quickly transferred to the boarding party's launch. His brief passage through the flexible tunnel connecting the two craft allowed him a glimpse of space through its transparent windows. There was Shearwater, the planet he had left yesterday, a full bright dot looking like Jupiter as seen from Earth—except that Shearwater appeared against a backdrop of pearly, soft, faint clouds of whitish nebula, the nebula whose slow drift had cut this solar system off from the galactic world for almost fifty standard years. And somewhere in the dazzle sunward must be the crescent of Lorenzoni, the war-torn world that was his goal, but he had no time to try to pick it out.

He was calmly unresisting as burly marines aboard the launch shoved him into a space that must have been meant as a closet and locked the door on him. Capture meant nothing essential to Shen-yang, as far as the success of his mission was concerned. He had been going to visit both sides on Lorenzoni anyway, and if fate insisted that he drop in on the aggressors first, so be it.

He had just been beginning to know and like the Shearwater crew, a half-dozen experienced blockade runners whose swagger still had something self-conscious about it, and he hoped they would manage to come through this in good shape. Likely they would remain as prisoners aboard their own ship, while a Condamine prize crew brought her in. From what Shen-yang had heard of the war so far, there was some hope that they might get home later in a prisoner exchange. . . .

At last he heard the sounds of separation, as the launch departed from the captured smuggler. A minute later came the solid *chunk* of her arrival at her berth in what must be a sizable war vessel.

When Shen-yang was brought off the launch, the Condaminer captain was there to introduce himself, in stiffly correct style, and treat him to another penetrating glare. A minute or two later, in a room or cell almost big enough to be called a cabin, the captain—naturally enough wondering just what sort of diplomat he had bagged so accidentally and what the effect was going to be upon his own career—came to talk with him a little more.

"Your government does know I'm coming, Captain, though they'll no doubt be surprised when I show up in your custody. By the way, I hope the crew of the ship you just captured are being cared for properly?"

"Better than they deserve, in my opinion."

"What did they really have aboard as cargo? They told me it was only medical supplies, and I'd like to know if you found anything else."

The captain frowned, and his heavy jaw twitched, as if he might be having a hard time trying to re-program himself for diplomacy. "From the little bit I've seen so far," he admitted finally, "it looks as if that might be so. On this particular ship."

"Nobody denies that Shearwater ships bring in military cargo too. At least once in a while."

"Once in a while, huh?" And that ended the conversation for the present.

Faster-than-light travel being impossible this deep inside the gravitational well of a solar system, the approach to Lorenzoni took the patrol ship two more days. Free to spend a good deal of his time out of his tiny cabin, Shen-yang during this time got a good look at the nearing planet. It was an Earth-type ball circling a Sol-type sun, and it had been colonized, directly from Earth, a good many centuries ago.

With the slight magnification available from a viewport, he studied the land mass of Condamine when it was on nightside and drew the immediate conclusion that the

Condaminers feared no attack from space. The glow of a thousand cities and towns shone forth with open cheerfulness.

Some ten hours later he took another look, at considerably closer range, and caught Ungava, the other sizable continent, in darkness. The blackness enfolding it was eerie—it was not a cloud cover, for there was the ghostly reflected sparkle of the nebula off the great poisoned lakes, and the coastline showed distinctly. But there was not a sign of human civilization, under conditions where the light sparks of every town of twenty thousand or more should have been visible. Shen-yang was a traveled man, and this reminded him of Stone Age worlds and worlds where mindless creatures ruled supreme.

Even as he meditated upon the meaning of this darkness, there came a sudden pinpoint dazzle right in the middle of it. The flash was over in a moment, but he knew it had been there. Yet another nuclear strike from Condamine, he thought, as if they still feared the very space where their enemies' cities had once stood—feared that in that deep night one building stone might still be raised upon another.

The captain later confirmed his thoughts about the flash. "Yeah, we still hit 'em that way from time to time, when recon confirms some kind of buildup that would make a worthwhile target."

The captain drank some coffee and seemed not about to say more; so Shen-yang prodded him: "But isn't it obvious that the war is really over? I mean you hit them, as you put it, forty-six years ago, with everything you had. That's the way I've heard it." The captain's eyes flicked over at him, but not denying anything, and Shen-yang went on: "Their cities are all wiped out—right? Your cities are untouched. Their casualties in that first strike were more than one hundred million—isn't that so? God knows what they've been since or how many people are still alive inside Ungava."

A little snort. "Too bloody many."

"Your casualties in the whole war are nowhere near

that figure. Condamine has a population of between two and three hundred million people. Your industry is intact—"

"There's the terrorists." The captain's voice was milder than his looks. "Every week something is blown up."

"So? Maybe there's more of that than I've heard about. Look, I'm here trying to learn, to understand. When I say something you know is wrong, please straighten me out. Okay?"

"Okay."

"Now isn't your industry essentially intact?"

"Well, yes." The captain looked at him, and amplified: "But theirs is too, more than you'd think. They're dug in like you wouldn't believe now, and dispersed. Nothing centralized any more."

"You've seen how it is over there?"

A shrug. "Common knowledge."

"Ungava's not going to blast you, are they? And they're not going to invade you. I mean, if *your* three invasion tries on *their* continent couldn't settle the war—?"

"By God, I wish they'd try that."

"But they won't. So, they're not really all that dangerous to Condamine, not now at least. *Hasn't the war really been over, Captain, for the last forty-six years?*"

The other stood up, outraged though not surprised. His face had been grim before, but now it was beginning to look dangerous. "Tell that to my buddy, who was killed last month. He'll have a good laugh."

At the military spaceport on Condamine, Shen-yang walked down the ramp from the great sphere of the patrol ship, under a sunny sky tinged green near the horizon. A sprightly wind made banners snap; a good day, he thought, for a parade.

Three harried-looking civilians stood at the foot of the ramp, looking up it anxiously. At first glance Shen-yang knew they had come for him. Hurtling with them in a buried tubecar toward the capital city, Vellore, and the foreign minister who waited there to see him, Shen-yang chatted with the three and lamented the fact that this mode of travel kept him from appreciating the beauties of the countryside. Aboard ship he had been told this was the best season to see the blooms.

They assured him that he would have a chance, tomorrow or the next day. They were relieved that he accepted his capture in space so equably and had no real maltreatment to complain of. His own thought was that he who chooses to ride with smugglers must take some chances. He had not come for a sterile protocol tour but to find out what was going on.

"Have you read Orwell?" his boss at the foundation, a hundred light-years distant, had asked him just before he left.

"Orwell. Yes, a little anyway."

"Remember the bit in *1984*, where a man is asked to envision the future as 'a boot, stamping on a human face, forever'? That bit's always stuck in my mind."

"I can well imagine." Now that it was mentioned, he did recall it.

"I think the world I'm sending you to look at may furnish an example. Nick—what's the most terrible conclusion you can imagine for a war?"

"I don't know. Everybody killed on both sides."

"That's bad, all right. But what we're looking at on Lorenzoni may be something more Orwellian and therefore—*I* think—even worse. What about no conclusion at all? The winner knocks out the loser with the first punch and then goes on beating until his victim dies—and then goes on beating some more."

"Ungava's certainly not completely dead."

"That's what the Condaminers say. I think they're keeping the so-called conflict going, to distract their own people from other matters. Just what, I don't know."

"That ploy is common enough in history. What did you think of the Ungavan envoy?" The first ship out of the Lorenzoni-Shearwater system when the nebula parted had brought such a personage, pleading the cause of his tormented people to the galaxy.

Dr. Nicobar considered, brushing back long gray hair from her eyes. "He's a very good talker. He tells how, somehow, dug in against the hail of missiles, working wonders of medical research against radiation poisoning— all good achievements due to the High Leader, of course— Ungavan life and heroic resistance go on. He understates, or gives the impression that he's understating. He—I don't know, I wanted to like him and I couldn't, quite. For a man who represents an absolute dictatorship, he's perhaps just a little too good, too gentle-saintish, to be taken at face value."

"And what about the man from Condamine?" He had come out on the second ship.

"In the brief exchange I had with him, he didn't seem to want to talk about the war at all, just about Condamine's rejoining the League of Galactic Nations. I'm going to talk to him again, of course. But, meanwhile, there's a ship leaving tomorrow to go in, and I want us to have a representative on it. Here's your diplomatic card. Go there and see for yourself, and think for yourself, and report personally to me when you come out."

In the streets of Vellore the war—if it was a real war—seemed as remote as something on another planet. In every block electronic posters burned energy from street level up to twenty stories high or higher, urging the people to smash Ungava, not to waste, not to talk loosely of military secrets, not to grumble about the rules. But all these exhortations seemed to Shen-yang to be largely set at naught by the stores, full of good things to buy; the theaters and houses of entertainment, varied enough to suit any taste and any credit balance, doing a mass business; and by the people themselves.

The streets were full of folk who obviously enjoyed a wide choice of clothing and personal decoration and of vehicles in which to travel. They were busy, and they looked basically healthy and certainly well-fed. Just a

touch glassy-eyed, perhaps—but Shen-yang saw that
often enough at home, in the larger cities at any rate.

The people from the foreign ministry had a hotel
room ready for him in one of the bigger and fancier inns
on a main street of the capital. With the small bag of
personal effects he had so far retained through thick
and thin, he moved in, announcing a tiredness which
certainly seemed likely enough under the circumstances,
and was left alone. Five minutes later he moved right
out again. In the first place, he was morally certain—
although he had no technical means of proving it—that
they had bugged his room. In the second place, he
wanted to see just how his hosts would react. And in
the third place, he wanted to make what free and
unofficial contact he could manage with the citizens.

He left word at the desk of his departure and mentioned that he would call back, saying where he could
be reached when he had picked himself another hotel.
Reason for leaving, he gave none.

Apparently free of all restraint and even observation,
he walked the crowded thoroughfares briefly, then settled himself in another hotel, chosen at whim from half
a dozen that looked inviting. The men from the ministry had thoughtfully established electronic credit for him,
and there was no problem about paying. The room he
got this time was a lot smaller but looked just as comfortable. He left his bag in it and walked out again, to
try a little mingling with the people.

Across the street, in the public bar of yet a third
hotel, a young woman with a startlingly beautiful face
gave him the eye so insistently that he decided to
accept Fate again. Shortly she was walking with him
back to his room.

When the door had closed behind them, he cleared
his throat and said, "You may have heard this before."

"You're not a stickman," she opined, raising an
eyebrow.

"If that means am I with the police, no, I'm not. I
just meant that all I really want to do is talk."

In her face amusement began to struggle with other

things and eventually prevailed. "As a matter of fact," she said at last, "that's all I really wanted to do myself."

He started to offer money, but she pantomimed it away, at which point he began to watch her very alertly.

She said, "Mr. Shen-yang . . ." and paused there to let him appreciate the fact that she already knew his name. "I am sorry your trip was interrupted so unpleasantly but glad that you got to Lorenzoni in one piece. I represent what the rulers of Condamine call the Underground. Dirty Ungavan sympathizers."

"Ah. Are there many of you in Vellore?"

She waved aside the question, preferring to speak of something she considered more important. "If you go out again in the next hour—walk clear of Middle Street. It would be your most direct route from here to the foreign ministry, should you be going that way. But do not take it."

He nodded. "All right. But why?"

"Now I must go. They will soon be here to keep a watch on you again."

He nodded again.

When the door had closed behind the girl, it would have been easy to imagine that she had never been here.

He looked at his timepiece and sighed. His appointment at the foreign ministry was in just half an hour.

A quarter of an hour later, he was given the chance to show his diplomatic card again. When the Condamine police had looked at it and had talked quietly on their radios to some invisible authority, they saluted and let him go on his way at once, brushing the dust of the recent spinbomb blast from his new clothing and shaking his head in an effort to dispel the ringing ache that the explosion had installed immediately inboard from his right ear.

He assumed the thing had been a spinbomb because other kinds of explosives were now too easy to detect. He calculated that he must have been leaving his new hotel just about the time the nameless terrorist was setting down the bomb on Middle Street and quietly pulling its axis pin and walking on, colorless and invisible in the crowd. Shen-yang had just bypassed Middle Street and gone on around a corner when someone brushed the bomb in its no doubt innocent-looking container, or traffic shook the walk enough to make it wobble, and its tiny flywheels, counter-rotating inside their vacuum bottle with a rim speed equal to a substantial proportion of the velocity of light, disintegrated. If it had been a small nuke instead of a tiny spinner, Shen-yang supposed, the ministry three blocks away might have gone up with a sizable surrounding chunk of city, instead of a mere storefront or two. But certainly the police would have detected a nuke before it had been carried into the middle of the city.

The blast seemed to have made no great impression on the vast majority of the folk hurrying busily through the streets. No one who was not bleeding seemed to take it all that hard. It was evidently something that happened from time to time, like rain, and the business of getting and spending had to go on.

The foreign ministry was no bigger than a large house and tastefully ornate, set apart from the city around it only by a simple-looking fence and a narrow belt of lawn. There were uniformed guards at the door, keen-looking though they did not seem to be actually doing much. They gave Shen-yang and his card a simple looking over and courteously directed him on his way; if he underwent any other inspection, the means by which it was accomplished were imperceptible.

The elevator went down instead of up, down for almost twenty levels. Maybe, after all, a small nuke three blocks away would not have taken out the ministry's most important parts.

Only a little late, Shen-yang reached the proper office, where he had to wait about thirty seconds before being passed on in. His appointment was with Minister Hondurman himself, who came around his desk with hand outstretched to offer greetings. He was a large, dark man, very correctly dressed, with a handsome face beginning to go puffy.

One of the first things Shen-yang said was: "I bring you personal greetings from Director Nicobar—she regrets that urgent business kept her from coming herself."

"Yes . . . we did know each other once, in school. How long ago that was . . . but how is Dr. Nicobar?"

"In good health. Extremely busy. It sometimes seems that the whole galaxy is bringing the Peace Foundation jobs these days. We arbitrate, we investigate, we publish a great deal."

"I am well aware that great advantages can accrue from your endorsement. That was true even before we were cut off here."

"It is more true now, Minister Hondurman. We have more real power in the galaxy than do the governments of some small worlds. If, when we make our formal investigation of this war on Lorenzoni, we can report a reasonable settlement, it will in fact go a long way to help your government rejoin galactic society—which I understand you are eager to do." Hondurman was waiting silently, and Shen-yang went on: "Frankly, while the war continues, I don't see how any favorable report can be made."

The minister, unsurprised, nodded and took thought. Then he asked, "What did they tell you on Shearwater about the war?"

"Next to nothing. They expected I would be going directly from there to Ungava, and I suppose they thought the High Leader would prefer to present his own case."

"We can make travel arrangements with Ungava, if you still wish to go on and see him."

"Of course I do."

Hondurman nodded again and made a note to himself on the surface of his desk, which seemed constantly awash with electronic projections of one kind or another. "Believe me, Mr. Shen-yang." He coughed. "My government would like to end the war, when it can be done honorably and decently. We have not yet found a way."

Shen-yang gestured disagreement. "Why not simply end the bombardment and the raids?"

"We have in fact several times suspended such activities. But Ungavan operations against us are out of our control, and while they persist, the war goes on. Did you hear the blast in the street not half an hour ago?"

"Very well; in fact I am still hearing it." He explained just how close he had been.

The other rose and came around the desk, concerned. "But you should have said something. Do you need medical attention?"

"I don't think so."

"My own physician is not far away. I wish you would allow me to call her."

"If you like, but later. Now, do these terrorist attacks really amount to a war waged against you? Do they compare to what your forces have done and are still doing to Ungava?"

Hondurman shrugged. "I'll show you some things. See if you think they add up to a war or not."

The charts and figures began to appear, like some conjurer's props, projected on walls, spewed in printape from the desk. They detailed Ungavan attacks on fishing vessels, on shipping, on mining and drilling operations in all the oceans of the world. Terrorist bombs in Condamine cities. Condamine aircraft (unarmed recon ships and transports, Hondurman claimed them to be) shot down. Hit-and-run raids by small forces against the Condamine coast. Ungavan atrocities in the planet's ministates, small societies trying to cling to independence and neutrality. More atrocities against any of the people dwelling in Ungava who cooperated in the least degree with Condamine. All in all, if it were true, it certainly added up to a lot of killing and a lot of damage. Not a hundred million dead, of course. Not the destruction of a great industrial society.

At last Shen-yang broke into the flow of data with a question. "How do you suppose they can keep going, making such a war effort as you describe? After attacks like those you have made and are still making?"

"Mr. Shen-yang, have you studied the history of strategic bombardment? It has never broken the will of any people to fight."

"Of course it has never before been applied quite so—thoroughly—has it? Minister Hondurman, I'd like to pass on for your comment some figures recently given the Peace Foundation by the first Ungavan envoy to the galaxy. They concern that first missile strike of yours."

The man across the desk nodded, poker-faced, and Shen-yang began to produce the data he had been carrying in his memory. How many missiles Condamine had delivered, without warning, in that first awesome blow. How many cities were roasted, how much land and water poisoned, how many tens of millions of the Ungavan people had died in the first ten minutes—and how many more in the next hour, the next day, the next year. . . .

"Let us suppose," Hondurman interrupted coldly, "for the sake of argument, that all this is substantially correct. What is the point you wish to make from it?"

"Simply this. The war is effectively over. You won it a long time ago. How can that poor battered remnant of a people pose any real threat to you? Sure, as long as Shearwater supports them with material, they can burrow under the mountains, cling to life, to some kind of military organization. They can even carry on harassing operations against you. But what do you want of them before you will make peace?"

"It is not what we want of them, sir, but what they want of us. Peace talks have been convened many times—I really forget how many. Talks are presently suspended, as long as our present government remains in office. This is the latest Ungavan condition for resuming peace talks, sir, that we replace our government!"

"All right." Shen-yang could picture the fanatic Ungavan leaders—utter, bitter fanatics they must be by now, and one could hardly blame them—making such demands, in sheer all-out defiance. "But why do you really need a peace conference at all? Why not simply *stop?*"

"We could stop. But they would not. They would continue, a bombing here, a raid there. Sooner or later we would strike at them again." Hondurman made a curiously helpless gesture.

"Excuse me, sir, but I find that hard to believe. If you really let them know it was all over. Ceased building ICBMs or long-range cruise missiles. Offered them some reparations, which it would seem you can afford."

Hondurman was silent, listening attentively, and Shen-yang pressed on: "According to the Ungavans' figures, which I notice you don't deny, they can have very little left in the way of heavy industry and not a lot in the way of natural resources. I repeat, don't you think the war is really over?"

"They keep a war machine going," the minister answered stolidly. "They have great help from Shearwater, whose government is bitterly opposed to ours, for historical reasons which you may or may not—"

"I've read some of the history of your system."

"Good. However, an all-out inter-planetary war remains unthinkable, in this system or elsewhere. There is simply too much—"

"I've read the theories on that, too. What I have never read anywhere is any reason for the Ungavans' fighting on if you stopped."

"Well—you will have to ask them about that, I suppose."

"I intend to."

"Excuse me, Mr. Shen-yang, you said a moment ago that you did not see what real threat they pose to us. Are you aware that they still have their own strategic missiles?"

A silence began to grow. Shen-yang fingered his aching right ear, wondering if it might have played him false. Then he understood, or thought he did. "You mean they are starting now to build some? Or to import some from Shearwater?"

"No. I mean that the Ungavans still have more than a thousand of their own ICBMs emplaced, mostly in hardened sites—have had them since before the war. Some have been knocked out by our missiles, of course. I am not at liberty to quote you our best intelligence estimates of how many remain—but a thousand would be a good, fair, round figure."

There was silence again. Shen-yang noticed that his chair squeaked if he rocked in it.

His ears were evidently working fine. Either something in his brain was badly askew, though, or something in this world. "Let me see if I understand. Your official claim is that Ungava still possesses a sizable strategic strike force, intact after more than forty years of pounding by nuclear missiles—"

"Excuse me." The minister leaned forward. "It is important that you understand, there had not been forty years of continuous pounding, as you call it. If we had built missiles and fired them as fast as we could for forty years, both we and the Ungavans would long since have perished from radiation poisoning, and there would be no world of Lorenzoni to fight about—no world that anyone could live on."

"I understand that," said Shen-yang stiffly. "I have some military experience."

"Ah? Very good. Proceed."

"You say they have a sizable strategic strike force, still intact. *But* in more than forty years of war, in which you have hit them again and again with similar weapons, they have never fired even one of these missiles at you."

"That is correct."

"Can you explain why?"

"They fear to tip the environmental balance. You see, it can be shown mathematically—or so my experts tell me—that the long-term effects of another mass launching of missiles will be worse for Ungava than for us, regardless of where the missiles land." Was there, in the minister's almost immobile face, a glint of some brand of humor? "Of course for a first-hand answer, you will have to ask the Ungavans themselves."

His trip began next day with a flight from Vellore to an advanced military base, set amid the chalky cliffs of the southern coast. The next leg of his journey passed aboard a fast courier-recon plane, which deposited him upon a barren ocean islet, then took off in a hurry, headed back the way it had come, and vanished in a moment.

Surf pounded tranquilizingly, but then some wild sea creature screamed as if in torment. Waiting on the flat, lichen-spotted rock, Shen-yang studied the horizon and tried to use the time for thought. He still could not believe in the existence of the Ungavan strategic missiles—those utter, bitter fanatics would have used them, sometime in the past forty years. Themselves held on the rack of war, year after year, by a merciless enemy—they would have struck back as hard as possible. No claim had ever been made that they were superhumanly forgiving, and it was unreasonable that they should be so reluctant to add some pollution to the atmosphere.

He could hear the Ungavan aircraft coming before he spotted it; it was moving somewhat more slowly than the Condamine courier. Shen-yang waved as the smooth metal shape made one leisurely pass overhead. He felt a little foolish for his wave when the aircraft had landed and he had walked to it and found it was unmanned.

A glassy canopy had retracted, above an empty, spartan seat and a small space for luggage. Shen-yang climbed in, and as his weight came down into the seat, the glass slid closed again above his head. A moment later he was airborne. The plane flew at a good speed, close above the waves. It turned smoothly a couple of times, avoiding a line of squalls.

In time a coastline grew, ahead. He thought his vehicle slowed somewhat as the land drew nearer—to give him a good look?

There, just inland among rocky hills, was ground-zero of some horrendous blast, a decade or more old. Glassy and sterile hectares were surrounded by the stumps of crags and recent, tender life in the form of scattered, stunted-looking greenery.

Farther from the central scar, the stumps of buildings, half-buried now in drifted sand, made a larger ring. This, then, had been a city, and probably a harbor. There were no signs that humans had ever tried to reoccupy the place.

He rode on. His homework-reading had informed him that the whole Ungavan continent was hardly more than one great, wide range of mountains. Between the barren peaks and crests, long valleys, some still fertile, twisted or ran nearly straight, marked here and there by narrow lakes. Now he could see people and machines working in some of the sheltered lowlands, tending or gathering crops. As his aircraft bore him through one valley at low altitude, he could see how some of the farmers looked up at his roaring passage, while others kept their attention on the earth. A few times he passed small buildings, never large enough to house the numbers of people he beheld.

The landing strip, he saw upon approaching it, looked like a plowed field too—no, it *was* a plowed field. Whatever his craft put down in the way of landing gear engaged the shallow furrows neatly, and the landing felt pleasantly slow and safe, if not exactly smooth.

His canopy slid back. People in drab, ill-fitting uniforms were all around him, smiling, most of them talking at the same time in accents newly strange to Shen-yang's ears. His ride had come to a stop under cover of a great tree. He was being helped out, and in a moment he was standing within a chest-high revetment between great rocks decorated with twin portraits of the High Leader. Leafy branches made a visually impenetrable cover overhead and hung on all sides in a shaggy veil. Welcome clamored on all sides, and there was no counting the hands held out for him to shake. The general impression was of youth, eagerness, and energy.

When a girl handed him a hot drink and some simple food, Shen-yang noticed what he thought were radiation keloids on her arm and side. He thought the scars were not boldly enough undraped to be meant for intentional display. He supposed the whole countryside must be chronically hot. Well, before leaving home he had taken what medical steps he could in the way of radiation prophylaxis for himself.

They led him to a car, a mass of twenty or more people all enthusing at the same time about the rare privilege that he was being granted. The privilege was a talk with the High Leader himself; the young folk dropped their envious voices to a whisper whenever they mentioned that old man by his title or his name.

Four or five got into the car with him, and they were off. The road twisted and turned, seemed to be inside a tunnel as often as not, but still gave him a good chance to see the countryside. Not that there was anything much different from what he had already seen. Blast-marks, crops, workers, rocky hills. Here and there the entrance to some other tunnel, enigmatically unmarked. Once an organized gaggle of children pelted the speeding car with flowers and waved more pictures of the leader at it. The pictures and the flowers and some of the growing crops possessed the only bright colors to be seen below the sky. Everyone wore drab clothing, and everyone looked busy.

He was taken to the High Leader at once, and, despite all the awed foreshadowing, with practically no ceremony. He found that old man waiting for him in a simply furnished cave, a great chamber beneath an immensely beetling brow of limestone and about one third open to the air.

There were two simple chairs and one small table in the cave, and a cluster of cables passing crudely through it at the back. Shen-yang found himself left alone there with a toughly stout and greatly aged man, whose long white sideburns, a personal trademark, looked exactly as they did in all the pictures. What the pictures could not show was in the eyes.

They were seated, Shen-yang at a little distance from the old man and his table, upon which he seemed to like to rest his calloused, age-grooved hands, as if it were a lectern.

"And did you have a pleasant journey across the ocean?"

"Pleasant enough. I marvel at how well your air service runs. It must be difficult to keep it going."

The old man appeared pleased. "Mr. Shen-yang, there is really no secret to how we keep things going. We rely not upon our machines but upon our people. That is why we shall win this war in the end."

Shen-yang thought to himself that had his aircraft failed in midflight, no mass of a hundred or a million peasants rushing out to catch him in their arms would have helped in the least. So, on the surface level, what the old man had just said was nonsense. But Shen-yang thought that there were other levels in the statement, and in those other levels somewhere there was truth.

Still, he was not going to let it pass unchallenged. "You do have machines, though, and to some extent you do depend upon them."

"We use complex machinery when it is available and when it suits our plans. We do not use it when it is not suitable; therefore we do not need it, and our victory does not depend upon it."

If this old man, thought Shen-yang, tells me that this mountain we are under will turn to jelly in the next minute, my mouth will fall open with surprise when it does not. Dare I—*can* I—say to *this* man that the war is over?

The leader, after a courteous pause, was going on. "The enemy, on the contrary, has all along relied upon machines to crush us. That is why he must fail in the end."

"Your losses no doubt have been terrible."

"They have been great. I myself have walked for a kilometer on the dead bodies of my people, because there was no space between dead bodies to put down one's feet. That was after the blast and firestorm at

Kinjanchunga. But it is not huge losses that sap a people's will." Whatever words the old man said seemed to come out of his mouth engraved upon eternal slabs of granite. "What saps their will is a too-great concern with things that do not matter."

Shen-yang hitched his hard chair a little closer. "What matters—" he began and had a thought in mind that he could never afterwards recall because it was melted in a vast disruption of the world. A blue-white welder's torch came on to seal the sky, with one electric flick, across the entrance to the cave, and Shen-yang had a mad and trivial thought *I didn't mean it about the jelly*, and then the whole mountain made a fist and struck him in the mouth.

His chin was bleeding. Both of his ears now rang numbly. What sound had just come and gone was already as far beyond memory as it had been beyond hearing in its passage. He got up from where he found himself on hands and knees on the smooth cave floor and saw the High Leader, a fussy housekeeper, setting up his small table and his own old chair again. If the leader had been in the least damaged, or even excited by the blast, he did not show it.

With commotion, there were suddenly a dozen, a score, of frightened men's and women's faces looking in around one rocky corner and another. Not one looked for a moment at Shen-yang, but he was free to study them—the faces of people who had briefly felt their souls in peril but who were once more convinced of their salvation when they saw their God was still alive, unhurt, and with His people.

The old man had a sharp, practical-sounding question or two for them, in the local tongue, which Shen-yang could not follow. Answers were received and orders issued. The people as they turned away now looked elated by this new challenge.

Turning back to his guest, the old man addressed him once more in their common tongue. "More missiles may be on their way. It seems the Condaminers have tagged you with a tracer of some kind for them to home on, something our own search devices failed to detect, planted on you, your clothing, or perhaps your luggage. Doubtless they calculated that you would be having a talk with me shortly after your arrival here. To kill me, they will spare no effort." He turned toward the rear of the cave, gesturing Shen-yang to follow. "Their superior technology, you see. And you see that again it avails them nothing."

Around a fold of rock, an aide was standing by an open door. A moment later the three of them were descending in an elevator, which looked as neat as anything in Hondurman's foreign ministry.

"Here we will be safer." After the old man had said that, no missile in the world would dare to touch them.

When they got out of the elevator at its lowest level, Shen-yang looked about him, at the size and shape of the place in which he found himself, at the instruments ranked below the clock and the leader's portrait, at the texture of the walls that spoke to an expert eye of super-toughness.

The leader looked at him, started to say something, and then waited, bright eyes probing.

"This is what we used to call a technicians' bay," Shen-yang announced in a slow voice. "And—through that door—there will be an intercontinental ballistic missile waiting in its silo."

His host made a grave gesture of assent.

"You have them, then," said Shen-yang. "Do you really have a thousand?"

Again, the confirmation.

"Then, all this time . . . why didn't you fire them when you could?"

"When I could, Mr. Shen-yang?" The leader's face shivered into a thousand wrinkles, became that of a smiling, wise old demon. And he raised, on a chain that hung around his neck, the carven symbol of his party and his faith. Shen-yang could see the tiny studs projecting from it, coded secretly no doubt, so that one man alone possessed the power, day or night, to. . . .

"When I could? There is nothing to prevent my firing

them now—more than eleven hundred strategic missiles. But I chose not to fire, forty-six years ago. And as of this moment, that is still my choice."

Shen-yang felt more dazed by those absent blasts than by the real ones he had endured. "To—to save the atmosphere—?"

The old man smiled. "No, we can survive that, too, if need be. Our people's medicine is working on the problems and will solve them. Besides, already only the resistant ones of us are left. No, we have another reason for not launching.

"Our greatness is born of great adversity and nurtured on it. When we have blown away the Condaminers' cities and more than half their lives, what is left of them will be stronger and harder to defeat than they are now. Why, Mr. Shen-yang, should I so strengthen my foe? Their leaders, in their hearts, would be delighted if I did."

Shen-yang thought of Vellore, indefensibly open to the sky, to cruise missile and MIRV, to laser-reflecting warheads. He thought of the buried, hardened nerve centers and wondered if Hondurman himself ever came up above the ground.

I want to go home, thought Shen-yang, with a physical revulsion for this place so strong he almost started for the elevator. *Away from this world of madmen*.

The aide was approaching, a bright red wireless communicator of some kind in his hand. The old man took it with a nod and said into it at once: "Do you call now to see if I am still alive?" Even as he spoke, there came another godlike blast far above; the living rock around them shook and trickled powder. "Of course I am alive. How can you slay a man, who is an idea first of all, with a machine?"

A few more words were exchanged. Then the fleshy old arm held out the device to Shen-yang. "There is someone who wishes a few words with you."

When he held the thing for his own use, Hondurman's face was visible in its little screen, and Hondurman's voice came through. "My government's deepest apologies, Mr. Shen-yang, if any military action of ours has in fact endangered you. Of course you knew that you were entering a combat zone—"

"I'm still alive," he interrupted. "By the way, you were right about the missiles here."

A slight bow was visible. "It appears that you too were right, all along. Our Council of Ministers has just been reorganized, and it now agrees to the Ungavan conditions for peace talks to resume. Our new government deplores the latest launchings, disclaims responsibility for them, and will take disciplinary action against the officers responsible. Our official position is that the war is essentially over and the situation must be normalized before our world rejoins the galaxy."

"I was right about its being over, yes. But wrong about one other thing." Shen-yang paused. "So, you're changing leaders to get the peace talks going? That's what losers do, you know."

The eyes in the small screen were haunted. "And just what else, sir, did you suppose we were?"

Goodlife

"It's only a machine, Hemphill," said the dying man in a small voice. Hemphill, drifting weightless in near-darkness, heard him with only faint contempt and pity. Let the wretch go out timidly, forgiving the universe everything, if he found going out easier that way. Hemphill kept on staring out through the port, at the dark crenelated shape that blotted out so many of the stars.

There was probably just this one compartment of the passenger ship left livable, with three people in it, and the air whining out in steady leaks that would soon exhaust the emergency tanks. The ship was a wreck, torn and beaten, yet Hemphill's view of the enemy was steady. It must be a force of the enemy's that kept the wreck from spinning.

Now the young woman, another passenger, came drifting across the compartment to touch Hemphill on the arm. He thought her name was Maria something.

"Listen," she began. "Do you think we might—"

In her voice there was no despair, but the tone of planning; and so Hemphill had begun to listen to her. But she was interrupted.

The very walls of the cabin reverberated, driven like speaker diaphragms through the power of the enemy forcefield that still gripped the butchered hull. The voice of the berserker machine came:

"You who can still hear me, live on. I plan to spare you. I am sending a boat to save you from death."

The voice changed tones from word to word, being fragments of the voices of human prisoners the machine had taken and used. Bits of human emotion sorted and fixed, like butterflies on pins. Hemphill was sick with frustrated rage. He had never heard a berserker's voice in reality before, but still it was as familiar as an old nightmare. He could feel the woman's hand pull away from his arm, and then he saw that in his rage he had raised both his hands to be claws, then fists that almost smashed themselves against the port. The thing, the damned thing wanted to take him inside it. Of all people in space it wanted to make him prisoner.

A plan rose instantly in his mind and flowed smoothly into action; he spun away from the port. There were warheads, for small defensive missiles, here in this compartment. He remembered seeing them.

The other surviving man, a ship's officer, dying slowly, bleeding through his uniform tatters, saw what Hemphill was doing in the wreckage, and drifted in front of him interferingly.

"You can't do that. You'll only destroy the boat it sends . . . if it lets you do that much. There may be other people . . . still alive here . . ."

The man's face had been upside down before Hemphill as the two of them drifted. As their movement let them see each other in normal position, the wounded man stopped talking, gave up, and rotated himself away, drifting inertly as if already dead.

Hemphill could not hope to manage a whole warhead, but he could extract the chemical-explosive detonator, of a size to carry under one arm. All passengers had put on emergency spacesuits when the unequal battle had begun; now he found himself an extra air tank, and some officer's laser pistol, which he stuck in a loop of his suit's belt.

The girl approached him again. He watched her warily.

"Do it," she said with quiet conviction, while the three of them spun slowly in the near-darkness, and the air leaks whined. "Do it. The loss of a boat will weaken it, a little, for the next fight. And we here have no chance, anyway."

"Yes." He nodded approvingly. This young woman understood what was important: to hurt a berserker. To smash, burn, destroy—to kill it finally. Nothing else mattered very much.

He pointed to the wounded mate, and whispered: "Don't let him give me away." She nodded silently. It might hear them talking. If it could speak through these walls, it could be listening.

"A boat's coming," said the wounded man, in a calm and distant voice.

"Goodlife!" called the machine, voice cracking between syllables, as always.

"Here!" He woke up with a start, and got quickly to his feet. He had been dozing almost under the dripping end of a drinking-water pipe.

"Goodlife!" There were no speakers or scanners in this little compartment; the call came from some distance away.

"Here!" He ran toward the call, his feet shuffling and thumping on metal. He had dozed off, being tired; even though the battle had been only a little one, it had created extra tasks for him, servicing and directing the commensal machines that roamed the endless ducts and corridors repairing damage. It was small help he could give, he knew.

Now his head and neck bore sore spots from the helmet he had had to wear, and his body was chafed red in places from the unaccustomed covering he had to put on it when a battle came. This time, happily, there had been no battle damage at all.

He came to the flat glass eye of a scanner and shuffled to a stop, waiting.

"Goodlife, the perverted machine has been destroyed, and the few badlives left are helpless."

"Yes!" He jiggled his body up and down in happiness.

"I remind you, life is evil," said the voice of the machine.

"Evil is life, I am Goodlife!" he said quickly, ceasing his jiggling. He did not think punishment impended, but he wanted to be sure.

"Yes. Like your parents before you, you have been useful. Now I plan to bring other human beings inside myself, to study them closely. Your next use will be with them, in my experiments. I remind you, they are badlife—we must be careful."

"Badlife." He knew they were creatures shaped like himself, existing in the world beyond the machine. They caused the shudders and shocks and damage that made up a battle. "Badlife—here." It was a chilling thought. He raised his own hands and looked at them, then turned his attention up and down the passage in which he stood, trying to visualize the badlife become real before him.

"Go now to the medical room," said the machine. "You must be immunized against disease before you approach the badlife."

Hemphill made his way from one ruined compartment to another, until he found a gash in the outer hull that was plugged nearly shut. While he wrenched at the obstructing material, he heard the clanging arrival of the berserker's boat, come for prisoners. He pulled harder, the obstruction gave, and he was blown out into space.

Around the great wreck were hundreds of pieces of flotsam, held near it by tenuous magnetism or perhaps by the berserker's forcefields. Hemphill found that his suit worked well enough. With its tiny jet he moved around the shattered hull to where the boat had come to rest.

The dark blot of the berserker machine came into view against the starfields of deep space, battlemented like a fortified city of old, and far larger than any such city had ever been.

He could see that the berserker's boat had somehow found the right compartment and clamped itself to the wrecked hull. It would be gathering in Maria and the wounded man. Fingers on the plunger that would set off his bomb, Hemphill drifted closer.

On the brink of death, it annoyed him that he would never know with certainty that the boat was destroyed. And it was such a trifling blow to strike, such a small revenge.

Still drifting closer, holding the plunger ready, he saw the puff of decompressed air-moisture as the boat disconnected itself from the hull. The invisible forcefields of the berserker surged, tugging at the boat, at Hemphill, at half a hundred bits of wreckage that were within meters of the boat.

He managed to clamp himself to the boat before it was pulled away from him. He thought that he had an hour's supply of air in his tank, more than he would need.

The berserker pulled him toward itself.

They were relics of some ancient galactic war, some internecine struggle between unheard-of races. They were machines set to seek out and destroy life, and each of them bore weapons that could sterilize an Earth-sized planet in two or three days.

Earthmen had spread out among the stars of a little section of an arm of the galactic spiral. Now they reeled back under the emotionless assault of the machines; planets and whole systems were depopulated.

Humans fought back when they could. The passenger ship, intercepted far from help, had had no chance, but three or four warships could circle a machine like wolves around a bear, could match missiles and computer speeds with it for long minutes, and—sometimes—could win. For the enemy was old, and damaged by warfare through

unknown centuries and systems. Possibly many of them
had been destroyed before their swarm descended upon
Earthly humanity. The machines surviving had learned,
as machines can learn, to avoid tactical error, and to
never forgive the mistakes of an opponent. Their basic
built-in order was the destruction of all life encountered, but each machine's strategic schemes were un-
predictable, being controlled by the random atomic
disintegrations of some long-lived radioactive isotope,
buried in the center of the mechanism.

Hemphill's mind hung over the brink of death, as his
fingers held the plunger of his bomb. The night-colored
enemy was death in his mind. It was as old as a meteor-
ite, perhaps two hundred kilometers around its bulging
middle. The black, scarred surface of it hurtled closer
in the unreal starlight, becoming a planet toward which
the boat fell.

Hemphill still clung to the boat when it was pulled
into an opening that could have accommodated many
ships. The size and power of the berserker were all
around the man, enough to overwhelm hate and courage alike.

His little bomb was a pointless joke. When the boat
touched at a dark internal dock, Hemphill leaped away
and scrambled to find a hiding place.

As he cowered on a shadowed ledge of metal, his
hand wanted to fire the bomb, simply to bring death
and escape. He forced his hand to be still. He forced
himself to watch while the two human prisoners were
sucked from the boat through a pulsing transparent
tube that passed through a bulkhead. Not knowing
what he meant to accomplish, he pushed himself in the
direction of the tube. He glided through the dark enormous cavern almost weightlessly; the berserker's mass
was enough to give it a small natural gravity of its own.

Within ten minutes he came upon an unmistakable
airlock, which seemed to have been cut, along with a
surrounding section of hull, from some Earth warship,
and set into the bulkhead.

Inside an airlock would be as good a place as he was likely to find for the bomb. He got the outer door open and went in, apparently without triggering any alarms. If he destroyed himself here, he would deprive the berserker of . . . of what? Why should it need an airlock at all?

Not for prisoners, thought Hemphill, if it sucks them in through a tube. Hardly an entrance built for enemies. He tested the air inside the lock, and opened his helmet. For air-breathing friends, the size of human beings? That was a contradiction. Everything that lived and breathed must be a berserker's enemy—except, of course, the unknown beings who had sometime built it, and loosed it to do what damage it might.

It was thought they were extinct, or unreachably distant in space and time. No defeated and boarded berserker had been found to carry a crew, or to have a place or purpose for a living crew.

The inner door of the lock opened, and artificial gravity came on. Hemphill walked into a narrow and badly lighted passage, his fingers ready on the plunger.

"Go in, Goodlife," said the machine. "Look closely at each of them."

Goodlife made an uncertain sound in his throat, like a servomotor starting and stopping. He was gripped by a feeling resembling hunger, or the fear of punishment— because he was going to see life forms directly now, not as old images on a stage. Knowing the reason for the unpleasant feeling did not help. He stood hesitating outside the door of the room where the badlife was being kept. He had put on his suit again, as the machine had ordered. The suit would protect him if the badlife tried to damage him.

"Go in," the machine repeated.

"Maybe I'd better not," Goodlife said in misery, remembering to speak well and clearly. Punishment was always less likely when he did.

"Punish, punish," said the voice.

When it said the word twice, punishment was very

near. As if already feeling in his bones the wrenching
pain-that-left-no-damage. He opened the door quickly
and stepped in.

He lay on the floor, bloody and damaged, in strange
ragged suiting. And at the same time, he was still in the
doorway. His own shape was on the floor, the same
human form he knew, but now seen entirely from outside. It was more than an image—far more—for it was
himself now bi-located. There, here, himself, not
himself—

Goodlife fell back against the door. He raised his arm
and tried to bite it, forgetting his suit. He pounded his
suited arms violently together, until there was bruised
pain enough to nail him to himself where he stood.

Slowly the terror subsided. Gradually his intellect
could explain it and master it. This is me, here, in the
doorway. That, *there*, on the floor—that is another life.
Another body, corroded like me with vitality. One far
worse than I. That one on the floor is badlife.

Maria Juarez had prayed continuously for a long time,
her eys closed. Cold impersonal grippers had moved
her this way and that. Her weight had come back, and
there was air to breathe when her helmet and suit were
carefully removed. She opened her eyes and struggled
when the grippers began to remove her inner coverall;
she saw that she was in a low-ceilinged room, surrounded by man-sized machines of various shapes. When
she struggled they paused briefly, then gave up undressing her, chained her to the wall by one ankle, and
glided away. The dying mate had been dropped at the
other end of the room, as if not worth the trouble of
further handling.

The man with the cold eyes, Hemphill, had tried to
make a bomb and failed. Now there would probably be
no quick end to life.

When she heard the door operate she opened her
eyes again, to watch without comprehension while the
bearded young man in the ancient spacesuit went through
senseless contortions in the doorway, and finally came

forward to stand staring down at the dying man on the floor. The visitor's fingers moved with speed and precision when he raised his hands to the fasteners of his helmet, but the helmet's removal revealed ragged hair and beard framing an idiot's slack face.

He set the helmet down, then scratched and rubbed his hairy head, never taking his eyes from the man on the floor. He had not yet looked at Maria, and she could look nowhere but at him. She had never seen a face so blank on a living person. This was what happened to a berserker's prisoner.

And yet—and yet. Maria had seen the brainwashed before, ex-prisoners on her own planet. She felt this man was something more—or something less.

The bearded man knelt beside the mate, with an air of hesitation, and reached out to touch him. The dying man stirred feebly, and looked up without comprehension. The floor under him was wet with blood.

The stranger took the mate's limp arm and bent it back and forth, as if interested in the articulation of the human elbow. The mate groaned and struggled feebly. The stranger suddenly shot out his metal-gauntleted hands and seized the dying man by the throat.

Maria could not move or turn her eyes away, though the whole room seemed to spin slowly, then faster and faster, around the focus of those armored hands.

The bearded man released his grip and stood erect, still watching the body at his feet.

"Turned off," he said distinctly.

Perhaps she moved. For whatever reason, the bearded man raised his sleepwalker's face to look at her. He did not meet her eyes, or avoid them. His eye movements were quick and alert, but the muscles of his face just hung there under the skin. He came toward her.

Why, he's young, she thought. Hardly more than a boy. She backed against the wall and waited, standing. Women were not brought up to faint on her planet. Somehow, the closer he came, the less she feared him. But if he had smiled once she would have screamed, on and on.

He stood before her, and reached out one hand to touch her face, her hair, her body. She stood still; she felt no lust in him, no meanness and no kindness. It was as if he radiated an emptiness.

"Not images," said the young man, as if to himself. Then another word, sounding like: "Badlife."

Almost, Maria dared to speak to him. The strangled man lay on the deck a few meters away.

The young man turned and shuffled deliberately away. She had never seen anyone who walked like him. He picked up his helmet and went out the door without looking back.

A pipe streamed water into one corner of her little space, where it gurgled away through a hole in the floor. The gravity seemed to be set at about Earth level. Maria sat leaning against the wall, praying and listening to her heart pound. It almost stopped when the door opened again, but only a machine entered, to bring her a large cake of pink and green stuff that seemed to be food. The machine walked around the dead man on its way out.

She had eaten a little of the cake when the door opened again, very slightly at first, then enough for a man to step quickly in. It was Hemphill, the cold-eyed one from the ship, leaning a bit to one side as if dragged down by the weight of the little bomb he still carried under his arm. After a quick look around he shut the door behind him and crossed the room to her, hardly glancing down as he stepped over the body of the mate.

"How many of them are there?" Hemphill whispered, bending over her. She had remained seated on the floor, too surprised to move or speak.

"Who?" she finally managed.

He jerked his head impatiently. "Them. The ones who live here inside *it*, and serve it. I saw one of them coming out of this room, when I was out in the passage. It's fixed up a lot of breathing space for them."

He showed Maria how the bomb could be made to explode, and gave it to her to hold, while he began to burn through her chain with his laser pistol. They exchanged information on what had happened. She did not think she would ever be able to pull the plunger and kill herself, but she did not tell that to Hemphill.

Just as they stepped out of the prison room, Hemphill had a bad moment when three machines rolled toward them from around a corner. But the things ignored the two frozen humans and rolled silently past them, going on out of sight.

He turned to Maria with an exultant whisper: "The damned thing is three-quarters blind, here inside its own skin!"

She only waited, watching him with frightened eyes.

With the beginning of hope, a vague plan was forming in his mind. He led her on, saying: "Now we'll see about that man. Or men." Was it too good to be true, that there was only one of them?

The corridors were badly lit, with uneven jogs and steps in them. Carelessly built concessions to life, he thought. He moved in the direction he had seen the man take.

After a few minutes of cautious advance, Hemphill heard the shuffling footsteps of one person ahead, coming nearer. He handed the bomb to Maria again, and pressed her behind him. They waited in a dark niche.

The footsteps approached with careless speed, a vague shadow bobbing ahead of them. The shaggy head swung so abruptly into view that Hemphill's metal-fisted swing was almost too late. The blow only grazed the back of the skull; the man yelped, staggered off balance, and fell down. He was wearing an old-model spacesuit, with no helmet.

Hemphill crouched over him, shoving the laser pistol almost into his face. "Make a sound and I'll kill you. Where are the others?"

The face looking up at Hemphill was stunned—worse than stunned. It seemed more dead than alive, though the eyes moved alertly enough from Hemphill to Maria and back, disregarding the gun.

"He's the same one," Maria whispered.

"Where are your friends?" Hemphill asked.

The man felt the back of his head, where he had been hit. "Damage," he said tonelessly, as if to himself. Then he reached up for the pistol, so calmly and steadily that he was nearly able to touch it.

Hemphill jumped back a step, and barely kept himself from firing. "Sit still or I'll kill you! Now tell me who you are, and how many others are here."

The man's putty face showed nothing. He said: "Your speech is steady in tone from word to word, not like that of the machine. You hold a killing tool there. Give it to me, and I will destroy you and—that one."

It seemed this man was only a brainwashed ruin, instead of an unspeakable traitor. Now what use could be made of him? Hemphill moved back another step, slowly lowering the pistol.

Maria spoke to their prisoner. "Where are you from? What planet?"

A blank stare.

"Your home. Where were you born?"

"From the birth tank." Sometimes the tones of the man's voice shifted like the berserker's, as if he were some fearful comedian, mocking it.

Hemphill uttered an unstable laugh. "From a birth tank, of course. What else? *Where are the others?*"

"I do not understand."

Hemphill sighed. "All right. Where's this birth tank?" It was someplace to start.

The place looked like the storeroom of a biology lab, badly lighted, piled and crowded with equipment, laced with pipes and conduits. But perhaps no living technician had ever worked here.

"You were *born* here?" Hemphill demanded.

"Yes."

"He's crazy."

"No, wait." Maria's voice sank to an even lower whisper, as if she was frightened anew. She took the hand of the slack-faced man, and he bent his head to stare at their touching hands.

"Do you have a name?" she asked, as if of a lost child.

"I am Goodlife."

"I think it's hopeless," put in Hemphill.

The woman ignored him. "Goodlife? My name is Maria. And this is Hemphill."

No reaction.

"Who were your parents? Father? Mother?"

"They were goodlife, too—they helped the machine. There was a battle, and badlife killed them. But they had given cells of their bodies to the machine, and from them it made me. Now I am the only goodlife."

"Great God," whispered Hemphill.

Silent, awed attention seemed to move Goodlife when threats and pleas had not. His face changed in awkward grimaces; then he turned to stare into a corner. For almost the first time, he volunteered a communication: "I know they were like you. A man and a woman."

Hemphill wanted to sweep every cubic meter of the surrounding mechanism with his hatred; he looked around at every side and angle of the room.

"The damned things," he said, his voice cracking like the berserker's own. "What they've done to me. To you. To everyone."

Plans seemed to come to him when the strain of hating was greatest. He moved quickly to put a hand on Goodlife's shoulder. "Listen to me. Do you know what a radioactive isotope is?"

"Yes."

"There will be a place, somewhere, where the machine decides what to do next—what strategy to follow. A place holding a block of some isotope with a long half-life. Probably near the center of the machine. Do you know of such a place?"

"Yes, I know where the strategic housing is."

"Strategic housing." Hemphill mounted to a strong new level. "Is there a way for us to reach it?"

"You are badlife!" He knocked Hemphill's hand away,

awkwardly. "You want to damage the machine, and you have damaged me. You are to be destroyed."

Maria took over, trying to soothe. "Goodlife—we are not bad, this man and I. Those who built this machine are the badlife. Someone built it, you know—some living people built it, long ago. They were the real badlife."

"Badlife." He might have been agreeing with Maria, or accusing her.

"Don't you want to live, Goodlife? Hemphill and I want to live. We want to help you, because you're alive, like us. Won't you help us now?"

Goodlife was silent for a few moments. Then he turned back to face them and said: "All life thinks it is, but it is not. There are only particles, energy, and space, and the laws of the machines."

Maria kept at him. "Goodlife, listen to me. A wise man once said: 'I think, therefore I am.'"

"A wise man?" he questioned, in his cracking voice. Then he sat down on the deck, hugging his knees and rocking back and forth. He might have been thinking.

Drawing Maria aside, Hemphill said: "You know, we have a faint hope now. There's plenty of air in here, there's water and food. There are warships following this thing—there must be. If we can find a way to disable it, we can wait and perhaps be picked up in a month or two."

She watched him silently for a moment. "Hemphill, what have these machines done to you?"

"My wife—my children." He thought his voice sounded almost indifferent. "They were on Pascalo, three years ago; there was nothing left. This machine, or one like it."

She took his hand, as she had taken Goodlife's. They both looked down at their joined fingers, then raised their eyes, smiling briefly together at the similarity of action.

"Where's the bomb?" Hemphill thought aloud suddenly, spinning around.

It lay in a dim corner. He grabbed it up again, and strode over to where Goodlife sat and rocked.

"Well, are you with us? Us, or the ones who built the machine?"

Goodlife stood up, and looked closely at Hemphill. "They were inspired by the laws of physics, which controlled their brains, to build the machine. Now the machine has preserved them as images. It has preserved my father and mother, and it will preserve me."

"What images do you mean? Where are they?"

"The images in the theater."

The right course seemed to be to accustom him to cooperation, win his confidence, learn about him and the machine. Then, on to the strategic housing.

"Will you guide us to the theater, Goodlife?"

It was by far the largest air-filled room they had yet found, with a hundred seats of a shape usable by Earth-descended humanity, though Hemphill guessed it had been built for someone else. The theater was elaborately furnished and well lighted. When the door closed behind them, the ranked images of intelligent creatures brightened into life upon the stage.

The stage became a window into a vast hall. One person stood forward at an imagined lectern. He was a slender, fine-boned being, topologically like a man except for the single eye that stretched across his face, with a bright bulging pupil that slid to and fro like mercury.

The speaker's voice was a high-pitched torrent of clicks and whines. Most of those in the ranks behind him wore a kind of uniform. When he paused, they whined in unison.

"What does he say?" Maria whispered.

Goodlife looked at her. "The machine has told me that it has lost the meaning of the sounds."

"Then, may we see the images of your parents, Goodlife?"

Hemphill, watching the stage, started to object. But

then he realized that Maria was right—the sight of this fellow's parents might be more immediately helpful.

Goodlife found a control somewhere.

Hemphill was surprised momentarily that the parents appeared only in flat projected pictures. First the man was there, against a plain background, blue eyes and neat short beard, nodding his head with a pleasant expression on his face. He wore the lining coverall of a spacesuit.

Then the woman was there, holding some kind of cloth before her for covering, and looking straight into the camera. She had a broad face and red braided hair. There was hardly time to see anything more before the alien orator was back, whining faster than ever.

Hemphill turned to ask: "Is that all? All you know of your parents?"

"Yes. Now they are images; they no longer think that they exist. The badlife killed them."

The creature in the projection was assuming, Maria thought, a more didactic tone. Three-dimensional charts of stars and planets appeared near him, one after another, and he gestured at them as he spoke. He had vast numbers of stars and planets on his charts to boast about; she could tell somehow that he was boasting.

Hemphill was moving toward the stage a step at a time, more and more absorbed. Maria did not like the way the light of the images reflected on his face.

Goodlife, too, watched the stage pageant, which perhaps he had seen a thousand times before. Maria could not tell what thoughts might be behind his meaningless face, which had never had another human face to imitate. On impulse she took his arm again.

"Goodlife, Hemphill and I are alive, like you. Will you help us now? Then we will always help you." She had a sudden mental picture of Goodlife rescued, taken to a planet, cowering among the staring badlife.

"Good. Bad." His hand reached to take hold of hers; he had removed his suit gauntlets. He swayed back and forth as if she attracted and repelled him at the same time. God, she wanted to scream and wail for him, to tear apart with her fingers the mindlessly proceeding metal that had made him what he was.

"We've got them!" It was Hemphill, coming back from the stage, where the recorded tirade went on unrelentingly. He was exultant. "Don't you see? He's showing what must be a complete catalogue, of every star and rock they own. It's a victory speech. But when we study those charts we can find them, and track them down and *reach* them!"

"Hemphill!" She wanted to calm him back to concentration on immediate problems. "How old are those—pictures up there? What part of the galaxy do they show? Or were they even made in another galaxy? Will we ever be able to tell?"

Hemphill lost some enthusiasm. "Anyway, it's a chance to track them down; we've got to save this information." He pointed at Goodlife. "He's got to take me to what he calls the strategic housing; then we can sit and wait for the warships, or maybe get off this damned thing in a boat."

She stroked Goodlife's hand, soothing a baby. "Yes, but he's confused. God, how could he be anything else?"

"Of course." Hemphill paused to consider. "You can handle him much better than I."

She didn't answer.

Hemphill went on: "Now you're a woman, and he appears to be a physically healthy young male. Calm him down if you like, but somehow you've *got* to persuade him to help me. Everything depends on it." He had turned toward the stage again, unable to take more than half his mind from the star charts. "Go for a little walk and talk with him; don't get far away."

And what else was there to do? She led Goodlife from the theater while the dead man on the stage clicked and shouted, cataloguing his thousand suns.

Too much had happened, was still happening, and all at once he could no longer stand to be near the badlife.

Goodlife found himself pulling away from the female, running, flying down the passages, toward the place where he had fled when he was small and strange fears had come from nowhere. It was the room where the machine always saw and heard him, and was ready to talk to him.

He stood before the attention of the machine, in the chamber-that-has-shrunk. He thought of the place so, because he could remember it clearly as a larger room, where the scanners and speakers of the machine towered above his head. He knew the real change had been his own physical growth; still, this compartment was set apart in a special association with food and sleep and protective warmth.

"I have listened to the badlife, and shown them things," he said, fearing punishment.

"I know that, Goodlife, for I have watched. These things have become a part of my experiment."

What joyous relief! The machine said nothing of punishment, though it must know that the words of the badlife had shaken and confused him. He had even imagined himself showing the man Hemphill the strategic housing, and so putting an end to all punishment, for always.

"They wanted me—they wanted me to—"

"I have watched. I have listened. The man Hemphill is tough and evil, powerfully motivated to fight against me. I must understand his kind, for they cause much damage. He must be tested to his limits—to destruction. He thinks himself free inside me, and so he will not think as a prisoner. This is important."

Goodlife peeled off his irritating suit; the machine would not let the badlife in here. He sank down to the floor and wrapped his arms around the base of a scanner-speaker console. Once, long ago, the machine had given him a thing that was soft and warm when he held it. He closed his eyes.

"What are my orders?" he asked, sleepily. Here in this chamber all was steady and comforting, as always.

"First, do not tell the badlife of these orders. Then,

do what the man Hemphill tells you to do. No harm will come to me."

"He has a bomb."

"I watched his approach, and I disabled his bomb, even before he entered to attack me. His pistol can do me no serious harm. Do you think one badlife can conquer me?"

"No." Smiling, reassured, he curled into a more comfortable position. "Tell me about my parents." He had heard the story a thousand times, but it was always good.

"Your parents were good; they gave themselves to me. Then, during a great battle, the badlife killed them. The badlife hated them, as they hate you. When they say they like you, they lie, with the evil untruth of all badlife.

"But your parents were good, and each gave me a part of their bodies, and from them I made you. Your parents were destroyed completely by the badlife, or I would have saved even their nonfunctioning bodies for you to see. That would have been good."

"Yes."

"The two badlife have searched for you; now they are resting. Sleep, Goodlife."

He slept.

Awakening, he remembered a dream in which two people had beckoned him to join them on the stage of the theater. He knew they were his mother and father, though they looked like the two badlife. The dream faded before his waking mind could grasp it firmly.

He ate and drank, while the machine talked to him.

"If the man Hemphill wants to be guided to the strategic housing, take him there. I will capture him there, and later let him escape to try again. When finally he can be provoked to fight no more, I will destroy him. But I mean to preserve the life of the female; you and she will produce more goodlife for me."

"Yes!" It was immediately clear what a good thing

that would be. They would give parts of their bodies to the machine, so new goodlife bodies could be built, cell by cell. And the man Hemphill, who punished and damaged with his fast-swinging arm, would be destroyed.

When he rejoined the badlife, the man Hemphill barked questions and threatened punishment until Goodlife was confused and a little frightened. But Goodlife agreed to help, and was careful to reveal nothing of what the machine planned. Maria was more pleasant than ever; he touched her whenever he could.

Hemphill demanded to be taken to the strategic housing. Goodlife agreed at once; he had been there many times. There was a high-speed elevator that made the eighty-kilometer journey easy.

Hemphill paused, before saying: "You're too damned willing, all of a sudden." Turning his face to Maria. "I don't trust him."

This badlife thought he was being false! Goodlife was angered; the machine never lied, and no properly obedient goodlife could lie.

Hemphill paced around, and finally demanded: "Is there any route that approaches this strategic housing in such a way that the machine cannot possibly watch us?"

Goodlife thought. "I believe there is one such way. We will have to carry extra tanks of air, and travel many kilometers through vacuum." The machine had said to help Hemphill, and help he would. He hoped he could watch when the male badlife was finally destroyed.

There had been a battle, in some time that could hardly be related meaningfully to any Earthly calendar. The berserker had fought some terrible opponent, and had taken a terrible lance-thrust of a wound. A cavity three kilometers wide at the widest, and eighty kilometers deep, had been driven in by a sequence of shaped atomic charges, through level after level of machinery, deck after deck of armor, and had been stopped only by the last inner defenses of the buried, unliving heart. The berserker had survived, and crushed its enemy, and soon afterward its repair machines had sealed over the outer opening of the wound, using extra thicknesses of armor. It had meant to gradually rebuild the whole destruction, but there was so much life in the galaxy, and so much of it was stubborn and clever. Somehow, battle damage accumulated faster than it could be repaired. The great hole was used as a conveyor path, and never much worked on.

When Hemphill saw the blasted cavity—what little of it his tiny suit-lamp could show—he felt a shrinking fear that was greater than any in his memory. He stopped on the edge of the void, drifting there with his arm instinctively around Maria. She had put on a suit and accompanied him, without protest or eagerness, without being asked.

They had already come an hour's journey from the airlock, through weightless vacuum inside the great machine. Goodlife had led the way through section after section, with every show of cooperation. Hemphill had the pistol ready, and the bomb, and fifty meters of cord tied around his left arm.

But when Hemphill recognized the once-molten edge of the berserker's great scar for what it was, his delicate new hope of survival left him. This, the damned thing had survived. This, perhaps, had hardly weakened it. Again, the bomb under his arm was only a pathetic toy.

Goodlife drifted up to them. Hemphill had already taught him to touch helmets for speech in vaccum.

"This great damage is the one path we can take to reach the strategic housing without passing scanners or service machines. I will teach you to ride the conveyor. It will carry us most of the way."

The conveyor was a thing of forcefields and great rushing containers, hundreds of meters out in the enormous wound and running lengthwise through it. When the conveyor's forcefields caught the people up, their weightlessness was more than ever like falling, with occasional vast shapes, corpuscles of the berserker's bloodstream, flickering past in the near-darkness to show movement.

Hemphill flew beside Maria, holding her hand. Her face was hard to see inside the helmet, but she did not seem to be looking at him. There was no need.

This conveyor was another mad new world, a fairy tale of monsters and flying and falling. Hemphill fell past his great fear, into a new determination. I can do it, he thought. The thing is blind and helpless here. I will do it, and I will survive if I can.

Goodlife led them from the slowing conveyor, to drift into a chamber hollowed in the inner armor by the final explosion at the end of the ancient lance-thrust. The chamber was an empty sphere thirty meters across, from which cracks radiated out into the solid armor. On the surface nearest the center of the berserker, one fissure was as wide as a door, where the last energy of the enemy's blow had driven ahead.

Goodlife touched helmets. "I have seen the other end of this crack from inside, at the strategic housing. It is only a few meters from here."

Hemphill hesitated for only a moment, wondering whether to send Goodlife through the twisting passage first. But if this was some incredibly complex trap, the trigger of it might be anywhere.

He touched his helmet to Maria's. "Stay behind him. Follow him through, and keep an eye on him."

The fissure narrowed as Hemphill followed it, but at the end it was still wide enough for him to force himself through.

He had reached another vast hollow sphere, the inner temple. In the center was a complexity the size of a small house, shock-mounted on a web of girders that ran in every direction. This could be nothing but the strategic housing. There was a glow from it like flickering moonlight; forcefield switches responding to the random atomic turmoil within, somehow choosing what human shipping lane or colony would be next attacked, and how.

Hemphill felt a pressure rising in his mind and soul,

toward a climax of triumphal hate. He drifted forward, cradling his bomb tenderly, starting to unwind the cord wrapped around his arm. He tied the free end delicately to the plunger of the bomb as he approached the central complex.

I mean to live, he thought, to watch the damned thing die. I will tape the bomb against the central block, that so-innocent-looking slab in there, and I will brace myself around fifty meters of these heavy metal corners, and pull.

Goodlife stood braced in the perfect place from which to see the heart of the machine, watching the man Hemphill string his cord. Goodlife felt a certain satisfaction that his prediction had been right, and that the strategic housing was approachable by this one narrow path of the great damage. They would not have to go back that way; when the badlife was captured, all of them could ride up in the air-filled elevator Goodlife used when he came here for maintenance practice.

Hemphill had finished stringing his cord. Now he waved his arm at Goodlife and Maria, who clung to the same girder, watching. Hemphill pulled on the cord. Of course, nothing happened. The machine had said the bomb was disabled, and the machine would make very certain in such a matter.

Maria pushed away from her place beside Goodlife, and drifted in toward Hemphill.

Hemphill tugged again and again on his cord. Goodlife sighed impatiently, and moved his arms and legs. There was a great cold in the girders here; he could begin to feel it now through the fingers and toes of his suit.

At last, when Hemphill started back to see what was wrong with his device, the service machines came from where they had been hiding, to seize him. He tried to draw his pistol but their grippers moved far too quickly.

It was hardly a struggle that Goodlife saw, but he watched with interest. Hemphill's figure had gone rigid in the suit, obviously straining every muscle to the limit. Why should the badlife try to struggle against steel and atomic power? The machines bore the man effortlessly away, toward the elevator shaft. Goodlife felt an uneasiness.

Maria was drifting, her face turned back toward Goodlife. He wanted to go to her and touch her again, but suddenly he was a little afraid, as before when he had run from her. One of the service machines came back from the elevator to grip her and carry her away. She kept her face still turned toward Goodlife. He turned away from her, a feeling like punishment in the core of his being.

In the great cold silence, the flickering light from the strategic housing bathed everything. In the center, a chaotic block of atoms. Elsewhere, engines, relays, sensing cells. Where was it, really, the great machine that spoke to him? Everywhere, and nowhere. Would these new feelings, brought by the badlife, ever leave him? He tried to understand himself, and could not begin.

Light flickered on a round shape among the girders a few meters away, a shape that offended Goodlife's sense of the proper and necessary in machinery. Looking closer, he saw that it was a space helmet.

It was as if he knew that this was an ultimate thing that he had found, before he knew what it was. He felt a certainty. He had expected this, known it all along, known it all his lifetime, in his bones. It seemed a lifetime before he could move toward it.

The motionless figure was wedged only lightly in an angle between frigid beams, but there was no force in here to move it.

He could hear the suit creak, stiff with great cold, when he grabbed it and turned it. Unseeing blue eyes looked out at Goodlife through the faceplate. The man's face wore a neat short beard.

"Ahhh, yes," sighed Goodlife inside his own helmet. A thousand times he had seen the image of this face.

His father had been carrying something heavy, strapped carefully to his ancient suit. His father had carried it this far, and here the old suit had wheezed and failed.

His father, too, had followed the logical narrow path of the great damage, to reach the strategic housing without being seen. His father had choked and died and frozen here, carrying toward the strategic housing what could only be a bomb.

Goodlife heard his own voice keening, without words, and he could not see plainly for the tears floating in his helmet. His fingers felt numbed with cold as he unstrapped the bomb and lifted it from his father . . .

Hemphill was too exhausted to do more than gasp as the service machine carried him out of the elevator and along the air-filled corridor toward the prison room. When the machine went dead and dropped him, he had to lie still for long seconds before he could attack it again. It had hidden his pistol somewhere, so he began to beat on the robotlike thing with his armored fists, while it stood unresisting. Soon it toppled over. Hemphill sat on it and beat it some more, sobbing and cursing.

It was nearly a minute later when the tremor of the explosion, racing from the compounded chaos of the berserker's torn-out heart, racing through metal beams and decks, reached the corridor, where it was far too faint for anyone to feel.

Maria, completely weary, sat where her metal captor had dropped her, watching Hemphill, pitying him and loving him.

He stopped his pointless pounding of the machine under him, and said hoarsely: "It's a trick, another damned trick."

Maria shook her head. "No, I don't think so." She saw that power still seemed to be on in the elevator, and she watched the door of it.

Hemphill went away to search among the now-purposeless machines for weapons and food. He came back, raging again. What was probably an automatic destructor charge had wrecked the theater and the starcharts. They might as well get away in the boat.

She ignored him, still watching an elevator door which never opened. Soon she began quietly to cry.

Young Girl at an Open Half-door

That first night there was a police vehicle, what I think they call a K-9 unit, in the little employees' lot behind the Institute. I parked my car beside it and got out. The summer moon was dull above the city's air, but floodlights glared at a small door set in the granite flank of the great building. I carried my toolbox there, pushed a button, and stood waiting.

Within half a minute, a uniformed guard appeared inside the reinforced glass of the door. Before he had finished unlocking, two uniformed policemen were standing beside him, and beside them a powerful leashed dog whose ears were aimed my way.

The door opened. "Electronic Watch," I said, holding out my identification. The dog inspected me, while the three uniformed men peered at my symbols and were satisfied.

With a few words and nods the police admitted me to fellowship. In the next moment they were saying good-bye to the guard. "It's clean here, Dan, we're gonna shove off."

The guard agreed they might as well. He gave them a jovial farewell and locked them out, and then turned

back to me, still smiling, an old and heavy man, now
adopting a fatherly attitude. He squinted with the effort
of remembering what he had read on my identification
card. "Your name Joe?"

"Joe Ricci."

"Well, Joe, our system's acting up." He pointed.
"The control room's up this way."

"I know, I helped install it." I walked beside the
guard named Dan through silent passages and silent
marble galleries, all carved by night lights into one-
third brilliance and two-thirds shadow. We passed
through new glass doors that were opened for us by
photocells. Maintenance men in green uniforms were
cleaning the glass; the white men among them were
calling back and forth in Polish.

Dan whistled cheerfully as we went up the wide
four-branched central stair, passing under a great skylight holding out the night. From the top landing of the
stair, a plain door, little noticed in the daytime, opens
through classical marble into a science-fiction room of
fluorescent lights and electronic consoles. In that room
are three large wall panels, marked Security, Fire, and
Interior Climate. As we entered, another guard was
alone in the room, seated before the huge security
panel.

"Gallery two-fifteen showed again," the seated guard
said in a faintly triumphant voice, turning to us and
pointing to one of the indicator lights on the panel. The
little panel lights were laid out within an outline of the
building's floor plan. "You'd swear it was someone in
there."

I set down my kit and stood looking at the panel,
mentally reviewing the general layout of the security
circuitry. Electronic Watch has not for a long time used
anything as primitive as photocells, which are relegated
to such prosaic jobs as opening doors. After closing
hours in the Institute, when the security system is
switched on, invisible electric fields permeate the space
of every room where there is anything of value. A cat

cannot prowl the building without leaving a track of disturbances across the Security panel.

At the moment all its indicators were dim and quiet. I opened my kit, took out a multimeter and a set of probes, and began a preliminary check of the panel itself.

"You'd swear someone's in two-fifteen when it happens," said the guard named Dan. Standing close and watching me, he gave a little laugh. "And then a man starts over to investigate, and before he can get there it stops."

Of course there was nothing nice and obvious wrong with the panel. I had not expected there would be; neat, simple troubles are too much to expect from the complexities of modern electronic gear. I tapped the indicator marked 215 but its glow remained dim and steady. "You get the signal from just the one gallery?" I asked.

"Yeah," said the guard in the chair. "Flashing a couple times, real quick, on and off. Then it stays on steady for a while, like someones's just standing in the middle of the room over there. Then like he said, it goes off while a man's trying to get over there. We called the officers and then we called you."

I put the things back in my kit and closed it up and lifted it. "I'll walk over there and look around."

"You know where two-fifteen is?" Dan just unwrapped a sandwich. "I can walk over with you."

"That's all right, I can find it." I delayed on my way out of the room, smiling back at the two guards. "I've been here in the daytime, looking at the pictures."

"Oh. You bring your girl here, hey?" The guards laughed, a little relieved that I had broken my air of grim intentness. I know I often strike people that way.

Walking alone through the half-lit halls, I found it pleasant to think of myself as a man who came there in two such different capacities. Electronics and art were both in my grasp. I had a good start at knowing everything of importance. Renaissance Man, I thought, of the New Renaissance of the Space Age.

Finding the gallery I wanted was no problem, for all of them are numbered plainly, more or less in sequence. Through rising numbers, I traversed the Thirteenth Century, the Fourteenth, the Fifteenth. A multitude of Christs and virgins, saints and noblemen watched my passage from their walls of glare and shadow.

From several rooms away I saw the girl, through a real doorway framing the painted one she stands in. My steps slowed as I entered gallery two-fifteen. About twenty other paintings hang there, but for me it was empty of any presence but hers.

That night I had not thought of her until I saw her, which struck me then as odd, because on my occasional daytime visits I had always stopped before her door. I had no girl of the kind to take to an art gallery, whatever the guards might surmise.

The painter's light is full only on her face, and on her left hand, which rests on the closed bottom panel of a divided door. She is leaning very slightly out through the half-open doorway, her head of auburn curls turned just an inch to her left but her eyes looking the other way. She watches and listens, that much is certain. To me it had always seemed that she is expecting someone. Her full, vital body is chaste in a plain dark dress. Consider her attitude, her face, and wonder that so much is made of the smile of Mona Lisa.

The card on the wall beside the painting reads:

REMBRANDT VAN RIJN
DUTCH 1606-1669
YOUNG GIRL AT AN OPEN HALF-DOOR
dated 1645

She might have been seventeen when Rembrandt saw her, and seventeen she has remained, while the faces passing her doorway have grown up and grown old and disappeared, wave after wave of them.

She waits.

I broke out of my reverie, at last, with an effort. My eye was caught by the next painting, Saftleven's *Witches'*

Sabbath, which once in the daylight had struck me as amusing. When I had freed my eyes from that I looked into the adjoining galleries, trying to put down the sudden feeling of being watched. I squinted up at the skylight ceiling of gallery two-fifteen, through which a single glaring spotlight shone.

Holding firmly to thoughts of electronics, I peered in corners and under benches, where a forgotten transistor radio might lurk to interfere, conceivably, with the electric field of the alarm. There was none.

From my kit I took a small field-strength meter, and like a priest swinging a censer I moved it gently through the air around me. The needle swayed, as it should have, with the invisible presence of the field.

There was a light gasp, as of surprise. A sighing momentary movement in the air, something nearby come and gone in a moment, and in that moment the meter needle jumped over violently, pegging so that with a technician's reflex my hand flew to switch it to a less sensitive scale.

I waited there alone for ten more minutes, but nothing further happened.

"It's working now; I could follow you everywhere you moved," said the guard in the chair, turning with assurance to speak to me just as I re-entered the science-fiction room. Dan and his sandwich were gone.

"Something's causing interference," I said, in my voice the false authority of the expert at a loss. "So. You never have any trouble with any other gallery, hey?"

"No, least I've never seen any—well, look at that now. Make a liar out of me." The guard chuckled without humor. "Something showing in two-twenty-seven now. That's Modern Art."

Half an hour later I was creeping on a catwalk through a clean crawl space above gallery two-twenty-seven, tracing a perfectly healthy microwave system. The reflected glare of night lights below filtered up into the crawl space, through a million holes in acoustical ceiling panels.

A small, bright auburn movement, almost directly below me, caught my eye. I crouched lower on the catwalk, putting my eyes close to the holes in one thin panel, bringing into my view almost the whole of the enormous room under the false ceiling.

The auburn was in a girl's hair. It came near matching the hair of the girl in the painting, but that could only have been coincidence, if such a thing exists. The girl below me was alive in the same sense I am, solid and fleshy and three-dimensional. She wore a kind of stretch suit, of a green shade that set off her hair, and she held a shiny object raised like a camera in her hands.

From my position almost directly above her, I could not see her face, only the curved grace of her body as she took a step forward, holding the shiny thing high. Then she began another step, and halfway through it she was gone, vanished in an instant from the center of an open floor.

Some time passed before I eased up from the strain of my bent position. All the world was silent and ordinary, so that alarm and astonishment would have seemed out of place. I inched back through the crawl space to my borrowed ladder, climbed down, walked along a corridor and turned a corner into the vast shadow-and-glare of gallery two-two-seven.

Standing in the brightly lit spot where I had seen the girl, I realized she had been raising her camera at a sculpture—a huge, flowing mass of bronze blobs and curved holes, on the topmost blob a face that looked like something scratched there by a child. I went up to it and thumped my knuckles on the nearest bulge of bronze, and the great thing sounded hollowly. Looking at the card on its marble base I had begun to read—RECLINING FIGURE, 1957—when a sound behind me made me spin round.

Dan asked benignly: "Was that you raising a ruckus in here about five minutes ago? Looked like a whole mob of people was running around."

I nodded, feeling the beginning of a strange contentment.

Next day I awoke at the usual time, to afternoon sunlight pushing at the closed yellow shades of my furnished apartment, to the endless street noises coming in. I had slept well and felt alert at once, and I began thinking about the girl.

Even if I had not seen her vanish, it would have been obvious that her comings and goings at the Institute were accomplished by no ordinary prowlers' or burglars' methods. Nor was she there on any ordinary purpose; if she had stolen or vandalized, I would most certainly have been awakened early.

I ate an ordinary breakfast, not noticing much or being noticed, sitting at the counter in the restaurant on the ground floor of the converted hotel where I rented my apartment. The waitress wore green, although her hair was black. Once I had tried half-heartedly to talk to her, to know her, to make out, but she had kept on working and loafing, talking to me and everyone else alike.

When the sun was near going down, I started for work as usual. I bought the usual newspaper to take along, but did not read it when I saw the headline PEACE TALKS FAILING. That evening I felt the way I supposed a lover should feel, going to his beloved.

Dan and two other guards greeted me with smiles of the kind that people wear when things that are clearly not their fault are going wrong for their employer. They told me that the pseudo-prowler had once more visited gallery two-fifteen, had vanished as usual from the panel just as a guard approached that room, and then had several times appeared on the indicators for gallery two-twenty-seven. I went to two-twenty-seven, making a show of carrying in tools and equipment, and settled myself on a bench in a dim corner, to wait.

The contentment I had known for twenty-four hours became impatience, and with slowly passing time the tension of impatience made me uncontrollably restless. I felt sure that she could somehow watch me waiting; she must know I was waiting for her; she must be able to see that I meant her no harm. Beyond meeting her, I had no plan at all.

Not even a guard came to disturb me. Around me, in paint and bronze and stone and welded steel, crowded the tortured visions of the Twentieth Century. I got up at last in desperation and found that not everything was torture. There on the wall were Monet's water lilies; at first nothing but vague flat shapes of paint, then the surface of a pond and a deep curve of reflected sky. I grew dizzy staring into that water, a dizziness of relief that made me laugh. When I looked away at last, the walls and ceiling were shimmering as if the glare of the night lights was reflected from Monet's pond.

I understood then that something was awry, something was being done to me, but I could not care. Giggling at the world, I stood there breathing air that seemed to sparkle in my lungs. The auburn-haired girl came to my side and took my arm and guided me to the bench where my unused equipment lay.

Her voice had the beauty I had expected, though with a strange strong accent. "Oh, I am sorry to make you weak and sick. But you insist to stay here and span much time, the time in which I must do my work."

For the moment I could say nothing. She made me sit on the bench, and bent over me with concern, turning her head with something of the same questioning look as the girl in the Rembrandt painting. Again she said, "Oh, I am sorry."

"S'all right." My tongue was heavy, and I still wanted to laugh.

She smiled and hurried away, flowed away. Again she was dressed in a green stretch suit, setting off the color of her hair. This time she vanished from my sight in normal fashion, going around one of the gallery's low partitions. Coming from behind that partition were flashes of light.

I got unsteadily to my feet and went after her. Rounding

the corner, I saw three devices set up on tripods, the tripods spaced evenly around the *Reclining Figure*. From the three devices, which I could not begin to identify, little lances of light flicked like stings or brushes at the sculpture. And whirling around it like dancers, on silent rubbery feet, moved another pair of machine-shapes, busy with some purpose that was totally beyond me.

The girl reached to support me as I swayed. Her hands were strong, her eyes were darkly blue, and she was tall in slender curves. Smiling, she said, "It is all right, I do no harm."

"I don't care about that," I said. "I want only—not to tangle things with you."

"What?" She smiled, as if at someone raving. She had drugged me, with subtle gases in the air that sparkled in my lungs. I knew that but I did not care.

"I always hold back," I said, "and tangle things with people. Not this time. I want to love you without any of that. This is a simple miracle, and I just want it to go on. Now tell me your name."

She was so silent and solemn for a moment, watching me, that I feared that I had angered her. But then she shook her head and smiled again. "My name is Day-ell. Now don't fall down!" and she took her supporting arm away.

For the moment I was content without her touching me. I leaned against the partition and looked at her busy machines. "Will you steal our *Reclining Figure?*" I asked, giggling again as I wondered who would want it.

"Steal?" she was thoughtful. "The two greatest works of this house I must save. I will replace them with copies so well made that no one will ever know, before—" She broke off. After a moment she added, "Only you will know." And then she turned away to give closer attention to her silent and ragingly busy machines. When she made an adjustment on a tiny thing she held in her hand, there were suddenly two *Reclining Figures* visible, one of them smaller and transparent but growing larger, moving toward us from some dark and distant space that was temporarily within the gallery.

I was thinking over and over what Day-ell had said. Addled and joyful, I plotted what seemed to me a clever compliment, and announced, "I know what the two greatest works in this house are."

"Oh?" The word in her voice was a soft bell. But she was still busy.

"One is Rembrandt's girl."

"You are right!" Day-ell, pleased, turned to me. "Last night I took that one to safety. Where I take them, the originals, they will be safe forever."

"But the best—is you." I pushed away from the partition. "I make you my girl. My love. Forever, if it can be. But how long doesn't matter."

Her face changed and her eyes went wide, as if she truly understood how marvelous were such words, from anyone, from grim Joe Ricci in particular. She took a step toward me.

"If you could mean that," she whispered, "then I would stay with you, in spite of everything."

My arms went round her and I could feel forever passing. "Stay, of course I mean it, stay with me."

"Come, Day-ell, come," intoned a voice, soft, but still having metal in its timbre. Looking over her shoulder, I saw the machine-shapes waiting, balancing motionless now on their silent feet. There was again only one *Reclining Figure*.

My thoughts were clearing and I said to her, "You're leaving copies, you said, and no one will know the difference, before. Before what? What's going to happen?"

When my girl did not answer, I held her at arms' length. She was shaking her head slowly, and tears had come into her eyes. She said, "It does not matter what happens, since I have found here a man of life who will love me. In my world there is no one like that. If you will hold me, I can stay."

My hands holding her began to shake. I said, "I won't keep you here, to die in some disaster. I'll go with you instead."

"Come, Day-ell, come." It was a terrible steel whisper. And she stepped back, compelled by the machine-voice now that I had let her go. She said to me, "You must not come. My world is safe for paint, safe for bronze, not safe for men who love. Why do you think that we must steal—?"

She was gone, the machines and lights gone with her.

The *Reclining Figure* stands massive and immobile as ever, bronze blobs and curved holes, with a face like something scratched on by a child. Thump it with a knuckle, and it sounds hollowly. Maybe three hundred years' perspective is needed to see it as one of the two greatest in this house. Maybe eyes are needed, accustomed to more dimensions than ours; eyes of those who sent Day-ell diving down through time to save choice fragments from the murky wreckage of the New Renaissance, plunged in the mud of the ignorant and boastful Twentieth Century.

Not that her world is better. *Safe for paint, safe for bronze, not safe for men who love.* I could not live there now.

The painting looks unchanged. A girl of seventeen still waits, frozen warmly in Rembrandt's light, three hundred years and more on the verge of smiling, secure that long from age and death and disappointment. But will a war incinerate her next week, or an earthquake swallow her next month? Or will our city convulse and die in mass rioting madness, a witches' Sabbath come true? What warning can I give? When they found me alone and weeping in the empty gallery that night, they talked about a nervous breakdown. The indicators on the Security panel are always quiet now, and I have let myself be argued out of the little of my story that I told.

No world is safe for those who love.

The Adventure Of The Metal Murderer

It had the shape of a man, the brain of an electronic devil.

It and the machines like it were the best imitations of men and women that the berserkers, murderous machines themselves, were capable of building. Still, these man-shapes and woman-shapes were obviously fraudulent when under close inspection by members of any known human society.

"Only twenty-nine accounted for?" the supervisor of defense demanded sharply. Strapped into his combat chair, he sat looking through the information screen before him into space. The nearby bulk of Earth was armored in the dun brown of defensive forcefields, and the flagship was hugging it as closely as had the first astronauts' capsules a thousand years before.

"Only twenty-nine." The flat admission of the answer arrived on the flagship's bridge amid a sharp spattering of electrical noise. The skirmish just concluded had left enough radiation in nearby space to fry the signals of even the best communicators. The tortured voice continued: "And it's quite certain now that there were thirty to begin with."

"Then where's the other?"

There was no immediate reply.

All of Earth's defensive forces were still at something close to full alert, though the attack had been tiny, no more than an attempt at infiltration, and it seemed to have been thoroughly defeated. Berserkers, remnants of some ancient interstellar war, were mortal enemies of everything that lived, and the greatest danger to humanity that the universe had yet revealed.

The moon was rising now, its apparent motion greatly accelerated by the flagship's own fast orbit. And now, much closer than the moon, a small blur leaped over Earth's dully shielded limb, hurtling along a course that would bring it within a few hundred kilometers of the supervisor's craft. This was Power Station One, a tamed black hole. In times of peace the power-hungry billions of the planet drew from it half their necessary energy. Station One was visible to the eye only as a flowing, slight distortion of the stars beyond. The flagship's mass detectors had already recognized it, though; two decks below the bridge, engines murmured with the autopilot's nudging, moving the ship to give that subtle blur more elbow room.

Another report was coming in. "We are searching space for the missing berserker android, Supervisor."

"You had damned well better be."

"The infiltrating enemy craft had padded containers for thirty androids, as shown by computer analysis of its debris. We must assume that all containers were filled."

Life and death were in the supervisor's tones: "Is there any possibility at all that the missing unit got past you to the surface?"

"Negative, Supervisor." There was a slight pause. "At least we know it did not reach the surface in our time."

"Our time? What does that mean, babbler? How could—ah."

The black hole flashed by. Not really tamed, though men sometimes described it with that word, to help put their own doubts to rest. Just harnessed, more or less. Moving that enigmatic monster into a handy orbit had not been easy.

Suppose—and given the location of the skirmish, the supposition was not unlikely—that berserker android number thirty had been propelled, by some accident of combat, right at Station One. It could easily have entered the black hole. According to the latest theories, it might conceivably have survived that process, to re-emerge into the universe intact, projected out of the hole as its own tangible image, in a burst of virtual-particle radiation.

Theory dictated that, in such a case, the re-emergence must take place before the falling-in.

The supervisor issued orders crisply. At once, his computers on the world below, the Earth Defense Conglomerate of awesome reputation, took up the problem, giving it highest priority. What could one berserker android do to Earth? Probably not much. But to the supervisor, and those who worked for him, defense was a sacred task. The temple of Earth's safety had been horribly profaned.

To produce the first answers took those machines eleven minutes.

"Number thirty did go into the black hole, sir. Neither we nor the enemy could very well have foreseen such a result, but—"

"What is the probability that the android emerged intact?"

"Because of the peculiar angle at which it entered, approximately sixty-nine percent."

"That high!"

"And there is a forty-nine percent chance that it will reach the surface of the Earth intact, in functional condition, at some point in our past. However, the computers do add one reassuring note. As the enemy device must have been programmed for some subtle attack upon our present society, it is not likely to be able to do much damage at the time and place where it—"

"Your skull contains a vacuum of a truly intergalactic

order. *I* will tell *you* and the computers when it has become possible for us to feel even the slightest degree of reassurance! Meanwhile, get me more figures."

The next word from the ground came twenty minutes later. "There is a ninety-two percent chance that landing of the android on the surface, if it occurred was within one hundred kilometers of fifty-one degrees, eleven minutes, north latitude; zero degrees, seven minutes, west longitude."

"And the time?"

"Ninety-eight percent probability of January 1, 1880 CE, plus or minus ten standard years."

A land mass, a great clouded island, was presented to the supervisor on his screen, marked with a green ring and crosshairs.

"Recommended course of action?"

It took the Ed Conglomerate an hour and a half to answer that.

The first two volunteers perished in attempted launchings before the method could be perfected. When the third was ready he was called in, just before launching, for a last private meeting with the supervisor.

The supervisor looked him up and down, taking in his outlandish dress, strange hair-styling, and all the rest. He did not ask if the volunteer was ready, but began bluntly: "It has now been confirmed that whether you win or lose back there, you will never be able to return to your own time."

"Yes, sir." Training had ingrained the ancient speech patterns so thoroughly in the volunteer that now the words of his native language emerged half strangled from his throat. "I had assumed that would be the case."

"Very well." The supervisor cleared his own throat, and consulted data spread before him. "We are still uncertain as to just how the enemy is armed. Something subtle, no doubt, suitable for a spy or saboteur on our contemporary Earth—in addition, of course, to the superhuman physical strength and speed you must expect to face. There are the scrambling or the switching mindbeams to be considered; either could damage any human society. There are the pattern bombs, designed to disable our defense computers by seeding them at close range with pure, random information. There are always possibilities of biological warfare—you have your disguised medical kit? Yes, I see. And, of course, there is always the chance of something new."

"Yes, sir." The volunteer agent looked as ready as anyone could look. The supervisor went to him, opening his arms for a ritual farewell embrace.

He blinked away some London rain, pulled out his heavy, ticking timepiece, as if only checking the hour, and stood on the pavement before the theater like a man waiting for a friend. The instrument he held throbbed with a silent, extra vibration in addition to its ticking. This special signal had now taken on a character that meant the enemy machine was very near indeed, probably within a radius of fifty meters from where the agent stood.

A poster nearby said:

THE IMPROVED AUTOMATION CHESSPLAYER
MARVEL OF THE AGE
UNDER NEW MANAGEMENT

"The real problem, sir," proclaimed one top-hatted man nearby, in conversation with another, "is not whether a machine can be made to win at chess, but whether it may possibly be made to play at all."

No, that is not at all the real problem, sir, the agent from the future thought. But count yourself fortunate that you can still believe it is.

He bought a ticket and went in. On exhibit inside there were a number of clockwork devices, some of an ingenuity that the man from the future would have found really intriguing, under other circumstances. When a sizable audience had gathered there was a short lecture, by a man in evening dress, who had something at once predatory and frightened about him, despite the glibness and the rehearsed humor of his talk.

At length the chessplayer itself appeared, a desklike box with a figure seated behind it, the whole assembly wheeled out on stage by assistants. The figure was that of a man in Turkish garb, quite obviously a mannequin or dummy of some kind, and it bobbed slightly with the motion of the rolling desk, to which its chair was somehow fixed. Now the agent could feel the excited vibration of his watch without even putting a hand into his pocket.

The predatory man cracked another joke, dabbed at his forehead with a handkerchief, and from several chessplayers in the audience who raised their hands— the agent was not among them—selected one to challenge the automation. The volunteer went up on stage, where black and white pieces were being set out on a board fastened to the rolling desk or table, and the doors in the front of the desk were being opened to show that there was nothing but mechanism inside.

The agent noted that there were no candles on this desk, as there had been on Maelzel's, a few decades earlier. Maelzel's mechanical chessplayer had been a fraud, of course, and candles had been needed on its box to mask the odor of burning wax from the candle needed by the man so cleverly hidden inside amid the dummy gears. It was still too early in the century, the agent knew, for electric lights, at least the kind that would be handy for such a hidden man to use. Add the fact that this chessplayer's opponent was allowed to sit much closer than Maelzel's had ever been, and it became a pretty safe deduction that the box and figure on this stage contained no hidden man.

Therefore . . .

He might, if he stood up in the audience, get a clear shot at it right now. But he could not be sure how it was armed. Who would stop it, if he tried and failed? Already it had learned enough to survive in nineteenth-century London; already it had found itself a niche. Doubtless it had already killed, to further its designs.

"Under new management," indeed. With the agent out of the way it could safely bide its time until it had discovered how to do the greatest damage to Victorian humanity with whatever armament it had.

No, now that he had located the enemy, he must plan as thoroughly as it was planning, and work as patiently. Deep in thought, he left the theater amid the crowd at the conclusion of the performance, and started on foot back to the rooms which he had just begun to share in Baker Street. A minor difficulty at launching into the black hole had cost him some of his equipment, including most of his forged money. There had not been time as yet for his adopted profession to bring him much income, so he was, for the time, in straitened financial circumstances.

He must plan. Suppose, now, that he approached the man who ran the chessplayer show, who by now ought to have begun to understand what kind of a tiger he was riding. The agent might approach him in the guise of—

A sudden tap-tapping came in the agent's watchpocket, a signal quite distinct from any his fake watch had previously generated. This one meant that the enemy had managed to detect his detector, was indeed locked onto it and tracking.

There was sudden sweat on his face now, mingling with the drizzle, as he began to run. It must have discovered him in the theater, though probably it could not single him out amid the crowd. Avoiding horse-drawn cabs, four-wheelers, and an omnibus, he turned out of Oxford Street to Baker Street, and slowed to a fast walk for the short distance remaining. He could not throw away the telltale watch, for he would be unable to track the enemy without it. But neither dared he retain it on his person . . .

As the agent burst into his sitting room, his new roommate looked up, with his usual, somewhat shallow smile, from a leisurely job of taking books out of a crate and putting them on shelves.

"I say," the agent began, in mingled relief and urgency, meanwhile leaning against the doorjamb for a moment's rest, "something rather important has come up, and I find there are two errands I really must undertake at once. Might I impose one of them on you?"

The agent's own brisk errand took him no farther than just across the street. There, in the doorway of Camden House, he shrank back, trying to breathe silently. He had not moved three minutes later when from the direction of Oxford Street there approached a tall figure that the agent suspected was not human. The lower portion of its face was muffled in a white scarf or bandage, and its hat was pulled down. It paused briefly in front of 221B, seemed to consult a watch of its own, then rang the bell. Had the agent been sure it was his quarry, he would have shot it in the back. But without his watch, he would have to get a better look to be sure.

After a moment's questioning from the landlady, the figure was admitted. The agent waited about two minutes. Then he drew a deep breath, gathered up his considerable courage, and went after it.

The thing standing alone at a window turned to face him as he entered the sitting room. Now he was sure of what it was, from the mere expression of the eyes above the bandaged lower face. Not the Turk's eyes, but not human, either.

The white swathing muffled its gruff voice. "You are the doctor?"

"Ah, it is my fellow-lodger that you want." The agent threw a careless glance toward the desk where he had locked up the watch, the desk on which some papers bearing his roommate's name were scattered. "He is out at the moment, as you see, but we can expect him presently. I take it you are a patient."

The thing said, in its wrong voice: "I have been referred to him. It seems that the doctor and I share a certain common background. Therefore, the good landlady has let me wait in here. If my presence is no inconvenience?"

"Not in the least. Pray take a seat, Mr—?"

What name the berserker might have given, the agent never learned. The bell sounded below, suspending conversation. He heard the servant-girl answering the door, and a moment later his roommate's brisk feet upon the stairs. The death machine took a small object from a pocket, and sidestepped a little to get a clear view past the agent toward the door.

Half turning his back upon the enemy, as if with the casual purpose of greeting the man about to enter, the agent casually drew from his own pocket a quite functional briar pipe, which was designed to serve another function, too. Then he turned his head and fired the pipe at the berserker from under his own left armpit.

For a human being he was uncannily fast, and for a berserker, the android was meanly slow and clumsy, being designed for imitation and not primarily for dueling. Their weapons triggered at the same instant.

Explosions racked and destroyed the enemy, blasts shatteringly powerful but compactly limited in space, self-damping so as to be almost silent.

The agent was hit, too. He staggered, knowing with his last clear thought just what kind of weapon the enemy had carried—the switching mindbeam. Then for a moment he could no longer think at all. He was dimly aware of being down on one knee, and of his fellow-lodger, who had just entered, standing stunned a step inside the door.

At last the agent could move again, and shakily pocketed his pipe. The ruined body of the enemy was almost vaporized already. It had been built to self-destruct when damaged badly, that humanity might never learn its secrets. Already it was no more than a puddle of heavy mist, warping in slow tendrils out through the slightly open window to mingle with the fog.

The man still standing near the door had put out a hand to steady himself against the wall. "The jeweler . . . did not have your watch," he muttered dazedly.

I have won, thought the agent dully. It was a joyless

thought because with it came slow realization of the price of his success. Three-quarters of his intellect, at least, was gone irrecoverably, the superior pattern of his brain-cell connections scattered . . . No. Not scattered. The switching mindbeam would have reimposed the pattern of his neurons somewhere farther down its pathway . . . *there*, behind those gray eyes with their newly penetrating gaze.

"Obviously, sending me out for your watch was a ruse." His roommate's voice was suddenly crisper, more assured than it had been. "Also, I perceive that your desk has just been broken into, by someone who thought it mine. And that you, sir, are not exactly what you represent yourself to be." The tone softened somewhat. "Come, man, I bear you no ill will. Your secret, if honorable, is safe with me."

The agent got to his feet, pulling at his sandy hair, trying desperately to think. "How—how do you know?"

"Elementary, my dear Doctor," the tall man said impatiently.

From The Tree Of Time

"Very well then," said Count Dracula. "If you wish a story with a touch of mystification, I can provide one."

It was on a raw, rainy spring night, not long ago, and the two of us were standing on a streetcorner of a northern city. Folk far madder and perhaps less probable than either the Prince of Wallachia or myself walked those streets as well. But in the presence of my companion I scarcely gave them a thought.

"I will be delighted," I replied (naturally enough), "to hear whatever tale you may wish to tell."

Dracula halted at a curb, the wet cold wind stirring his black hair as he stared moodily across the street. He had doubtless paused only to gather his thoughts, but a quartet of youths swaggering along on the other side of the street interpreted our hesitation as timidity. They loitered in their own walk, and one of their number called some obscenity in our direction. My companion did not appear to notice.

"I am sure you are aware" (he began his tale to me) "that with vampires, as with the greater mass of the breathing population, the vast majority are peaceable, law-abiding citizens. We seek no more, essentially, than

231

breathers do: bodily nourishment (any animal blood will do for sustenance); the contemplation of beauty, and affection, as nourishment for the soul; an interesting occupation; a time and place in which to rest (some native soil being, in our case, very important for that purpose).

"It makes me laugh"—he laughed, and across the street four youths simultaneously remembered pressing business elsewhere—"yes, laugh, to contemplate the preposterous attributes that have been bestowed upon my branch of the human race by those breathing legendizers who have never known even one of us at first hand. Of course I am not talking about you, my friend. I mean those who have learned nothing since the last century, when the arch-fool Van Helsing could imagine that the symbols and the substance of religion are to us automatically repellent or even deadly. As you know, that is no more true of us than of—of some of the breathing gangsters who once made this very city legend."

My friend paused, frowning, doubtless wishing that he had chosen some other comparison. I hastened to assure him that I would do all in my literary power to expunge from human thought the kinds of misinformation that he found so distasteful. He nodded abstractedly.

"Nevertheless" (he went on) "in our society as in yours, the rogue, the criminal, exists. I need not belabor the point that the psychopath who happens also to be a vampire is infinitely more dangerous than his mundanely breathing counterpart. Even apart from the fact that very few of your breathing people truly believe that we exist, effective countermeasures against our criminal element, while not impossible, appear to be uncommonly difficult for you to manage. The Cross, as I have said, is no deterrent at all—except perhaps to vampires of such religious nature that their consciences would be painfully affected by the sight—such probably do not pose you a major problem in any event.

"Garlic? Even less efficacious than it would be against some breathing ruffian—surely useful, if at all, only against the more fastidious and less determined. Mirrors? Useful to detect and identify us by our lack of any reflection; but with no application as weapons, except as they might be used to concentrate our great bane, natural sunlight. The older and tougher among us can bear *some* sun, you know, at least the cloudy, tempered sun of the high latitudes.

"Fire? By daylight, through which period we are compelled to retain whatever form we had at dawn—and moreover are likely to be resting in lethargic trance—yes, by daylight fire can be effective, whereas by night we easily avoid it.

"Ordinary bullets, blades of metal, clubs of stone, all can cause us momentary pain and superficial injury, but do us virtually no real damage at all. Any trifling harm inflicted soon disappears. Silver bullets are only advocated by those who confuse us with werewolves, or certain other creatures of the night.

"The best practical defense is doubtless to remain in your own house, admitting no one suspicious. No vampire may enter a true dwelling unless invited—but once invited, he or she may return at any time.

"And, if we consider the offensive means that ordinary breathing folk can hope to use successfully against us, almost the whole truth is contained in one short and simple word."

By now we were strolling again. My companion was of course impervious to the chilling effects of wind and rain, but I was shivering. Taking note of this, Dracula gestured as we were passing the door of a decent-appearing tavern, and gratefully I preceded him in. We were seated in a dim, snug corner with mugs of Irish coffee before us—his of course remained untouched throughout our stay—before he spoke again.

"That one word," he said, "is wood. Ah, wood, that oh-so-nearly magical stuff, that once was living and now is not. Ah, wood . . . and that leads me to the story that I wished to tell."

*   *   *

From an idea by Eric Saberhagen

It was (Dracula continued) almost a century ago, and in another great city, one grimier and in some ways grander than this one, that I made acquaintance—never mind now exactly how—with a certain professional investigator, a consulting detective whose name was then even better known than my own. We were an oddly matched pair, yet on good terms; he understood my nature better than most breathing folk have ever been able to do. Still I was greatly surprised one day when I received a message from him saying that he wished my help in a professional consultation. Naturally my curiosity was much aroused, and I agreed.

My friend the detective and I traveled down by train from London to a certain country estate in Kent. The house was a great gloomy pile, built during Elizabethan times. Its owner, besides being a man of considerable wealth, was something of an antiquarian, and also much interested in what he still called natural philosophy. It was not he, however, who had invited us to the estate, but his only child. She was a grown woman now, and married for a year. And it was she—whose real name I cannot tell you even now, for at the time I swore that it would never pass my lips—she who conducted us on our arrival, with urgent speed, into a closed room for a private consultation. The room was large, and mostly lined with books, with new electric lights in its far corners, and on the huge desk an old-fashioned oil lamp, whose rays fell on a collection of curious items evidently brought together from the ends of the earth. I saw a whale's tooth, a monkey's skull, along with other items I did not immediately recognize. A small table at some distance from the desk held a microscope and various specimens. Along with their burden of books, the room's many shelves held stuffed birds and animals.

"And now, your ladyship," began my friend the detective, "we are at your service. You may speak as freely before Dr. Corday here"—he glanced in my direction—"as before myself."

The lady, whose considerable beauty was obviously being worn away by some overwhelming fear or worry,

now appeared on the verge of collapse. "Very well."
She drew a deep, exhausted breath. "I must be brief,
for my father and my husband will both soon return,
and I must save them, if I can . . .

"The incident that haunts me, that has driven me to
the brink of madness, occurred almost exactly a year
ago, and in this very room. I must confess to you that
before I was married, or even knew Richard well, I
was—acquainted with—a man, named Hayden. I have
outlined to you already, sir, how that came to be—"

"You have indeed, your ladyship." My companion
gave an impatient nod. "Since our time is short, we had
better concentrate on what happened between you and
Hayden in this very room, as you say it was. That is the
aspect of the case in which I most value Dr. Corday's
consultation."

"You are right." Our hostess paused again to collect
herself, then plunged on. "I had not seen Hayden for
many months. I was beginning to manage to forget him,
when almost on the very eve of my wedding, he appeared here unexpectedly. I was alone in the house
except for a few servants, my father being engaged on
some last-minute business in London having to do with
the arrangements.

"Hayden, of course, knew that I was alone. And his
purpose in coming was of course an evil one. He had
brought with him some letters—they were foolish letters indeed—that I had written him in an earlier day.
The letters contained—certain things that could have
ruined me, had Hayden given them, as he threatened
to do, to my prospective husband. I protested my innocence. He admitted it, but read from the letters certain
phrases, words I had almost forgotten, that suggested
otherwise. Hayden would destroy me, he swore, unless—
unless 'Here and now in this very room' was how he
put it—I should—should—"

For a moment the lady could not continue. My friend
and I exchanged glances, of sympathy and determination, in a silent pledge that we would do everything
possible to assist her. It must be hard for folk with

experience only of the late twentieth century to grasp what a threat such letters could represent, to understand what impact the mere suggestion of a premarital affair could have had at that time and place, on one in her position. It would have been regarded by all her contemporaries as the literal ruin of the young lady's life.

"I was innocent," she repeated, when she was able to resume at last. "I swear to you both that I was. Yet that man had some devilish power, influence . . . I had broken free of it before, and as he faced me in this room I swore to myself that I would never allow it to gain the faintest hold on me again.

" 'Sooner or later you will have me,' the villain said, sneering at me. 'I have now been invited into your fine house, you see.' Those were his words, and I have puzzled over them; alas, a greater and more horrible puzzle was to come.

"I retreated to the desk—I stood here in front of it, like this. Hayden was just there, and he advanced upon me. I cried at him to stay away. My hand, behind me on the desk, closed on a piece of stone—much like this one." With that her ladyship raised what would now be called a geode from among the curios collected on the huge desk. "I raised it—like this—and warned him again to stop.

"Hayden only smiled at me—no, he sneered—as if the idea that I might refuse him, even resist him, were a childish fantasy that only a childish creature like myself—a mere woman—could entertain. He sneered at me, I say. His handsome face was hideously transformed, and it seemed to me that even his teeth were . . . were . . . and he came on toward me, his hands reaching out."

The lovely narrator raised her chin. "I—hit him, gentlemen. With the stone. With all my strength. And— God help me—I think it was as much because of the way in which he looked at me, so contemptuously, as it was because of anything I feared that he might do.

"I hit him, and he fell backward, with a broad smear

of blood across his forehead. I have the impression that only one of his eyes was still open, and that it was looking at me with the most intense surprise. He fell backward, and rolled halfway over on the carpet, and was still.

"I was perfectly sure, looking down at his smashed face, that he was dead. Dead, and I swear to you that at that moment I felt nothing but relief. For a moment only. Then the horror began. Not an intrinsic horror at what I had done—that came to me too, but later—but horror at the fact that what I had just done was certain to be discovered, and at other discoveries that must flow from that. Even though I might—I almost certainly would—be able to plead self defense and avoid any legal penalty, yet inevitably enough information must be made public to bring ruin down upon me—and disgrace upon Richard, whom I loved . . .

"I suppose that in that moment I was half mad with shock and grief. Not, you understand, grief for the one who, as I thought, lay dead—"

My friend interrupted. "As you thought?"

"As—let me finish, and in a moment you will understand."

"Then pray continue."

"My eye fell on the door of the lumber room—there." It was a plain, small, inconspicuous door, set in the wall between bookcases, some eight or ten feet from the desk. "I seized Hayden by the ankles—to take him by the hands would have meant touching his skin, and the thought of that was utterly abhorrent to me—and I dragged him into there."

"May I?"

"Of course."

Taking up the lamp from the desk, my friend moved to open the small door, which was unlocked. The lamplight shining in revealed a dusty storage closet. Its walls and floor were of stone, its ceiling of solid wood; there was no window, or any other door. The chamber was half-filled with a miscellany of boxes, crates, and bundles, none larger than a bushel, and all covered with a fine film of dust that might well have lain undisturbed for the past year.

Our client joined us looking in. She said: "The room was very much as you see it now. My father uses it chiefly for storage of things he has brought back from his various travels and then never finds time to catalogue, or else judges at second thought to be not worthy of display.

"I dragged Hayden—or his body—in there, and left him on the dusty floor. Understand that this was not part of any thought-out plan for concealing what I had done. It was only a shocked reaction, like that of a child trying to hide the pieces of a broken vase. Hardly aware of what I was doing, I came back here to the middle of the room, and picked up from the carpet the stone that had done the deed. I carried it into the lumber-room also, and threw it on top of that which lay on the floor already. I then came out of the lumber-room and closed its door, and locked it—though it is rarely if ever locked—with a key I knew was kept in the top drawer of my father's desk.

"Then, with a mind still whirling in terror, I looked around. The letters, where were they? Still in Hayden's pocket, for now I remember distinctly seeing him replace them there. It might be wise to get them out, but for the moment I could not think of touching him again.

"And there was blood on the carpet. I had noted that already, in my first frenzied panic. But now, as my mind made its first adjustment back toward sanity, I saw that the spots were only two or three in number, and so small against the dark pattern that no one entering the study casually would be in the least likely to notice them. Here, gentlemen, is where they were— over the past year they have faded almost to invisibility.

My companion had crouched down and whipped out a magnifying glass, with which he scrutinized closely the indicated section of the carpet. He stood up frowning. "Pray continue," he said again, his voice noncommittal.

"I was still hovering near the desk, in a state of near-panic, not knowing what to do, when as in a nightmare I heard a brisk knock on the door to the hall, and the voice of my beloved Richard. A moment later, before I could say anything at all, the hall door opened and Richard came in. From the look on his face, I knew immediately that he was aware at least of something gravely wrong.

"My fiance evidently already knew much more about Hayden than I had ever suspected. Perhaps the duke, Richard's father, had employed investigators—to this day I do not know what had made my dear one suspicious of me. But he was full of suspicion on that day, and with cause—though not with as great cause as he feared.

"Richard confronted me. 'He was seen coming in here, the man Hayden. Do you tell me that he is not here now?'

"I do not remember what I said in reply. I must however have looked the very picture of guilt.

"Richard looked quickly round the study, even peering behind pieces of furniture where a man might possibly have had room to lie concealed. It took him only a moment to do so; the furniture was then very much as it is now, and offered, as you can see, little in the way of hiding places.

"He tried the door of the lumber-room then, and I was sure for a moment that my heart had stopped.

" 'This door is locked. Do you know, Louise, where the key is kept?'

"I understood perfectly that he would force the door at once if no key were available. Silently I went to the desk, and got the key from the upper drawer, where, in my confusion I had just replaced it; I handed it to Richard, still without a word. At that moment I knew with certainty that final ruin was upon me, and I could not bear another instant the horror of waiting for the blow to fall. I thought that after Richard had seen what I had done, then, in that moment of his greatest shock,

I might appeal to him. I could only hope that he loved me as truly and deeply as I did him.

"But his gaze was black and forbidding as he took the key from my hand and turned away. He was in the lumber-room for only a few moments, but I need not tell you what an eternity they seemed to me. When he reappeared, his face was altered; yet even as I gazed at him in despair, a sudden new hope was born within my breast. For his new expression was not so much one of horror or shock, as one expressing a great relief, even though mingled with shame and bewilderment.

"For a moment he could not speak. Then 'Darling!,' he said at last, and his voice cracked, even as mine had moments earlier. 'Can you ever forgive me for having doubted you?'

"Without answering, I pushed past Richard to the door of the lumber-room. Everything inside, with one great exception, was just as I had seen it a few minutes earlier before I had locked the door. There were the dusty crates and cartons, untouched, certainly, by any human hand in the intervening time. There on the floor, in lighter dust and hardly noticeable, were the tracks left by my own feet on my first entrance, and by the horrible burden that I had dragged in with such difficulty. There was the stone with which I had struck the fateful blow—but the piece of stone lay now in the middle of the otherwise empty patch of bare floor. Of the body of the man I had struck down there was not the smallest trace."

My friend the detective emitted a faint sigh, expressing what in the circumstances seemed a rather inhuman degree of intellectual satisfaction. "Most interesting indeed," he murmured soothingly. "And then?"

"There is very little more that I can tell you. I murmured something to Richard; he, assuming my state of near-collapse was all his fault for behaving, as he said, brutally, made amends to the best of his ability. To make the story short, we were married as planned. Hayden's name has never since been mentioned between us. Our life together has been largely uneventful, and in all outward aspects happy. But I tell you, gentlemen—since that day I have lived in inward terror . . . either I am mad, and therefore doomed, and imagined the whole ghastly scene in which I murdered Hayden; or I did not imagine it. Then he was only stunned. He somehow extricated himself from that lumber-room. He is lying in wait for me. Somewhere, sometime . . . neither of you know him, what he can be like . . . he still has the letters, yet he has in mind some revenge that would be even more horrible . . . I tell you I can bear it no longer . . ." The lady sank into a chair, struggling to control herself.

The detective turned to me. "Dr. Corday, it is essential that we ascertain the—nature of this man Hayden." A meaningful glance assured me what sort of variations in nature he had in mind.

I nodded, and addressed myself to the lady, who had now somewhat recovered. "At what time of day, madam, did these events occur? Can we be absolutely sure that they took place after dawn and before sunset?"

The lady looked for a moment as if she suspected that madness was my problem instead of hers. "In broad daylight, surely," she replied at last. "Though what possible difference . . ."

I signed to my friend that I must speak to him in confidence. After a hurried apology to our client we withdrew to a far corner of the study. "The man she knocked down," I informed the detective there, "could not possibly have been a vampire, because of the force of the blow that felled him was borne in stone, to which we are immune. Nor could he, even supposing him to be a vampire, have shifted form in broad daylight, and escaped as a mist from that closet under the conditions we have heard described; nor could he in daylight have taken on the form of a small animal and hidden himself somewhere among those crates and boxes."

"You are quite sure of all that?"

"Quite."

"Very good." My friend received my expert opinion with evident satisfaction, which surprised me.

For my own part, it seemed to me that we were getting nowhere. "My life has been very long," I added, "and active, if not always well spent. I have seen madness . . . much madness. And I tell you that the lady here, if I am any judge, is neither mad nor subject to hallucinations."

"In that opinion I concur." Still my friend did not appear nearly as disconcerted as it seemed to me he should. There was, in fact, something almost like a twinkle in his eye.

"Then what are we to make of this?" I demanded.

"I deduce . . ."

"Yes?"

Again the twinkle. "That one of her father's trips abroad, before the wedding, took him to Arizona. But of course I must make sure." And with that, leaving me in a state that I confess approached speechlessness, my friend went back across the room.

He approached our client, who still sat wearily in her chair, and extended both his hands. When she took them, wonderingly, he raised her to her feet. "One more question," he urged her solemnly. "The stone with which you struck down Hayden—where is it now? Surely it is not one of those still on the desk?"

"No," the lady marveled. "I could not bear to leave it there." Going back to the door of the lumber-room, she reached inside, and from a shelf took down a pinkish stone of irregular, angular shape, a little larger than a man's fist. This she presented to my friend.

He turned it over once in his hands, and set it back upon the desk. A confident smile now transformed his face. "It is my happy duty to inform you," he said at once, "that the man you knew as Hayden will never bother you again; you may depend upon it."

Dracula paused here in his narration. "In a moment I was able to add my own assurances, for what they were worth, to those of the famed detective. That was after I had walked over to the desk and looked at the weapon for myself. I knew then that the man struck down with it could indeed have been a vampire; nay, that he must have been. For when he died of the effects of the blow, there on the floor of the lumber-room, his body, as is commonly the case with us, had at once undergone a dissolution to dust, and less than dust. His clothing, including the letters in his pocket, had, as would be expected, disappeared as well. No humanly detectable trace was left when the fiance opened the door a few moments later."

"A vampire?" I protested. "But, he was struck down with a stone . . ."

"I was looking," said Dracula softly, "at a choice Arizona specimen of petrified wood."

Inhuman Error

When the dreadnought *Hamilcar Barca* came out of the inhuman world of plus-space into the blue-white glare of Meitner's sun, the forty men and women of the dreadnought's crew were taut at their battle stations, not knowing whether or not the whole berserker fleet would be around them as they emerged. But then they were in normal space, seconds of time were ticking calmly by, and there were only the stars and galaxies to be seen—no implacable, inanimate killers coming to the attack. The tautness eased a little.

Captain Liao, strapped firmly into his combat chair in the center of the dreadnought's bridge, had brought his ship back into normal space as close to Meitner's sun as he dared—operating on interstellar, faster-than-light, c-plus drive in a gravitational field this strong was dangerous, to put it mildly—but the orbit of the one planet of the system worth being concerned about was still tens of millions of kilometers closer to the central sun. It was known simply as Meitner's planet, and was the one rock in the system habitable in terms of gravity and temperature.

Before his ship had been ten standard seconds in

normal space, Liao had begun to focus a remotely controlled telescope to bring the planet into close view on a screen that hung before him on the bridge. Luck had brought him to the same side of the sun that the planet happened to be on; it showed under magnification on the screen as a thin, illuminated crescent, covered with fluffy-looking perpetual clouds. Somewhere beneath those clouds a human colony of about ten thousand people dwelt, for the most part under the shelter of one huge ceramic dome. The colonists had begun work on the titanic project of converting the planet's ammonia atmosphere to a breathable one of nitrogen and oxygen. Meanwhile, they held the planet as an outpost of some importance for the interstellar community of all Earth-descended men.

There were no flares of battle visible in space around the planet, but still, Liao lost no time in transmitting a message on the standard radio and laser communications frequencies. "Meitner's planet, calling Meitner's. This is the dreadnought *Hamilcar Barca*. Are you under attack? Do you need immediate assistance?"

There came no immediate answer, nor could one be expected for several minutes, the time required for signals traveling at the speed of light to reach the planet, and for an answer to be returned.

Into Liao's earphones now came the voice of his detection and ranging officer, "Captain, we have three ships in view." On the bridge there now sprang to life a three-dimensional holographic presentation, showing Liao the situation as accurately as the dreadnought's far-ranging detection systems and elaborate combat computers could diagram it.

One ship, appearing as a small bright dot with attached numerical coordinates, was hanging relatively motionless in space, nearly on a line between *Hamilcar Barca* and Meitner's planet. The symbol chosen for it indicated that this was probably a sizable craft, though not nearly as massive as the dreadnought. The other two ships visible in the presentation were much smaller, according to the mass-detector readings on them. They were also both considerably closer to the planet, and moving toward it at velocities that would let them land on it, if that was their intention, in less than an hour.

What these three ships were up to, and whether they were controlled by human beings or berserker machines, was not immediately apparent. After sizing up the situation for a few seconds, Liao ordered full speed toward the planet—full speed, of course, in the sense of remaining in normal space and thus traveling much slower than light—and to each of the three ships in view he ordered the same message beamed: "Identify yourself, or be destroyed."

The threat was no bluff. No one took chances where berserker machines were concerned. They were an armada of robot spaceships and supporting devices built by some unknown and long-vanished race to fight in some interstellar war that had reached its forgotten conclusion while men on Earth were wielding spears against the saber-toothed tiger. Though the war for which the berserker machines had been made was long since over, still they fought on across the galaxy, replicating and repairing themselves endlessly, learning new strategies and tactics, refining their weapons to cope with their chief new enemy, Earth-descended man. The sole known basic in their fundamental programming was the destruction of all life, wherever and whenever they could find it.

Waiting for replies from the planet and the three ships, hoping fervently that the berserker fleet that was known to be on its way here had not already come and gone, leaving the helpless colony destroyed, Liao meanwhile studied his instruments critically. "Drive, this is captain. Can't you get a little more speed on?"

The answer came into his earphones: "No sir, we're on the red line now. Another kilometer per second and we'll blow a power lamp, or worse. This is one heavy sun, and it's got some dirty space around it." The ship was running now on the same space-warping engines that carried it faster than light between the stars, but this deep within the huge gravitational well surrounding Meitner's sun, the power that could be applied to them was severely restricted. The more so because here space was dirty, as the drive officer had said, meaning the interplanetary matter to be encountered within this system was comparatively dense. It boiled down to the fact that Liao had no hope of overtaking the two small vessels that fled ahead of him toward the planet. They, as it were, skimmed over shoals of particles that the dreadnought must plow through, flirted with reefs of drive-wrecking gravitational potential that it must approach more cautiously, and rode more lightly the waves of the solar wind that streamed outward as always from a sun.

Now the minimum time in which the largest, nearest vessel might have replied to the dreadnought's challenge had elapsed. No reply had been received. Liao ordered the challenge repeated continuously.

The communications officer was speaking. "Answer from the planet, captain. It's coming in code. I mean the simple standard dot-dash code, sir, like emergency signals. There's a lot of noise around—maybe that's the only way they can get a signal through." Powerfully and crudely modulated dot-and-dash signals could carry intelligence through under conditions where more advanced forms of modulation were simply lost.

Communications was on the ball; already, they had the decoded words flowing across a big screen on the bridge: DREADNOUGHT ARE WE EVER GLAD TO HEAR FROM YOU STOP ONE OF THE TWO LITTLE SHIPS CLOSING IN ON US MUST BE A BERSERKER STOP BETTER TRANSMIT TO US IN DOTDASH CODE STOP LOTS OF NOISE BECAUSE SUN IS FLARING AND WE COULDNT READ YOUR SIGNAL VERY WELL

The letters abruptly stopped flowing across the screen. The voice of the communications officer said: "Big burst of noise, captain. Signals from the planet are going to be cut off entirely for a little while. This sun is a very active flare star. Just a moment, sir. Now we're getting voice and video transmissions beamed to us from both small ships. But the signals from both ships are so garbled by noise we can't make anything out of them."

"Beam back to them in dot-dash, tell them they'll have to answer us that way. Repeat our warnings that they must identify themselves. And keep trying to find out what the ground wants to tell us." The captain turned his head to look over at his second officer in the adjoining combat chair. "What'd you think of that, Miller? 'One of the two little ships must be a berserker?'"

Miller, by nature a somewhat morose man, only shook his head gloomily, and saved his speech to make a factual report. "Sir, I've been working on identifying the two active ships. The one nearest the planet is so small it seems to be nothing more than a lifeboat. Extrapolating backward from its present course and position indicates it may well have come from the third ship—the one that's drifting—a couple of hours ago.

"The second little ship is a true interstellar vessel; could be a one-man courier ship, or even somebody's private yacht. Or a berserker, of course." The enemy came in all shapes and sizes.

Still no answer had been returned from the large, drifting ship, though the dreadnought was continuing to beam threatening messages to her, now in dot-dash code. Detection reported now that she was spinning slowly around her longest axis, consistent with the theory that she was some kind of derelict. Liao checked again on the state of communications with the planet, but they were still cut off by noise.

"Here's something, Captain. Dot-and-dash is coming in from the supposed courier. Standard code as before, coming at moderate manual speed."

Immediately, more letters began to flow across the number one screen on the bridge: I AM METION CHONGJIN COMMANDING THE ONE MAN COURIER ETRURIA EIGHT DAYS OUT OF ESTEEL STOP CANNOT TURN ASIDE I AM CARRYING VITAL DEFENSE COMPONENT FOR COLONY STOP LIFEBOAT APPROX 12 MILLION KM TO MY PORT AND AHEAD IS SAID BY GROUND TO BE CLAIMING TO BE THE SHIP CARRYING THE DEFENSE COMPONENT THEREFORE IT MUST REALLY BE A BERSERKER STOP IT WILL PROBABLY REACH COLONY AND BOMB OR RAM IT BEFORE I GET THERE SO YOU MUST DE-

STROY IT REPEAT DESTROY THE BERSERKER QUOTE LIFEBOAT
UNQUOTE MOST URGENT THAT YOU HIT IT SOON END MESSAGE

Miller made a faint whistling noise. "Sounds fairly convincing, chief." During briefing back at base, three standard days ago, they had been informed of the fact that the colony on Meitner's planet was awaiting shipment of a space inverter to complete and activate its defensive system of protective force-screens and beam-projecting weapons. Until the inverter could be brought from Esteel and installed, the colony was virtually defenseless; the dreadnought had been dispatched to offer it some interim protection.

Liao was giving orders to Armament to lock the C-plus cannon of the main battery onto the lifeboat. "But fire only on my command." Turning back to the second, he said: "Yes, fairly convincing. But the berserkers might have found out somehow that the space inverter was being rushed here. They might even have intercepted and taken over the courier carrying it. We can't see who we're talking to on that ship or hear his voice. It might have been a berserker machine that just tapped out that message to us.

The communications officer was on again. "Bridge, we have the first coded reply from the lifeboat coming in now. Here it comes on your screen."

WE ARE HENRI SAKAI AND WINIFRED ISPAHAN CARRYING THE DEFENSE MATERIAL NAMELY SPACE INVERTER THEY NEED ON THE PLANET STOP OUR SHIP THE WILHELMINA FROM ESTEEL WAS SHOT UP BY THE BERSERKER TWO DAYS AGO WHEN IT ALMOST CAUGHT US STOP THE BERSERKER OR ANOTHER ONE IS HERE NOW ABOUT 11 MILLION KM TO OUR STARBOARD AND A LITTLE BEHIND US STOP YOU MUST KEEP IT FROM GETTING TO US OR TO THE PLANET WHERE MAYBE IT COULD RAM THE DOME END MESSAGE

"Communications," the captain snapped, "how is this coming through? I mean, does this also seem like someone sending manual code?"

"No sir, this is very rapid and regular. But if you mean, captain, does that prove they're not human, it doesn't. In a lifeboat the transmitter often has a voice-to-code converter built in."

"And conversely, a berserker could send slowly and somewhat irregularly, like a man, if it wanted to. Thank you." The captain pondered in silence for a little while.

"Sir," Miller suggested, "maybe we'd better order both small ships to stop, until we can overtake and board them."

The captain turned his head to look at him steadily, but remained silent.

Miller, slightly flustered, took thought and then corrected himself. "Now I see the problem more fully, sir. You can't do that. If one of them is really carrying the space inverter, you don't dare delay him for a minute. A berserker fleet may materialize in-system here at any moment, and is virtually certain to arrive within the next six to eight hours. Our ship alone won't be able to do more than hit and run when that happens. Our fleet can't get here for another day. The colony will never survive the interval without its space inverter installed."

"Right. Even if I sent a fast launch ahead to board and inspect those ships, the delay would be too much to risk. And that's not all, Second. Tell me this. Is this conceivably just some misunderstanding? Could both of those ships really be manned by human beings?"

"Not a chance," the second answered promptly. "They both claim to be carrying the space inverter, and that can't be true. Those things just aren't ordered or built in duplicate or triplicate, and they both claim to be bringing it from the planet Esteel. The next question is, can both of our little targets be berserkers, trying to psych us into letting one of them get through? I'll keep trying to reach the ground, see if they can shed any more light on this."

"Good going."

In their earphones communications said: "Here's more from the ship that calls itself *Itruria*, bridge."

"Put it right on our screen."

REPEAT COLONY SAYS LIFEBOAT IS ALSO CLAIMING TO BE THE HUMAN ONE STOP IT MUST BE A BERSERKER IMPERATIVE

STOP YOU STOP THEM STOP WHAT DO YOU WANT ME TO DO
TO PROVE IM HUMAN STOP REPEAT MY NAME IS METION
CHONGJIN STOP IM ALONE ON BOARD HERE STOP WIFE AND
KIDS AT HOME ON ESTEEL IF THAT MEANS ANYTHING TO YOU
STOP REPEAT HOW CAN I PROVE TO YOU IM HUMAN END
MESSAGE

"Easy," Captain Liao muttered to himself. "Father a
human child. Compose a decent symphony. In the next
forty minutes or so." That was approximately the time
left before at least one of the ships would be able to
reach the planet. Liao's mind was racing to formulate
possible tests, but getting nowhere. Berserkers had
awesome powers, not only as physical fighting machines,
but as computers. He was not certain that a battery of
psychologists with several days to work would be able
to say with certainty whether it was a living man or a
lying Berserker that answered their questions in dot-dash.

Time passed. Hurtling through silence and near-
emptiness at many kilometers per second, the ships
very slowly changed the positions of their symbols in
the huge holographic presentation on the bridge.

"Now more from the *Wilhelmina*'s lifeboat, captain."

"Run that on the top of the screen, will you, and put
any more that comes in from *Itruria* on the bottom."

HENRI AND WINIFRED HERE STOP COLONY TELLS US OTHER
SHIP IS CLAIMING TO BE FROM ESTEEL CARRYING DEFENSE
COMPONENTS AND REQUESTING LANDING INSTRUCTIONS STOP
IT MUST BE LYING STOP IT MUST BE A BERSERKER STOP MAYBE
THE SAME ONE THAT ATTACKED OUR SHIP TWO DAYS AGO. . .

The message ran on and despite some irrelevancies
and redundancies it outlined a story. The *Wilhelmina* (if
the story was to be believed) had been on an interstellar cruise, carrying a number of young people on some
kind of student exchange voyage or postgraduate trip.
Somewhere on the outskirts of the solar system that
contained the heavily industrialized planet Esteel, a
courier ship bound out for Meitner's had approached
and hailed the *Wilhelmina*, had in fact commandeered
her to complete the courier's mission. Berserkers were

in pursuit of the courier and had already damaged her extensively.

... AND WE WERE ON OUR WAY HERE WITH THE IN-VERTER WHEN ONE OF THE BERSERKERS ALMOST CAUGHT UP AGAIN TWO STANDARD DAYS AGO STOP WILHELMINA WAS BADLY SHOT UP THEN CREW ALL KILLED STOP WE ARE ONLY TWO LEFT ALIVE STOP TWO HISTORY STUDENTS STOP WE HAD TERRIBLE PROBLEMS ASTROGATING HERE BUT MADE IT STOP LIVING IN LIFEBOAT AND WORKING RIDDLED SHIP IN SPACESUITS STOP YOU CANT STOP US NOW AFTER ALL WEVE BEEN THROUGH STOP YOU MUST DESTROY THE BERSERKER SHIP STOP WE WILL REACH PLANET BEFORE IT DOES I THINK BUT IT WILL BE ABLE TO HIT THE DOME BEFORE THE SPACE INVERTER CAN BE INSTALLED STOP WE ARE GOING TO KEEP SENDING UNTIL YOU ARE CONVINCED WERE HUMAN. . .

The message from the lifeboat went on, somewhat more repetitiously now. And at the same time, on the bottom of the screen, more words from *Etruria* flowed in:

IVE TRIED TO CATCH THE BERSERKER LIFEBOAT AND SHOOT IT DOWN BUT I CANT STOP ITS UP TO YOU TO STOP IT STOP WHAT DO YOU WANT ME TO DO TO PROVE IM HUMAN. . .

The second officer sighed lightly to himself, wondering if, after all, he really wanted his own command.

"Communications, beam this out," the captain was ordering. "Tell them both to keep talking and give us their life histories. Birth, family, education, the works. Tell them both they'd better make it good if they want to live." On buttons on the arm of his chair he punched out an order for tea, and a moment later it came to him there through a little door, hot in a capped cup with drinking tube attached. "I've got an idea, Second. You study the background this so-called Esteeler spaceman Metion Chongjin gives us. Think up someplace you might have known him. We'll introduce you to him as an old friend, see how he copes."

"Good idea, chief."

"Communications here again, bridge. We've finally gotten another clear answer back from the ground. It's coming through now. We'll put it in the middle of your number one screen."

. . .IN ANSWER TO YOUR QUESTION NO THEY CANT BOTH BE BERSERKERS STOP AN HOUR AGO THERE WAS A BRIEF LETUP IN THE NOISE AND WE GOT ONE CLEAR LOOK AT A HUMAN MALE FACE ALIVE AND TALKING COGENTLY ANSWERING OUR QUESTIONS STOP NO POSSIBILITY THAT WAS A BERSERKER BUT UNFORTUNATELY BOTH SUSPECT SHIPS WERE SENDING ON THE SAME FREQ AND WE DONT KNOW FROM WHICH ONE THAT VOICE AND PICTURE CAME BUT WE DO KNOW THAT ONE OF THEM IS HUMAN. . .

"Damnation, how they've botched things up. Why didn't they ask the two men to describe themselves, and see which description fit what they saw?"

"This is communications again, bridge. They may have tried asking that, sir, for all we know. We've lost contact with the ground again now, even on code. I guess the solar wind is heating up. Conditions in the ionosphere down there must be pretty fierce. Anyway, here's a little more from the Itruria:

WHAT DO YOU WANT ME TO DO TO PROVE IM HUMAN STOP RECITE POETRY STOP MARY HAD A LITTLE LAMB STOP SAY PRAYERS I NEVER MEMORIZED ANY OF THEM STOP OKAY I GIVE UP STOP SHOOT US BOTH DOWN THEN END MESSAGE.

The second officer thumped a fist on the arm of his massive chair. "A berserker would say that, knowing that its fleet was coming, and the colony would be defenseless if we stopped the space inverter from getting to it."

Liao shrugged, and helped himself to a massive slug of tea. "But a human might say that, too, being willing to die to give the colony a few more hours of life. A human might hope that given a few more hours some miracle might come along, like the human fleet getting here first after all. I'm afraid that statement didn't prove a thing."

"I . . . guess it didn't."

After another good slug of tea, Liao put in a call to astrogation.

"Chief astrogator here, sir."

"Barbara, have you been listening in on this? Good. Tell me, could those two supposed history students, probably knowing little science or technology, have brought that ship in here? Specifically, could they have astrogated for two days, maybe fifty or sixty light years, without getting lost? I suppose the ship's autopilot was knocked out. They said they were living in the lifeboat and working the damaged ship in spacesuits."

"Captain, I've been pondering that claim, too, and I just don't know. I can't say definitely that it would be impossible. If we knew just how badly that ship was damaged, what they had to work with, we could make a better guess."

The captain looked back at his situation hologram. The apparently inert hulk that he had been told was the *Wilhelmina* was considerably closer now, lying as it did almost in *Hamilcar Barca*'s path toward Meitner's planet. The dreadnought was going to pass fairly near the other ship within the next few minutes. "As to that, maybe we can find out something. Keep listening in, Barbara." Turning to the second officer, Liao ordered: "You're going to be taking over the bridge shortly, Miller. I want us to match velocities with that supposed hulk ahead, and then I'm going over to her, in hopes of learning something."

"It might be booby-trapped, Captain."

"Then we'll have an answer, won't we? But I don't expect an answer will be found that easily. Also, get me a reading on exactly how much time we have left to decide which ship we're going to fire on."

"I've already had the computers going on that, sir. As of now, thirty-two and a quarter minutes. Then the lifeboat will either be down in atmosphere or around on the other side of the planet, and out of effective range in either case. The courier will take a little longer to get out of effective range, but . . ." He gestured helplessly.

"The courier being slower won't help us. We have to decide in thirty-two minutes."

"Chief, I just had an idea. Since the lifeboat is closer to the planet, if it was the berserker, wouldn't it have tried before we got here to head off the courier from the planet . . . oh. No good. No offensive weapons on the lifeboat."

"Right, except perhaps it has one bloody big bomb, meant for the colony, while the courier ship doubtless has some light armament, enough to deal with the lifeboat if it got in range. Still nothing proven, either way."

In another minute the silent ship ahead was close enough for telescopes on the dreadnought to pick out her name by starlight. It was *Wilhelmina*, all right, emblazoned near one end of her cigarlike shape. The dreadnought matched velocities with her smoothly, and held position a couple of kilometers off. Just before getting into a launch with a squad of armed marines to go over and inspect her, Liao checked back with the bridge to see if anything was new.

"Better hear this before you go," Miller told him. "I just introduced myself to Chongjin as an old buddy. This is his reply, quote: 'I honestly don't remember your name if I ever knew it, stop. If this was a test I guess I passed. Hurrah. Now get on with it and stop that berserker on the lifeboat . . .' and then the signal faded out again. Chief, our communication problems are getting steadily worse. If we're going to say anything more to either of those ships we'd better send it soon."

"How many minutes left, Second?"

"Just eighteen, sir."

"Don't waste any of 'em. The ship is yours."

"I relieve you, sir."

No signs of either life or berserker activity were apparent on the *Wilhelmina* as the launch crossed the space separating her from the dreadnought and docked, with a gentle clang of magnetic grapples. Now Liao could see that the reported damage was certainly a fact. Holes several meters in diameter had been torn in *Wilhelmina*'s outer hull. Conditions inside could hardly be good.

Leaving one man with the launch, Liao led the rest

of his small party in through one of the blasted holes,
swimming weightlessly, propelling themselves by whatever they could grip. He had briefed the men to look
for something, anything, that would prove or disprove
the contention that humans had driven this ship for the
last two days since she had been damaged.

Fifteen and a half minutes left.

The damage inside was quite as extensive as the
condition of the hull had indicated. Their suit lights
augmenting the sharp beams that Meiter's distant sun
threw into the airless interior, the boarding party spread
out, keeping in touch by means of their suit radios. This
had undoubtedly been a passenger ship. Much of the
interior was meant as living quarters, divided into single and double cabins, with accommodations for a couple of dozen people. What furnishings remained suggested
luxury. So far, everything said by the lifeboat's occupant was being proved true, but Liao as yet had no
clear evidence regarding that occupant's humanity, nor
even a firm idea of what evidence he was looking for.
He could only hope the evidence was here, and that he
would recognize it at first sight.

The interior of the ship was totally airless now, having been effectively opened to the stars by the repeated
use of some kind of penetration weapon. The ruin was
much cleaner than any similarly damaged structure on a
planet's surface could be. Loose debris had been carried out of the ship with escaping air, or separated from
her when her drive took her outside of normal space
and time, between the stars.

"Look here, Captain." The lieutenant in charge of
the marine squad was beckoning to him.

Near the center of the slender ship the lieutenant
had found a place where a wound bigger than any of the
others had pierced in, creating, in effect, an enormous
skylight over what had been one of the largest compartments on board. Probably it had been a lounge or
refectory for the passengers and crew. Since the ship
was damaged, this ruined room had evidently provided
the most convenient observation platform for whom-

ever or whatever had been in control. A small, wide-angle telescope, and a tubular electronic spectroscope, battery-powered and made for use in vacuum, had been roughly but effectively clamped to the jagged upper edge of what had been one of the lounge's interior walls, and now formed a parapet against infinity.

The lieutenant was swiveling the instruments on their mountings. "Captain, these look like emergency equipment from a lifeboat. Would a berserker machine have needed to use these, or would it have gear of its own?"

The captain stood beside him. "When a berserker puts a prize crew on a ship, it uses man-sized, almost android machines for the job. It's just more convenient for the machines that way, I suppose—more efficient. So they could quite easily use instruments designed for humans." He swung his legs to put his magnetic boots against the lounge's soft floor, so that they held him lightly to the steel deck beneath, and stared at the instruments, trying to force more meaning from them.

Men kept on searching the ship, probing everywhere, coming and going to report results (or rather, the lack of them) to Liao at his impromptu command post in what had been the lounge. Two marines had broken open a jammed door and found a small airless room containing a dead man who wore a space suit. Cause of death was not immediately apparent, but the uniform collar visible through the helmet's faceplate indicated that the man had been a member of *Wilhelmina*'s crew. And in an area of considerable damage near the lounge another suitless body was discovered wedged among twisted structural members. This corpse had probably been frozen near absolute zero for several days and exposed to vacuum for an equal length of time. Its death had also been violent. After all this it was hard to be sure, but Liao thought that the body had once been that of a young girl who had been wearing a fancy party dress when she met her end.

Liao could imagine a full scenario now, or rather two of them. Both began with the shipload of students, eighteen or twenty of them, perhaps, enjoying their interstellar trip. Surely such a cruise had been a momentous event in their lives. Maybe they had been partying as they either entered or were about to leave the solar system containing the planet Esteel. And then, according to Scenario One, out of the deep night of space came the desperate plea for help from the damaged and harried courier, hotly pursued by berserkers that were not expected to be in this part of the galaxy at all.

The students would have had to remain on board the *Wilhelmina*, there being no place for them to get off, when she was commandeered to carry the space inverter on to Meitner's planet. Then urgent flight, and two days from Meitner's a berserker almost caught up, tracking and finding and shooting holes in *Wilhelmina*, somewhere in the great labyrinth of space and dust and stars and time, in which the little worlds of men were strange and isolated phenomena. And then the two heroic survivors, Henri and Winifred, finding a way to push on somehow.

Scenario Two diverged from that version early on; it was simpler and, at first glance, more credible. Instead of the *Wilhelmina* being hailed by a courier and pressed into military service, she was simply jumped by berserkers somewhere, her crew and passengers efficiently wiped out, her battered body driven on here ahead of the main berserker fleet in a ploy to forestall the installation of the space inverter and demolish the colony before any help could reach it. Scenario One was the more heroic and romantic, Two the more prosaic and businesslike. The trouble was that the real world was not committed to behaving in either style but went on its way indifferently.

A man was just now back from inspecting *Wilhelmina*'s control room. "Almost a total loss in there, sir, except for the drive controls and their directional settings. Artificial gravity's gone, astrogator's position is wiped out, and the autopilot, too. Drive itself seems all right, as far as I can tell without trying it."

"Don't bother. Thank you, mister."

Another man came to report, drifting upside down before the captain in the lack of gravity. "Starboard forward lifeboat's been launched, captain. Others are all still in place, no signs of having been lived in. Eight-passenger models."

"Thank you," Liao said courteously. These facts told him nothing new. Twelve minutes left now, before he must select a target and give the command to fire. In his magnetic boots he stood before the telescope and spectroscope as their user had done, and looked out at the stars.

The slow rotation of the *Wilhelmina* brought the dreadnought into view, and Liao flicked his suit radio to the intership channel. "Bridge, this is captain. Someone tell me just how big that space inverter is. Could two untrained people manhandle it and its packing into one of those little eight-passenger lifeboats?"

"This is the armaments officer, sir," an answer came back promptly. "I used to work in ground installations, and I've handled those things. I could put my arms around the biggest space inverter ever made, and it wouldn't mass more than fifty kilograms. It's not the size makes 'em rare and hard to come by, it's the complexity. Makes a regular drive unit or artificial gravity generator look like nothing."

"All right. Thank you. Astrogation, are you there?"

"Listening in, sir."

"Good. Barbara, the regular astrogator's gear on this ship seems to have been wiped out. What we have then is two history students or whatever, with unknown astronomical competence, working their way here from someplace two days off, in a series of c-plus jumps. We've found their instruments, apparently all they used—simple telescope and spectroscope. You've been thinking it over. Now, how about it? Possible?"

There was a pause. "Possible, yes. I can't say more than that on what you've given me."

"I'm not convinced it's possible. With umpteen thousand stars to look at, their patterns changing every time you jump, how could you hope to find the one you wanted to work toward?" *Ten minutes.* Inspiration struck. "Listen! Why couldn't they have shoved off in the lifeboat, two days ago, and used its autopilot?"

Barbara's voice was careful, as always. "To answer your last question first, chief, the lifeboat autopilots on civilian ships are usually not adjustable to give you a choice of goals; they just bring you out in the nearest place where you are likely to be found. No good for either people or berserkers intent on coming to Meitner's system. And if *Wilhelmina's* drive is working, it could take them between the stars faster than a lifeboat could.

"To answer your first question, the lifeboats carry aids for the amateur astrogator, such as spectral records of thousands of key stars, kept on microfilm. Also often provided is an electronic scanning spectroscope of the type you seem to have found there. The star records are indexed by basic spectral type—you know, types O, B, A, F, G, K, and so on. Type O stars, for example, are quite rare in this neck of the woods, so if you just scanned for them, you would cut down tremendously on the number of stars to be looked at closely for identification. There are large drawbacks to such a system of astrogation, but on the other hand, with a little luck, one might go a long way using it. If the two students are real people, though, I'll bet at least one of them knows some astronomy."

"Thank you," Liao said carefully, once again. He glanced around him. The marines were still busy, flashing their lights on everything and poking into every crevice. *Eight minutes.* He thought he could keep the time in his head now, not needing a chronometer.

People had lived in this lounge, or rec room, or whatever it had been, and enjoyed themselves. The wall to which the astrogation instruments were now fastened had earlier been decorated, or burdened, with numerous graffiti of the kinds students seemed always to generate. Many of the messages, Liao saw now, were in English, an ancient and honorable language still fairly widely taught. From his own schooldays he remembered enough to be able to read it fairly well, helping himself out with an occasional guess.

CAPTAIN AHAB CHASES ALEWIVES, said one message proceeding boldly across the wall at an easy reading height. The first and third words of that were certainly English, but the meaning of the whole eluded him. Captain Liao chases shadows, he thought, and hunches. What else is left?

Here was another:

                                      WORLD
                         WHOLE
                THE
           WISH
       CLASSMATES
     NOBLE
   HIS
  AND
OSS

And then nothingness, the remainder of the message having gone when Oss and his noble classmates went and the upper half of this wall went with them.

"Here, Captain! Look!" A marine was beckoning wildly.

The writing he was pointing to was low down on the wall and inconspicuous, made with a thinner writing instrument than most of the other graffiti had been. It said simply:

Henri & Winifred

Liao looked at it, first with a jumping hope in his heart, and then with a sagging sensation that had rapidly become all too familiar. He rubbed at the writing with his suited thumb; nothing much came off. He said: "Can anyone tell me in seven minutes whether this was put here after the air went out of the ship? If so, it would seem to prove that Henri and Winifred were still around then. Otherwise, it proves nothing." If the berserker had been here, it could easily have seen those names and retained them in its effortless, lifeless memory, and used them when it had to construct a scenario.

"Where are Henri and Winifred now, that is the question," Liao said to the lieutenant, who came drifting near, evidently wondering, as they all must be, what to do next. "Maybe that was Winifred back there in the party dress."

The marine answered: "Sir, that might have been Henri, for all that I could tell." He went on directing his men, and waiting for the captain to tell him what else was to be done.

A little distance to one side of the names, an English message in the same script and apparently made with the same writing instrument went down the wall like this:

Oh
Be
A
Fine
Girl
Kiss
Me
Right
Now
Sweetie

Liao was willing to bet that that particular message wasn't written by anyone wearing a space helmet. But no, he wouldn't make such a bet, not really. If he tried, he could easily enough picture the two young people, rubbing faceplates and laughing, momentarily able to forget the dead wedged in the twisted girders a few meters away. Something about that message nagged at his memory, though. Could it be the first line of an English poem he had forgotten?

The slow turn of the torn ship was bringing the dreadnought into view again. "Bridge, this is captain. Tell me anything that's new."

"Sir, here's a little more that came in clear from the lifeboat. I quote: 'This is Winifred talking now, stop. We're going on being human even if you don't believe us, stop.' some more repetitious stuff, Captain, and then this: 'While Henri was navigating I would come out from the lifeboat with him and he started trying to teach me about the stars, stop. We wrote our names there on the wall under the telescope, stop. If you care to look you'll find them, stop. Of course that doesn't prove anything does it, stop. If I had lenses for eyes I could have read those names there and remembered them . . .' It cuts off again there, chief, buried in noise."

"Second, confirm my reading of how much time we have left to decide."

"Three minutes forty seconds, sir. That's cutting it thin."

"Thanks." Liao fell silent, looking off across the universe. It offered him no help.

"Sir! Sir! I may have something here." It was the marine who had found the names; he was still closely examining the wall.

Looking at the wall where the man had aimed his helmet light, near the deck below the mounted instruments, Liao beheld a set of small, grayish, indented scratches, about half a meter apart.

"Sir, some machine coming here repeatedly to use the scopes might well have made these markings on the wall, whereas a man or woman in a spacesuit would not have left such marks, in my opinion, sir."

"I see." Looking at the marks, which might have been made by anything—maybe furniture banged into the wall during that final party—Liao felt an irrational anger at the marine. But of course the man was only trying to help. He had a duty to put forward any possibly useful idea that came into his head. "I'm not sure these were made by a berserker, spaceman, but it's something to think about. How much time have we left, Second?"

"Just under three minutes, sir. Standing by, ready to fire at target of your choice, sir. Pleading messages still coming in intermittently from both ships, nothing new in them."

"All right." The only reasonable hope of winning was to guess and take the fifty-fifty chance. If he let both ships go on, the bad one was certain to ram into the colony and destroy it before the other could deliver the key to the defenses and it could be installed. If he destroyed both ships, the odds were ten to one or worse that the berserker fleet would be here shortly and accomplish the same ruin upon a colony deprived of any chance of protecting itself.

Liao adjusted his throat muscles so that his voice, when it came out, would be firm and certain, and then he flipped a coin in his mind. Well, not really. There were the indented scratches on the bulkhead, perhaps not so meaningless after all, and there was the story of the two students' struggle to get here, perhaps a little too fantastic. "Hit the lifeboat," he said then, decisively. "Give it another two minutes, but if no new evidence turns up, let go at it with the main turret. Under no circumstances delay enough to let it reach the planet."

"Understand, sir," said Miller's voice. "Fire at the lifeboat two minutes from your order."

He would repeat the order to fire, emphatically, when the time was up, so that there could be no possible confusion as to where responsibility lay. "Lieutenant, let's get the men back to the launch. Continue to keep your eyes open on the way, for anything . . ."

"Yes, sir."

The last one to leave the ruined lounge-observatory, Liao looked at the place once more before following the marines back through the ship. Oh, be a fine girl, Winifred, when the slug from the c-plus cannon comes. But if I have guessed wrong and it is coming for you, at least you'll never see it. Just no more for you. No more Henri and no more lessons about the stars.

The stars . . .

Oh, be a fine girl . . .

O, B, A, F, G, K . . .

"Second officer!"

"Sir!"

"Cancel my previous order! Let the lifeboat land. Hit the *Etruria*! Unload on that bloody damned berserker with everything we've got, right now!"

"Yessir!"

Long before Liao got back to the launch, the c-plus cannon volleyed. Their firing was invisible, and inaudible here in airlessness, but still he and the others felt the energies released pass twistily through all their bones. Now the huge leaden slugs would begin skipping in and out of normal space, homing on their tiny target, far outracing light in their trajectories toward Meitner's planet. The slugs would be traveling now like de Broglie wavicles, one aspect matter with its mass magnified awesomely by Einsteinian velocity, one aspect waves of not much more than mathematics. The molecules of lead churned internally with phase velocities greater than that of light.

Liao was back on the dreadnought's bridge before laggard light brought the faint flash of destruction back.

"Direct hit, Captain." There was no need to amplify on that.

"Good shot, Arms."

And then, only a little later, a message got through the planet's ionospheric noise to tell them that the two people with the space inverter were safely down.

Within a few hours the berserker fleet appeared in-system, found an armed and ready colony, with *Hamil-car Barca* hanging by for heavy hit-and-run support. They skirmished briefly, and then decided to decline battle and depart. A few hours after that, the human fleet arrived and decided to pause for some refitting. And then Captain Liao had a chance to get down into the domed colony and talk to two people who wanted very much to meet him.

"So," he was explaining, soon after the first round of mutual congratulations had been completed, "when I at last recognized the mnemonic on the wall for what it was, I knew that not only had Henri and Winny been there, but that he had in fact been teaching her something about astronomical spectroscopy at that very place beside the instruments—therefore, after the ship was damaged."

Henri was shaking his youthful head, with the air of one still marveling at it all. "Yes, *now* I can remember putting the mnemonic thing down, showing her how to remember the order of spectral types. I guess we use mnemonics all the time without thinking about it much. Every good boy does fine, for the musical notes. Bad boys race our young girls—that one's in electronics."

The captain nodded. "Thirty days hath September. And 'Barbara Celarent' that the logicians still use now and then. Berserkers, with their perfect memories, probably don't even know what mnemonics are, much less need them. Anyway, if the berserker had been on the *Wilhelmina*, it would've had no reason to leave false clues. No way it could have guessed that I was coming to look things over."

Winifred took him by the hand. "Captain, you've given us our lives, you know. What can we ever do for you?"

"Well. For a start . . ." He slipped into some English he had recently practiced: "You might be a fine girl, sweetie, and . . ."

Martha

It rained hard on Tuesday, and the Science Museum was not crowded. On my way to interview the director in his office, I saw a touring class of schoolchildren gathered around the newest exhibit, a very late-model computer. It had been given the name of Martha, an acronym constructed by some abbreviation of electronic terms. Martha was supposed to be capable of answering a very wide range of questions in all areas of human knowledge, even explaining some of the most abstruse scientific theories to the layman.

"I understand the computer can even change its own design," I commented, a bit later, talking to the director.

He was proud. "Yes, theoretically. She hasn't done much rebuilding yet, except to design and print a few new logic circuits for herself."

"You call the computer 'she,' then. Why?"

"I do. Yes. Perhaps because she's still mysterious, even to the men who know her best." He chuckled, man-to-man.

"What does it—or she—say to people? Or let me put it this way, what kind of questions does she get?"

"Oh, there are some interesting conversations." He

paused. "Martha allows each person about a minute at one of the phones, then asks him or her to move along. She has scanners and comparator circuits that can classify people by shape. She can conduct several conversations simultaneously, and she even uses simpler words when talking to children. We're quite proud of her."

I was making notes. Maybe my editor would like one article on Martha and another on the museum in general. "What would you say was the most common question asked of the machine?"

The director thought. "Well, people sometimes ask: 'Are you a girl in there?' At first Martha always answered 'No,' but lately she's begun to say: 'You've got me there.' That's not just a programmed response, either, which is what makes it remarkable. She's a smart little lady." He chuckled again. "Also, people sometimes want their fortunes told, which naturally is beyond even Martha's powers. Let me think. Oh yes, many people want her to multiply large numbers, or play tic-tac-toe on the electric board. She does those things perfectly, of course. She's brought a lot of people to the museum."

On my way out I saw that the children had gone. For the moment I was alone with Martha in her room. The communicating phones hung unused on the elegant guardrail. I went over and picked up one of the phones, feeling just a little foolish.

"Yes, sir," said the pleasant feminine voice in my ear, made up, I knew, of individually recorded words electronically strung together. "What can I do for you?"

Inspiration came. "You ask *me* a question," I suggested.

The pleasant voice repeated: "What can I do for you?"

"I want you to ask me a question."

"You are the first human being to ask me for a question. Now, this is the question I ask of you: What do you, as one human being, want from me?"

I was momentarily stumped. "I don't know," I said finally. "The same as everyone else, I guess." I was wondering how to improve upon my answer when a sign lit up, reading:

CLOSED TEMPORARILY FOR REPAIRS
PARDON ME WHILE I POWDER MY NOSE

The whimsy was not Martha's, but printed by human design on the glass over the light. If she turned the repair light on, those were the only words that she could show the world. Meanwhile, the phone I was holding went dead. As I moved away I thought I heard machinery starting up under the floor.

Next day the director called to tell me that Martha was rebuilding herself. The day after that I went back to look. People were crowding up to the guardrail, around new panels which held rows of buttons. Each button, when pushed, produced noises, or colored lights, or impressive discharges of static electricity, among the complex new devices which had been added atop the machine. Through the telephone receivers a sexy voice answered every question with clearly spoken scraps of nonsense, studded with long technical words.

Intermission

Atoms do not age. They either exist or they do not. Then do molecules get old and tired? Do genes?

In the last twilight of the Sun the answer regarding genes became clear. It was stored in the investigating machines' memories, until the time of live intelligence came again.

Ten-Word Autobiography

Fred Saberhagen was alive when born. He means to continue.

Earthshade

When Zalazar saw the lenticular cloud decapitate the mountain, he knew that the old magic in the world was not yet dead. The conviction struck him all in an instant, and with overwhelming force, even as the cloud itself had struck the rock. Dazed by the psychic impact, he turned around shakily on the steep hillside to gaze at the countenance of the youth who was standing beside him. For a long moment then, even as the shock wave of the crash came through the earth beneath their feet and then blasted the air about their ears, Zalazar seemed truly stunned. His old eyes and mind were vacant alike, as if he might never before have seen this young man's face.

"Grandfather." The voice of the youth was hushed, and filled with awe. His gaze went past Zalazar's shoulder, and on up the mountain. "What was that?"

"You saw," said Zalazar shortly. With a hobbling motion on the incline, he turned his attention back to the miracle. "How it came down from the sky. You heard and felt it when it hit. You know as much about it as I do."

Zalazar himself had not particularly noticed one small

271

round cloud, among other clouds of various shape around what was, in general, an ordinary summer sky. Not until a comparatively rapid relative movement, of something small, unnaturally round, and very white against the high deep blue had happened to catch the corner of his eye. He had looked up directly at the cloud then, and the moment he did that he felt the magic. That distant disk-shape, trailing small patches of ivory fur, had come down in an angled, silent glide that somehow gave the impression of heaviness, of being on the verge of a complete loss of buoyancy and control. The cloud slid, or fell, with a deceptive speed, a speed that became fully apparent to Zalazar only when the long path of its descent at last intersected age-old rock.

"Grandfather, I can feel the magic."

"I'm sure you can. Not that you've ever had the chance to feel anything like it before. But it's something everyone is able to recognize at once." The old man took a step higher on the slope, staring at the mountain fiercely. "You were born to live with magic. We all were—the whole human race. We're never more than half alive unless we have it." He paused for a moment, savoring his own sensations. "Well, I've felt many a great spell in my time. There's no harm in this one—not for us, at least. In fact, I think it may possibly bring us some great good."

With that Zalazar paused again, experiencing something new, or maybe something long-forgotten. Was it only that the perceived aura of great spells near at hand brought back memories of his youth? It was more than that, probably. Old wellsprings of divination, caked over by the years, were proving to be still capable of stir and bubble. "All right. Whatever that cloud is, it took the whole top of the mountain with it over into the next valley. I think we should climb up there and take a look." All above was silent now, and apparently tranquil—except that a large, vague plume of gray dust had become visible above the truncated mountain, where it drifted fitfully in an uncertain wind.

The youth was eager, and they began at once. With

his hand upon a strong young arm for support when needed, Zalazar felt confident that his old limbs and heart would serve him through the climb.

They stopped at the foot of an old rock slide to rest, and to drink from a high spring there that the old man knew about. The midsummer grass grew lush around the water source, and with a sudden concern for the mundane, Zalazar pointed this out to the boy as a good place to bring the flocks. Then, after they had rested in the shade of a rock for a little longer, the real climb began. It went more easily for Zalazar than he had expected, because he had help at the harder places. They spoke rarely. He was saving his breath, and anyway, he did not want to talk or even think much about what they were going to discover. This reluctance was born not of fear, but of an almost childish and still growing anticipation. Whatever else, there was going to be magic in his life again, a vast new store of magic, ebullient and overflowing—and feeding the magic, of course, a small ocean at least of *mana*. Maybe with a supply like that, there would be enough left over to let an old man use some for himself . . . unless it were all used up, maintaining that altered cloud, before they got to it . . .

Zalazar walked and climbed a little faster. *Mana* from somewhere was around him already in the air, tantalizingly faint, like the first warm wind from the south before the snow has melted, but there indubitably, like spring.

It was obvious to the old man that his companion, even encumbered as he was by bow and quiver on his back and the small lyre at his belt, could have clambered on ahead to get a quick look at the wonders. But the youth stayed patiently at the old man's side. The bright young eyes, though, were for the most part fixed on ahead. Maybe, Zalazar thought, looking at the other speculatively, he's a little more frightened than he wants to admit.

Maybe I am, too, he added to himself. But I am certainly going on up there, nevertheless.

At about midday they reached what was now the mountaintop. It was a bright new tableland, about half a kilometer across, and as flat now as a certain parade ground that the old man could remember. The sight also made Zalazar think imaginatively of the stump of some giant's neck or limb; it was rimmed with soil and growth resembling scurfy skin, boned and veined with white rocks and red toward the middle, and it bubbled here and there with pure new springs, the blood of Earth.

From a little distance, the raw new surface looked preternaturally smooth. But when you were really near, close enough to bend down and touch the faint new warmth of it, you could see that the surface left by the mighty plane was not *that* smooth. It was no more level, perhaps, than it might have been if made by a small army of men with hand tools, provided they had been well supervised and induced to try.

The foot trail had brought them up the west side of what was left of the mountain. The strange cloud in its long, killing glide had come down also from the west, and had carried the whole mass of the mountaintop off with it to the east. Not far, though. For now, from his newly gained vantage upon the western rim of the new tabletop, Zalazar could see the cloud again.

It was no more than a kilometer or so away, looking like some giant, snow white, not-quite-rigid dish. It was tilted almost on edge, and it was half sunken into the valley on the mountain's far side, so that the place where Zalazar stood was just about on a horizontal level with the enormous dish's center.

"Come," he said to his young companion, and immediately led the way forward across the smoothed-off rock. The cloud ahead of them was stirring continually, like a sail in a faint breeze, and Zalazar realized that the bulk of it must be still partially airborne. Probably the lower curve of its circular rim was resting or dragging on the floor of the valley below, like the basket of a balloon ready to take off. In his youth, Zalazar had seen balloons, as well as magic and parade grounds. In his youth he had seen much.

As he walked, the raw *mana* rose all around him from

the rawly opened earth. It was a maddeningly subtle emanation, like ancient perfume, or warm air from an oven used yesterday to bake the finest bread. Zalazar inhaled it like a starving man, with mind and memory as well as lungs. It wasn't enough, he told himself, to really do anything with. But it was quite enough to make him remember what the world had once been like, and what his own role in the world had been.

At another time, under different conditions, such a fragrance of *mana* might have been enough to make the old man weep. But not now, with the wonder of the cloud visible just ahead. It seemed to be waiting for him. Zalazar felt no inclination to dawdle, as he sniffed the air nostalgically.

There was movement on the planed ground just before his feet. Looking down without breaking stride, Zalazar beheld small creatures that had once been living, then petrified into the mountain's fabric by the slow failure of the world's *mana*, now stirring with gropings back toward life. Under his sandaled foot he felt the purl of a new spring, almost alive. The sensation was gone in an instant, but it jarred him into noticing how quick his own strides had suddenly become, as if he too were already on the way to rejuvenation.

When they reached the eastern edge of the tabletop, Zalazar found he could look almost straight down to where a newly created slope of talus began far below. From the fringes of this great mass of rubble that had been a mountaintop, giant trees, freshly slain or crippled by the landslide, jutted out here and there at deathly angles. The dust of the enormous crash was still persisting faintly in the breeze, and Zalazar thought he could still hear the last withdrawing echoes of its roar . . .

"Grandfather, look!"

Zalazar raised his head quickly, to see the tilted lens-shape of the gigantic cloud bestirring itself with new apparent purpose. Half rolling on its circular rim, which dragged new scars into the valley's grassy skin below, and half lurching sideways, it was slowly, ponderously making its way back toward the mountain and the two who watched it.

The cloud also appeared to be shrinking slightly. Mass in the form of vapor was fuming and boiling away from the vast gentle convexities of its sides. There were also sidewise gouts of rain or spray, that woke in Zalazar the memory of ocean waterspouts. Thunder grumbled. Or was it only the cloud's weight, scraping at the ground? The extremity of the round, mountain-chopping rim looked hard and deadly as a scimitar. Then from the rim inwards the appearance of the enchanted cloudstuff altered gradually, until at the hub of the great wheel a dullard might have thought it only natural.

Another wheel turn of a few degrees. Another thunderous lurch. And suddenly the cloud was a hundred meters closer than before. Someone or something was maneuvering it.

"Grandfather?"

Zalazar spoke in answer to the anxious tone. "It won't do us a bit of good to try to run away." His own voice was cheerful, not fatalistic. The good feeling that he had about the cloud had grown stronger, if anything, the nearer he got to it. Maybe his prescient sense, long dormant, had been awakened into something like acuity by the faint accession of *mana* from the newly opened earth. He could tell that the *mana* in the cloud itself was vastly stronger. "We don't have to be afraid, lad. They don't mean us any harm."

"They?"

"There's someone inside that cloud. If you can still call it a cloud, as much as it's been changed."

"*Inside* it? Who could that be?"

Zalazar gestured his ignorance. He felt sure that the cloud was inhabited, without being able to say how he knew, or even beginning to understand how such a thing could be. Wizards had been known to ride *on* clouds, of course, with a minimum of alteration in the material. But to alter one to this extent . . .

The cloud, meanwhile, continued to work its way closer. Turn, slide, ponderous hop, gigantic bump, and scrape. It was now only about a hundred meters beyond the edge of the cliff. And now it appeared that something new was going to happen.

The tilted, slowly oscillating wall that was the cloudside closest to the cliff had developed a rolling boil quite near its center. Zalazar judged that this hub of white disturbance was only slightly bigger than a man. After a few moments of development, during which time the whole cloud-mass slid majestically still closer to the cliff, the hub blew out in a hard but silent puff of vapor. Where it had been was now an opening, an arched doorway into the pale interior of the cloud.

A figure in human shape, that of a woman nobly dressed, appeared an instant later in this doorway. Zalazar, in the first moment that he looked directly at her, was struck with awe. In that moment all the day's earlier marvels shrank down, for him, to dimensions hardly greater than the ordinary; they had been but fitting prologue. This was the great true wonder.

He went down at once upon one knee, averting his gaze from the personage before him. And without raising his eyes he put out a hand, and tugged fiercely at his grandson's sleeve until the boy had knelt down, too.

Then the woman who was standing in the doorway called to them. Her voice was very clear, and it seemed to the old man that he had been waiting all his years to hear that call. Still, the words in themselves were certainly prosaic enough. "You men!" she cried. "I ask your help."

Probably *ask* was not the most accurate word she could have chosen. Zalazar heard himself babbling some reply immediately, some extravagant promise whose exact wording he could not recall a moment later. Not that it mattered, probably. Commitment had been demanded and given.

His pledge once made, he found that he could raise his eyes again. Still the huge cloud was easing closer to the cliff, in little bumps and starts. Its lower flange was continually bending and flowing, making slow thunder against the talus far below, a roaring rearrangement of the fallen rock.

"I am Je," the dazzlingly beautiful woman called to them in an imperious voice. Her robes were rich blue, brown, and an ermine that made the cloud itself look gray. "It is written that you two are the men I need to find. Who are you?"

The terrible beauty of her face was no more than a score of meters distant now. Again Zalazar had to look away from its full glory. "I am Zalazar, mighty Je," he answered, in a breaking voice. "I am only a poor man. And this is my innocent grandson—Bormanus." For a moment he had had to search to find the name. "Take pity on us!"

"I mean to take pity on the world, instead, and use you as may be necessary for the world's good," the goddess answered. "But what worthier fate can mortals hope for? Look at me, both of you."

Zalazar raised his eyes again. The woman's countenance was once more bearable. Even as he looked, she turned her head as if to speak or otherwise communicate with someone else behind her in the cloud. Zalazar could see in there part of a corridor, and also a portion of some kind of room, all lined in brightness. The white interior walls and overhead were all shifting slightly and continually in their outlines, in a way that suggested unaltered cloudstuff. But the changes were never more than slight, the large-scale shapes remaining as stable as those of a wooden house. And the lady stood always upright upon a perfectly level deck, despite the vast oscillations of the cloud, and its turning as it shifted ever closer to the cliff.

Her piercing gaze returned to Zalazar. "You are an old man, mortal—at first glance, not good for much. But I see that there is hidden value in you. You may stand up."

He got slowly to his feet. "My lady Je, it is true that once my hands knew power. But the long death of the world has crippled me."

The goddess's anger flared at him like a flame. "Speak

not to me of death! I am no mere mortal subject to Thanatos." Her figure, as terrible as that of any warrior, as female as any succubus of love, was now no more than five meters from Zalazar's half-closed eyes. Her voice rang as clearly and commandingly as before. Yet, mixed with its power was a tone of doomed helplessness, and this tone frightened Zalazar on a deeper level even than did her implied threat.

"Lady," he murmured, "I can but try. Whatever help you need, I will attempt to give it."

"Certainly you will. And willingly. If in the old times your hands knew power, as you say, then you will try hard and risk much to bring the old times back again. You will be glad to hazard what little of good your life may have left in it now. Is it not so?"

Zalazar could only sign agreement, wordlessly.

"And the lad with you, your grandson. It he your apprentice, too? Have you given him any training?"

"In tending flocks, no more. In magic?" The old man gestured helplessness with gnarled hands. "In magic, great lady Je? How could I have? Everywhere that we have lived, the world is dead. Or so close to utter deadness that—"

"I have said that you must not speak to me of death! I will not warn you again. Now, it is written that both of you must come aboard. Yes, both; there will be use for both." And, as if the goddess were piloting and powering the cloud with her will alone, the whole mass of it now tilted gently, bringing her spotless doorway within easy stepping distance of the lip of rock.

Now Zalazar and Bormanus with him were surrounded by whiteness, sealed into it as if by mounds of glowing cotton. While cushioned firmness served their feet as floor or deck, as level always for them as for their divine guide, who walked ahead. Whiteness opened itself ahead of her, and sealed itself again when Bormanus had passed, walking close on Zalazar's heels.

The grinding of tormented rock and earth below could no longer be heard as the Lady Je, her robes of ermine and ultramarine and brown swirling with her long strides, led them through the cloud. Almost, there was no sound at all. Maybe a little wind, Zalazar decided, very faint and sounding far away. He had the feeling that the cloud, its power and purpose somehow regained, had risen quickly from the scarred valley and was once more swiftly airborne.

Je came to a sudden halt in the soft, pearly silence, and stretched forth her arms. Around her an open space, a room, swiftly began to define itself. In moments there had grown an intricately formed chamber, as high as a large temple, in which she stood like a statue, with her two puny mortal figures in attendance.

Then Zalazar saw that there was one other in the room with them. He muttered something, and heard Bormanus at his side give a quick intake of breath.

The bier or altar at the room's far end supported a figure that might almost have been a gray statue of a tormented man, done on a heroic scale. The figure was youthful, powerful, naked. With limbs contorted, it lay twisted on one side. The head was turned in a god's agony so that the short beard jutted vertically.

But it was not a statue. And Zalazar could tell, within a moment of first seeing it, that the sleep that held it was not quite—or not yet—the sleep of death. He had been forbidden to mention death to Je again, and he would not do so.

With a double gesture she beckoned both mortals to cross the room with her to stand beside the figure. While Zalazar was wondering what he ought to say or do, his own right hand moved out, without his willing it, as if to touch the statue-man. Je, he saw, observed this, but she said nothing; and with a great effort of his will Zalazar forced his own arm back to his side. Meanwhile, Bormanus, at his side, was standing still, staring, as if unable to move or speak at all.

Je spoke now as if angry and disappointed. "So, what buried value have you, old man? If you can be of no help in freeing my ally, then why has it been ordained for you to be here?"

"Lady, how should I know?" Zalazar burst out. "I am sorry to disappoint you. I knew something, once, of magic. But . . ." As for even understanding the forces that could bind a god like this, let alone trying to undo them . . . Zalazar could only gesture helplessly. At last he found words. "Great lady Je, I do not even know who this is."

"Call him Phaeton."

"Ah, great gods," Zalazar muttered, shocked and near despair.

"Yes, mortal, indeed we are. As well you knew when you first saw us."

"Yes, I knew . . . indeed." In fact, he had thought that all the gods were long dead, or departed from the world of humankind. "And why is he—like this?"

"He has fallen in battle, mortal. I and he and others have laid siege to Cloudholm, and it has been a long and bitter fight. We seek to free his father, Helios, who lies trapped in the same kind of enchantment there. Through Helios's entrapment, the world of old is dying. Have you heard of Cloudholm, old mortal? Among men it is not often named."

"Ah. I have heard something. Long ago . . ."

"It stifles the *mana*-rain that Helios cast ever on the Earth. With a fleet of cloudships like this one, we hurled ourselves upon its battlements—and were defeated. Most of the old gods lie now in tormented slumber, far above. A few have switched sides willingly. And all our ships save this one were destroyed."

"How could they dare?" The words burst from Bormanus, the first he had uttered since boarding the cloud-vessel. Then he stuttered, as Je's eyes burned at him: "I mean, who would dare try to destroy such ships? And who would have the power to do it?"

The goddess looked at the boy a moment longer, then reached out and took him by the hand. "Lend me your mortal fingers here. Let us see if they will serve to drain enchantment off." Bormanus appeared to be trying to draw back, but his hand, like a baby's, was brought out forcibly to touch the statue-figure's arm. And Zalazar's hand went out on its own once more. This time he could not keep it back, or perhaps he did not dare to try. His fingers spread on rounded arm-muscle, thicker by far than his own thigh. The touch of the figure made him think more of frozen snake than flesh of god. And now, Zalazar felt faint with sudden terror. Something, some great power, was urging the freezing near-death to desert its present captive and be content with Zalazar and Bormanus instead. But that mighty urging was mightily opposed, and came to nothing. At last, far above Zalazar's head, as if between proud kings disputing across some infant's cradle, a truce was reached. For the moment. He was able to withdraw his hand unharmed, and watched as Bormanus did the same.

The goddess Je sighed. It was a world-weary sound, close to defeat yet still infinitely stubborn. "And yet I am sure that there is *something* in you, old man . . . or possibly in your young companion here. Something that in the end will be of very great importance. Something that must be found . . . though I see, now, that you yourselves can hardly be expected to be aware of what it is."

He clasped his hand. "Oh great lady Je, we are only poor humans . . . mortals . . ."

"Never mind. In time I will discover the key. What is written anywhere, I can eventually read."

Zalazar was aware now of a strong motion underneath his feet. Even to weak human senses it was evident that the whole cloud was now in purposeful and very rapid flight.

"Where are we going?" Bormanus muttered, as if he were asking the air itself. He was a very handsome youth, with dark and curly hair.

"We return to the attack, young mortal. If most of our fleet has been destroyed, well, so too are the defenses of Cloudholm nearly worn away. One more assault can bring it into my hands, and set its prisoners free."

Zalazar had been about to ask some question, but now a distracting realization made him forget what it was. He had suddenly become aware that there was some guardian presence, sprite or demon he thought, melded with the cloud, driving and controlling it on Je's commands. It drew for energy on some vast internal store of *mana*, a treasure trove that Zalazar could only dimly sense.

Now, in obedience to Je's unspoken orders, the light inside the room or temple where they stood was taking on a reddish tinge. And the cloud-carvings were disappearing from what Zalazar took to be the forward wall. As Je faced in that direction, pictures began to appear there magically. These were of a cloudscape first, then of an earthly plain seen from a height greater than any mountain's. Both were passing at fantastic speed.

Je nodded as if satisfied. "Come," she said, "and we will try your usefulness in a new way." With a quick gesture she opened the whiteness to one side, and overhead. A stair took form even as she began to climb it. "We will see if your value lies in reconnoitering the enemy."

Clinging to Bormanus's shoulder for support, Zalazar found that the stairs were not as hard to negotiate as he had feared, even when they shifted form from one step to the next. Then there was a sudden gaping purple openness above their heads. "Fear not," said Je. "My protection is upon you both, to let you breathe and live."

Zalazar and Bormanus mounted higher. Wind shrieked thinly now, not in their faces but around them at some little distance, as if warded by some invisible shield. Then abruptly the climbing stair had no more steps. Zalazar thought that they stood on an open deck of cloud, under a bright sun in a dark sky, in some strange realm of neither day nor night. The prow of the cloudship that he rode upon was just before him; he stood as if on the bridge of some proud ocean vessel, looking out over deck and rounded bow, and a wild vastness of the elements beyond.

Not that the ship was borne by anything as small and simple as an earthly sea. The whole globe of Earth was already so far below that Zalazar could now begin to see its roundness, and still the cloudship climbed. All natural clouds were far below, clinging near the great curve of Earth, though rising here and there in strong relief. At first Zalazar thought that the star-pierced blackness through which they flew was empty of everything but passing light. But presently—with, as he sensed, Je's unspoken aid—he began to be able to perceive structure in the thinness of space about him.

"What do you see now, my sage old man? And you, my clever youth?" Je's voice pleaded even as it mocked and commanded. Her fear and puzzlement frightened Zalazar again. For the first time now he knew true regret that he had followed his first impulse and climbed a chopped-off mountain. Where now was the good result that prescience had seemed to promise?

"I see only the night ahead of us," responded Bormanus. His voice sounded remote, as if he were half asleep.

"I . . . see," said Zalazar, and paused with that. Much was coming clear to him, but it was going to be hard to describe. The cloud structures far below, so heavy with their contained water and their own mundane laws, blended almost imperceptibly into the base of something much vaster, finer, and more subtle— something that filled the space around the Earth, from the level of those low clouds up to the vastly greater altitude at which Zalazar now stood. And higher still . . . his eyes, as if ensnared now by those faery lines and arches, followed them upward and outward and ever higher still. The lines girdled the whole round Earth, and rose . . .

And rose . . .

Zalazar clutched out for support. Obligingly, a stanchion of cloudstuff grew up and hardened into place to meet his grasp. He did not even look at it. His eyes were fixed up and ahead, looking at Cloudholm.

Imagine the greatest castle of legend. And then go beyond that, and beyond, till imagination knows itself inadequate. Two aspects dominate: first, an almost invisible delicacy, with the appearance of a fragility to match. Secondly, almost omnipotent power—or, again, its seeming. Size was certainly a component of that power. Zalazar had never tried to, or been able to, imagine anything as high as this. So high that it grew near only slowly, though the cloudship was racing toward it at a speed that Zalazar would have described as almost as fast as thought.

Then Zalazar saw how, beyond Cloudholm, a thin crescent of moon rose wonderfully higher still; and again, beyond that, burned the blaze of sun, a jewel in black. These sights threw him into a sudden terror of the depths of space. No longer did he marvel so greatly that Je and her allied powers could have been defeated.

"Great lady," he asked humbly, "what realm, whose dominion is this?"

"What I need from you, mortal, are answers, not questions of a kind that I can pose myself." Je's broad white hand swung out gently to touch him on the eyes. Her touch felt surprisingly warm. Her voice commanded: "Say what you see."

The touch at once allowed him to see more clearly. But he stuttered, groping for words. What he was suddenly able to perceive was that the sun lived at the core of a magnificent, perpetual explosion, the expanding waves of which were as faint as Cloudholm itself, but nonetheless glorious for that. These waves moved in some medium far finer than the air, more tenuous than even the thinning air that had almost ceased to whistle with the cloudship's passage. And the waves of the continual slow sun-explosion bore with them a myriad of almost infinitesimal particles, particles that were heavy with *mana*, though they were almost too small to be called solid.

And there were the lines, as of pure force, in space. In obedience to some elegant system of laws they bore the gossamer outer robes of the sun itself, to wrap the Earth with delicate energy . . . and the *mana* that flowed outward from the sun—great Zeus but there was such a flood of it!

The Earth was bathed in warmth and energy—but not in *mana*, Zalazar suddenly perceived. That flow had been cut off by Cloudholm and its spreading wings. (Yes, Zalazar could see the pinions of enchantment now, raptor-wings extending curved on two sides from the castle itself, as if to embrace the whole Earth—or smother it.) Through them the common sunlight flowed on unimpeded, to make the surface of the world flash blue and ermine white. But all the inner energies of magic were cut off . . .

Zalazar realized with a start that he was, or just had been, entranced and muttering, that someone with a mighty grip had just shaken his arm, that a voice of divine power was urging him to speak up, to make sense in what he reported of his vision.

"Tell clearly what you see, old man. The wings, you say, spread out from Cloudholm to enfold the Earth. That much I knew already. Now say what their weakness is. How are they to be torn aside?"

"I . . . I . . . the wings are very strong. They draw sustaining power from the very flow of *mana* that they deny the Earth. Some of the particles that hail on them go through—but those are without *mana*. Many of the particles and waves remain, are trapped by the great wings and drained of *mana* and of other energies. Then eventually they are let go."

"Old fool, what use are you? You tell me nothing I do not already know. Say, where is the weakness of the wings? How can our Earth be fed?"

"Just at the poles. There is a weakness, sometimes, a drooping of the wings, and there a little more *mana* than elsewhere can reach the Earth."

Suddenly faint, Zalazar felt himself begin to topple. He was grabbed, and upheld, and shaken again. "Tell more, mortal. What power has created Cloudholm?"

"What do I know? How can I see? What can I say?"

He was shaken more violently than before, until in his desperate fear of Je he cried: "Great Apollo himself could not learn more!"

He was released abruptly, and there was a precipitous

silence, as if even Je had been shocked by Zalazar's free use of that name, the presence of whose owner only his mother Leto and his father Zeus could readily endure. Then Zalazar's eyes were brushed again by Je's warm hand, and he came fully to himself.

Cloudholm was bearing down on them. "And Helios is trapped up there?" Zalazar wondered aloud. "But why, and how?"

"Why?" The bitterness and soft rage in Je's voice were worthy of a goddess. "Why, I myself helped first to bind him. Was I made to do that, after opposing him and bringing on a bitter quarrel? I do not know. Are even we deities the playthings of some overriding fate? What was Helios's sin, for such a punishment? And what was mine?"

Again Zalazar had to avert his gaze, for Je's beauty glowed even more terribly than before. And at the same time he had to strive to master himself, hold firm his will against the hubris that rose up in him and urged him to reach for the role of god himself. Such an opportunity existed, would exist, foreknowledge told him, and it was somewhere near at hand. If he only . . .

His internal struggle was interrupted by the realization that the cloudship no longer moved. Looking carefully, Zalazar could see that it had come to rest upon an almost insubstantial plain.

Straight ahead of him now, the bases of the walls of Cloudholm rose. And there was a towering gate.

Je was addressing him almost calmly again. "If your latent power, old mortal, is neither of healing nor of seeing, then perhaps it lies in the realm of war. That is the way we now must pass. Kneel down."

Zalazar knelt. The right hand of the goddess closed on his and drew him to his feet again. He arose on lithely muscular legs, and saw that the old clothing in which he had walked the high pasturelands had been transformed. He was clad now in silver cloth, a fabric worked with a fine brocade. His garments hung on him as solidly as chain mail, yet felt as soft and light as silk. They were at once the clothing and the armor of a god.

In Zalazar's right hand, grown young and muscular, a short sword had appeared. The weapon was of some metal vastly different from that of his garments, and yet he could feel that its power was at least their equal. On his left arm now hung a shield of dazzling brightness, but seemingly of no more than a bracelet's weight.

The front of the cloudship divided and opened a way for the man who had been the old herdsman Zalazar. The thin cloudstuff of the magic plain swirled and rippled round his boots of silver-gray. His feet were firmly planted, and though he could plainly see the sunlit Earth below, he knew no fear that he might fall.

He glanced behind him once, and saw the cloudship altering, disintegrating, and knew that the nameless demon who had sustained it had come out now at Je's command, to serve her in some other way.

Then Zalazar faced ahead. He could see, now, how much damage the great walls of Cloudholm had sustained, and what had caused the damage. Other cloudships, their insubstantial wreckage mixed with that of the walls they had assailed, lay scattered across the plain and piled at the feet of those enduring, fragile-looking towers. Nor were the wrecked ships empty. With vision somehow granted him by Je, Zalazar could see that each of them held at least one sleep-bound figure of the stature of a god or demigod. They were male or female, old-looking or young, of diverse attributes. All were caught and held, like Phaeton, by some powerful magic that imposed a quiet, if not always a peaceful, slumber.

Now, where was Je herself? Zalazar realized suddenly that he could see neither the goddess nor her attendant demon. He called her name aloud.

Do not seek me, her voice replied, whispering just at his ear. *Make your way across the plain, and force the castle gates. With my help you can do it, and I shall be with you when my help is needed.*

Zalazar shrugged his shoulders. With part of his mind he knew that his present feelings of power and confidence were unnatural, given him by the goddess for her own purposes. But at the same time he could not deny those feelings—nor did he really want to. Feeling enormously capable, driven by an urge to prove what this divine weapon in his new right hand could do, he shrugged his shoulders again, loosening tight new muscles for action. Beside him, Bormanus, who had not been changed, was looking about in all directions alertly. With one hand the lad gripped tightly the small lyre at his belt, but he gave no other sign of fear. Then suddenly he raised his other hand and pointed.

Coming from the gates of Cloudholm, which now stood open, already halfway across the wide plain between, a challenger was treading thin white cloud in great white boots.

Zalazar, watching, raised his sword a little. Still the goddess was letting him know no fear. He who approached was a red-bearded man, wearing what looked like a winged Nordic helmet, and other equipment to match. He was of no remarkable height for a hero, but as he drew near Zalazar saw that his arms and shoulders, under a tight battle harness, were of enormous thickness. He balanced a monstrous war hammer like a feather in one hand.

I should know who this is, Zalazar thought. But then the thought was gone, as quickly as it had come. Je manages her tools too well, he thought again, and then that idea too was swept from his mind.

The one approaching came to a halt, no more than three quick strides away. "Return to Earth, old Zalazar," he called out, jovially enough. "My bones already ache with a full age of combat. I yearn to let little brother Hypnos whisper in my ear, so I can lie down and rest. I don't know why Je bothered to bring you here; the proper time for humans to visit Cloudholm is long gone, and again, is not yet come."

"Save your riddles," Zalazar advised him fearlessly. This, he thought, in a moment of great glory and pride, this is what it is like to be a god. And in his heart he thanked Je for this moment, and cared not what might happen in the next.

"Oho," Redbeard remarked good-humoredly. "Well, then, it seems we must." The sword and hammer leapt together of themselves, with a blare as of all war-trumpets in the world, and a clash as of all arms. It lasted endlessly, and at the same time it seemed to take no time at all. Zalazar thought that he saw Redbeard fall, but when he bent with some intention of dealing a finishing stroke, the figure of his opponent had vanished. Save for Bormanus, who had prudently stepped back from the clash, he was apparently alone.

Well fought! Je's voice, from invisible lips, whispered beside his ear. There was new excitement in the words, an undertone of savage triumph.

Zalazar, triumphant too—and at the same time knowing an undercurrent of dissatisfaction, for these deeds were not his of his own right—moved on toward the open gate. He had gone a dozen strides when something— he thought not Je—urged him to look back. When he did, he could now see Redbeard, hammer still in hand, stretched out upon the cloud. There was no sign of blood or injury. At Redbeard's ear a winged head was hovering, whispering a compulsion from divine lips. And on the face of the fallen warrior there was peace.

Why do you pause? Je demanded in her hidden voice. She required no answer, but Zalazar must go on. All Je's attention, and Zalazar's, too, was bent now upon the open castle gate. It slammed shut of itself when he was still a hundred strides away. Now he could see that what he had taken for carved dragon heads on either side of the portal were alive, turning fanged jaws toward him.

Zalazar glanced at the lad who was walking so trustingly at his side, and for the first time since landing on the cloud-plain he knew anxiety. "Lady Je," he prayed in a whisper, "I crave your protection for my grandson as well as for myself."

I give what protection I can, to those I need. And I foresee now that I will need him, later on . . .

The dragons guarding the gate stretched out their necks when Zalazar came near; fangs like bunched knives drove at him. The shield raised upon his left arm took the blows. The sword flashed left, lashed right.

Zalazar stepped back, gasping; he looked to see that Bormanus, who had kept clear, was safe. Then Zalazar willed the swordblade at the great cruciform timbers of the gate itself. They splintered, shuddered, and swung back.

Je's triumph was a shrill scream, almost soundless, inarticulate.

Zalazar knew that he must still go forward, now into Cloudholm itself. He balanced the shield upon his left arm, hefted the sword again in his right hand. He drew a deep breath, of ample-seeming air, and entered the palace proper.

He came to door after door, each taller and more magnificent than the last, and each swung open of itself to let him in. Around him on every hand there towered shapes that should have been terrible, though he could see them only indistinctly. Something told him which way he must go. And he pressed on, through one royal hall and chamber after another . . .

. . . until he had entered that which he knew must be the greatest hall of all. At the far end of it, very distant from where he stood, Zalazar saw the Throne of the World. It was guarded by a wall of flame, and it was standing vacant.

As Zalazar's feet brought him closer to the fire, he saw that it was centered on a plinth of cloud that supported another manlike figure, similar to that of tortured Phaeton but larger still.

It is Helios, said Je's disembodied whisper. *Pull him from the flames, restore him to his throne, and* mana *will rain upon the Earth again.*

The flame felt very hot. When Zalazar probed it with his sword, it pushed the swordblade back. "But what power is this that imprisons him? Je?"

Do not ask questions, mortal. Act.

Zalazar stalked right and left, seeking a way around the flames or through them. The figure inside them did not seem to be burned or tormented by the terrible heat, only bound. Zalazar, as he approached the tongues of fire, had to raise first one hand, and then his shield, to try to protect himself from radiance and glare. The only way to reach the bound god seemed to be to leap directly into the flames, or through them.

Zalazar tried. Unbearable pain seared at him, and the tongues of flame seized him like hands and threw him back. The instant he was clear of the flames, their burning stopped; he was unharmed.

Je shrieked words of compulsion in his ear. Zalazar wrapped himself in his silvery cloak, raised his shield, brandished his sword, and tried again. And was thrown back. And yet again, but all to no avail. And still Je made him try. She stood near now in her full imaged presence.

Yet again the tongues of fire gripped Zalazar, and hurled him flying, sprawling. When Zalazar saw that the metal of his shield was running now in molten drops, he cried aloud his agony: "Spare me, great Je! what will you have from me? Only so much can you make of me—so much and no more."

"I will make whatever I wish of you, mortal. We are so near, so very near to victory!" Her gaze turned to Bormanus, and she went on: "There is a way in which we can augment our power, as I foresaw. Murder will feed great magic."

Zalazar came crawling along the floor, toward the goddess's feet. He made his hand let go the sword. Only now he realized that no scabbard for it had ever been given him. "Goddess, do not demand of me that I kill my own flesh and blood. It will not bring you victory. I was never a great wizard, even in my youth. No Alhazred, no Vulcan the Shaper. Though even before I met you I had convinced myself of that. A warrior? Conqueror? No, I am not Trillion Mu either, though I have killed; your demon's power and yours could sustain me in combat for a time even against Thor Redbeard himself. But I cannot do more. Even murder will not give me power enough. And if it could, I will not—"

In fishwife rage, Je lost her self-control. "What are you, thing of clay, to argue with me?" She grabbed Bormanus and forced him forward, bent down so that his neck was exposed for a swordstroke. "Earth is mine to deal with as I will, and you are no more than a clod of earth. Kill him!"

"Destroy me if you will, goddess. If you can. I will not kill him."

Je's eyes glowed, orange fire from a volcano. "I see that I have maddened you with my assistance, until you think you are a demigod at least. You are not worth destruction. If I only withdraw my sustaining power, you will both fall back to earth and be no more than bird-dung when you land. Where will you turn for help if I abandon you?"

Zalazar, on his feet again, turned, physically, looking for help. The half-melted shield now felt impossibly heavy, weighing his left arm down. The brocade of his god-garments hung on him now like lead. The last time the flames had thrown him, some of their pain had remained in his bones. At a thought from Je, the cloud-floor of the palace would open beneath his feet. He would have a long fall in which to think things over.

The Throne of the World was empty, waiting. No help there. But still he was not going to murder.

Je's voice surprised him in its altered tone. It was less threatening now. "Zalazar, I see that I must tell you the truth. It need not be Helios that you place on the Throne when you have gained the power. It could be me."

"You?"

"The truth is that it could even be yourself."

"I?" Zalazar turned slowly. Looked at the throne again, and thought, and shook his head. "I am only a poor man, I tell you, goddess. Alone and almost lost. If it is true that I can choose the Ruler of the World, well, it must be some cruel joke, such as you say that even gods are subject to. But if the choice is truly mine to make, I will not give it you. As for taking it myself, I should not. I have no fitness, or powers, or wealth, or even family."

Silence fell in Cloudholm. It was an abrupt change; a stillness that was something more than silence had descended. Zalazar waited, eyes downcast, holding his breath, trying to understand.

Then he began to understand, for the last three words that he himself had spoken seemed to be echoing and re-echoing in the air. All his life he had been a poor nomad, with no family at all.

Even the flames of Helios's prison seemed to have cooled somewhat, though Zalazar did not immediately raise his head to look at them. When it seemed to him that the silence might have gone on for half an hour, he did at last look up.

He who had walked with Zalazar as his companion had at last taken the lyre from his belt, and the others were allowed to recognize him now.

Je had recoiled, cringing, herself for once down on one knee, with averted gaze. But Zalazar, for now, could look.

White teeth, inhumanly beautiful and even, smiled at him. "Old man, you have decided well. One comes to claim the throne in time, and Thanatos will be overcome, and your many-times-great-grandsons will have to choose again; but that is not your problem now. I send you back to Earth. Retain the youth that Je has given you—it is fitting, for a new age of the world has been ordained, though not by me. And memories, if you can—retain them too. Magic must sleep."

Bright, half-melted shield and silver garments fell softly to the floor of cloud, beside the sword. Zalazar was gone.

The bright eyes under the dark curls swept around. The god belted his lyre and unslung his bow. There was a great recessional howling as Je's demon-servant fled, and fell, and fled and fell again.

Je raised her eyes, in a last moment of defiance. The

winged head of Hypnos, already hovering beside her ear, silently awaited a command.

"Sleep now, sister Je. As our father Zeus and our brothers and sisters sleep. I join you presently," Apollo said.

Recessional

From the window of his high hotel room, sixty dollars a day at convention rates, he could look between other buildings to see a small piece of the ocean. Within the mirror where he looked when shaving there was another window with another square of sea, and an hourly newscast came on that morning just as he was starting to shave. Razor in hand he listened while the voice of the woman announcer went through a few details of what she called the grisly discovery. The thing somehow got to him, enough to keep him from concentrating properly either on shaving or on what he ought to say when he appeared on the panel in a couple of hours. Not only that, it stayed with him after he finished getting ready and left the room.

The radio really hadn't given many facts. The body of a woman of indeterminate age had been washed up on a beach somewhere down in the Keys, which put it, he supposed, almost a hundred miles to the southwest of Miami Beach. An unnamed authority was quoted to the effect that the body might have been in the water as long as several years. He thought at first that the newscaster had probably got that garbled somehow, but then mention was made of pockets of cold, uncirculating water to be found in certain depths, in which unusual preservative action could be expected.

One reason for the grisly discovery remaining with him all morning, he supposed, was that his panel topic was "Science in Science Fiction," and he hoped to be able to work that "unusual preservative action" into what he had to say. He felt a little uncomfortable about this panel, as he really was no scientist, though he read the professional journals fairly often and popularizations a lot, and his stories tended to be thick with scientific jargon. He thought some of the readers liked the jargon better than the stories, and he loved it himself, really, which was why long ago he had begun to use so much of it. For him it had always made a kind of poetry.

Some of the other people on the panel were not only real scientists, but writers as well. They talked quantum mechanics. They talked espistemology. He wasn't sure at first that he remembered what that meant. He wondered for a little while if he was going to have to sit there like a dummy for long minutes at a time. So as soon as the chance came, he got in a few words that shifted the subject to alternate universes. Anybody could talk about that.

Suppose, he thought to himself, looking out over the heads of the audience in the far last row while some argument between two other panelists droned on, just suppose that body could have been five years in the sea. How far could a body drift in five years? Well, certainly not through the Panama Canal. When, in the early afternoon, he got back to his room, he looked out at what little he could see of the one great ocean that went all the way around the world, and thought about that body again. They hadn't said what, if anything, the woman had been wearing. He couldn't quite shake the subject, it seemed to have set up a resonance of some kind inside his head. Time passed, what seemed like a lot of time as he sat waiting in his room, but the phone call from another hotel room that he was expecting failed to come.

So he left the convention earlier than he had planned, left it that very afternoon, driving north through summer Florida. Going to the convention, he told himself, had been more trouble than it was worth. In the old days, the cons ran three days, no more, and were relaxed and friendly. Now each one he went to seemed like some damned big business in itself. Just getting away on his own was something of a relief.

A day and a half later, waking up early in his motel room in Atlanta, he put in a call to his agent in New York. The agent would be back in the office in half an hour, the girl thought, and would call him back then. Waiting for the agent to call back, he took a shower, and when he came out of the shower, dripping, turned on the radio.

Listening, he experienced something of an inward chill.

". . . thought to have been in her early twenties, recovered from the Chattahoochie some twenty miles north of Atlanta. The condition of the body made it impossible to determine immediately if there were any marks of violence. Sheriff's officers said that the body might have been in the water for as long as several months. Attempts at identification . . ."

The phone rang. It was the agent, for once communicating even earlier than expected. And with good news: money was coming through, even more money than they had been looking for, and he could afford a trip, a wander across the country, if he felt like one. He hadn't really felt like one for several years, not since he had been living alone, but he felt like one now, before he went home and got back to work. Not that New York or any place else was really home. He had reached the stage of being down to mailing addresses.

The Interstate impelled him west. He liked driving his car, he usually liked machines. Quantum mechanics. Epistemology. That was what they talked about on panels nowadays. In the old days they had talked about relativity sometimes, but then you could figure that almost no one knew what they were talking about. He should have taken the time, before coming to the convention, to read up a little more on current work. That way he could have at least sounded a little more intelligent. He would settle in for a day or two of reading when he got home.

A feeling was growing in him that the convention he had just left had marked some kind of turning point, a new departure in his life. Something had changed. Whether it was for better or worse had yet to be discovered. For richer, for poorer. He was never going to get married again, that much he felt pretty sure about, not even when his status as a widower became finally and fully legal and official, as one of these years it would. Was it two years now, or three? Conventions were still good for providing a little fun in bed, and that was all he needed. Then next day he waited in his room and the phone refused to ring as scheduled. Well, maybe it was just as well.

He didn't really know where he was driving now, he just wanted to get off for a few days. On a new course. Alternate universe. When he had brought up that hoary old science fiction concept on the panel, one of the real scientists, almost condescending though he was trying not to sound that way, had admitted aloud that some experiments in particle physics carried out within the last ten years even suggest that physical reality may depend, in some sense, to some extent, on human consciousness. If that was true, the writer had thought, listening, if that could be true, how was it possible for everybody to remain so calm about it? But thus spake a real live quantum mechanic. The Bell inequality, whatever the hell that was. The spin of elementary particles . . .

The car radio assured him that gas supplies were good everywhere across the country, though prices showed no sign of coming down. Tourist business was suffering. He was going to have no trouble finding a motel room, wherever he went.

At Birmingham he decided to head on west for a while, and stayed with Interstate 20 going southwest to Jackson. Hell of a country to be driving through in the summer in search of fun or relaxation. But the car was nicely air conditioned, a space capsule whose interior guarded its own sounds and atmosphere, keeping noise and dust and rain and heat all nicely sealed outside. What showed on the windows could almost be no more than pictures from outside, computer presentations.

In Vicksburg he located a bottle of bourbon and took it to bed with him. A lot less trouble than a woman. But then to his own surprise he discovered that he didn't feel like drinking much, even after the long drive. He took a couple of sips, then let the bottle sit. He turned on the television, got some local talk show. Talk shows were usually his favorite, they provided humanity at just about the right distance. They proved that the human race was still around somewhere, alive, not too terribly far away. But when you wanted, you could turn them off.

". . . for your research at the battlefield cemeteries?" the host was asking.

"Well, the opportunity came about because of some new road construction in the park." The speaker was a well-dressed man in the prime of life, mustached, relaxed, superior. He enjoyed talking like this. He was reminiscent of some of the people on the convention panel. "In the process of excavation for the road, some previously unknown 1863 military burials came to light, and we applied for permission to use some of the skulls in our tests, the same kind of tests we had been developing for the archaeological work on Indian sites. There were twenty-seven of the Civil War skulls altogether, all completely unidentified. We think they were divided about evenly between Union and Confederate."

"And you got the same results with these, as with the older subjects, that had been in the ground for maybe thousands of years?"

"Better, in many cases. The bone frequently was much better preserved than in the older specimens. We were able to get some very interesting results indeed. The trace elements in the bone that resonate with the NMR . . ."

Jargon, of any scientific field, could still soothe him like poetry. Better than poetry. He sipped at his bottle and set it back on the table and got ready to drift toward sleep.

". . . beauty of the whole thing, you see, is that the visual cortex of the brain need not be intact, or even present."

"That's the real discovery, then."

"That's part of it. Apparently what no one had suspected all along was that the hard bone of the skull itself has another purpose besides that of mere protection."

They had him drifting toward wakefulness again. Why hadn't he heard anything about any of this before? It sounded revolutionary. He wanted to hear it now.

". . . bone perhaps serves as a kind of backup memory storage system, at least in human skulls. We don't know yet if it works the same way in other mammals."

"Then there should be applications of this outside the field of archaeology, wouldn't you say?"

"Oh, yes, definitely. Police work, for instance. Medicine. X-rays will still have their place, of course. But in medicine the NMR is soon going to replace the X-ray for most purposes, because it doesn't involve ionizing radiation; X-ray always presents some element of risk. Anyway, a police laboratory, say, can set up an unidentified skull and obtain from it images of scenes that the person actually saw when alive."

"That's spooky. Would you get, maybe, the last thing they saw before they died? Wasn't there some nineteenth-century theory that by photographing a dead person's eyes the image of the last thing they saw in life could be recovered?"

"Yes. There's a Kappling short story about it. But that's all sheer superstition. This is something entirely different."

Not *Kappling*, you numbskull, you mean Kipling. But the word had been so clear and deliberate. Some affected pronunciation? Some in-joke? No one was laughing.

". . . a thing like this to be acceptable as legal evidence, I wonder."

"I'm no lawyer, but I do know that police all over the country are already trying it out. I think that sooner or later it's bound to be accepted fully. The weight of accumulated evidence is going to silence the objections."

"What objections are there? If you can obtain a good picture, as you say you can, doesn't that prove you're right?"

"Well, a few pretty bright people were worried, at first, when they realized what we were doing. There were arguments that what we were doing could start to unravel the whole fabric of physical reality. There's a kind of resonance factor operating, and the more people you have doing similar experiments—especially on similar subjects—the more likely it seems to be that there will be a concentration, a focusing of the effects of many separate experiments upon one subject."

"How can that be?"

"We don't know. But if reality can depend in some sense upon human consciousness, then maybe the existence, the form, of an individual human consciousness depends also upon the reality surrounding it. Or the realities, if you prefer."

"You said there was no harmful radiation, though."

"Right. All the physical objections have now been pretty well taken care of. The main objection now is to the fact that our best pictures are partially subjective. That is, we obtain the best readings from a human skull when we use another skull, the observer's own, as a kind of resonator."

"The observer's own skull? Give me that again, will you?"

"All right." But there ensued a thoughtful pause. The scientist chewed his mustache.

The host, avoiding dead air time if nothing else, interjected: "With NMR you *do* project waves of some kind into the body, into whatever's being examined—?"

"Yes. NMR scans are a proven means of probing inside matter. They've been used now for thirty years."

"And, tell me again, NMR stands for—?"

"Nuclear magnetic resonance. All that we actually

project into the body, the specimen, or whatever, is a strong magnetic field. This causes the nuclei of certain atoms inside the specimen to line up in certain ways. Then, when the imposed field is removed, the nuclei flip back again. When a nucleus flips back it emits a trace of radiation that registers on our detectors, and from all these traces our computer can form a picture."

"No harmful radiation, though."

The scientist smiled. "Do you have a sort of a *thing* about radiation?"

"Most people do, these days."

"Well, no, it's not harmful. Now what we've discovered is that when the observer's own skull is used as a kind of magnetic resonator, then pictures, images, are actually induced in the observer's own visual cortex. He sees a finer, sharper version of what the computer can otherwise extract from the specimen and put up on a stage in the form of a holographic projection. But we can't yet repeat the results as consistently as we'd like. When you scan a specimen skull more than once, you're likely to get a different picture every time. So the question is, is what the human experimenter claims to see really the same as that blurry picture that the computer puts up on the hologram stage?"

"I wish you could have brought some pictures along to show our audience."

"By the time I photographed the hologram, and then you ran it through your cameras and so on here, onto their sets at home, they would be seeing a picture of a picture of a not very good picture."

"Maybe next time?"

"Maybe next time. But as I say, it's not really all that informative when the first image is blurry."

"And you can't get the same picture twice?"

"The structure of the skull, the specimen, is changed minutely by the very act of reading it. There are various interpretations of why and how this whole thing works at all. It surprised the hell out of a lot of us when we first began to realize what was happening. And even worried a few people, as I say: can time and space become unraveled? Do we tend to get different readings each time because we are reaching for similar atoms, similar skulls, in adjoining universes? The theoretical physicists think it has to do with coupling through electron spin resonance, that's ESR. The ligand field of each particle expands indefinitely, they say now, which is going to open up a whole new field of research."

"Superhyperfine splitting," commented the host, nodding sagely, and got a laugh in the studio. He was obviously harking back to something that had earlier snowed him and the audience as well.

The scientist shook his head and smiled tolerantly. He murmured something that was lost in the subsiding laughter.

"*I* see," added the host. He continued to nod in a way that meant he had given up on trying to see, especially after that ligand field. "But do you think you'd be able to help the police discover, for instance, who this young woman is whose body came down the Mississippi today? They say she might have been in the water for several weeks. Wearing a yellow bikini and—"

His jerking hand at last found the right switch on the unfamiliar set. The picture died, in an erratically shrinking white dot-spark, that lashed about for a moment as if trying to escape its glassy prison.

The departure of the voices left a hollowness in the air of the dark motel room. Other murmurings came in from other rooms not far away. The carpet under his knees felt rough and dusty. He might have just got up calmly and walked over to the set to turn it off, if he wanted it off. But there had been a bad moment there, bad enough to make him lunge and crawl.

He stood up, stiffly. On the bedside table the bottle waited, hardly started. No. He was all right. No, just a moment of panic there, such as sometimes came when he was drifting off to sleep. He had thought that at last, after months of learning to sleep alone again, he was all through with midnight panics. Just one small sip now, and even without that he was tired enough to sleep.

Then, tomorrow, he would drive again. He could drive anywhere he wanted to. Things were all right . . .

In the morning he knew that he was not going to follow the great river north, up to the great lakes. Yesterday the plan in the back of his mind, as well as he could remember it, had been to do something along that line. But enough of water, and watery places. He would go on west, and put the big rivers and the lakes behind him.

In Shreveport he sat in a plastic booth, eating plastic-tasting food, and abruptly realizing that in the booth next to him sat two state police officers. Whether it was more nearly impossible that they had already been there, unseen by him, when he sat down, or that they had walked in past him without his knowing it, he couldn't estimate.

". . . she mighta been from way upstream somewheres. The Doc, he says days in the water. White gal. Just a lil ol bathing suit on. No wounds, nothing like that."

"Well, the Red can be worse'n the Mississippi even, when it rains enough. It's been like pourin' piss out'n a boot up there in Oklahoma."

Back in his car, moving on the highway, he realized that somehow he must have paid the restaurant cashier. Otherwise the two state troopers would already be in hot pursuit.

Fifty-five was the law, and maybe in some places they cared about that. But once he got to Texas he felt sure that nobody was going to give a damn. He opened her up.

Greenery and rivers dried up and blew away in the hot wind of his passage. Signs indicated where to turn to get to Midland, Odessa, Corsicana. Nazareth. If a name existed in the universe, if a name was even conceivable, and maybe sometimes if it was not, it could be found somewhere in the vastness of Texas, applied to a small town.

He slept in a motel somewhere, in a room where he turned on no radio or television. And sometime after that he crossed a border that lay invisibly athwart the unfamiliar lunar landscape and found that he was in New Mexico. Maybe he had never come exactly this way before. He couldn't remember things being quite this barren even here.

Signs told him he was nearing Carlsbad. The highway topped a stark rise to disclose an unexpected wall of greenery waiting for him, not far ahead. Pecos River, a small sign added. He drove across a highway bridge over the river, which was for this part of the country so wide and full that he was astonished by it until he saw the dam.

If he tried to go any farther tonight he was going to drive right off the road somewhere in exhaustion. And yet, once settled in the Carlsbad Motel, he couldn't sleep. He had to know first what was happening. No, not quite right. He had to know if he was going to have to admit to himself that something was happening. Maybe he was just going a little crazy from being alone too much in summer heat. If that was all, he should just stay in one cool room for a day and a night and sleep.

He forced himself to turn on the ten p.m. television news, and he listened to the whole half hour attentively, and there was not a word about drowned bodies anywhere. He started to relax, to feel that whatever had started to happen to him was over. When the news was over, he found a talk show, on another channel that came in by cable from the west coast. Show biz people and famous lawyers sat around a table. During the first commercial he roused himself and went out to get half a pint of good bourbon. To hell with being so careful, you could probably drive yourself crazy that way. Tonight he was going to drink. He had the feeling that things were going to be all right after all.

He thought he had turned off the television set, but the voices were busy when he came back with the whisky. The same host, but evidently a new segment of the show, for the guests were different.

The scientist had no mustache, but he was certainly a scientist, and he even looked a little like that one on the other show. Well-entrenched in the world and imperturbable.

". . . from Cal Tech, going to talk with us a little about nuclear physics, quantum mechanics, the nature of reality, all kinds of good stuff like that there." Laughter in the studio followed, febrile and feeble at the same time, predictable as the outcome of a lab demonstration.

"The nature of reality," said another panelist. "You left that out." But it hadn't been left out. Didn't they even listen to each other's words?

Someone else on the panel said something else, and they all laughed again.

"Speaking of reality, we'll be right back, after this."

The cable brought in a good many channels. Here was Atlanta. Who knew where they all came from? But he knew that he would have to switch back.

". . . pretty well accepted now by everyone in the field that it can't have any effect on the general perception of reality, what people generally experience as reality, no matter how many of these experiments you have going on around the world at the same time, or how many of them are concentrated on the same type of subject. The concentration effect, if there is one, sort of goes off somewhere; we can't even trace where it goes."

"You're saying that in effect you fire a volley off over the fields . . ."

". . . and it could possibly hit someone, but the chance is very small."

"Endor, did you say a moment ago?"

"The Witch of Endor?" another guest put in, archly, oh they were sharp out there on the coast, and there was more reflexive laughter, from people who recognized their cue, even if they didn't know what they were laughing about.

"ENDOR is an acronym," the scientist with no mustache was explaining, "for electron-nuclear double resonance. You see, it seems now that resonance is set up not only in the real atoms but in virtual atomic particles in nearby time-frames. The implications are enormous. Someday, theoretically, we could each have our own personal universe to carry around with us, tuned to our own skulls, our own perceptions. The original idea was only to measure the hyperfine . . ."

Flying a little high on bourbon now, and getting doses of jargon like that one, he needed only a few more sips from the bottle before he drifted off. To wake up, as it seemed, almost at once, with daylight coming in round the motel drapes. The airconditioner was humming already, the television had somehow been turned off. He lay there feeling better than he had dared to expect. Jargon is the thing, he thought. Jargon is definitely in. Where the hell have I been the last few days, anyway? But it seemed to be over now, whatever it had been.

He thought: I'm going to have to try to get on some talk show myself.

Taking his time in the warm morning, he listened without much apprehension to what scrapes of news the radio was willing to give up. No drowned bodies anywhere. He went out and breakfasted. As far as he could tell from looking out across the landscape away from town, he might still have been in Texas. But in town there were trees, and lawns, though the grass when he looked at it closely was of an unfamiliar variety.

Driving away from the motel, he was still unsure about whether to head north, east, or west. South—Mexico—he didn't want. On impulse he drove a couple of blocks toward the massed trees, the river. Above the dam it looked like an eastern river, wide and full and slow-moving, and there for some distance the banks were lined with expensive-looking houses. There was the sound of a motorboat, and in a moment a crack in the green wall showed a skier passing on the brown water. Nearby was a city park; he entered and drove through it slowly. There was a small sand beach, already in use in the day's heat.

There was also a police car, and a small but steadily growing crowd, fed by running children who were not interested just now in swimming. Between the standing bodies he caught a single glimpse of brown hair, yellow cloth. Bare, tanned arms being worked up and down by arms in blue policeman's sleeves.

He remembered to gas up the car and have the oil checked before heading on west. He was worried. But somehow he didn't seem to be as worried as he ought to be. He had the feeling that he was forgetting, putting behind him, a lot, an awful lot of recent happenings. Nothing essential, though. Excess baggage. Part of the feeling of strangeness was no doubt due to the fact that he was just coming out of a bad time. Even if he hadn't been on good terms with her lately, it was only to be expected that such a loss would leave him in a shocked condition for several weeks. But he was starting to come out of it now.

Later that day, he was almost at Tucson when he realized where he was going.

At home in San Diego, he watched the sun go down into the one great ocean, just as once, long ago, he had watched it rise. On the Atlantic horizon, he could remember there had been pink-gray nothingness, and then, instantly out of nowhere, a spark. Now at the last instant of sunset the shrinking sun became what looked like that identical same, long-remembered spark. And then, then night.

This house was his, this house right on the beach, only a hundred feet from water at high tide. Decades ago his parents had first rented then bought it, and he had hung onto it as an investment. This afternoon as soon as he got into town he had driven past the place on an impulse. It had looked unoccupied, though he had been sure that it was rented. He was going to have to talk to the agent about that in the morning.

The place had looked completely deserted from the outside, but when he had let himself in with the key he always kept, it was hard to be sure whether it was currently being lived in or not. There were furnishings, not all of them unfamiliar. Pictures on the walls, some of which he could remember.

He turned on a couple of lights after watching the sunset. A little food in the kitchen cabinets, a little in the refrigerator. As if some people might just have moved out, not bothering to take everything or use it up.

He went out again, through the French windows, to sit in a lawn chair on the patio overlooking the sea. The ocean, never quite silent, was now almost invisible in the gathering darkness. The smell of it brought back to him no memories that were peculiar to this place. He had looked at and smelled the sea in too many other, different places for that. The one great ocean that went on and on.

Through low clouds there came suddenly the half-familiar, half-surprising sound of a slow Navy plane from the air station not far away. One of the search and rescue craft, and it sounded like it was heading out. Would they commence a search at night? That seemed unlikely, but there were always new devices, new techniques. Anyway, they wouldn't be using a plane to look for her, she hadn't gone out in a boat. And if they hadn't started to look for her last night, when she walked out, they wouldn't be starting now.

He paused, trying to clear his thoughts. How could they have started any search last night? He still, up to this minute, hadn't told anyone how she had gone. Not yet . . .

If you can't stand your own life, he had said to her, *then I suggest you put an end to it. I have an interesting life of my own that's going to take all my time.* The room seemed still to echo with the words.

The waves were getting a little louder now, rolling invisibilities up the invisible beach.

He went into the house and turned up the volume of the television slightly; he could not really remember having turned it on. The voices from the talk show came with him as he went outside again, onto the seaward patio. The hyperfine and superhyperfine splittings could now be measured accurately, but that was only the start. Police forces all over the country were using the technique on unidentified bodies every day, with great success. Nobody worried any more that the technique might offer any danger to the fabric of the world. The implications were really vast. The ligand fields expanded without limit. The voices continued to follow as he opened the gate in the low wall and walked down a slope of sand to meet the still invisible burden of the waves.

Rob a Pharaoh and you've made an enemy
not just for life . . . but for *all time*.

FRED SABERHAGEN
PYRAMIDS

Tom Scheffler knew that his great uncle,
Montgomery Chapel, had worked as an Egyptologist
during the 1930s, and after that had become a
millionaire by selling artifacts no one else could
have obtained. Scheffler also knew that the old
man, fifty years later, was still afraid of some
man—some *entity*—known only as Pilgrim. But
what did that mean to Scheffler, an impoverished
student with the chance to spend a year "house-
sitting" a multi-million-dollar condo?

What Scheffler didn't know—and would learn
the hard way—was that Pilgrim was coming back,
aboard a ship that traveled both space and time,
headed for a confrontation in a weirdly changed
past where the monstrous gods of ancient Egypt
walked the Earth. And where Pharaoh Khufu,
builder of the greatest monument the world had
ever known, lay in wait for grave robbers from
out of time . . .

JANUARY 1987 • 65609-0 • 320 pp. • $3.50

"Everybody is asking: How do we knock out ICBM's? That's the wrong question. How do you design a system that allows a nation to defend itself, that can be used, even by accident, without destroying mankind, indeed, must be used every day, and is so effective that nuclear weapons cannot compete with it in the marketplace? That's the right question."

THE MOON GODDESS AND THE SON

DONALD KINGSBURY

The great illusion of the Nuclear Peace is that there will be no war as long as neither side wants war. We have neglected to find a defense against nuclear weaponry—but we cannot guarantee that a military accident will not happen. We argue that defense is impossible and disarmament the only solution—but we know no more about how to disarm than we know how to shoot down rocket-powered warheads.

Exploring these situations is what science fiction does best, and author Donald Kingsbury is one of its stricter players. Every detail is considered and every ramification explored. His first novel, *Courtship Rite*—set in the far future—received critical acclaim. His new novel takes place during the next thirty years.

In the 1990s the Soviets, building on their solid achievements in Earth orbit, surge into ascendancy by launching the space station Mir. Mir in time becomes Mirograd, a Russian "city" orbiting only a few hundred miles above North America. Now the U.S. plays desperate catch-up in the space race they are trailing.

THE MOON GODDESS AND THE SON is the story of the men and women who will make America great again. "Kingsbury interweaves [his] subplots with great skill, carrying his large cast of characters forward over 30-odd years. Neither his narrative and characterization nor his eye for the telling detail fall short. . . . An original mind and superior skill have combined to produce an excellent book."—*Chicago Sun-Times*

416 pp. • 55958-3 • $15.95

THE MOON GODDESS AND THE SON is available wherever quality hardcovers are sold, or order directly by sending a check or money order for $15.95 to Baen Books, 260 Fifth Avenue, New York, N.Y. 10001.

TRAVIS SHELTON
LIKES BAEN BOOKS
BECAUSE THEY TASTE GOOD

Recently we received this letter from Travis Shelton of Dayton, Texas:

> I have come to associate Baen Books with Del Monte. Now what is that supposed to mean? Well, if you're in a strange store with a lot of different labels, you pick Del Monte because the product will be consistent and will not disappoint.
>
> Something I have noticed about Baen Books is that the stories are always fast-paced, exciting, action-filled and seem to be published because of content instead of who wrote the book. I now find myself glancing to see who published the book instead of reading the back or intro. If it's a Baen Book it's going to be good and exciting and will capture your spare reading moments.
>
> Another discovery I have recently made is that I don't have any Baen Books in my unread stacks—and I read four to seven books a week, so that in itself is a meaningful statistic.

Why do you like Baen Books? Drop us a letter like Travis did. The person who best tells us what we're doing right—and where we could do better—will receive a Baen Books gift certificate worth $100. Entries must be received by December 31, 1987. Send to Baen Books, 260 Fifth Avenue, New York, N.Y. 10001. And ask for our free catalog!